Megan Clawson was born and raised in Boston, Lincolnshire. A beefeater's daughter, her heart was ensnared by the city of London at a young age, and she moved to study English with Film at King's College in 2018. Whilst there, she fell in love with her own royal guard. Now, she still resides in the Tower of London, alongside her little dog Ethel – and works as an English Tutor and a TV and film extra, alongside her writing. *Falling Hard for the Royal Guard* is her debut novel.

Falling Hard for the Royal Guard

MEGAN CLAWSON

avon.

Published by AVON
A division of HarperCollins*Publishers*
1 London Bridge Street
London SE1 9GF

www.harpercollins.co.uk

HarperCollins*Publishers*
Macken House
39/40 Mayor Street Upper
Dublin 1
D01 C9W8
Ireland

A Paperback Original 2023
1
First published in Great Britain by HarperCollins*Publishers* 2023

A catalogue copy of this book is available from the British Library.

ISBN: 978-0-00-855441-5

Typeset in Birka by Palimpsest Book Production Limited, Falkirk, Stirlingshire

Printed and Bound in the UK using 100% Renewable Electricity
at CPI Group (UK) Ltd

For Gingers/Red Heads/Carrot Tops/Gingas/people that are told they look like every ginger celebrity ever,

Because we deserve to be the main character every once in a while. Freckles and all.

Author's note

The Tower of London has seen many residents over its millennium, but it's frequently the unwilling guests that we remember. Most people don't realise that beyond the moat, the fortress walls, and the portcullises, there is a village and there always has been. Even now in 2022, a whole community of people hang out their washing in the places that royalty once walked, park their cars on top of the gone-by sites of executions, walk their dogs through a moat now far more welcoming than the cesspit it previously was, and come together in a bar just like their predecessors in every century before.

The beefeaters themselves are, in my eyes, the Tower of London personified. Without them, the Tower would lose the beating heart that they have maintained and nurtured for the last five hundred years. They are a constant in our nation, something we can so easily take pride in. Beyond their Tudor bonnets and ruffs, they are men and women who have served the most part of a lifetime in uniform, men and women who aren't made rich by their devotion but still carry out each of their duties with impeccable discipline – they are our culture.

The King's Guards are at the very beginning of this long service. Despite being one of the most iconic images that springs to mind when you think of Great Britain, the guards are still mystery to many. Contrary to popular belief, they aren't statues, they can speak. Once they take off that bearskin and tunic, these are young soldiers, moved away from all they have ever known, young people that are still making their mistakes, still learning through being thrown into life at the deep end. Yet when you get the privilege of seeing them, they are pristine, disciplined, nothing short of perfection.

I am one of the very few people that have been able to call the Tower of London my home. Within its walls, I finished my degree, fell in love, and wrote this book. Everything I know of the Tower has been passed down to me from my father, a beefeater, and his colleagues. Every conversation I have with them ends with me learning something new, whether it is the detailed history of a single brick or the tales of their own exploits somewhere across the world. With this novel, I want to offer a new perspective on some of Britain's most recognisable iconography. The many guards I have met through the years have been some of the strongest men, but also the most vulnerable, and the beefeaters have a sort of depth that you could only understand after a tipsy chat over a pint with them. I want to do them justice by making this book as honest and accurate as possible. But ultimately *Falling Hard for the Royal Guard* is a work of fiction. The names and events are all fiction-alised. My personal story with the Tower stays between me and the walls that hold the secrets of our history, but I hope this one will be a good enough substitute.

A Map of the Tower of London

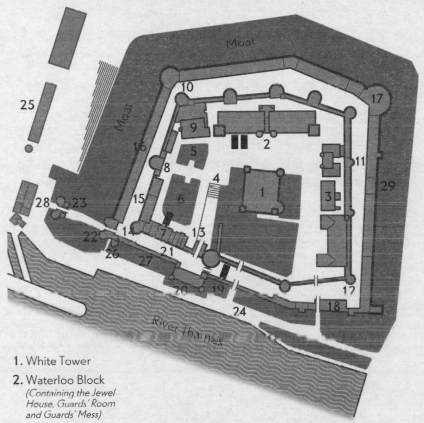

1. White Tower
2. Waterloo Block
   (Containing the Jewel House, Guards' Room and Guards' Mess)
3. Old Hospital Block
4. Broadwalk Steps
5. Scaffold Site
6. Tower Green
7. King's House
8. Beauchamp Tower
9. Chapel
10. Devereux Tower
11. Constable Tower
12. Salt Tower
13. Bloody Tower
14. Bell Tower
15. Mint Street
16. Casemates
17. Brass Mount
18. The Keys
19. Middle Drawbridge
20. Traitors' Gate
21. Water Lane
22. Byward Tower
23. Middle Tower
24. Tower Wharf
25. Ticket Office
26. Byward Postern/ Sally Port
27. Pet Cemetery
28. Entrance
29. Maggie's House
▌ Guard sentry boxes

Chapter 1

*T*he sun always leaves the East Casemates first. It gets
  swallowed up by the western side of the White Tower,
locked in its dungeon and liberated at dawn to the sound of
the ravens' cries. To move through the castle at this time is
to be undisturbed. Residents hide at the hearths of their fires
and don't bother to distinguish between passer-by and
wandering spirit. There is little difference anyway.

I wander the south lawn alone, the dew-soaked strands
of grass slip between my bare toes and around my ankles as
I glide freely under the moonlight. Standing in her shadow,
I drink in the glowing stone of the White Tower and lose
myself in the shadowed arches of the windows as the twilight
breeze pushes me further towards her.

Only the sound of soft laughter disturbs me. I whip around,
my damp red hair cloaking my face in the motion. But I see no
one, I feel no one. The sound crescendos until it becomes abusive,
only growing louder, more animated as I begin to squirm.

*

1

Laugh, lick, laugh, lick.

I open my eyes with a start, before quickly clamping them shut again as the bright sunlight claws abusively at my vision from the window. The dampness on my feet spreads up my bare legs until it finally settles on my face. Working up the strength to prise open my eyelids again with a groan, I come face to furry face with my cat, who really has no concept of personal space. I rub my saliva-soaked feet against my bedsheets as I give Cromwell a playful scratch behind the ears. I can only work up enough anger to grimace at the slimy coating over my toes, the tortoiseshell ball of fluff absolutely impossible to tell off.

Giggle, Giggle, Giggle.

In my drowsy state, the sinister laughter has turned into . . . oh *balls*! I have to peek over the top of Cromwell's fuzzy head to notice a pair of boys in their late teens and their high-tech DSLR camera upon the east wall peering back at me. My obnoxiously wide-open window provides absolutely zero cover to hide the fact my boobs have escaped my tank top and are practically waving back in my frantic fatigue. The Cheshire-cat smile appearing either side of the bulky tourist camera is all the confirmation I need to throw myself out of my bed and onto the floor.

Leopard-crawling across my carpet, I have to dodge empty glasses and random articles of clothing like I'm on a military assault course to escape the laughter that still reverberates from the inner wall. When I'm sure I'm out of sight, I flop dramatically onto my back on the floor, berating myself over all of the ways I could have resolved this situation, like simply cocooning myself in my duvet, actually remembering to close the curtains or, like any normal person, just readjusting the tank top that had betrayed me. It's all well and good thinking of these solutions now that I already have a carpet burn across my chest.

Without warning, my mum's voice reverberates through my mind, and I flinch at the clarity of it, almost half believing – half hoping – she were in the room: 'You know, Maggie, for a lass with brains you really do have no common sense.' Ah yes, the phrase that haunted every moment of my teenage idiocy. It feels just that little bit more tragic now in my late twenties.

'Mags, is that you? You not at work today?' my dad's voice echoes up the stairs. It reaches me as I'm sprawled in just my baby pink knickers across the landing carpet, too full of embarrassment to have moved.

Hang on. What time is it? I grasp for my burgundy work shirt that has been screwed up on the floor since the end of my shift yesterday. The creased blouse now shielding me from onlookers, I reach for my phone: 9.53 a.m. I was meant to start work almost an hour ago. Stuffing my face into the carpet, I groan loudly making my dad laugh as he now stands in my doorway. Like me, he is only half dressed for work. A graphic T-shirt embellished with a joke only fit for a pudgy middle-aged dad splashes the words *with a body like this, who needs hair?* across his chest. Navy trousers sit just above his belly, clinging on by a set of straining red braces. His red beard, speckled with white, has been left tucked into the neck of his T-shirt, as though it has been tossed on without a second thought. He's still missing his Tudor bonnet and navy tunic. Right

3

now, he looks like Father Christmas's rebellious younger brother, a far cry from the fit and clean-cut British Army soldier that he had been for twenty-two years.

I hadn't thought my dad could get any more eccentric than when he sold his house to live on a narrow boat, but here we are, living in the Tower of London where he managed to obtain the most obscure job he could find: a beefeater – or a Yeoman Warder if you want to be fancy. The result? He spends most of his days showing tourists around the Tower of London, bragging about being the monarch's bodyguard, subtly omitting the 'ceremonial' prefix in his title. I am pretty sure he chose the job based on the fact that there is none other out there with a uniform so bizarre. He was more excited than he'd ever admit hopping into the ruff and tights of his ceremonial dress, which is sewn together with the finest gold thread. He sprouted his ginger beard and popped out a little round belly as soon as he stepped over the threshold, really taking a method approach to his new role. It only took a matter of weeks for him to look like he had stepped out of the print of a novelty tea towel that you find in the tourist tat shops across London. And he loves it.

'Oh, bloody hell!' I dart around the room, desperate to find the trousers I had discarded somewhere in the dark after waking up from my 'ten-minute bit of shut-eye' at 3 a.m. Finding them lodged down the back of my bed, I only have enough time to wedge my toothbrush between my jaws and say a very brief and garbled goodbye to Dad before running down the five flights of stairs to the front door. Racing though I am, I can't bring myself to forgo my usual routine of saying a whispered 'love you' to Mum, and I pause briefly in the hallway on my way out, spending precious seconds staring at her photo. She looks exactly how I remember her: her hair windswept and wild, with a smile pinching so tightly at her cheeks that her eyes disappear into it as well. Sighing as I reluctantly tear myself away, I give her a sad smile in return and resume my manic morning. Too late to grab a coat I just sprint, hoping that the March breeze might aid even slightly in taming my hair.

'Morning!' I call to each one of the beefeaters that I pass on the way. My next-door neighbour Richie, half dressed, like a mirror image of my dad in his T-shirt, braces, and salt and pepper beard, waters his array of out-of-control flowers in front of the house. He waves back with his free hand, absentmindedly sloshing water across his boots with the other in the process. Continuing my mad dash, I pass Linda as she steps out from the wide front door of Brass Mount in the east corner of the casemates. I am pretty sure Linda is the only person in the world who can say she lives in an old artillery tower from which they fired the cannons back in the day. She places her Tudor bonnet upon her perfectly sleek bun and shouts her greetings, knowing far better than to corner me for a conversation on my daily rush to work.

Having conquered the cobbles, I make it onto the path over the drawbridge. It takes all of my strength to not bend down to stroke Timmy, Beefeater Charlie's Newfoundland, as they both emerge after a morning of chasing seagulls in the moat.

'Mornin', darlin'!'

'Morning, Charlie! Can't stop or Kev'll have my head!' He laughs and gives me a mock salute as I overtake him.

Timmy tries to join me on my panicked dash. Being the size of a black bear, his paws thump audibly against the floor and his whole body moves in a wave with the motion. His excitable tail adding a *Total-Wipeout*-style obstacle for me to vault. His giant tongue lolls out the side of his mouth and leaves a splodge of saliva on the hem of my trousers.

With work in my sights, it's only Ben, the gardener, I have left on my checklist of hellos.

'Good morning, Ben! The lines in the lawn this morning . . .' I kiss the tips of my fingers in an exaggerated 'chef's kiss' motion.

He just laughs in acknowledgement and waves me on to work.

Panting, I slide through the door of the ticket office, far too late to be excused as fashionably late, and sweating as though I'd fallen asleep inside a sauna. Edging towards my seat, I glance furtively around, hoping against hope that I might still get away with my tardy arrival.

'Margaret Moore . . .' I tense – no such luck. 'How can someone who literally lives at the place they work *still* be late? You may live in a castle but don't expect me to treat you like the princess you think you are.' I could hear my boss before I could see him.

'I am so, so sorry, Kevin, I really am. I didn't realise the—' He cuts me off with a hand shoved so close to my face I can smell that he has already been to the café for a

6

bacon butty and chased it down with a secret fag behind the storehouse.

I stop trying to plead my case. When Kevin is in this mood, there's no talking to him and I already know the punishment I'll end up with: a trip down into the White Tower's cellar to place the day's cash into the safe. I shudder at the thought. It wouldn't be so bad if it weren't nearly one thousand years old with a lighting system almost as dated. Not that newer lights would make much of a difference: no one ventures down the creaking staircase without first closing their eyes and running like a child fleeing from the monsters that reach for their heels on the way to bed, and no one goes in any deeper than they must. Centuries-old bottles of wine remain stored for a rainy day by nobility dead and buried, protected by the instinctive human fear of the dark.

With a flick of his wrist, Kevin shoos me away to my designated ticket booth, his fool's gold bangle clattering against his 'Realex' as he does so. Thankfully each booth is secluded from the other by partitions and faces the street outside, so I am only seen by the general public when I childishly mock his gestures in a farce-like performance. I slump down in my chair, and, catching a glimpse of my reflection in the glass, unsuccessfully attempt to smooth down the halo of frizz on top of my head. Damp strands cling to my face and red flyaway hairs tickle at my nostrils. I tuck the rest of it down the back of my shirt to get it out of the way of my desk and it itches at the waistband of my trousers.

Plastering a fake smile across my face, I welcome my

very first customer: 'Good morning and welcome to His Majesty's Royal Palace and Fortress, the Tower of London. How many tickets can I get for you today?'

The day passes as usual: I say the same thing so many times that it no longer sounds like English, I push buttons on the computer, print things off, dodge my colleagues, and try my absolute hardest to hold on to the last few scraps of my soul before my job destroys them. Today, however, did have the added excitement of having to read-just my knickers after a quick toilet break and a persistent wedgie revealed that I had managed to put them on backwards this morning.

Then when the long clock hand finally crawls its way towards the end of the day, at just five minutes to close there is, of course, someone else with their face pressing up against the glass of my booth. Already six years deep into the Facebook profile of a girl I went to primary school with after noticing she has posted a few cryptic statuses about the father of her kids, I recite the usual script without looking up: 'I am afraid the Tower closes at 5 p.m. today. We do reopen tomorrow at 9 a.m. if you'd still like to visit.'

'Margo, it's me . . .'

I freeze. Only one person calls me Margo. And it's the last person I want to see right now – especially in this dishevelled state. No, absolutely not! This could not be further than the post-break-up, I-am-totally-fine-without-you-and-yes-I-already-have-a-new-man-can't-you-tell-from-my-sexy-glow-because-I'm-definitely-FINE meeting I have spent the last few weeks planning out in my daydreams.

The meeting that I've been bracing myself for. I look up into the eyes of my ex-boyfriend.

He leans into the glass. The dragon tattoo that splays across his wrist, the same one that I helped him design, is partially covered by a series of woven bracelets and a few old festival wristbands and tucked beneath the cuff of a creased pink shirt. The rings on his thumb and forefinger – ones I gifted him for various birthdays and anniversaries over the seven years of our relationship – clash as he sweeps his dark hair behind his ear.

'If anyone sees you here, Bran, you'll end up buried in that moat behind you by thirty-two beefeaters. You see that camera above me? I can guarantee Lesley and Simon from security will have already seen your face and are putting the Grenadier Guards on standby as we speak.' That isn't strictly true. Lesley and Simon are more likely laughing as their own little reality show gets just that tiny bit more exciting. The whole office will have heard of Bran's visit by tomorrow morning.

'Margo . . .'

'Don't call me that.'

'Maggie, I just wanted to talk. The flat doesn't feel the same without you. I'm sorry you feel like this, but I've given you a month, just like I said.'

For a while after we broke up, after he had exhausted all of his other options and realised that they weren't as good as they seemed when he had the adrenaline of hiding it from his girlfriend, these unannounced visits came like clockwork.

Unluckily for me, Bran got himself a job in some boring office in the financial district just across the river, which means he is just a bridge away from ruining my day. I don't really know what he does at work, something to do with numbers and taxes, but he seems to have enough spare time in his day to harass me, so it can't be that important. On this day a month ago, he told me he wouldn't come for thirty days in what I can only assume was an attempt at triggering the 'absence makes the heart grow fonder' philosophy. But here we are again.

Worst of all, it is almost working. From seeing his face almost every day for seven years, to being left alone only to brood over old memories that seem just that little bit shinier and happier through the rose-tinted lens of nostalgia, I *have* missed him.

'Just please come home. Where you belong.'

I almost laugh at that. I have to admire my ex-boyfriend's attempt at trying to convince me that our zone-five apartment, wallpapered with black mould and filled with the ghosts of his infidelity is a better place for me to live than a royal palace. Once upon a time just a single second of sensitivity would be enough to convince me to do anything – and he knows it. It's his trojan horse, a façade of intimacy filled with the pain that he will only unleash once he's seduced me into letting him through the walls that only exist to keep him out in the first place. As he contorts his face into that of a man broken, I have to work hard to remind myself that I'd rather live out my days in Rudolf Hess's stone cell of the Bell Tower than sleep in the bed that swallowed up my misery each night. I want to believe it, believe in my strength.

'I *need* you,' he breathes as the climax of his emotional atom bomb.

A tear escapes his dark eyelashes and slips down his tanned face. He leaves it there drying, to lay siege to the battlements that he made me build. In that tear I see us. I see seven years of my life, seven years of memories. He is everything that I know of adulthood. He is both my pain and my peace.

My heart acts before my brain can arrest it and chain it to the scrap of dignity and sense I have left. Intuitively, I open the door to the ticket office and before I can see sense, I find my hand on his face, catching the tears for him. That damned horse.

Somewhere at the back of my mind warning bells are ringing, but it's too late now. It infuriates me how natural this feels. How touching him brings me the most comfort that I have had in weeks. We used to be able to spend days on end inside the house, living in each other's pockets, contented with just being together. If either one of us didn't feel like facing the world, we wouldn't. Not a single word would have to be uttered for us to know; we'd just clamber back under the duvet together, recharge and bring the equilibrium back into our lives for the next day. When I lost Mum, we didn't share a word for three days straight. He took leave from work and simply held me, until . . .

As he embraces me, my gaze lands on one of the cameras, and I am finally drawn back down to reality. The paranoia takes over and I begin to think that whoever is sitting behind the monitor, watching my dignity and strength slip away, has lost another bit of respect for me. Although I suppose they can't think any worse of me than I already think of myself. My brain is racing with every disgusting

11

insult to condemn my own actions, but they just swim around in his tears and are carried off down the Thames.

He pulls back, his eyes casting over me, taking me in. I curse inwardly again at how not according to plan this is going: I had managed a strip-wash in the disabled loos on my break, but no amount of effort would save my hair from its feral mess, and no amount of lavender hand soap could quite get the smell of this morning's exercise out of my shirt. Staring at my face in a glass reflection all day has done little but confirm that I really do look a wreck.

'I had no idea you'd taken the break-up so hard, Margo,' he announces after a pause.

'Uh . . . what?' His grip is weak, so it doesn't take too much for me to draw away from him.

'You know, like letting yourself go and stuff; not putting in any effort because you're heartbroken. You don't even have to say anything, and I already know you've missed me.'

I stare at him. When I don't respond he places his hands on my burning cheeks and continues, eagerly: 'Have you not been eating either? You look like you've lost weight . . . It's kinda hot.'

I don't even have to snap myself out of my moment of weakness; he has managed to do it for me, just by being exactly himself. My face must be scarlet by now. That's the disadvantage of being a ginger; no matter how good my poker face, my freckled skin changing colour like a chameleon uncovers my emotions every time.

'Margo? I would still put on perfume, though. You still have that expensive one I bought you for your birthday a few years ago, right?' He babbles on. The One Direction perfume he bought me six years ago sits in my dad's bathroom, used as an air freshener . . . 'The natural scent thing isn't quite as sexy.'

I falter. I want so desperately to scream in his face, to shout every swearword I have ever picked up from my childhood hanging around military bases. But Bran always seems to have the ability to silence me. I don't trust my own emotions and the words are anchored in my throat.

Before I can find my voice, a rapping sound diverts my attention, as Kevin knocks impatiently on the ticket booth window. Forgetting to turn on the microphone, he shouts noiselessly through the security screen, no doubt reminding me of my punishment to fulfil for this morning's late arrival – which, of course, is the real reason why I look like I've 'let myself go'.

Bran strokes back my hair and his ring snags on a knot. I wince at the pull, but he unsurprisingly doesn't seem to notice, and kisses me on the forehead, muttering something about letting me get back to work and that he will see me again soon. With my tongue still failing me, I offer a weak smile in response. And with that, he turns on the heel of his black Chelsea boot and struts away, quickly disappearing over Tower Hill. Finally coming to my senses, and frustrated at my feebleness, I shout after him, or really just in the direction of his exit, for those damned long legs mean he is probably already at the Tube station by now.

'I haven't lost any bloody weight, they're just baggy trousers!'

Chapter 2

The last thing I want to do after a surprise encounter with a ghost from my not-so-distant past is to walk straight into the White Tower for an escapade with a few real ones. Unfortunately, I have no other choice; Kevin has already packed me up with a tatty bag filled with today's takings and was sucking on a cigarette at the bus stop before I could even grovel.

Psyching myself up, I stride with purpose down Water Lane, attempting to think up all of the ways I could defend myself against some disturbed ghost that's been trapped in a dungeon for a few centuries. The only weapon I have to hand is a half-melted Snickers bar from the work vending machine, so unless the bodiless spirit is allergic to nuts, I don't stand a chance.

Sighing, I try a different tack, reminding myself of my dad's sage advice: 'We're Northerners,' he'd say. 'If we can manage a conversation with Londoners, then talking to a few wandering spirits is a doddle. They'll actually see

14

you as their friend, and we're used to never getting a reply.'

When he first admitted these ghost-facing tactics, in all deadly seriousness, I laughed at him, thinking it another of his whims picked up from the Channel Twelve conspiracy theory documentaries he watches on repeat. But every day since he told me, I have asked the smog dust in my bedroom how it's doing whenever I ever hear a noise that I can't quite explain – and he's right. It *is* comforting.

The money sits uncomfortably heavy in the bag across my shoulder, the loose coins jingling with each step, drawing everyone's eyes to me as they escape the walls of work. I can't help but feel a bit nervous with such a stash. In my mind, I am Colonel Blood, the only man to ever steal the Crown Jewels by stuffing them into his trousers, just waiting for King Kevin to catch me and throw me into the dungeon. I'd take the Bloody Tower dungeon over this cellar any day.

When I reach the White Tower, I have to pass through the armoury first. I stare longingly at rows on rows of ancient armour, shields, weapons as I travel further and further into the underbelly of the castle. With each floor descended, the light grows darker and darker until I reach the basement that glows under the synthetic buzz of orange lamps.

I hesitate in the doorway. The oak door is scratched with age and deliberately slashed with deep X-shaped runes or 'witches' marks' that were meant to ward off evil spirits. After a few experiences with the cold draughts behind that door, I think the Tower needs to ask those medieval carpenters for their money back.

Gathering my courage, I press down on the lever on the handle and with a slight wiggle I hear the latch on the other side spring up, the metallic clash echoing around the empty space on the inside. As I use my shoulder to force it open, its shriek ricochets down the hallway into the dimly lit space where I stand.

Clutching the bag of cash to my chest, I step tentatively onto the stairs. I swear that even they are out to get you. They sit crooked and uneven, tempting you to fall, and I will my eyes to adjust more quickly to the gloom.

Five steps in and I feel pressure on my shoulder, like a hand, just resting. I can't tell if it's guiding or threatening. My heart throbs in my head and beats hard in my chest.

'Hi there.' I speak into the darkness, desperately hoping for no reply. 'I'll get out of your hair really quick, I promise. Kevin is making me do this – you know what he's like. A . . . real . . . bloody . . . arsehole!' I ramble into the void, getting increasingly erratic as I pray the ghosts love a bit of bitching as much as the girls in the break room do.

A cold draught whips past my ear and lifts my hair from around my face.

'Okey-dokey, hurrying up, not a problem at all. Nope, no problemo. Totally going to hurry up now.' I run down the rest of the stairs and just about make it to the last one before stumbling and hurling myself headfirst into the solid steel safe. With my hands still occupied gripping the bag of cash like a shield, my forehead collides with the cold metal, and I have to blink several times before I can see through the pain.

Uttering a few expletives that the ex-sailors in the

16

Yeoman body would be proud of, I throw the takings into the safe, slam it shut and scarper, on all fours, back up the stairs.

'Have a lovely evening, n-n-night!' I shout again to the phantom audience, yanking closed the door behind me. Locking everything back up as quickly as my trembling fingers will allow, I jog up three flights of spiral stairs and emerge with a heaving chest and a sprinkling of sweat across my already bruising forehead.

I look around the courtyard, now deserted by all except the conspiracy of ravens. You are never alone in the Tower, never without a pair of beady black eyes watching you. They practically own the place. There's an ancient prophecy that if the ravens leave the Tower of London, then the White Tower shall crumble and the kingdom shall fall. So, it is actually quite a relief to see them stealing a sandwich crust out of the bin or to hear them cawing loudly in the mornings because it supposedly means we're all safe for another day.

I lock eyes with Regina, one of the ravens, and I blush; she's most definitely judging me for my erratic ejection from the castle door. I'm sure the cameras caught it too. Trying hard to brush it off, I straighten my blouse and speed-walk across the cobbles. The spring breeze stings against the fresh wound on my head, the bruise throbbing down across my temple. I lightly stroke it, to soothe it in the way my mother would when I was a child, but the placebo effect doesn't seem to work so well when I do it. Living and breathing each day and night within these ancient walls means my feet could carry me through its

17

maze with my eyes closed and so I hide under my hair, too embarrassed to parade my stupidity in such a prestigious place as this.

Clear of the White Tower's intimidating gaze, I prepare myself to flee down the Broadwalk Steps – which are now just up ahead – like Cinderella at midnight. I romanticise this moment of my day almost every night in my lucid dreams, so I close my eyes and, still moving forwards, calm myself by relaxing into my imagination.

'Ow. Oh, fuck. Oh, bloody hell.'

If I hadn't already given myself a concussion on the side of the safe, I certainly have now. One of the Victorian streetlamps has managed to migrate forward by about two metres, and I think I just shook every bone in my body walking into it.

'Oh, you bloody fool, what on earth are you doing with yourself!' I berate myself, furious at my own ineptitude.

'Excuse me?' the lamppost spits back. My eyes fly open. I may believe in ghosts, but I am definitely not concussed enough to believe that lampposts can talk.

I push all of the hair out of my face to get a better look at the source of the voice. A man stares back at me, and he's furious. His phone is held tightly to his ear, and his expression is pulled tight with aggravation, his jaw twitching from the strength with which he grits his teeth. At first glance his tailored blazer, unbuttoned and flashing a pristinely ironed white shirt, gives him an air of authority, one of those men that you instantly submit to. But upon closer inspection, he mustn't be much older than me. His umber hair is shaved low and neatly at the sides, but the

18

top flaunts soft curls that he has clearly made a boyish attempt to tame, but which explode in an unruly mass at his crown.

But it's his eyes that knock the wind out of my chest momentarily. They are Catherine wheels of jade and pietersite that sit like gemstones behind a fanning of dark lashes. I follow their every micromovement like a hypnotist's medallion. Only the deepening frown lines at his brow snap me out of my trance, as I realise that my mouth has been agape for some time. Well done, Maggie. Now you not only look like a clown in front of the most attractive man you've ever laid eyes on, but now he most definitely thinks you're an idiot too.

I finally come to my senses and clock that, in the commotion, I have managed to relieve his hands of a glossy wooden box that now lies cracked open on the concrete. The clearly expensive contents shimmer in the low light of the night. My stomach drops. Both of us rush to pick it up at the same time; his voluminous hair does nothing to cushion the blow as our heads collide in the process. Pain splits through my already tender skull, sending specks of light across my vision. The stranger grimaces in his own pain as I notice for the first time that his hands are gripping my arms, the only thing preventing me from falling back onto the concrete.

Awkwardly shuffling out of his grip, I make another grab for the box but, of course, his long limbs reach it before me, and he snaps it shut before I can pull my fingers away. My fiercely bitten nails throb from the pressure, and I press them against my palm with a hiss. The only positive thing to come out of this exchange is the fact that my freshly injured fingertips are proving a fine distraction from the pain in my head.

The man's phone is still wedged against his ear, propped up by his shoulder as he emotionlessly resumes his side of the conversation with the faceless interlocutor. He doesn't pay attention to the way I clutch at my pinched digits.

'I'll call you back, Father. Yes, I have it here. Yes, sir.' He stands back up to his full height as he slides the phone into his pocket.

'Oh shit, no. I'm so sorry, I didn't . . . I don't . . . I . . . I . . .' I bluster as his full attention shifts to me.

'Who do you think you are talking to me like that? And don't you look where you're going?'

Every single syllable is perfectly formed, not a colloquialism in sight. Even the king could be insulted by him and still be impressed by his enunciation and intonation. With that, I remember where we are stood; in the eyeline of the King's House, the Constable of the Tower's residence. The man who inhabits those walls is the monarch's eyes and ears within the Tower, Lord Herbert. His retirement from leading the entirety of the British Army consists of hosting dinner parties inside the Tower for every important man, woman, and child who ever places their feet upon British soil. And I am almost one hundred per cent sure that I have just insulted one of his guests. Perhaps a gentleman with a title? Or at least the rich ambassador of some country that could have me 'disappear' before the sun rose again.

He glances down at the box; it's slightly battered on one

corner, the varnish is chipped, and rough splinters peek out of the side. Running a hand through his hair, he is visibly distressed. He only looks away from me to pinch the bridge of his nose, muttering to himself. His stony exterior crumbles as he bends down again to pick up each fragment that had been left behind. A lump rises in my throat and I can't tell if I want to cry or be sick.

'No, sir, absolutely not. I wasn't insulting you! I was talking to myself!' I try so hard to cover up the Yorkshire twang in my apology, but I stand no chance in erasing my offence now. I am done for. I point at the box. 'I can pay! For a new one . . .'

This is a complete lie. If the box is as expensive as it looks, I would have to rob a bank to replace it. Thankfully, he doesn't acknowledge any of this and opens the box to inspect its contents. A row of sapphires, strung together by a delicate chain of silver glitters back at him. The man lets out a sigh of what seems to be relief as I suck in yet another anxious breath that pulls the rug from under me. After pushing the precious stones back into a uniform row he thrusts a hand through his hair and, before I can say anything else to dig myself out of the hole I have launched myself into, this intimidatingly beautiful man about turns and marches away on his perfectly polished brogues.

My hands tremble slightly as I watch him move across the courtyard; my fingertips throb as I try and shake away the slight sting left behind from the meeting. As I look on, the golden clock chimes for six o'clock. It is perched at the heart of the Jewel House, the longest building of the Tower that stretches across almost the full length of the north of the courtyard – the building that the stranger disappears behind. Once I can no longer see the wide expanse of his back, nor hear the sharp echo of his shoes as they pound against the cobbles, I flee the scene with such speed that I'm out of breath when I finally stumble through my front door.

'All right, Maggie love?' Dad calls from his armchair upstairs. 'Get lost, did you?' I can hear the smile in his voice.

'Kevin . . . again . . .' I shout back up. He doesn't reply but I hear his deep grumble as I picture him chuntering to himself about all of the parts of my boss he dislikes the most.

Actually, Dad was the reason that Kevin took rather a strong distaste to me after my first few weeks on the job. My dad caught him in a precarious position with the deputy governor around the back of the Jewel House. Dad didn't tell me, or anyone else, what had happened – not until it was last week's news and common knowledge anyway – but when word got out about the affair a few weeks later, Kevin put two and two together and made five and instantly chose me as his scapegoat. Kevin has since made a special effort to make my days at work less enjoyable than a night with Henry VIII, and of course, his loyal subjects – my colleagues – are led by him in every sense.

Without interrupting his meditations on this topic, I head straight for the shower. It takes me until the hot water runs out before I finally feel my blood pressure returning to a healthy level for the first time since I awoke.

No longer smelling like the boys' changing rooms in

my old high school, I sit silently on my balcony with a much-needed cup of tea, milk, and one sugar, sitting steaming on the parapet.

Lucie, the youngest and most energetic of the ravens, is perched on the battlements eyeing me. Her sleek black feathers glow blue in the moonlight as she shakes them out and smooths them down with her long beak. Behind me, Cromwell lets out a muted yowl as he stares out of the window of my bedroom, his furry brow furrowed in frustration at having to sit behind a glass prison when he could be ruffling some feathers. Little does he know that it is actually him I am protecting. Lucie sits regally, the size of a Jack Russell, and would swallow my furry snack whole given half the chance.

She hops across the wall, chirruping in conversation, before lightly tapping her beak against the sleeve of my pyjamas. I run a finger across the top of her head in the way I know she likes, and she clicks melodically in satisfaction. Still, Cromwell paws at the window and licks it every now again for a bit of backup, jealous at the lack of attention.

'He's as much of an idiot as his mum, that one.' I motion to the saliva-soaked window with a jerk of my head. Lucie continues to stare, as though she listens and understands.

'Why can't I just have one normal day, eh? I reckon that this tops it all though.'

I rub the lump on my forehead, and I can't decide if it is the pain or the reminder of the embarrassment that causes me to wince. I bring the mug of tea to my lips and my soft sigh blows the steam away from my face.

'You know, sometimes I wish I were a bird too. I would fly away before anyone could come close and just sit upon the highest wall and observe the chaos from afar. Although, knowing me, I'd be the first ever bird to be afraid of heights: I'd just sit in the nest forever until a storm blows me out of it.'

Lucie's pearly black eyes stay fixed as she cocks her head questioningly. I pull out one of the patio chairs from under the small table and sit beside her.

'Come on then, I'll tell you what happened.'

Chapter 3

My third alarm of the morning is the one that finally pulls me from another night of dreaming. I haul myself from bed; there is no way that I'm going to let Kevin have the satisfaction of being able to lumber me with his punishment for tardiness today. Glancing in the mirror, I see that the lump on my head has settled into a lovely black and purple bruise that cups my eye as if I've attempted to give myself a Mike Tyson tattoo in felt-tip pen, with my eyes shut. I'm still thinking about the events of last night as I climb into the shower. Getting ready takes a good hour, plaiting my hair out of my face and ironing my uniform, as I try to push the stranger's angry eyes from my mind.

Popping my head around the living room door, I say goodbye to Dad. He is propped up in his armchair in the corner, the empty plate in his hand doing little to catch the custard cream crumbs that are trapped like flies in his spider-web beard. His red braces frame yet another gaudy

T-shirt as he waves back absentmindedly, too busy watching another rerun of an Eighties police drama and muttering to himself about how he used to have the same shoes and mullet as the detective inspector.

Like clockwork, Richie is already outside, attending to his flower bed.

'G'morning!' I smile at him. He is so engrossed in picking off the dead petals of his roses that he looks startled when he sees me – although, quite honestly, the fact I actually look semi-human and am not sprinting out of the door this morning could easily be the reason for his surprise. He waves and replies in a thick Cornish accent that requires a moment of thought to translate in my head. I imagine him in another life as a farmer, spending each day walking between row on row of his new crop, muttering in an accent only the soil and the birds can understand.

With ten minutes to spare before my shift, I decide to take the 'scenic' route to work. This time, before I reach the East Bastion, I slip just behind the garages and up the stairs of a hidden passageway. Like every set of stairs in this place, they have their very own built-in defensive system that has an almost one hundred per cent success rate: they're so wonky I can't walk up more than three at a time without almost face-planting into the concrete. The passageway is wide but enclosed. The bare brick is constantly damp, and the sound of an eerie drip syncopates with the echo of my footsteps. An orange light glows in the corner and casts shadows across every edge in the proximity.

It's not until I see the light right at the end that my

chest leaps slightly in fear. As the top of the tunnel breaks away, a set of wire baboon sculptures sit atop the walls. Their metallic mouths are twisted into a primal scream, their barbarous teeth glinting in the morning sunlight. I never take this passage at night for that reason: their bodies always seem to transform in the moonlight. The stars fill the chicken-wire spaces in their eyes and a menacing aura overtakes them. I can't help but envisage them coming to life in a *Night at the Museum* spectacle, wreaking havoc across the Tower grounds and taking no prisoners in their fantastical mob.

Once upon a time, the Tower really was home to such creatures in its former years as a menagerie, filled with exotic animals brought as gifts for monarchs by monarchs, chained behind the walls. Elephants, lions, polar bears and monkeys, all akin in their imprisonment, left alone to destroy each other and anyone else in the crossfire. I'd pity them if their commemorative sculptures didn't make me – a grown-up with an actual job who pays actual taxes – afraid of chicken wire.

Finally clear of the parade of baboons, I'm into the courtyard and face to face with the White Tower again. In the morning light, the stone has a nobility about it. Each crumbling brick shines like the jewels of a crown: beautifully unique in isolation, but blindingly magnificent as a collective. The Union flag waves its royal wave from the summit, as it proudly flies over the city of London. Despite being long since eclipsed by glass skyscrapers filled with the same old beige and magnolia offices, the Tower refuses to be drowned out. Though not as tall and sophisticated as its neighbours, there is a beauty in its historic strength that can't be replicated. Once you stand at its foot, there is no single building more imposing, nor more magnificent than the White Tower. To stand in its shadow is to feel as though you're transported to a different time; just to look upon it feels like a privilege only fit for a royal.

Dressed head to toe in black, the cleaners wield brooms and litter grabbers at its base as they fight the never-ending battle to keep the ground worthy enough to stand beneath the Tower's beauty. I offer a 'good morning' to each of them, and the size of their smiles would never so much as hint at the fact that their day began before the stars had even retreated.

One of the workers switches off their leaf blower to speak to me. 'Saw you took a tumble last night! You all right?' I have never seen his face before – I certainly don't know his name – but I'm guessing through the magic of twenty-four-hour surveillance, he knows more about me than I do. This happens a lot, hence why my dreams of isolation are such a solace. Walking through these cobbled streets knowing they are always watching makes even a trip to the shops an anxious task, especially when you're a clumsy oaf like me.

Saving face, I point to my own battered head and laugh. 'Just a little bruise, mostly on my pride but the rest of me is well, thank you.' My smile is exaggerated, false, as he laughs. I don't stick around for the conversation to continue; it was nice enough for him to ask about my wellbeing, but it's done little more than reignite my embarrassment.

As I approach the Jewel House, I notice that the King's Guards are already on sentry duty. Each one is an exact copy and paste of the other. I see barely a glimmer of life in them as their regimented stance is unwavering, even without the eyes of the tourist analysing their every move for a sign of life. Their red tunics are embellished with golden buttons so perfectly polished that the Tower's reflection sits inside each one. Each guard carries a rifle propped up in the palms of their hands and its sharpened bayonet sits in their peripheral vision. I can tell that the blade too has seen its owner bent over it with a cloth doused in silver polish for hours upon hours; its tip captures the light and glows like it's molten. The bearskin caps obscure the majority of their faces, and I'm sure the inky fur must tickle at their ears. It looks like it would be the most annoying fringe in the world; I'd fail my training instantly by blowing the stray hairs out of my eyes like a frustrated toddler.

Five different infantry regiments stand guard here: the Coldstream, the Grenadiers, the Scots, the Welsh, and the Irish. They rotate around the royal palaces of London, taking it in turns to stand watch over the grounds and its precious contents for a few days at a time. Sometimes even the Royal Air Force, the Royal Navy, and the Gurkhas swap in for a turn, the blue-grey uniforms of the RAF, the bright white hats of the Navy, and the curved kukri carried by the Gurkhas offering a welcome change.

Glancing at my watch and noting I'm still running ahead of time, I observe today's two guards for a while, attempting to decipher which regiment they belong to. Scanning down their uniforms I come to the conclusion that they are from the Grenadier Guards. To the untrained eye, the striking

29

uniforms of each of the regiments look indistinguishable, but I can tell these lads are 'Grens' as a bright white plume juts out from the side of their bearskin, their buttons are equally spaced, and their collars are embroidered on each side with what they call 'a grenade fired proper'– though to me they just look like a pair of shuttlecocks.

With not a tourist in sight, the scene feels timeless and the pair of them stood there together could be the muse for an oil painting; if I could capture this moment right now, it wouldn't be too hard to convince someone that it was centuries old.

Eventually, I walk past them, analysing their uniforms like an officer ready to send them to His Majesty for inspection. I reach the second of the pair and I notice that he towers above the other. His nose is strong and straight, and his jawline is sharp enough that it looks like it could cut straight through the metal curb chain of his bearskin. He is the blueprint of a soldier in every way. Peering out from beneath the dark hair, his eyes are impossible not to notice. The blue-green of his irises seems to glow against his pale face as they too refrain from much movement, just a slow blink over his disciplined forward stare.

Something in them feels familiar. It's a uniform and stance I have seen a thousand times, but I can't help but recognise those eyes . . . I shake my head. I've probably just seen him here before. I have a knack of remembering (and fantasising) over the few handsome soldiers that rotate in and out of these walls: there was a rather stunning group of Canadian troops that came once, and I distinctly remember it being even harder than usual to get to work on time as I'd spend just a little too long admiring their beautifully wide shoulders. I do occasionally ask my dad if there are plans for them to return any time soon, but I certainly don't mind making do with this certain set of Grenadiers today.

I only take a few steps past the guard before I stop dead in my tracks. No. It can't be. It surely can't be him. Those eyes. I *do* remember those eyes. Forgetting where I am for a moment, I half shuffle, half moonwalk backwards until I am stood face to face with the guardsman. His broad chest cloaked in red towers over me as I squint at his face. It is him. It's Lord Lamppost – the terrifying posh guy from last night that I almost bulldozed over in my fit of idiocy. The terrifying posh guy who really did not take kindly to said bulldozing. I rub the tips of my fingers instinctively, the purple of my nail a reminder that our disagreeable meeting wasn't in fact a dream.

But how can it be him? A gentleman who could rival a prince with his elocution and have me believe he could possess the political power to make me disappear is a . . . guardsman? An infantry soldier? Don't get me wrong, it's a highly respectable job, but one usually undertaken by working class lads who didn't have the easiest time at school and need a little more discipline in their lives. Although, thinking back to his harshness, he does seem like he could use a few extra lessons in politeness.

Before I can process the information that I am not going to be arrested for accidentally assaulting a member of the royal family, the statuesque face . . . *winks?*

He just winked at me!

Letting out a little yelp of surprise, I stumble over my feet and power-walk away as quickly as I possibly can. Why the bloody hell am I stupid enough to forget that behind all of that wool and fur is an actual human being? One who can see me as much as I can see him! I fan my face with my hands, the heat of my shame prickling across my cheeks. Can I not just have one day without being a complete and utter social car crash? It's not even 9 a.m.!

As soon as I reach work, Kevin, of course, has to make matters worse by commenting on the freakish redness of my face, which, naturally, makes me blush an even deeper shade of crimson. I am too preoccupied replaying that stupid wink over and over in my head to respond and slump down into my chair. The heaviness of the movement, which is no doubt doubled by the ever-growing weight of my shame, forces some sort of demonic screech from the old chair, and I send a silent prayer to the gods that it will just put me out of my misery altogether and swallow me into its itchy cushion. Although, on second thought, I am almost certain that this is Kevin's seat that he attempts to strategically swap with everyone else's in the office to get rid of, and I don't particularly fancy being that close to anything that he has had his arse on top of.

Signing onto my computer, the same familiar tabs automatically reappear. I have four different job-hunting websites permanently open, using any spare second of the day to apply for jobs I actually want to do for the rest of my life. This morning, refreshing each of them at least three times presents not one offer that could provide me with a much-needed escape from my embarrassment or my stagnation.

Before long, a customer at the window distracts me from scrolling through the list of rejection notifications that are forming quite the collection in my inbox. A man knocks at the glass, his lips pursed and intermittently muttering. I suppose I have no other choice but to do my job, and so I plaster on my best fake smile and launch into the usual spiel: 'Good morning, sir. Wel—'

'Two adults, three children. You've already kept me waiting so be quick about it, would you.'

My smile retracts into a grimace as I turn to my computer. Minimising the tab 'Jobs: Heritage Manager', I deflate back into my place and do as my wonderful customer demands.

After the hundredth customer, all as charming as the first, my mouth is dry from the strain of forcing a smile. Escaping to the kitchen, my mind wanders back to this morning and the array of colourful variations on the 'you massive buffoon' self-talk resumes.

Not lumbered with any torturous punishment today, when 5 p.m. rolls around, I decide to take a stroll to the Tower's pet cemetery – conveniently located about as far from the guards' post as you can get. Now I'm not usually one to enjoy a gothic Mary-Shelley-style jaunt in a grave-yard but the pet cemetery has a private peace about it. Not many people remember it exists so it's a quiet retreat from the bustling village behind the walls. You're always accompanied by the red blinking eye of the camera in the corner, of course, but the only time I'm not is when I use the bathroom, so you get used to being watched.

The pet cemetery resides in a quiet, overgrown section of the moat. They had to turn the defensive moat into a welcoming garden a couple of hundred years ago after it turned into London's greatest cesspit and ended up killing more people inside the Tower than it did trespassers on the outside. This part of the moat isn't quite as wide as the rest and the dense vegetation flanked by high walls gives it a feeling of seclusion, like a tiny forest in the middle of the city.

Miniature gravestones skirt around the bottom of the walls and the engraved names of cats and dogs of times gone by peek out from behind mossy blankets. Right at the back of the cemetery is a bench that has been consumed by ivy; vines wrap around the wooden slats so tightly that it too looks like it sprouted straight out of the ground with Mother Nature as its only carpenter.

Woven into the landscape is the ravenmaster. She sits in the very corner of the bench, draped in foliage, and her layers of sage-coloured cardigans camouflage her against her surroundings. The soil of her black hair sprouts wiry shoots of white and, even in the spring warmth, is tucked into a burgundy scarf and a bark-coloured skirt completes the look, flowing over woollen tights that disappear into a ragged pair of leather boots planted into the ground like the roots of a tree. I've never seen anyone so readily belong to the earth in the way that she does. You could walk straight past her and not believe anything other than the fact she grew there, just as the flowers and weeds did.

I can sometimes lose myself in here, sat next to her in silence as ravens fly in and out to peck gently at the seeds in her hair with no concept of the passage of time. She says very little – although when she does, everyone listens as though they're hearing the words of a prophet. Instead, she reserves most of her conversation for her birds. I've seen her sit for hours talking to them, sharing a packet of digestive biscuits, dunking hers into a cold cup of tea and theirs into a polystyrene cup of animal blood. I truly believe they talk to her too. She has a strange wisdom, as if she watches everything unfold inside the Tower from a bird's eye view.

I take my usual seat beside her wordlessly. She prefers it this way, viewing small talk as a waste of language. Instead, she places a pinch of sunflower seeds on my thigh and after a short while of stillness, a small blackbird lands on my work trousers and cleans them up one by one. As quickly as it arrived, it flies away again with nothing left to prove it ever happened at all.

We sit like this for a while until a small evening breeze begins to creep under the folds of my work blouse. As I stand, her gravelly voice sounds – barely audible over the noise of the city: 'Don't be afraid of the heights, child. Your wings will always catch you before you even think to flap them.' This is another one of her abstract philosophies.

I'm never sure what to say but I point at the bruise on my face and laugh. 'I wish you'd told me that last night.'

She rolls her eyes in good humour but doesn't quite crack a smile. I raise my hand to bid her goodnight and she lifts hers in return.

Chapter 4

*P*earls press against my neck like cold fingertips. The breeze carries flurries of blossom across the courtyard and sprinkles the tiny petals into my hair like confetti showered over a bride. My corset forbids me to slouch as I perch myself on the stone wall. Propped up by the whale-boned seams, I have no choice but to sit high and proud overlooking Tower Green. The dark Tudor beams of the King's House wrap its glowing white panels in shadow. It too looks like it's straining to escape its fetters. The sentry box outside is unguarded, the house is unprotected. But there is no one around to protect it from. The tranquillity of lightless London guards me. The candle-free night shrouds my smiles in the darkness and hides my face from view. The anonymity of the night is my greatest comfort.

Darkness transforms the tall window at the heart of the Beauchamp Tower into a gaping void, and in the shadows it appears glassless and endless. The stone steps are lit up by a tall gas lamp. A figure lingers beneath it, illuminated only by the irregular flicker of the flame. Every evening I have walked these walls alone; it has been my solace to explore unnoticed. Despite the intrusion on my sanctum, the sight of a stranger doesn't unnerve me. Instead of fleeing, I am pulled towards them. I don't fear them, nor do I fear being seen by them.

As I inch closer, I notice the light catch in the contours of a chiselled face. Sharp cheekbones cast shadows across his masculine features and the moonlight seems to roll around in his green-blue irises. His dark curls shimmer with ribbons of red as they sit clumsily over his head. I'm close enough to touch him now. I outstretch my hand but, just as my fingertips are about to land on his cotton shirt, he disappears as though he was never there to begin with.

I wake with a start. I am so used to that dream, it's comfortable – it's like home. Every night, it's the same. I'm alone, I'm always alone. How has he followed me into my dreams? I'm almost certain that it was him, the guard, Lord Lamppost. Thoughts of him raced around my head all last night, and I fell asleep filled with guilt over his broken box, despite his rudeness and the subsequent wink. It seems my conscience has managed to follow me into my dreams.

Thinking of him and our perplexing meetings fills me with such an uncommon assortment of emotions. The wink is what confuses me most. Was it supposed to be some sort of peace offering? And yet, that doesn't ring true. He was *so* angry during our first meeting; he surely wouldn't be so jovial now. Something about it all reminds me of school – the way the popular boys would be dared to flirt with the girls who never stood a chance, only for a laugh with all of their friends. I was always that girl. The embarrassed impulse to see him again, to confront him, surges through me.

Throwing on my work uniform, my mind is set on going to see him this very instant. Although I haven't quite decided which stance to take. Do I grovel, so I don't get a six-figure invoice dropped through my letterbox for some expensive family heirloom I have accidentally destroyed? Or do I reproach him, for injuring me without a care and trespassing on my unconscious fantasies?

I look feral, I know I do, but I can't stop myself. I throw on a pair of shoes and run out of the house. So preoccupied with hoping the green-eyed guardsman is there again this morning, I only notice the rain when it's too late. It's already soaked through my blouse and droplets slide slowly down my arms.

Once I reach the sentry, the stone of anxiety in the pit of my stomach sits heavy, my anger dissipating under it. He's there. Just as I did yesterday, I stand before him as though I am challenging him to a duel.

'Okay, right, erm, good morning. Just want to start by saying I'm mad. By which I mean angry mad, not like crazy mad – although I know that's something a mad person would say, and I *am* talking to a stranger who can't talk back to me when I'm completely wet through but . . . hi, I'm Margaret. Well, actually, everyone just calls me Maggie. Margaret sounds a bit like your nan doesn't it.' I'm babbling. I'm totally babbling. Get it together, Mags, for God's sake. 'And . . . I wanted to apologise to you. Like I say, I'm mad at you, but also myself for being a massive idiot. The other day was really not my day and you caught me, or more I caught you, when I was in a bit of a bad spot. I can't tell you how sorry I am about the, you know . . .' I flap a hand wildly, attempting to refer to the jewellery box. 'And the swearing was directed one hundred per cent towards myself. To be fair I thought you were a lamppost for a good minute, if that makes it better?'

I pause for a response, forgetting myself again. For his part, though, he's ever the professional and just continues his regimented stare, as if I'm part of the landscape. If I am then I'm definitely one of those diseased pigeons, you see walking around with six toes on one foot and no toes on the other. 'Yeah, no, of course, if anything that's another insult. God, I'm awful at this. Anyways, please don't report me or anything. My dad's a beefeater here you see, and if I need a telling-off, it's him who gets it in the neck. I'd offer to pay if I could, I really would, but I work in that little ticket office on the hill and I am pretty sure the box alone costs more than my annual salary. And you know what a soldier's wage is, and a beefeater's is little better, so I couldn't even ask my dad or anything. I'd offer to polish your boots or something to make up for it, but it seems like you're pretty well covered on that front.' I point down at his boots and see myself warped in the toecap: my hair is stuck flat to my face, and I can't tell if the bead of water rolling down my forehead is rain or a nervous sweat. He doesn't look down. 'I really am sorry. Truly.' Not so much as a blink. 'Okay, well, have a nice day. Don't go standing around all day – you'll get varicose veins.' You'll get varicose veins? Honestly, if he decides to unload the entire magazine of his rifle into my back as I walk away, I think I'll thank him.

I don't really know what I expected the outcome to be, seeing as the poor guy can't even speak to tell me to 'get lost' if he wants to, but seeing as he broke his military code to wink at me – to embarrass me – I thought I might get a little flicker of acknowledgement.

With that, I stop in my tracks. The repressed anger bubbles back up again and, without thinking, I march back to him. This time, I try to straighten out the nervous slouch in my posture that I had shrunk to in my instinctive atonement. 'Actually. Before I go, I just wanted to say, that, well . . . you hurt me. When you picked up that box, you trapped my fingers, and as much as I feel horrendous for what happened, you could have at least had the decency to apologise.'

I pause for a moment, almost waiting for him to shout, or point his rifle towards me, but he is still. 'And, um, you walked into me too. You are just as much to blame as I am. You should look where you . . . just be careful when you are on the phone. And, well, yes. I just think, yeah . . .' I trail off and give him one of those tight 'you all right?' smiles that you do when you pass an acquaintance in the street and want to be polite but also want to avoid any actual conversation at all costs. With a sigh, I turn around again and don't look back.

My throat constricts in the aftermath of the confrontation. A silly little tear springs to my eye, and try as I might to cough it away, it abseils its way down my silly little face, and I end up tasting it and all of its salty shame. I'm thankful to the rain for masking it. I'm not upset that a man who I knew would get fired for talking to me didn't talk to me. I'm frustrated. I'm frustrated that I fail in spectacular fashion at everything I try. That I can't ever seem to execute any of my plans without losing all confidence halfway through and regretting every decision I ever made up until that point. I'm frustrated that each attempt I make to improve myself, I just get closer and closer to accepting that my idiocy is terminal.

The worst of all, I'm frustrated that every second of my embarrassment is broadcast in real time, in HD, to a whole room of people who replay it and show it off like it's an underground cinema and I'm their biggest star. Last winter, I even caught a pair of the Jewel House staff giggling over an edit someone had made of me slipping on the cobbles. Granted, the combination of music and slow-motion did make for a rather funny show, but at this point I can't even pee without worrying that I'm going to wake up to a video of it shared around the group chat.

Given my mission-like approach to the morning, I'm actually early to work for once and I'm grateful that I've beaten Kevin in I have enough time to stand under the hand dryer in the bathrooms before he can make a sarcastic comment about me swimming through the Thames to get to work. The padding of my bra is unsalvageable, though, and leaves two rather unflattering damp splodges on my chest as if I had been uncontrollably lactating. Luckily for me, my hair is enough of a distraction that I'm sure no one will notice my boobs. The undirected heat of the dryer has given me a wild Eighties blow-out, even after plaiting it and adding even more water to smooth it down, it bursts out of the braids in a curly bonnet of baby hairs.

By the time I emerge, my other colleagues have arrived and are sat around the staff room, giggling over a cup of tea.

'Oh my Goddess, this is too good! She has *no* shame! Soaking wet too!' Andy is in hysterics. She's twenty-seven but hasn't quite gotten over her 'I'm so weird and quirky' phase from school. Nor has she grown out of the bitching in the playground phase. Her blouse is intentionally frayed and burned at the bottom and a black leather choker holds a heavy metal ring around her neck. If we were still at school, she would have bullied me for listening to Taylor Swift because anything 'mainstream is a product of capitalism designed to brainwash you'. Yet, she buys her crystals on Amazon.

'Jules in the press office told me that she saw her harassing him. Proper flirting and that. *How* embarrassing!' Samantha cuts herself off, laughing too hard. She is always the one playing Chinese whispers – each day she arrives to work with her 'Paul's Boutique' handbag full of gossip that somehow turns into a dramatic soap opera storyline inside the hot pink lining.

My gut tells me they're talking about me. They haven't seen me yet but my stomach twists painfully and I debate sliding back through the toilet door. Just as I begin to creep backwards, Kevin bursts into the room. The door slams against the wall and small flakes of manila paint scatter onto the floor. As my colleagues snap their heads to the source of the noise, they spot me hovering in the corner, and Andy looks across at her partner in crime and feigns a gasp into her hand.

Andy has always been a little more malicious than the others. Samantha once let it slip that she had a soft spot for Bran whilst we were still dating. He had joined me at a few of the work parties as moral support and she managed to convince herself that he was a better match for her than someone like me. Luckily for me – or as it turns out, perhaps, unluckily – I think she is the only girl he has ever rejected and, thus, she absolutely despises me for it. Her rejection didn't stop her from stalking around every time he would pick me up from work or 'drunk' texting him in the early hours. I still get a little sick feeling each time I see her, but I've never had the guts to challenge her over it. Turns out, it's much easier to get the confidence to square up to someone when they are contractually obliged to neither move nor speak.

'Right get to work, you lot. Ooh 'ello, Margaret, bit early for you int it? Got something exciting to get out of bed for?' He looks over to the others and winks an exaggerated wink, and their responding chorus of abhorrent giggling cuts through me. I can do nothing except take a seat in the furthest ticket booth from them and think over all of the different witty comments I could have used to wipe the arrogant grins from their faces.

Imagining various scenarios of strapping Andy, Samantha and Kevin to a trebuchet and catapulting them across the river occupies most of my morning. There is one inside the moat opposite the ticket office, tempting me.

The slew of visitors is slow today, so I sit with my chin propped up in my palm, trying not to lose my mind. The best thing about working in central London is the people-watching: figuring out each person's story just from the way they look, the confidence in their stride, their inter-action with the world around them. The only positive about spending each and every day cooped up in a glass fishbowl is the fact that I can see every person that walks up to the Tower and around it. Tourists from across the globe file in in their herds. They're always armed with a camera that they're not too sure how to use and armoured in their khaki shorts. Locals are occasionally thrown into the mix too: men in suits try to outdo one another in their mono-tone received pronunciation, seeing how much corporate jargon they can cram into one sentence. Occasionally one of those really annoying people who have their lives together enough to go jogging around the sights over their lunch hour sails past. Show-offs.

An elderly couple shuffles along the cobbles. Frail and hunched over himself, the husband offers an arm to his wife, which she holds on to, to steady herself. She doesn't seem to be gripping hard enough for the arm to be making any difference to her; he certainly wouldn't be able to catch her if she fell. I like to think she holds his arm to make him feel like he can still protect her and care for her. Perhaps when they were young lovers, he walked her across the city, arm in arm. The doting husband who always came to his wife's aid. But the more I look, the more I'm convinced that the nameless wife has never been the kind to need saving. To me, she seems the capable kind, strong-willed. Maybe she just knew how much it pleased her husband to feel needed, so she'd take his arm but secretly do all of the heavy lifting herself. I have no idea if I'm any good at this game. They could be brother and sister for all I know, but fantasising takes my mind off of my own mortifying moments of the week so far.

By the time the old couple amble out of my eyeline, and I cast my gaze around to decide which clueless member of the public I will create a story for next, they've all stopped still. A Mexican wave of smartphones and cameras are thrust in front of most of their faces, each one pointed towards the same spot. It is likely a celebrity; they're hardly a rare find around here, although it's never anyone interesting. I lean forward in my seat anyway to see if I can work out what all of the fuss is about. Just in case Henry Cavill has finally seen all of my thirst tweets and is coming to sweep me off my feet. You never know . . .

Emerging from the crowd is one of the King's Guards. He is still clad in his bright red tunic and the hobnails in the bottom of his drill boots clink against the pavement with each perfectly even stride, but his bearskin hat has been swapped out for a forage cap and the peak bends low over his brow, obscuring him from curious onlookers. His posture is robotic, rigid, and his attention never diverts from the path before him. I don't think I've ever seen a man so elegant. Not only does his uniform mark him out from the rest, but he is easily a head of height above them all.

As though it was rehearsed, the tight crowd clears a pathway to allow him to pass through. The captivated audience follow him with the lenses of their cameras as he marches straight by them. Seemingly unperturbed by the sheer number of eyes upon him, the guard has become a walking landmark.

'See! I told you they were real!' enthuses a wide-eyed child stood close to my window. His strong American accent goes unacknowledged by the boy beside him who continues to stare at the soldier, open-mouthed, as though he'd just seen some superhero step out of the pages of a comic book.

The guardsman stops abruptly outside of the ticket office, leans back slightly, and surveys the signage. Getting over their excitement that they managed to see a guardsman in the wild, the sightseers slowly disperse, leaving just a nosy few behind to continue their staring.

He leans into the glass of the first window, out of my line of sight for now. Swinging back on my chair, I strain to hear Samantha's end of the conversation from within the office.

'You're sure you've got the right person, love? Right, okay then.' I can hear her tapping her acrylic nails against the desk. He's asking for someone, and whoever it is has piqued Samantha's interest.

'She in trouble then, is she?' She can't help herself, always collating her gossip; this will make tonight's 'going-home headlines' in the cloakroom. Whatever the soundless guardsman says next offends her, her nails stop their intrigued tapping. 'Ooh, I was just asking. Jesus! Down the other end.'

Only when the guard begins to stride down the row of

windows, heading for mine, do I recognise him. Panic sets in as the same unblinking and unmoving face I hounded only this morning inches closer and closer towards me, with those same intimidating features. Is he coming to tell me off? Come to give me a taste of my own medicine? Oh God, what do I do? Just as I hop up off my seat, ready to escape into the back room, a knock on the window makes me jump.

'Margo!' A familiar voice comes muffled through the glass. Now I'm almost wishing I had taken my chances with a telling-off from a King's Guard because this is the only worse alternative I could think of.

Bran presses his palms flat against the glass. The metal cufflinks of his freshly pressed white shirt tap an irregular beat with each little movement he makes and, try though I might to look past him, he fills my eyeline.

'Can we talk?'

I shake my head.

'Come on, babe,' he whines.

'I'm working, Bran.' He looks around at the people forming a queue behind him.

'Well, you won't be able to serve anyone until you've spoken to me, so let's just do this quickly shall we?' A sick feeling hangs in my stomach, and I realise that if I don't want to cause a scene then I have to appease him.

After sliding down the blind to my booth, I slip out of the building and meet my ex-boyfriend on the street outside.

'What do you need, Bran?' My voice is flat and blunt.

'I wanted to see you. Oh God, Margo, I miss you so

much.' He takes a lunge towards me, seemingly with the intention of taking my hand, but I dodge his advances.

'This is wasting my time. I need to get back to work. My break finished twenty minutes ago,' I lie and head back towards the office, but he catches me by the arm and prevents me from taking another step.

'Margo—'

'Please let go of me. I really can't do this here.'

'What happened to your face?' he asks, staring at my bruise. I instinctively lift a hand to touch it. 'Did someone hurt you?'

'No, not at all. I fell into that stupid safe. Can you please just let go?'

'Come on, Margo. I came to see you. I promised you I would.' I try to pull against his grip, but he only uses that as an opportunity to drag me closer. I stumble a little and have to place a hand against him to steady myself.

He takes that as an invitation to lean in for a kiss, but just before he reaches me, I turn my face away, so he misses his mark and ends up planting his unwanted lips on my cheek.

My eyes remain fixed open and with my face at this angle, my gaze is caught and locked in the stare of the same guardsman who was here only minutes before. He has clearly been interrupted in his journey back inside as he stands at the main gate, ignoring a group of tourists who have encircled him, no doubt trying to get a selfie. The guardsman doesn't look away as we stare at one another and it is me who breaks the connection as the realisation of Bran's lips still resting against my cheek hits home, and the fact I have embarrassed myself in front of this man yet again materialises into an intense feeling of vertigo. I push my ex-boyfriend away and rush back inside my booth, slamming the door and locking it before he can break through my resolve again.

Panting, I stand with my back pressed against the door. Bran wouldn't be able to get past the lock but the sick feeling that climbs through me pushes me to do everything I can to get away from the cause. My chest heaves and I have to press my palm against it to calm myself.

'It's okay, I'm okay.' I repeat to myself in an affirming whisper until my chest calms and the rising sense of doom eases.

Groaning, I knock on my forehead with the base of my palm. But I don't get to ruminate over my idiocy or curse at the universe for long, as Kevin emerges from his office with his rat-like eyes narrowed, I quickly snap up the blind, revealing myself to the public again.

'Back to work,' he spits through gritted teeth – and I mean literally spits. It's disgusting. A sunbeam that pries its way into the gloomy office lights up the tiny droplets as they shoot out of his tight lips and splatter to the floor. A sharp gesture of his thumb points me in the familiar direction. I repress the urge to salute him sarcastically as he pretends that he is some drill sergeant as opposed to a ticket-booth manager whose greatest responsibility is selecting the month's stationery out of a catalogue. And, yes, most of our work is done on the computer . . .

As expected, there is hardly a mad rush of people queueing down the street, desperate to get into a medieval castle on a Tuesday afternoon. In fact, for the next three hours I serve a grand total of four people, and one of them mistook us for a tourist information desk and asked me where the closest toilet is. That guardsman doesn't return either. Perhaps I was premature in my panic and it wasn't me he was looking for after all. At least that's one less thing to worry about, but the lack of work to do frees up plenty of time to think about Bran to the extent that when five finally crawls around, my legs are jittering beneath the desk and itching to get away.

Looking out of the window to check if the coast is clear of creeping exes, I slip out of the office and walk quickly back into the Tower. Security guard Bob gives me a smile as I walk in and my tenseness eases. No one can follow me in; I am safe over this threshold.

Unencumbered by the heavy bag of money, I take the scenic route back home again, down Water Lane, through the Bloody Tower archway, and up the Broadwalk Steps into the courtyard. I make it just far enough up the stairs that I can just see the fluffy tops of the guards' bearskins as they finish up their last sentry duty of the day when I hear my name being called again.

'Margo! Wait!'

'Oh, for f—' I mutter to myself as Bran jogs through the archway towards me.

Not wishing to air my dirty laundry in the middle of the palace, I continue on, but his long legs catch up to me just as I pass the two manned sentry boxes outside of the Jewel House.

He takes my arm prisoner in his grip once again and I pull hard against him.

'How did you even get in here?' I say through gritted teeth, trying my hardest not to draw even more attention to us.

'Andy let me in.' He motions to the stairs as Andy and Samantha finally catch up, leaning closely into one another as they watch us and whisper. I clench my fists so tightly that my bitten-down nails press into the skin of my palm.

'Why did you run away earlier? After all I have done for you, I don't deserve being cast aside like that.' A cold hollowness spreads through me. He is referring to Mum.

Again, I try my hardest to yank my arm from his iron grip. Again, I am hauled back into his grip with more force that knocks my tears over the ledge of my eyes to deluge my face. He leans close to me.

'STAND BACK!' a voice booms around the courtyard. We both jump, Bran so surprised he immediately releases me. I find the source of the voice; one of the guardsmen stands before the sentry box composing and resetting his stance by slapping his boots against the concrete and resuming a controlled and frigid posture. His eyes are the only thing to compromise his impartiality. He eyes Bran and I as we stare back, stunned.

The voice had echoed across the Tower and alerted any final stragglers leaving work to our position. The round face of the doctor peeks out between the net curtains of his house just behind Bran. My breath catches in my chest, and I massage my fingers across the palms of my hands; they glide over the dampness with ease, and I knead them together at such a pace that they dry out again.

And then I do the only thing I am good at. I run away.

Well, actually, I am most definitely *not* good at running; I do more of a speed walk across the courtyard towards my nearest exit behind the Jewel House. Twenty paces feels like miles. My feet become heavier with each step, the tears flowing freely down my face. I couldn't feel more exposed in this moment if I was naked.

The guards both watch me as I have to walk closer to them to flee. The one closest to the exit, the one who had simultaneously come to my rescue and yet made everything so much worse, watches me as I closely pass him. My bleary eyes track across his face, which is taut and expressionless; his features add another weight to my humiliation.

I stop before him and roughly wipe the tears out of my eyes with the bottom of my palm. Those same swirls of pietersite come into focus. I am becoming far too familiar with those eyes.

The sob that rattles through my chest pulls me away from him. As I make my way towards my home – my own personal fortress – I throw a glance over my shoulder to check that I am not being followed and see Godders, a beefeater still dressed in his uniform, with his bonnet pressed between his arm and round belly, escorting Bran back down the steps. A small mercy.

Chapter 5

'I wish I'd slapped him,' I say to Lucie from the doorway of my balcony. She does a little dance with her lustrous neck and chitters agreeably. 'Or at least said something cool, like . . . I don't know: "The only thing you deserve is a night in the pillory faced with thirty beefeaters and a bucket full of raven crap."'

The prim and proper corvid looks away as if embarrassed. 'Okay, okay, maybe just a permanent stay in the White Tower cellar.' She flaps her wings in approval.

'Mum did always like him though,' I say, a little more deflated. 'They used to cook together . . . well, she would cook and get him to do all of the washing up and peel all of the veg. She hated that bit. I think he just liked it because he never saw much of his own mum. Mine practically adopted him.'

Cromwell leaps up into my lap and I have to restrain him as he notices his nemesis. I stroke down his nose. 'He is the only boyfriend I'll ever have who will have met my mum.' My cat's rough tongue rakes across my finger lovingly. 'You know . . .' I chuckle, though not because it is funny, far from it. 'I think he cried as much as I did when she died. He used to get up halfway through the day and swap the pillows around on each side, because we both would soak them through. We'd just lay together for days in silence; neither of us wanted to be spoken to, and neither of us wanted to speak. I never loved him more than I did in those months.' I roughly swipe the silent tears from my cheeks. 'Probably because I didn't have to listen to the usual amount of crap that he spouts out of that stupid mouth of his.'

Cromwell leaps off my lap as I stand up. 'Anyway . . . I have better things to think about.' I pick up my history book that's splayed open on the patio table. The cover boasts a battered ship with a terrifying woman at its helm. Her hair is waved from the sea salt and sprouts out from beneath a leather tricorne hat. 'Pirate women are far more interesting than reminding myself that, in the space of three days, the same stranger has witnessed me embarrass myself more times than I have left the Tower grounds this week.'

For the sixth time today, Bran's name lights up on my phone, accompanied with an obnoxious vibration that grinds like a pneumatic drill against my desk. After lifting it up only to roll my eyes and switch it off, I arm myself with a pen and little sticky notes and hop back into bed, recommencing my usual day-off position.

After a few hours, I finish the book and heave it shut. Due to my extensive note taking, it now boasts at least a thousand more words than it had when it was printed and is almost double the thickness. With a severe cramp in my hand, I finally decide to emerge from my room.

'All right, kid?' Dad greets me as I awkwardly stand in the living room doorframe. 'Can I get you anything? You want me to cook us some tea?' He goes to stand up, but I put my hand up to stop him.

'It's okay, I'll just grab something quick.' He sinks back down and gives me a sad smile.

'Okay, love. You make sure you're eating proper though, all right?' I nod and carry on to the kitchen. With an armful of a random assortment of snacks I descend the next set of stairs and sit in the room I think of as Mum's room.

She never actually lived here, but I know she would have loved it. A castle would have suited her – I'm sure she was royalty in a past life. No matter how much money we had, no matter if her clothes all came from the sale rack of a charity shop, she always carried herself with such an air, such confidence, that you had no doubt she was anything but a star.

When she died, we brought most of her stuff from the old house and set it up in here. Her photos cover the walls, and odd knick-knacks that she picked up on her travels fill the shelves. I like to eat my tea, surrounded by her, or at least what she left behind. We would always eat as a family when she was still with us; some nights we'd wait up until midnight for Dad to come home so we could eat with him. Mum would fill me with little nibbles to keep me going but we'd both be so excited to hear about his day that we wouldn't mind. It feels like I'm eating with her again when I sit in this room, surrounded by all of her things.

Waiting until I hear the soft hum of the TV upstairs silenced, I pass Dad on the stairs. He will follow the foot-steps that I have just left behind and spend a few moments in the crowded room before he shuts the door tight until tomorrow.

'Night, darling.'

'Night, Dad.'

I wake up late. Again. My alarm was set for once, but after a continuous onslaught of calls from my ex that continued late into the night, I had no choice but to switch off my phone for a second time, and this time leave it off.

As I rush between the inner walls and across the court-yard, I hang my head low, my hair curtaining my face as I pass the guards on duty. I have no idea if it is the same guard today – for all I know the regiments have swapped and I am hiding from some oblivious Welsh Guard – but I would rather not take my chances.

I am ten minutes late when I finally stumble through the door, but thankfully, I still beat Kevin so as far as he knows I was actually ten minutes early. Until Samantha inevitably grasses me up anyway.

As I take my seat, I switch my phone back on and prepare myself for the tsunami of Bran's bullshit. Even when he isn't seeing how many times he can call me in a minute, his is the only name that ever frequents my phone. I was that insufferable girl at uni whose boyfriend became her life. All of Bran's friends became my friends, as I lived my life trying to be as close to him as possible. Right up until our break-up, I spent every waking moment I could with him, never making plans with anyone else so I'd be free for him.

Before I knew it, I had pushed away every single one of my own friends – made worse by uni ending and proximity no longer forcing me to at least say the occasional hi. By the time we lived together, if Bran had other plans, I could spend days not speaking to another living soul. I suppose I thought that if I isolated myself, showed him that he was my world, that I loved him more than anyone else in my orbit, then maybe I, in turn, would be enough for him.

I wasn't of course. And now, now I don't have him, don't have his friends or his life, my phone is as dry as a pack of Digestive Biscuits when Dad forgets to twist the sleeve closed. I watch the lives of my old friends through photos on social media and long for one of them to reach out, hoping that they might read my mind and do what I can't find the courage to.

I'm not even sure why I bothered switching it back on. It rings straight away, and when I have finished watching it ring out, a message follows it.

Bran: *Please answer my calls, Maggie. x*

Just as I slide my phone back into my pocket, with the message unanswered, it buzzes again.

Bran: *Please x*

Clawing at every scrap of willpower I have, which isn't a lot, I throw it into the drawer of my desk. My fingers itch to look at it again, to reply, but I busy myself staring out of the window. Instead, I while away the morning, tuning out the persistent buzzing and fantasising that I am some oppressed princess, locked away from the world. I imagine scenarios of a handsome prince rushing to save me and slaying the evil Queen Kevin and his two-headed dragon.

'Maggie. Maggie!' he'd say, his voice raspy from the exertion of his fight, doing that breathy thing that they do in films when the hero finally finds the heroine and is so overcome by his love that all he can do is hold her and repeat her name. He would sweep my hair out of my eyes and lift my chin with his blood-soaked hands, his blue-green eyes screaming every word he can't say. He'd lean in, and whisper . . .

'Ma'am!' A bang on the glass startles me out of my daydream just before it gets to the good bit. The arm that had previously propped up my chin, slips from the end of the edge of the table and I end up with a face full of my computer keyboard.

'Oh, shit.' The guardsman stands on the other side of the glass, his fist still lifted from rapping on the window, frozen in shock of my unintentional attempt to knock myself out. 'Are you okay?'

His eyes are wide, and I can see in the reflection of the glass that mine are a mirror image. I rub my forehead, the bruise from the other night still tender. Nodding, I smile through my embarrassment, the adrenaline of seeing him masking the pain.

Stood to attention with his forage cap tucked neatly under his arm, he is dressed in his tunic, his white buff belt tight around his waist. He is tense, both in his military discipline and also his face, which flashes with expressions of anxiety. Ochre curls spill over his forehead and he pushes them back, giving me a clearer look at his eyes and the tiny beauty spot just above his left eyebrow. There's another on his neck too, just above his collar. And at the bottom of his lip. Mum always used to say that marks like that are where your soul mate had kissed you in a past life, and that's why I was covered in freckles. *'You were as loved in that life as you are in this one,'* she would say as she kissed all over my face playfully.

'Yes, fine. Sorry about that,' I say, rubbing my face again. I am pretty sure I can feel little dents in my cheek left by the plastic keys. 'Away with the fairies . . .'

He clears his throat and stands up a little straighter. The crease in between his eyebrows is smoothed as he reassumes his emotionless expression, clearly readying himself to tell me off for accosting him the other day in the rain.

'Can I help you? You know you don't need to buy a ticket to get in, right?' I joke, in an attempt to dispel any lingering agitation on his part. Of course, he doesn't laugh.

'I . . .' he begins but trails off. He fidgets slightly and bends closer to my window. 'I just wanted . . .' He stops again and places his cap down on the ledge of the booth.

'Hang on.' The guardsman collects himself as I speak and moves back from the window. Locking my computer and grabbing my phone from the drawer, I meet him outside the booth. Being well over five foot nine myself, I'm always used to feeling like a giant stood next to literally anyone. But this gentleman must be at least six foot three and his air of superiority adds another six inches on top. For most people, feeling small is demeaning, but for me, feeling small allows me to hide, to feel protected from the subconscious pull of eyes that always seem to follow me. I feel safe stood in his shadow.

'I can hardly hear anything in there,' I say as I reach him. It's a white lie; it *is* slightly more muffled but, above all, it just makes everything feel a bit awkward when having conversations that aren't simply a transaction of tickets and money. I ignore the gnawing feeling of turbulence in my stomach.

He clears his throat again. 'I came yesterday, ma'am—'

'Please, call me Maggie. I mean, you can if you want to. "Ma'am" always registers in my brain as "Mum" and makes me feel old.'

He only nods his head stoically and continues: 'But they said that it was your day off yesterday. And the day before that, but I caught you at a . . . busy time.' Here it comes: quite literally a royal telling-off. Shielding my face behind my hair, I nibble at the inside of my cheek and prepare myself for the incoming lecture.

'I came to apologise for our very first meeting.' His eyes flick to my hand for a moment, and then to the greenish bruise across my forehead. Surprised at the turn the conversation has taken, I tuck the purplish nails into my fist and smile at him. 'I am utterly mortified thinking of how I treated you. Knowing I injured you and then conducted myself so impertinently is an unforgivable act and I would understand if you couldn't accept my sincerest apologies. Please just know it was completely out of character and the result of a particularly bad day.'

'Snap!' I try to defuse some of the tension between us, sensing he has as much desire to be here as a child who has been forced to apologise to their next-door neighbour for kicking a football over the fence. 'Really, it's fine. Thank you for your apology. I suppose now we're even.'

He relaxes for a moment, but it isn't long until his expression shifts again and his seriousness resumes. 'I also came yesterday because I wanted to make sure you . . . I know I upset you, again, in the courtyard with your . . . that guy. I thought that I should perhaps come and see if you're okay. And apologise . . . again.' He averts his eyes at the last part.

'Oh God, no . . ., absolutely not. Please, you were just doing your job. I understand.' My face is on fire.

'Not really. I was . . . well, it doesn't matter. I shouldn't have got involved. It's not my place to come between you and your . . ., partner.' He struggles for the words.

'Ex,' I correct him. 'I should really be thanking you. Although, next time could you try and do it just a little bit more quietly? I think you almost gave me a heart attack.' I leave out the part where all of the unwanted attention has been the talk of the Tower for two days now.

'I . . . think your phone is ringing,' he says, calling my

attention to the loud buzzing in the pocket of my trousers. 'I'll, erm, let you get . . . I should probably . . .' He places his cap back on his head, readying himself to leave.

'Oh, don't worry about it. That will be said ex.' I give an exasperated chuckle. 'You'd think he's working in a call centre and I'm the only caller with the number of times he's rung these last few days.' A brief frown creases the guardsman's face. 'Hopefully he will get bored soon,' I awkwardly add, slipping my hand into my pocket to discreetly decline the call.

'So, you're really okay? After the whole . . .' He gestures again to my bruised fingertips.

'Absolutely fine.' Aside from the typhoon of anxiety swirling in my stomach, of course.

'I'm glad.' He coughs. 'Maggie,' he adds with a glimmer of a smile.

'I knew you could drop the formalities!' I tease.

He visibly relaxes, sighing as though he'd been holding his breath with tension.

'I really do appreciate you coming here. And, hey, sorry for harassing you at work the other day. I have no idea what came over me.' I had a weird dream about him is what actually came over me, but I can hardly go around telling that to strangers – I'd end up on a register.

'It can be pretty boring stood there for two hours at a time when the only people speaking to you are just shouting things to try and get you to move, so you made it interesting. I didn't mind,' the guardsman replies, with a little shrug, and the slight twitch at the corners of his lips gives me a hint that he is more human than his ironing-board posture would suggest. I feel a strange sense of achievement and I can't help but beam up at him.

'I'm so sorry. I realise that I never even asked *your* name?'

The nameless soldier doesn't get a chance to reply.

'Margo!' a voice booms from across Tower Hill. 'Who the hell is that?'

I want to scream. When Bran reaches us, he is panting, his phone clutched tightly in his hand.

'Bran, please. I'm busy.' I motion back to my empty office and the queue that has begun to grow at Andy's window.

He leans close to me, gripping my arm. 'Busy flirting with soldiers?' He tries to tug me away.

'Maggie?' The guard addresses me as he stands even more rigidly than before, if that's possible. Bran acknowledges him with a reproachful glance from head to toe. I swallow hard at the rising lump in my throat, but my intense embarrassment and his tightening grip push the tears closer and closer to the edge, threatening to spill.

'I'm really sorry, sir,' I address the guard with a penitent expression.

Bran scoffs in his face and turns back to me with a Machiavellian grin. 'So, this is why you've been ignoring my calls, is it? I was already on my way over here when you finally answered, and I could hear every last word of your embarrassing little attempt at chatting him up.' His grip tightens and I wince.

'What? No . . . I . . . Bran . . .' My whole body burns in embarrassment as words fail me again and I throw a glance over my shoulder; Kevin, Andy and Samantha are all pressed against the glass of one of the ticket booths,

63

jostling with each other to get a slightly better view. I avert my gaze to the chewing gum on the pavement, desperately trying not to cry or throw up. 'Please, you're hurting me.' I place my free hand on his, which is still clamped around my fingers. He doesn't release me, only brings me even closer to him and is just about to continue his jealous accusations when he is swiftly interrupted.

The guardsman clears his throat, and I ready myself for whatever awkward excuse he's going to use to flee the situation. 'I'm only going to tell you this once: take your hands off of her, apologise, and fuck off.' I snap my eyes up to him in shock. He doesn't even look at Bran but holds eye contact with me. His boyish nerves seem to have vanished, and I shiver under the intensity of his stare.

Bran scoffs. 'I've heard that you lot aren't quite the brightest of the bunch, so I'll spell it out for you: my girlfriend here is happy to see me, aren't you, Margo? We have plans. I don't need some posh guy in a stupid costume giving me orders. Go back to what you're good at – stand still and shut up.'

'You aren't my boyfriend,' I mumble timidly. The idea of an ally acts as a shot of adrenaline, helping me to find my voice again.

'Come on, Margo, you don't know what you're saying because this stranger is making you uncomfortable. Let's go talk.' He tries to pull me painfully by the arm, and I resist as much as I can.

'That's funny, because Maggie and I have lunch plans. Perhaps you got the date wrong?' He steps forward and places his hand firmly on Bran's shoulder, his wide palm swallowing up my ex-boyfriend's skinny frame. 'Now I believe I told you to let go of her . . .' He continues in a whisper that I try but fail to hear. Whatever he says, it's effective. The tight grip on my hand is released and I rub it uncomfortably.

'Fine. I'll call you, Margo. Just answer it this time okay, baby?' And with that, Bran shuffles off the way he came – although not before the guardsman waves sarcastically.

He angles himself back towards me and asks if I'm okay, the intimidating glare completely dissipated. It takes me a while to formulate any words. The events of the past few days swim around in my eyes, caught in the riptide of tears that are becoming harder and harder to contain. I try to apologise but the embarrassment is tightening my chest, and I find myself gasping for air.

He goes to take my arm carefully. 'Do you mind?' he asks tentatively, and when I nod my head, he guides me to a bench at the back of the ticket office. We sit in a comfortable silence for a while whilst I compose myself.

'You never have to apologise for things like that . . . to anyone.' He breaks the silence and I give him a small smile.

'Thank you. And thank you for that out there too, sir . . .'

'Freddie. Please call me Freddie.' After a pause he stands up and looks at me expectantly. 'Come on then.'

Noticing my confusion he continues: 'I mean I know we don't actually have lunch plans, but you look like you need a drink. Although sadly the strongest thing I can offer you whilst we are both on duty is a coffee.'

He offers me his hand to help me up and I accept with a smile.

Nestled between office blocks just behind the Tower is a ruined church: St Dunstan in the East. Bombed out in the Second World War, its medieval pillars still stand, reclaimed by ivy and climbed by wisteria that blossoms in a violet explosion. Without its roof it should feel exposed, but the springtime has rebuilt it in its patchworks of nature. Trees hang so heavy with vegetation that it shields you from the bustle of the city and transports you to a timeless tranquillity. Robbed of its stained glass, the windows allow streams of light to pass through the Gothic arches, which glow under the warm gaze of the sun. Despite its state of disrepair, there is something even more divine about it. How can such a tragedy transform something already perfect into something magical? It is London's Garden of Eden.

With our hands awkwardly clutching at our warm paper cups, Freddie and I sit side by side on one of the ruined walls. It's clear that neither of us really knows what to say. What do you say to the stranger you had repeatedly embarrassed yourself in front of, and who just saved you from your unhinged ex-boyfriend?

I scan down his body, desperately looking for some sort of conversation prompt. His posture, even sat down, is perfect. I'm starting to think his uniform must have some sort of built-in rod or even a corset that makes it impossible to slouch. He is careful not to let the backs of his perfectly buffed and polished boots touch the wall at the heels. Even in his downtime, he acts as if he's on duty. I wonder if he even sleeps like Dracula, as still and stiff as the wood of his coffin.

'I really wouldn't look at you and say that you're a hot chocolate kind of guy,' I settle for, teasing him as he tries to suck whipped cream out of the little hole of the plastic lid.

He lowers his cup and clears his throat. 'You think that a guardsman can't enjoy a hot chocolate because it isn't masculine enough?' He is so perfectly well spoken that he could be reciting the Yellow Pages and still be intimidating.

Oh, shit. Well done, Maggie. The one thing I seem to know best is how to drop myself in it!

'I'm kidding! You don't have to look so terrified.' He laughs a little as I breathe a sigh of relief, shooting him an amused look. 'If you think this is surprising, you should see what I order at a bar.'

'You're a pink gin kind of guy?'

'Even worse: cocktails.'

After a short laugh, it goes quiet again. I suppose it shouldn't be too much of a surprise that a man who chose a career where he would be punished for interacting with anyone isn't much of a conversationalist. This time, though, it's a comfortable silence. I sip at my coffee, and my anxiety from the day's events slowly dissipates.

'Has he always been like . . . *that*?' Freddie asks suddenly, as though he had been thinking about it for a while and never meant for it to it slip out. He backtracks: 'Wait . . . you don't have to answer that. It's not my business. I shouldn't have gotten involved. Again.'

'You just put him in his place more than I ever did in seven years! I don't mind you asking questions.' He looks relieved and stares back into his paper cup as I continue: 'To be honest, I'm not sure. That must sound so silly to someone like you because he practically has the word "arsehole" scribbled across his forehead these days, but . . . I suppose he made me feel special. It was good for the first few years. We were at uni together, and we were never apart. I'd have done anything for him, and he would have done anything for me. And he helped me through . . . a lot. But when we graduated, things started to change. He got this job at the bottom of the heap in some finance company. I only met his colleagues once, but that was even too much. If you ever needed to explain toxic masculinity to anyone, you could just show them those idiots. After that, he got worse and worse. He had no control at work, no cool reputation, so he took control at home, and became "one of the lads" by destroying the person he was and subsequently me.'

I can feel my heartbeat pounding in my ears. I know I should stop there, but something about Freddie's calm composure makes me want to keep going. He still doesn't say a word, or drop his poker face, but I can tell he's listening intently – and it's been so long since I've had someone other than a raven to talk to about all of this.

'But I stayed anyway . . . It's so much harder than I thought to recognise that the guy I imagined was the love of my life is just . . . not very nice. I spent every single day believing that the man I had laughed with, leaned on, loved . . . was still in there. That maybe if I kept reminding him that he loved me, if I was the perfect girlfriend and devoted myself to him, he would see the error of his ways, and he might just come back to me. But I realise now that he couldn't have ever loved me if he could watch me fall apart in front of him over and over again. It felt like he was as addicted to my tears as I was to running back to him. I don't know what I thought would happen. All I know is, back then, I would have chosen that life a million times over rather than go it alone. I'd lost someone else, someone very close to me, and . . . I just couldn't face losing him too. But it was too late – I already had.'

I've shared too much. He still doesn't look at me. His gaze remains fixated on the dregs of chocolate that he swills around the bottom of his cup.

'I should have just stuck with my cat.' I laugh awkwardly, hoping to defuse the tension that has settled over us. As expected, he doesn't laugh along.

'So, was it you who left him?'

'Technically yes, although I didn't have much choice. After the third affair, I told my dad and half an hour later Dad, and Richie and Godders – two of the other beefeaters – turned up at our flat with Godders's little green Mini Cooper and shipped me and all of my stuff back here. I was just grateful that Bran wasn't home, or he'd have been marched through Traitors' Gate straight into the Bloody Tower.'

'Mmhmm,' Freddie hums quietly. I can't tell if I'm boring him or not, but I feel compelled to continue.

'He didn't take it all too well though, and he's been coming to the Tower a lot to try to win me back. He came the other day too – the day I bumped into you for the first time. All lovely and sweet, telling me he missed me and stuff. All of that happened just before I had to go down into the haunted cellar, and you know the rest. Like I said, that really wasn't my day. My mind was in a million different places. Actually, on that note . . . can we start again?'

He finally looks at me as I extend my hand for him to shake. His hand swallows mine in a firm grip.

'Good afternoon, ma'am. My name is Guardsman Freddie. It's a pleasure to make your acquaintance.'

I laugh at his formality, surprised that he's playing along with my charade.

'Hi, Freddie. My name is Maggie Moore and if you call me ma'am one more time, I'll have no choice but to pour what's left of my coffee over your lovely woollen tunic.'

He chuckles. 'Okay, Maggie it is then – although, just in case . . .' He takes my cold cup from my hands and tosses it in the bin beside him, along with his own. 'Now, Maggie, can you please explain to me why on earth you were in a haunted cellar?'

Enjoying the lighter tone our conversation has taken, I recount the whole story from the beginning.

'So, it is really haunted?'

'I think so. I haven't exactly seen any see-through floaty people, but I've certainly felt them. Even if it's not haunted, it's the creepiest place you will ever find yourself in. It isn't just me either! No one ever goes down voluntarily – hence they use it as a punishment. Anyway, enough about me. I know absolutely nothing about you.'

'There isn't too much to share to be honest. I'm a royal guard and I stand around all day not speaking – though I'm almost always inwardly laughing or swearing – at tourists who do all kinds of things to get me to move. My hobbies include people-watching, trying not to fall over when I march up and down – much harder than it looks by the way – and on really exciting days, I get to shout: "Make way for the King's Guard" at unsuspecting strangers.'

I laugh along, but internally I can't help but question his response. Somehow, he has managed to tell me about himself, without actually telling me anything about himself. I feel like a bit of a fool for oversharing as much as I have now. He must be one of those people who actually has a filter when talking to strangers and doesn't just tell a poor young man off the street about their tragic love life. No wonder he looked as if I'd just cornered him on the street like one of those charity people, who, if you make the mistake of making eye contact, talk for twenty minutes about blind donkeys or something or other until you feel so bad that you end up donating a small fortune just to be polite.

Not only am I too open, but I am also far too nosy. This 'Freddie' is turning into quite the enigma and, I must admit, I am intrigued. Having read far too many novels, when I meet someone who won't just tell me their life story after five minutes of meeting, I can't help but imagine that they're hiding a massive secret. Maybe he's a secret agent and if he told me he'd have to kill me . . . or he's one of those terrifying people who genuinely enjoys listening to jazz.

The more responsible part of my brain decides not to pry. Plus, if he is some sort of spy, I'd quite like to keep my life – and if he likes jazz then I would have to leave.

'Did I ruin anything important?' I ask nervously, changing the subject. 'The box, I mean.'

'Oh, no. Don't worry yourself about that. An order . . . errand for my father.' He gives me a tender smile and then looks back down to his hands as they rest against his thighs. 'I didn't like the box much anyway.'

I release the tension in my shoulders and relax. A smile, a real smile, feels its way onto my face.

'How are your fingers?' Freddie scans over my hands, and I offer him the one he is looking for, my nail still a faint purple.

'Still here. Not dropping off any time soon.' I wiggle them to demonstrate. He nods wordlessly.

'Pen?' His voice cuts through the short silence. I frisk my trousers, brows knitted slightly in confusion. Finding a slightly chewed-up biro in my back pocket, I offer it to him reluctantly.

'No, I mean your hands.' I follow his eyes and notice the tiny flecks of ink splatter across my fingers and thumbs that he's referring to – remnants of my day off messily annotating my history books.

'Ah . . .' I say. My voice is muffled as I lick my thumb and attempt to rub it off. 'I like to, erm, make notes in books when I read them. I get a little bit carried away.'

'It looks like you've missed the page completely,' he remarks, a cheeky smile ghosting his face.

'If you think that's bad, you should see the other guy.'

I grin and look back to my speckled hands, the ink merging with the freckles across my knuckles.

'What do you like to read? Or rather, what are your favourite books to deface?' He doesn't take his eyes off me now, and I can't help but blush under the intensity of his gaze.

'Anything with wide enough margins to make a note of when the words on a page stir a physical emotion inside of me. I find it fascinating that the ways we organise twenty-six of the same letters in black and white on a page can actually change you, can make you feel something.' I allow my eyes to meet his, but falter and avert them again. 'Most of all, I'm a real history geek, so I read anything about history, either fact or fiction, even a bit of fantasy, and plenty of romance. Although I do have to note all of the historical inaccuracies too.'

He chuckles. 'I'm the same with any film or TV programme that features the military. Did you ever see that one episode of *Sherlock* about the King's Guard? He was meant to be a Grenadier Guard, but they had him in a Welsh Guard's tunic, and a Scots Guard's bearskin. I still can't let that go.' As he talks animatedly, I watch him closely. His hands fidget slightly in his lap, almost as if he's holding himself back from bringing them into the conversation. 'You must love the guards' library? Although, I'm sure writing in one of those books must be punishable by death.'

I blink at him, confused.

'You haven't seen it?' he guesses from my expression.

'I didn't even know we had a library,' I admit, feeling a

little betrayed that my dad has never told me. Perhaps he knew that I would never leave if I did see it.

'Oh, yes, of course. You wouldn't know about the guards' Mess.'

'Guards' Mess?' I am royally intrigued now.

'There is a huge library filled with centuries-old leather-bound books beneath the guardroom in the Waterloo barracks . . . the Jewel House, I mean. None of the other guys take much notice of the books. They're mostly just collecting dust.'

'I've always wanted to know what it's like up in that guardroom. That's the only place in the Tower that I'm not allowed to go, and I've never once heard stories about what you all get up to.'

'We like to keep it that way.' He laughs, a mischievous smile twitching at his lips. 'I tell you what, how about I sneak you in, so you can give the books the appreciation they deserve. My way of a real apology.' He points at my hand again.

'Really? You would? How?' I sit up straighter on the wall and angle my body to his.

He nods but doesn't meet my gaze. 'How do you think we've managed to retain our reputation as the mystery of the Tower for so long?' He gets to his feet in one swift motion, still attempting to suppress his coy smile. 'Anyway, speaking of guardsmen, I'm afraid I have to get back to work.'

'Yes, oh yeah, of course, me too. Those tickets won't sell themselves! And I'm not sure our good old King Charlie would be too pleased if his jewels got stolen because one of his guards was too busy having a hot chocolate in the park. Thank you, again, Freddie.'

He crams his curls back under his forage cap, stands to attention, and gives me a curt nod. 'When the time is right, I'll come and find you.' There's that bloody wink again. I chuckle lightly and shake my head as he strides away, not once looking back.

Walking back to work is almost painful. I'm already dreading all of the things Andy and Samantha will have to say, and Kevin too no doubt. At least my silly little life will be keeping them entertained.

I drag my phone out of my pocket and pull up my messages. Besides Bran, 'Mum' is the only recent conversation thread. Well, I'm not sure you can call it much of a conversation. Blue bubbles that hold my own words line the whole of the left side in a continuous pattern, never once interrupted by a reply as I scroll through months and months of texts. Mum can't respond to my texts; I know that well. But when she first passed, the hardest part of losing her was going through life doing all of the things we'd spend hours talking about and no longer being able to tell her. So, I just didn't stop. Every time I find myself thinking *I should tell Mum about this*, I do. Sometimes it's just a picture of Cromwell looking particularly cute, or doing something a little naughty, and others it is lines and lines of incoherent thoughts.

It's moments like this that make me realise how much I miss her. Moving up and down the country, following my dad to various military camps, meant it was always just me and her; we were each other's best friend, and it was almost perfect. There was no topic out of bounds, and she practically knew my secrets before I even knew them myself. She was the brunette version of me in every single way, and I suppose I'm not really sure who I am without her. With her gone, I feel like I'm screaming in the face of a world that can't – or won't – hear me.

Until today, her unanswered phone has been the most I have spoken to anyone in weeks. Lucie and Cromwell aside, of course. Since we lost Mum, things with Dad haven't been the same and we mostly stick to 'safe' topics like what's on telly. With everyone else, we get as far as small talk, a few questions about work from the nicer ones, and then the conversation ends before it's even properly begun. I am quite literally surrounded by thousands of people each day, yet I feel completely alone.

Scrolling past Mum's contact, the message feed ends abruptly, most texts having been received last Christmas from distant family members who decided to do away with cards. I gave up all of my friends to be Bran's girlfriend, without even realising I had pushed everyone away to be with him. Now, there's no one for me to turn to, no best friend to call after a dramatic day, or to cry to when all you need is for someone to listen and wipe away your tears.

Except Mum's phone. I send her another message, telling her about Freddie, giving her a brief history of our series of strange and awkward interactions, finishing it off with a rather detailed description of what he looks like – she would have appreciated that. I just hope to God that her phone number hasn't been given to someone else and they have been secretly reading all of my woes and secrets for the past couple of years because they will definitely find this new development a tad creepy.

When I get back to work, Kevin's grating voice shouts to me from across the office. I tune out what he says but it's followed by a chorus of childish laughter. I take no notice and slip back into my booth with a huff.

Sliding up the blind that exposes me to the general public once again, the shock of the sight before me throws me back into my chair, my heart stopping and restarting in my chest. The ghost of Anne Boleyn haunts my window, head intact – pearl necklace and all. Toppling onto the floor as the wheelie chair slides from under me, I land on my coccyx with a thud.

'Are you all right?' the Tudor queen asks as she plonks her iPhone onto the sill with concern.

With that, another almost identical ghost joins her in the window and a tiny child's version pops up at her feet, the headdress slipping over her eyes as she emerges. Anne Boleyn fanatics . . .

'Can we get tickets to see Anne, Mummy?' She waves a single rose towards me as I clamber back into my seat.

'Of course, darling, and you can lay that beautiful rose on her grave,' the biggest Anne says to the smallest. 'May we have three tickets please?'

Nodding my head, I do as the queens command and send them on their way. I watch as they pass through the parting crowd and offer dainty royal waves, playing their role with the utmost seriousness.

I desperately need a new job.

Chapter 6

B ran has attempted to call seventeen times in the five
days since our last meeting. The texts that accompany
the missed calls vary between 'please baby, I love you' and
'fuck you, slut'. He always was a charmer. Thankfully, the
threat of my huge soldier 'boyfriend' seems to have put
him off making a physical appearance again.

After my heart-to-heart with Freddie, his platoon was
replaced with the Coldstream Guards the very same afternoon and I have been kicking myself on all five lonely
evenings that I never asked for his number. *When the
time is right,* he'd said, but that's almost giving the ravenmaster a run for her money on the most arbitrary,
philosophical saying front. Being left to my own devices
with nothing exciting going on for almost a full week after
being teased with good conversation, I realise how much
I miss having someone to talk to. So, I am resorting to
something I always swore blind I'd never lower myself to.
I download Tinder.

I watch the little red square of shame as it sits unopened against my screensaver, which is a cute picture of Cromwell in a bow tie. He sits at my feet now, headbutting my leg as if to deter me from the pain of trying to navigate the online dating minefield. I give him a scratch behind the ears and click into the app. As it opens slowly, the little flame icon teasing me in the centre of the screen, I toy with the idea of just throwing my phone out of the window before it fully loads, but I have to admit there is a small part of me deep down that craves the attention of it. The fact that the only romantic affection I have received in the past few weeks is my ex-boyfriend calling me a 'slut' on WhatsApp fuels me to fill out all of the tedious admin of the sign-up process. As Mum always used to say: *'Just go for it, Mags, what's the worst that can happen?'* Although, she usually meant following my dreams, not swiping right on whatever the male population of London has to offer.

Essentially being my own prisoner in the Tower of London means I have a severe lack of photos of myself. My camera roll is crammed with thirteen thousand photos of Cromwell and pretty sunsets and only the odd horrendous selfie, where I've tried (and failed) to copy a few poses that some old high-school acquaintances post on Instagram. Every now and again I'll scroll past one of my failed attempts and have to pause for a moment to cringe. Each one somehow managed to turn out like the ones your middle-aged auntie posts on Facebook after she'd had one too many gins.

Sighing, I throw together a profile that consists of a

photo of me and my dad from a few years ago and a bio that just says 'London, 26'. And with that, I am ready to face the eligible bachelors.

Joshua, 29, is the first face to fill my screen. All of his photos are a variation of him lounged across a paddleboard in different exotic locations. Killing two birds with one stone, he flashes off both his abs and his money in one. All I can think about is how much he'd hate a woman like me whose weekends are spent eating and reading in the comfort of her dad's home. His bio is what really sells him as a left swipe though: *Just a nice guy looking for a nice girl, I guess. Seems it's a lot to ask these days.* I might know relatively little about dating, but it doesn't take a genius to work out that suggesting the majority of women aren't nice is probably not the way to bag yourself a date. Maybe he's hoping girls will be blinded by his torso and ignore his cynicism. *Left swipe.*

Next up is Ryan, 28. Like my own, his bio says little more than the town he lives in, not giving anyone much to work from, and I make a mental note to change mine when I can think of a way to sell myself like a stray dog in a shelter. His photos make me giggle as I realise that each one is posed at an angle where the main focal point of the picture is his tattooed bicep. Of course, a black-and-white rose and a hyper-realistic lion are all faded together with various clock cogs and are topped off with the unfortunately phrased *'I ain't not like the rest'* permanently etched across his chest. *Left swipe.*

Sam, 27. *Left swipe.* Jordan, 32. *Left swipe.* Azeem, 28. *Left swipe.* Richard, 45. *Left swipe . . .*

Andrew, 35, is the only profile I linger on for a while. He has a good selection of photos, and in each one he is front and centre beaming a great big smile, with his cheeks bunching at either side and his blue eyes pinched tight in real genuine elation. There's something trustworthy in his expression, and his is the first face I have scrolled to that I haven't inwardly questioned whether a date with him could end up with my body being discovered by a dog walker in the morning.

The soft curve of his chin is dappled with a light sprinkling of stubble and his dark hair is cut short and neat. His bio isn't even anything backhandedly insulting or self-pitying, it's actually somewhat funny – or funny enough that I let out a nose-breath in approval: *'Need help getting to the minimum spend on Deliveroo?'* There surely has to be a catch? There must be something wrong with him somehow? I scour his profile, self-sabotaging, trying to figure out his flaw. And there it is: *317km*. Of course, the one man who seems half-decent is almost two hundred miles away from me.

I give up. Not even bothering to swipe, I throw my phone onto my bed and sit beside Cromwell, who was curled up on the edge, peacefully slumbering through my academic analysis of disappointing Tinder profiles. Feeling my weight sit down beside him, he pops his head up and stares at me with his huge black eyes.

'How would you feel about us adopting about fifteen brothers and sisters for you and never leaving the house?' He stands up at the sound of my voice and slowly paces towards me, wobbling slightly with fatigue.

After climbing into my lap, he kneads my thigh like dough.

I sigh, petting the top of his head. 'Thanks, Crom.'

With nothing better to do on a Saturday evening, and giving up on the idea of finding myself a date, I leave my phone at home and take a short walk down to the Keys.

On the wall next to the East Drawbridge, an old pub sign creaks in the breeze. Painted on it is the leather-gloved hand of a beefeater as they carry King Charles's keys. The pub is named after the Ceremony of the Keys, the ceremonial locking up of the Tower that the beefeaters and the royal guard have undertaken every evening for centuries. A true spectacle of military discipline, it happens at the exact same time, to the very minute, each night. We are all confined to our houses when that time comes – although Cromwell has been known to try and join in, slinking around the feet of the soldier who is tasked with carrying the lantern to light the keyhole for the beefeater to lock. He has since been on house arrest every night between half nine and ten.

The only time the ceremony has ever been late was during the Blitz of the Second World War. A bomb was dropped in the Tower, knocking over the guards and the beefeater performing the ceremony – but they still managed to get up and complete their duty. And if coming within inches of being blown up wasn't already a pretty terrible way to spend your shift, they had to go and do admin straight after, writing directly to the king to inform him that the ceremony was delayed by just seven minutes. The king gave them some measly thanks but didn't forget to sign it off with 'never let it happen again'. And as it happens, they didn't – but I think that was probably less to do with the beefeaters and more to do with poor aim.

I suppose it's unsurprising then that they named the place they retired to when the ceremony was over after it. They used to have pubs on pretty much every corner of the Tower but now we're just left with the one, and it's the most exclusive bar that London has to offer; one can only attend with a personal invitation from a Yeoman Warder. But they don't mind me popping by as long as I buy them a pint of 'Treason' (their very own ale) every now and again.

I swing open the heavy wooden door and I am immediately greeted by the familiar sight of row upon row of beefeater memorabilia, paintings, and ornaments, which line the walls. Two human-less uniforms stand guard with partisans at the entrance. The windows of the internal doorways are etched with the image of crossed keys like the symbol of a secret organisation, which I suppose it is in a way. This is their base. But the thing that really draws your attention as soon as you push open the inner door is the colour. A shock of red leather adorns the room, accenting each chair, bench, and even the bar itself.

Yet the assault on the eyes doesn't end there; it is almost impossible to tell if the carpet is stained from many messy nights as it too is bright red and festooned with the plant badges from the countries that make up the United Kingdom. Roses, thistles, and shamrocks are all bound together by branches and sprout from a beautiful golden crown in the centre. The smell of snuff hangs in the air, a reminder of the parties that only recently preceded and, no doubt, will presently follow, the restful scene before me.

Charlie – my Newfoundland-owning neighbour – and Dad are joined by Godders, and they all prop up the bar on stools. Godders, the slightly shorter (and wider) of the three beefeaters leans over the beer pump, filling up his almost empty pint glass with whichever tap he can reach. The bottom of his arm pokes out of his collared shirt as he stretches, offering a glimpse of his sparkling watch, which is so swanky I'm sure only James Bond could ever pull it off. Godders is always donning something flashy and expensive and usually has a story to tell – and rest assured he will tell it, for hours and hours.

I take a stool on the other side of the L-shaped bar, looking across at the trio of beefeaters, who have a look of the Three Stooges about them, with their wild array of hairstyles, beards, and boyish behaviours.

As I do so, Godders glances at me with a nervous look of surprise – most likely worried that I am one of the more cantankerous beefeaters come to scold him for syphoning the goods – but his expression softens when he realises that it is just me. 'All right, Mags, how you doing, pet?' he asks in his thick Geordie accent.

'Aah, Maggie, you all right, lass?' Charlie adds, smiling sweetly. Charlie is like the grandad of this place and can always be found in the pub telling a tale or two of when he was a bagpiper for the Royal Regiment of Scotland. His stories hook you in, and – whilst I'm honestly not sure if it's just because they sound more dramatic in his Highland accent – I could listen to him for hours.

'Come to spend your Saturday night with the old boys have you, sweetheart?' My dad smiles.

'I thought I'd come and keep an eye on you three, make sure you aren't causing any trouble,' I reply, waggling my eyebrows at Godders playfully. He puts both hands up in surrender, the stolen goods filling his cheeks, his own wiry moustache overlaid with a foamy one that drips over his lips and down his bearded chin. We all give a hearty laugh. 'My round?' I offer and the three old men nod their heads enthusiastically.

In the continued absence of the barman, I shuffle around to the other side of the bar and pull the pints myself. 'What's happened to Baz anyway?' Also a beefeater, Baz is always the one to volunteer to run the bar. Never without his tweed flat cap, faded braces, or his Liverpool football shirt, he is as much a part of the décor as the bar itself.

'They had a few boys from his old regiment in last night for a party, and as soon as they found out he's one of theirs, every pint they bought they bought him one too. He's still out the back sleeping it off.' I picture Baz shooting gin across the room from between the gap in his front teeth, his go-to party trick after he's had a tipple or two.

'Some fancy lot from the Canadian Embassy are meant to be in later tonight so we said we'd "watch the bar" whilst he had a kip.' Dad giggles to his friends impishly. I notice all three of them slightly swaying on their stools.

'Of course you did.' I roll my eyes and shove a ten-pound note into the crack in the till before returning to my seat.

I listen to them for a while as they tipsily share

grumbles about the governor of the Tower, their boss, and a few of the other beefeaters. I don't know who coined the stereotype of middle-aged ladies loving their gossip, but they clearly haven't met any beefeaters in their late fifties.

'You see Lunchbox givin' his tour this morning? Turned up, nae socks and nae boots, just stood there with his hobbit feet out like nothing was amiss! I feel sorry for the wee bairns that had to stand so close to them.' Charlie feigns a gag at the end of his sentence. The other two share a look of disgust.

'You're joking?' Dad smooths his ginger beard around his smile with a large palm. 'Was he steamin'?'

'Nope, completely sober. Reckons he was getting a hot flush like his wife does.'

'Aye, a common tale of woe: the twenty-stone ex-marine in his sixties going through the bloody menopause. Idiot.' Godders shakes his head with a laugh that sounds like a chesty cough and takes another swig from his fast-depleting beer.

Contributing only a quiet laugh to the conversation, I just watch them and their animated interactions in awe. They are natural entertainers, their company being more hilarious and exciting than any big-budget Saturday night telly.

'How's life in the ticket office these days, Maggie?' Godders diverts their attention towards me this time.

Charlie nods his head. 'Aye, that Kevin still being an arsehole?'

'You took the words right out of my mouth. I can't stand it. You know, he told a customer this week that the Tower was built by Henry the Eighth. I almost got up and left right there.' The three beefeaters all grumble and shake their heads in disapproval.

'Who's hiring these clowns? And they won't even give my girl a job as a White Tower warden, even though she knows more than all of that bunch put together.' Dad looks at me sympathetically. I return an uncomfortable grimace, not quite sure what to say to his outburst of fatherly affection.

Thankfully he moves on just as swiftly: 'Although, that isn't as bad as the question I got asked by a tourist on Monday . . .' He waggles his eyebrows at Godders and Charlie who both roll their eyes.

'Do I even want tae know?' Charlie groans, clearly expecting to be pained by whatever my dad has to share.

'First of all, they asked me: "What is that bridge with those big towers on it called?" I replied: "That, unsurprisingly, madam, is Tower Bridge." To which she proceeded to add, no joke: "And does it go all the way across the river?"'

'Jesus Christ,' Godders mutters and does one of his spluttery laughs again.

The beer that I had been in the process of drinking sprays out of my mouth and across the bar. 'How do you even respond to that? I wonder what the bridges are like in her country.'

'What did you say?' Godders asks.

'Well, at first I thought she was joking, but then I realised she was waiting for an answer. The only thing I could think of to say was: "It's not called Tower Pier now, is it?"

To be honest, she still looked confused, but I just about managed to ask where she was from and get out of earshot before I died from laughing.'

They have a little book in the Byward Tower full of the stupid questions the beefeaters have been asked by tourists over the years, along with where said tourist came from. It gets brought out at one of the posh parties at the end of the year, with the best few printed out and handed around as a way of entertaining the guests. A personal favourite of mine is one that comes up far too often: 'Did they purposely build it close to the Tube station?' And it's almost always guaranteed either a facepalm or a belly laugh in response. Considering the Tower was built alongside a Roman wall by William the Conqueror in the 1080s, I highly doubt Willy was planning ahead to the 1960s and thinking about the convenience of tourist access . . .

'No points for guessing where she said . . .' The three beefeaters give me a knowing look, each of their eyes swimming in their drunkenness and shining in amusement. A rosy tint has spread across their cheeks and glows a deep red on the ends of their noses. Sat together in their row along the bar, they look like a string of Christmas lights.

The grandfather clock in the corner chimes 8 p.m. and just like the tiny bird in a cuckoo clock, Baz emerges from the back room, his sparse hair sticking up and over to the left in a thin wave. He smooths it down flat across the bald top of his head and covers it with his flat cap. Still rubbing his eyes sleepily and with his braces dragging on the floor behind him, he waddles up to the bar, pours himself a glass of gin and water and drops a vitamin C tablet into it with a plop.

'Feeling as rough as you look eh, Baz?' Dad slurs, receiving only a middle finger over the shoulder in response.

'You need a couple of extra hands tonight, Baz?' I ask, watching as he wrestles with his braces and wincing in sympathy when they get stuck on his shoulder and ping him in the face. 'I don't mind being the barmaid for the evening. I've got nothing better to do, and I don't fancy having to tuck this one into bed.' I use my thumb to point at Dad, whose head has begun drooping into a packet of pork scratchings that he'd managed to pinch from behind the bar without Baz noticing.

Successfully managing to fasten himself in, albeit with one strap that twists all down his back like a helter-skelter into his trousers, Baz walks over to my stool and ruffles my hair in appreciation. 'You are a brilliant, brilliant young lady. Cheers, Maggie.'

Smiling broadly, I wave him off and he waddles back into the room he came from, groaning as he swigs his hair-of-the-dog cocktail. I take his place behind the bar just as the first few guests filter in. Black suits and cocktail dresses flow into the room and soon form a huddle around the three men at the bar.

'Right, you bunch of old men.' I startle Godders, Charlie, and Dad who were each almost asleep. 'Go home and get a cup of tea down you. You're needing your beds and I've got work to do.'

Chapter 7

The only way that I'm able to respond to the knock at my bedroom door is with a grunt that is akin to that of a Neanderthal. My face is squished into my pillow with my body lying like a dead weight behind me. I'm still fully clothed in the jeans that I never took off last night and I already know that my makeup is smeared across my pillowcase. The only part of my body I can actually seem to feel is my head, as it pounds with a pain strong enough to numb the rest of me from the neck down.

My dad peeks around from behind the door. 'Good morning, beautiful.' Only a father could look at me right now – my hair surely defying gravity and melted into a sweaty pool of dehydrated skin – and still call me 'beautiful'. I can only let out another groan in response. I have as much brain power as a one-year-old, with the body and energy of a corpse, yet my dad – the man who was falling asleep sat up at 8 p.m. – looks fresh as a daisy. He waltzes into the room, carrying a much-needed cup of tea.

'How. You. Fine? Ugh.' I manage to grumble out into my pillow. Dad sits down on the end of my bed with a chuckle.

'I have had a hell of a lot of practice. I spent twenty-two years in the army where we'd go out drinking all night and I'd be outside at 6 a.m. without fail, boots polished, uniform ironed and still able to shoot straight.' He laughs as I groan again and he hands me my tea with two painkillers.

Mumbling a 'thank you', I swallow them and have to pause to make sure that they stay down.

'You got plenty of liquid tips then?'

'Let's just say I know why Baz always looks hungover now.' I rub my temples, trying to do anything to ease the throbbing. 'I had to keep pouring pints down the sink because they were buying me more than I could have physically drunk. I'm pretty sure they were trying to drown me from the inside.'

'You'll be fine once you get to work.' Work. More work. Fuck.

'I feel like vomiting every time I see Kevin on a good day. There is really no hope for me today is there?'

'Nope, but if you do, make sure you get it all over his shoes.' I make an attempt to laugh but it sends a shooting pain up my skull, which only makes my dad shake his head and stand up.

'I'll leave you to get ready.'

I stand in the shower for a little too long, having no desire to leave the comfort of the hot water as it washes away my hangover sweats and last night's makeup. Not risking having to run to work this morning, I eventually reluctantly pull myself away from the stream. Not wanting to put any more pressure on my fragile head, I leave my hair down and try to smooth it out, so it at least isn't sticking up in every direction.

As I go to dress myself, I discover that Dad has ironed my uniform for me and all of the stigma about living with your dad when you're in your late twenties is worth it for mornings like this. He does little things like this for me, since Mum died. I guess it's his own way of looking after me – a tough old veteran's way of caring. All of the things he should have done for me at age six and sixteen, he has started to do for me at twenty-six, making up for lost time.

By the time I finally make it outside, the cool breeze is a welcome relief. I have been taking the same route to work lately, up the secret passage and through the court-yard – a decision that *obviously* has nothing to do with any attempts to see if a certain regiment of guardsmen have returned.

Not that I am checking, but it is still the Coldstream Guards today. Their buttons are paired down their torsos. The plumes that jut out from their bearskins are a striking shade of red instead of the Grenadiers' white, and their collars are embroidered with a Garter Star. And the pang in my stomach is definitely a result of my messy evening, and not the sinking feeling of disappointment.

The sight of the ticket office gives my stomach another lurch and I almost wish that I was still drunk.

'Margaret, Margaret, Margaret.'

I roll my eyes, my back to my boss as he slinks around the corner tapping his nails together like a Bond villain. 'Kevin.' I nod in acknowledgement.

'You're here.' He sounds weirdly happy. A sinister grin is plastered across his face, and I can't decide if I should be scared.

'Yep, that's, erm, usually what happens when a boss asks one of their employees to come into work.' I really, really cannot be bothered to deal with him and his games this morning. My head pounds twice as hard after hearing his voice.

'Don't get smart with me, young lady.' Kevin is only three years older than me but absolutely loves diminutive phrases that make him seem like he has the authority and wisdom of a teacher. Except, just about the only thing he has in common with a teacher is the coffee breath. 'It's just Rachel in accounts said that you were working on the bar last night and Cameron in surveillance told her that he saw you stumbling home at 3 a.m.'

'Did he really?' I mutter under my breath, shaking my head in disbelief. Surely the multimillion-pound security system has better uses than spying on a young woman walking home?

'Hmm? Never mind. We just won a bet with the accounts team. They all put twenty quid on you calling in sick.'

'Well, that's brilliant isn't it . . .'

'Me and the girls will be off to Wetherspoons at midday, so you'll have to hold down the fort.' He skips away clapping his hands together in glee, like a child who has just stolen the dinner money of their weaker classmate.

'Glad I could be of service.' Behind his back, I give a sarcastic curtsey. 'Prick,' I add once he's out of earshot.

'What was that?' Kevin turns on his heel, the grin gone from his face and replaced with his usual look of malice. Maybe I misjudged how good his hearing is.

I backtrack, the ever-familiar feeling of panic beginning to catch up with me. 'Nothing, nothing. Have a good lunch.' I try to smile, but it comes out more as a grimace.

If I didn't feel like I had been freshly dug out of my grave, I might have said more. But I just acknowledge the sensation of a cold kind of emptiness as it spreads across my chest and get to work.

By the time lunchtime rolls around, I resemble a functioning member of society again. Just the peace of an office without Kevin, Andy, and Samantha is enough to cure anything. I'm almost glad that they have gone out on their little lunch date at my expense. Maybe I'll bring in a 'Maggie Roulette' to encourage them to go every day: red equals 'she actually looks like a human today'; black equals 'oh look, she's having another breakdown.' They'd pick black and win, and the more times they leave me alone over lunch, the odds of it becoming red improve.

'Good afternoon and welcome to His Majesty's Royal Palace and Fortress, the Tower of London. How many tickets can I get for you today?' I reel off the standard script to a customer who looks to be in her mid-forties. She and her three children all wear matching parka coats and each of their tiny faces are copied and pasted from the woman who is undeniably their mother.

'Is the king home today?' she asks, ignoring everything else I have just said.

'I am not sure, madam,' I answer, a little confused as to

94

why she'd think a girl who works in a ticket office would know any king's personal schedule.

'How do you not know if the king is home? You are literally sat facing his house all day.'

'The king doesn't – and never has – lived in the Tower of London, madam. Perhaps you are thinking of Windsor Castle? Or Buckingham Palace?'

'But there is a house inside called the King's House. I do my research.' Her three children nod their heads, like her own little backup army. I try and keep my composure.

'Ah I see, the King's House inside the Tower of London is called the King's House as it is where the monarch *could* stay if they wished. But it was actually built for the Lieutenant of the Tower; the Constable of the Tower is the one who lives there now. Our current king has never stayed there. He probably heard about all of the ghosts!' I waggle my eyebrows at the children whose bored expressions turn to surprise, the prospect of a ghost story piquing their interest as they share excited glances.

'Well, that's just false advertising,' she huffs.

'Sorry, madam. Do you still wish to visit the Tower today?'

'Well, I did come to see the king . . .' she grumbles. Her children nod their heads furiously 'But okay give me two adults and three children.'

Over her shoulder, I notice Bob from security hauling open the gates to make way for a military van. A man in his casual 'combats' uniform hops down from the tall, armoured vehicle and hands him a piece of paper. After a nod from Bob and a shake of their hands, the soldier hops back into the van and drives over the West Draw-bridge.

They're changing the guard over. It used to be every day, or every two days, that the regiment on guard here would get relieved of their duties. But recently I think they realised how impractical it is to uproot a group of young men and a truckload of uniform just for one night, so now each regiment spends a week at a time guarding my home. It's always pot luck who comes next – for us at least. I never know until Monday rolls around and I have to take an embarrassing glance at who the next lucky man is to see me running to work with as much grace as Captain Jack Sparrow, arms flailing and all.

I can't tell if it's the Grenadiers, Freddie's regiment. In their standard khaki uniform and berets, they are impos-sible to distinguish from this distance. And it's not as if I'm looking anyway . . .

'Erm, excuse me? Can we get our tickets please?' I snap out of my brief trance and back to my customer, who looks erratically around, trying to figure out what I was so fixated on. A giant of a man appears next to her and peers into the window of my booth, so close I can see his dark nose hairs.

I cough. 'Yes, sorry, of course, I'll just get those for you now.' Tapping a few keys on my computer, I print out their tickets and send them on their way. I lean forward across my desk, pressing my face against the glass to see if I can catch a glimpse of the van again but it has long gone.

The sudden presence of a fake-tan-stained hand, followed by a bang on the glass, startles me and I fall back into my seat. The Three Musker-Twits have returned from their pub lunch and are doubled over in laughter. My face flushes but I do manage to get a little satisfaction out of seeing Samantha massaging her hand in pain, her skinny hands no match for the inch-thick security glass. I suppose the peace was nice whilst it lasted.

All I can think about for the afternoon is the changing of the guard. The possibility that it may have been Freddie huddled into the back of that van, his bearskin in a box on his lap, puts me on edge. I'm nervous, but the good kind. Like when your fingers tingle at the prospect of something exciting, not the kind where you feel like you are only one anxious thought away from needing a fresh set of knickers.

With little to distract me, I get ahead of myself, imagining all of the things I could say to him if he decided to come and save me from my workplace hell again. I'd thank him, profusely. Maybe I could suggest going for coffee again, to pay him back for getting them before. Or I'd tell him that the Coldstream Guards are a hell of a lot more boring and absolutely terrible at standing still. He'd probably like that.

But what if he isn't actually interested in being my friend? He never asked for my number. Actually, he didn't so much as hint at it. What if he's just one of those Hugh Grant characters who is just a posh guy whose chronic politeness gets them into situations that they can't get themselves out of? Did I force him to sit and listen to all of my problems? Oh God . . . What if he went back to the guardroom and laughed at me with all of the other guards?

The excited tingle is rapidly turning into a nervous twitch of the bowel . . .

I feel like slapping myself in the face to snap myself out of my rumination hole. He asked *me* to go to coffee. And chances are, I am just freaking myself out only for it to be the blue-grey uniforms of the Royal Air Force Regiment on guard in the morning. Just chill the hell out, woman.

I finish work with a few hours of sunlight left, and decide, after my late night, to catch up on a few chores and hang out some washing, whilst we get a brief respite from the watchful gazes of tourists peering over the wall. As the beefeaters all trundle home, I peg my washing out on the line. This week, it is mostly my period pants, so large and comfortable I'm sure one of the ravens could make a good nest out of them.

I am halfway through hanging up a pair that have discoloured slightly from the wash, and from other things by the looks of it, when I am disturbed by the sound of an engine. Spinning around, I see a white minibus clattering loudly over the speedbump just outside of my house. Smiling to be polite, just in case I know the driver, I stare at it for a while, framed by my embarrassing load of washing. Twelve pairs of male eyes stare back at me. Almost without thinking, I whip the pair of my ugliest pants from the line and hold them behind my back, the pegs shooting off. One of them lands in my hair and wedges itself in the tangled mess. My heart thumps at my chest, my face stinging with humiliated heat.

That there is the minibus ferrying all of the guardsmen from their base in Westminster to their base in the Tower, and it drives painfully slowly. Clearly, the heavily armoured vehicle I saw earlier today was delivering only their masses of uniform or whatever other equipment you need when guarding a royal palace. I can see each smiling face as they get a good look at my knickers. And, lo and behold, Freddie is right at the back, closest to the window. Annoyingly – or perhaps fortuitously – he is the only one not looking at me. Instead, his attention is focused on the lads sat ahead of him, and I watch him punch one of them in the back of the head playfully after they make some inaudible comment, his lips almost a smile.

They finally pass, and when they eventually turn the corner at Linda's house, I pivot back to my washing and pull down every single pair of pants, scattering the pegs across the concrete. Rushing back into the house with an armful of underwear, I decide they will dry just fine slung over the metal headboard of my bed. But the damage is done, my cheeks are unfortunately still the same colour as the one sexy red lacy pair I own, and I fling myself face down between my pillows with a groan.

Chapter 8

Outside of the Jewel House, in his usual spot, I see his bearskin before I see him. It is as tall as the arch of the sentry box that he stands in front of, and I amuse myself imagining his elongated and broad frame having to bend down to step inside it. Hanging back, I hover by one of the signs that explains the history of the Old Hospital Block, to delay walking past. My legs feel weirdly jelly-like, and I'm worried I might faceplant at Freddie's feet if I tried to move now. Looking over my shoulder, I take furtive little glances. The other guard beside him sways slightly under the strain of stillness but Freddie remains statuesque. His gaze doesn't waver from staring straight forward so I know he doesn't see me, and I'm grateful for his professionalism.

To really sell the 'oh, fancy seeing you here' act, I pretend to look interested in the tourist information boards – even though, in reality, it is one I already have memorised. An old photograph balances out all of the text, rubble cluttering the whole left side of the frame, a memento of its 'redecoration' at the hands of a Luftwaffe bomb. I gaze up at the building now, remembering how the windows slope ever so slightly on the right side and that the brick is plaited in the middle – the dark polluted brick of the surviving side woven together with the light brick of the newly rebuilt version. It's almost seamless until you look closely, so perfectly imperfect.

What was once the hospital for all of the soldiers stationed here is now just apartments for the beefeaters. They're gorgeous, but I'm not sure I'd swap living in the casemates for their front-row view of the White Tower – not only because tourists are attracted to the bright blue front doors like moths drawn to a flame, but also because I dread to think how haunted they are. In their basement they still have all of the original trays used to stack the bodies in their very own morgue.

I'm getting distracted.

As the tourists filter in, I take my opportunity. Trying my best to fit into the crowd, I meet him again, coming to a dead stop in front of him. A foot-high fence separates us and despite it not being very physically imposing, I'm intimidated again. Actually, that might be something to do with the very tall man holding a gun with a massive knife strapped to the end, and the fact that I have embarrassed myself every time I've been in his vicinity.

Freddie shows no sign that he has seen me; he doesn't even look at me. I have to keep reminding myself that he's working. I'm not expecting any reaction from him what-soever. The last thing I want is to endanger his job.

The awkwardness of a conversation where only one of the interlocutors can acknowledge the other becomes apparent. I clear my throat. 'Did you know that the Old Hospital Block was bombed out? Well, half of it. That's why the left side looks a lot less wonky – they rebuilt it better than it was before.' I point to the building. Its two striking blue doors look out from over a raised terrace. Tall white windows line the entire way up, and despite its weather-worn brick and patchwork repairs, it is still a stunning example of Georgian sophistication. 'Oh, and you see those little black doors? They were actually the doors to the Tower morgue that they used in the Crimean War.' Freddie doesn't look. 'Is that a bit bleak for a Monday morning? Probably.'

I keep going, self-consciously. 'I just wanted to thank you, again. You left so quickly before I didn't even get the chance to offer to buy you a coffee in return. Or a hot chocolate . . . I don't discriminate.' His eyes flick to me briefly in a flash of amusement. The redness creeps onto my face yet again. 'But, yeah . . . erm, not many people would have done what you did for me. Plus, thanks to you, I had an excuse to escape from work, and my colleagues are arguably worse than my ex.'

He finally allows his eyes to settle on my face. The shadow of his bearskin has turned them into a dusky shade of pine, and it seems to darken his whole mien. I notice the muscle of his neck twitch against his curb chain, and I can feel myself faltering under his stare. I can't help but to lean into all of my internal nervous ramblings from before. My hands tremble as I feel the blood rush away from my face this time. Standing before him, expecting

102

nothing, yet still desiring something, his hard stare intimidates me.

My whole body lurches as if urging me to flee, to escape before he can properly reject me. Flitting my eyes across the grounds, I try to see if any familiar faces are bearing witness to me making yet another fool of myself. The beefeaters are all dotted around the courtyard, their wooden bonnets elevated above circles of school children and in between couples for photos; a few wardens stand on the steps of the White Tower, talking to each other in their short top hats and long coat tails; the blush-pink blazer of Rachel from accounts catches my eye as she climbs the Broadwalk Steps alongside a colleague I don't recognise. I'm fairly sure she's too engrossed to have seen me yet, but I grow agitated.

Just as I open my mouth to excuse myself, Freddie speaks first: 'Tonight.' It comes out as a mix between a whisper and a deep growl. His jaw is still firmly clamped together and only his top lip moves slightly to let the gravelly sound escape. 'Jewel House,' he adds in his staccato command. I can barely process the words. I can't believe he's talking to me, defying orders – risking everything – for me.

Glancing around quickly again, I check to see if any nosy tourists are close enough to hear. Thankfully, they all seem to be fixated on Merlin, one of the ravens who is hopping along the grass with a bacon sandwich wedged in between his beak. A young child points after him, sobbing, as his mother attempts to comfort him.

'Ten p.m.' Freddie finishes off his code, his face relaxing again into his absent stare.

'Okay. Come to the Jewel House tonight at 10 p.m.?' I repeat, more to myself but Freddie risks his position again to give a brisk nod. He is subtle but I notice how the fur of his bearskin bounces under the short, sharp motion. A warm tingle of excitement spreads across the bottom of my stomach again and I can't control the smile that pulls at my face. The time is right, and he wants to see me. He actually wants to see me.

My giddy spell is broken as the sound of his boots snapping together on the concrete and his palms slapping against his rifle as he stands to attention echoes through the courtyard. My body shudders in surprise and hundreds of heads snap towards us as he marches towards the parallel sentry box. His colleague on the other side does the same. Out of the corner of my eye, Rachel inches even closer; I can't tell if I've been spotted but I duck between a forming crowd of iPhones and tourists and make my getaway.

Despite my early outing, today is one of my rare days off and instead of spending it in bed, curtains drawn and cuddling with Cromwell like usual, I while away the hours just minorly freaking out. I don't have much in my wardrobe, but, within the first ten minutes of me getting home, the entire contents are sprawled across my bed. I hate to be the kind of person to obsess about how she looks, or what she should wear, but I really can't afford to look like an idiot. With that in mind, I push the array of comedic T-shirts to the side. Louis Theroux's sympathetic eyes stare at me from the black nylon and I almost feel bad for not wanting to wear it. Cromwell soon turns the pile into his bed for the afternoon and I get back to my panic.

I decide that if I'm going to have to hide in the shadows and avoid being seen, black jeans are always the safest option. I pair them with a slightly quirky patterned blouse and place the outfit over the banister ready to throw them on in exactly . . . ten hours.

'Come on, this way.' Freddie's head pops out from behind one of the cannons, his long arm waving me forward. After an entire day racing over every single possible outcome of this evening, mostly all terrible, I am finally here, creeping around the Jewel House like a rebellious teen sneaking out of their parents' house to drink blue WKDs in the local park.

Although, my parents were actually the kind to encourage that behaviour. I remember being fifteen and mentioning in passing that an acquaintance in my class at school was throwing a party whilst her parents were away, and that was it – Mum was bundling me into the car to get a crate of alcopops and offering to be my taxi. *'No matter what the time, the later the better. How about 4 a.m.?'* She was always worried I wasn't making enough friends and growing too anxious to leave the house. As much as she loved being my best friend, I knew she worried that deep down I would grow to resent the fact I didn't have anyone my own age.

Those nuclear-coloured drinks stayed in the pantry for a good few years and moved between at least three of our houses. I *did* stay up until 4 a.m. the night of the party, but that was because I was three-quarters of the way through *Northanger Abbey* and there was no way I was falling asleep before I knew whether Henry Tilney would rise up against his father to marry the woman below his station.

I think Mum would laugh now, seeing that all of my friends are fifty-something-year-old beefeaters and a few intelligent birds. But here I am, at the grand old age of twenty-six, finally sneaking out. Although I guess I *am* on my way to a secret library . . . so maybe some things don't change. Opening up our message thread, I quickly pop her a message and I imagine her broad smile upon receiving it, wherever she may be, her crooked bottom teeth peeking out from behind her lipstick and shaking her head with affection. Knowing how she would be proud of my tiny rebellion makes the thought of getting caught by Dad and the cameras slightly less daunting.

Checking that the coast is clear, I follow Freddie. The apprehension feels electric at the thought of doing something no one would have ever expected from me. I can't deny that it is oddly thrilling to behave so completely out of character. I ignore the voice in the back of my head that reminds me that only ten minutes ago I was dry-heaving into the bathroom sink, sick with anxiety.

Still dressed in his uniform, Freddie leads me to a small but heavy lead door on a shadowed corner of the Jewel House. I have to slide through it sideways, both my belly and my boobs snagging on the frame, and I have to shuffle a little to get free. I'm grateful for the darkness, the low-lit corridor concealing the red hue that has broken out across my cheeks.

Freddie escorts me down a narrow corridor. It's only

just wide enough for me to walk through comfortably, but the tall guardsman is forced to duck slightly, dodging low-hanging lamps, and skirting around thick paintings that are silhouetted against the walls. We walk in silence, and I strain my eyes to see what lies ahead but his wide back blocks my view. Instead, I take mental notes of the doors that line the walls, each one numbered like a hotel but all of them padlocked from the outside. Only the sound of our own footsteps and heavy breathing fills the space.

Cursing Freddie and his skyscraper legs, I feel like I'm about to break a sweat trying to keep up with his lengthy strides. The longer we amble down the corridor, the more my apprehension catches up with me. I came here knowing no more than the man who leads me, and I'm not totally sure what I have signed myself up for. What if it's a set-up? What if Andy and Samantha jump out from behind one of the doors, in a peal of their psychotic giggles?

After walking for what feels like miles, a small stream of light catches my attention as the corridor comes to an end. Deep laughter and muffled speech become audible. As Freddie turns to me, I see in the dim lighting that his brows are furrowed in a brief flash of confusion across his face – but, clearly clocking my own mirrored look of concern, he quickly switches out his worried expression for a broad grin. His teeth are perfectly straight, of course, and I smile back at him nervously.

We reach a door, and he turns to me. 'Okay, before we go in, I have to tell you that you are the first outsider who has ever been granted this privilege, and if you tell anyone, I know where you live . . .' He wiggles his eyebrows in jest.

Not sure how to respond, I simply nod my head with an exaggerated fervour, and, seemingly content with my answer, he wraps his hand around the doorknob.

'Oh, and by the way . . .' He swivels back round to me again and I, already committed to walking through his mystery door, plant my face into his chest, my hands skimming his torso and hitching on to the polished buff belt that wraps around his waist. Freddie catches me by the elbows as I stumble backwards, and as soon as my eyes meet his, he snatches back his hands as if regretting laying them on me at all. Muttering a quiet apology, I bring my own hands up to my chest, retracting into myself.

He doesn't finish what he was going to say and instead swings open the door. I have to blink through the sudden flood of light that was hidden behind the heavy oak, and I try and swallow down the awkwardness that has settled over us from our fumble in the corridor before he looks at me again and realises that my face is the colour of his tunic.

Freddie steps aside and I can finally see the room before me. We definitely were walking for a long while – seventy years back in time to be precise. Oxblood leather sofas have been pushed to the side of the room, and small bright-red tarnished patches across the arms and pillows hint at years and years of wear. Mahogany furnishings skirt the entire room, and a full-length dining table with all of its places neatly set has also been pushed to the back of the room, with crystal glasses and polished cutlery all lying untouched on the surface and dark wood chairs uniformly positioned at each placemat. A Regency-style chandelier fills the high ceiling, its teardrop prisms refracting light across the cornice carvings, casting tiny rainbows across the room like some heavenly dream. I almost want to ask Freddie if I'm dead and this is some sort of ghostly afterlife.

In the centre of the room is a roaring fireplace, the wooden mantel chipped and stained, but still ornamented with a stunning silver candlestick at each end. A golden frame is hung above it, depicting the Duke of Wellington wielding a sword in his decorated military uniform. He doesn't look out over the room but instead smoulders off to the side, as though in this place, his men are freed from his severe watch.

Freddie's expression is austere. The contours of his face have become even more prominent. His long straight nose, high cheekbones, and angular chin seem elevated, stronger. Dark lashes stand to attention and his well-trained eyes refuse to blink as he surveys the room. His comrades in varying arrays of undress filter across the room, and I gather from the low hum that they have just returned from completing the Ceremony of the Keys and various other patrols to secure the Tower. Their bearskins and white belts are strewn across the furniture. Two gentlemen cross the room, too engrossed in their conversation to notice me, one blond and one brunette. The blond slaps the other across the chest playfully as he sets to unbuttoning his tunic. Both of them, in perfect synchronisation, ruffle their hair with wide-open palms, and where it was slightly damp and flattened from their hats it now springs into life. Their pristine image crumples and the statuesque façade of the 'impenetrable' guardsman slips away.

'They weren't meant to be here.' Freddie's voice interrupts my gawping. Even his words are tense and stiff as he mutters to me from behind his teeth. My excitement has dwindled, left behind in the miles of corridor as an uneasiness settles over us.

'It's okay, I can just come back another . . .' I am cut off by the appearance of another man, towering over me.

'Guildford, are you keeping this beautiful lady all to yourself or are you going to introduce us?' One of the guards, completely free of his uniform and simply clad in a band T-shirt and a pair of sports shorts, claps Freddie on the shoulder and leans against him. His tanned bicep is enhanced by black tribal tattoos that flex as he gives Freddie a playful shake. The twang of an accent hangs ever so slightly on his words as he flings a pearly white smile in my direction.

'Ah, yes . . . Sorry! Maggie, this is Lance Corporal Mo Lomani.' I stretch out my freckled hand to shake his, giving Freddie a sideways glance as I do so.

'A pleasure to meet you, Maggie.' He kisses the top of my hand tenderly and I have to bring my other hand to my cheek to try and cover my blush. 'Although . . . I do normally like to know a girl's name before she lets me see her underwear.' He winks and there's certainly no use trying to cover my embarrassment now – even my hands are scarlet.

Freddie places a hand on his chest and guides his lips away from my knuckles. 'She's the daughter of a Yeoman Warder, Mo. She outranks you and I, so you better treat her like your superior. No funny business, you hear me?

The last thing you need is another regimental sergeant major on your back because your "charm" has got you in trouble.'

'Excuse me, ma'am.' Mo quickly stands to attention before me. Despite being the lower rank of the two, Freddie seems to hold the power.

'Please, I'm not a Yeoman Warder's daughter here. I am just plain old Maggie.'

Mo gives a chuckle and snakes his arm around my shoulders. He leans down to whisper in my ear and his breath tickles against my hair. 'Can you see why some of the lads have given him the nickname "Stiff"?' I glance at Freddie; his expression is still unreadable. 'Stiff' indeed.

I smile back at Mo and take a look around the room, my awkwardness easing as I realise the unexpected guests aren't such a terrible addition to the evening – especially with Freddie being about as talkative as he is when he is guarding the Crown Jewels.

'This place has been here all this time?' My geekiness takes over and I find myself practically bouncing in excitement. 'Whoa is that a real gun?' I point to the shotgun mounted on one of the walls.

'The whole Waterloo Block was built for soldiers in Wellington's garrison here.' Freddie too seems to ease as he notices my eagerness. 'He shut down most of the pubs in the Tower and introduced a strict curfew, so the guys here made their own little social space, hidden away from those up top. If I'm correct, it hasn't changed much since the nineteenth century.' The history nerd within me has just orgasmed. 'And yes, that is a real gun.' He grabs me softly by the wrist as I reach for the polished barrel. His fingers wrap effortlessly around my arm in such a tender touch that my skin instantly prickles at the contact. I quickly move out of his hold before he can notice, or before another strained atmosphere settles over us.

An expression that I can't translate flashes briefly across his face, but he turns away from me before I can study him further. Mo's hearty chuckle reminds me of his presence, and I shift my attention back to him.

'This place is amazing! You're going to have to drag me out at the end of the night.' My mind races, picturing centuries of guardsmen hiding out in here, just like we are now. I feel like I should have a cigar lit and a glass of whisky in my hand.

Three guys in the corner catch my eye. Tunics unbuttoned, they lean over various cases for musical instruments. One of them looks no older than seventeen but his skinny frame towers over everyone in the room. His cheeks are dotted with clusters of acne and his blond hair is shaved right down to just a fine fuzz on top of his head. He pulls out a battered fiddle and after pressing the rest to his chin, plucks the strings softly, as the man beside him uncases an Irish bodhrán drum. The drummer is only slightly smaller than the fiddler, but he is almost twice the width. His face seems set in a continuous smile as he listens to the conversations around him, although I notice he doesn't once join in himself. Their little string-and-percussion trio is completed by a guitarist. I don't have to get close to him to know that he'd make me look like a mountain in comparison. He is the same height as the drummer, even though

112

he's now seated and leaning over his drum. He straps his guitar over his shoulder and disappears behind it. Standing next to the beanpole of a guardsman, they don't even look like they are from the same species of man, let alone bandmates and colleagues.

'You're having a party?' I ask Mo as another guardsman brings a tray of drinks over to the band, who are tuning their instruments ready to play.

He gives me another cheeky smile. 'Let me introduce you to everyone else! They're all dying to meet the special guest.'

'Special guest?' My face burns and I look over to Freddie, but he is already on the other side of the room, walking further and further away from me. My sigh steals my smile and I traipse after Mo. I'm here now, I suppose. Freddie can just show me the library another day, if he still wants to.

Mo leads me over to the band first. 'This is Chaplin on the drum, Tiny on the fiddle, and Davidson on guitar. They will be our entertainment for this evening. Lads, this is "just plain old Maggie".'

I give them a shy wave as Mo leans into my ear again to add his own footnote to each of their profiles: 'Tiny is one of our "crows" (fresh out of training) and he hasn't spoken to a woman except his mum in six months so just try to ignore the staring thing.' Sure enough the lanky new recruit looks like a deer caught in the headlights, his mouth hanging open, and the only thing that snaps him out of his trance is the sound of his fiddle clattering to the floor. He scrambles to pick it up as Chaplin silently laughs and pats him on the back.

'I can't wait to hear you guys play. Are you all in the military band?'

I address Chaplin but it is Davidson who replies: 'Nope, Chaplin plays the bugle at the end of the Keys to sound "The Last Post" but this stuff is more of a hobby for us.'

'Chaplin is an Afghan vet. He, erm, doesn't really say anything anymore.' My heart sinks as Mo whispers to me again. Now stood so close to him, I notice the silver slither of a scar running across his cheek. It interrupts the six o'clock shadow of his dark facial hair, and his smile is ever so slightly lopsided as the tight scar drags at his lips – though that doesn't seem to stop the friendly grin being permanently plastered on his face. Stumbling over my thoughts I can't figure out what is the right thing to say. Do I apologise? Do I thank him for his service? Do I just not say anything more?

'I hope you're not one of those buglers who never quite managed to learn how to hit the high notes. I can hear them play it every night if I sit on my balcony and it always finishes up going . . .' I give an absolutely horrendous attempt to vocalise an out-of-tune 'Last Post'. They all laugh at my rendition, and Chaplin nods his head in recognition, silent amusement overtaking his face. They are no different to the beefeaters, except a lot less round and a lot less hairy. Buoyed, my anxiety starts to dissipate; I feel like tonight may just be a good night.

There seems to be a Freddie-shaped gap in the conversation, however. I can't quite give the others my full attention, and my eyes instinctively track around the room for his long limbs and dishevelled curls. Trying my hardest to listen to Davidson as he talks to me about the time when Chaplin had napped through the Ceremony of the Keys and had to quickly play 'The Last Post' from out of the guardroom window, I finally spot Freddie peering at us over the rim of a wide whisky glass. When his eyes catch mine, he averts them and moves fluidly across the room, disappearing again.

Mo must have noticed my unrest, and places a heavy hand on my shoulder, telling me to wait with the band for a moment. He crosses the room and through a thick curtain that I had just assumed to be a window.

I turn back to Davidson on the guitar. 'Do you have these kinds of parties often?' I try my best to fill the silence.

'Only on special occasions – birthdays and the like. Or sometimes we just fancy a bit of a drink, so . . . actually, it's probably most of the times that we're here.'

'Is tonight any special occasion?'

'Of course, you're here,' he says so casually that it is clear he makes up for his lack of height in charm. It works; I blush.

'Have you been a guardsman for long?' I ask once the fire across my cheeks subsides.

'I'm what they call a senior guardsman, so I've been here almost two years now,' Davidson says, straightening up with pride. 'Most of the others have only been out of training a year or so, some two. This is our first posting – eases us in gently. Plus, we do so much drill in training, we are better than most of the older lot at marching up and down, so they leave it to us. My time is almost up though, now.'

'Where will you end up once your posting here is done?'

'I'm not quite sure where's next. I just wait around for some posh bloke to tell me and do what he says. There's no point hoping because you don't get much of a choice.' He doesn't seem much affected by this, and I understand. When I was a kid, we'd not know one year to the next whether we'd get to stay in the house that we had only just unfinished unpacking the boxes in. Like Davidson says, it is just something about your life that you have to accept, and the sooner you come to terms with the fact your job is in fact your lifestyle, the easier it is.

Mo returns after a short while, his giant hands dwarfing a pair of martini glasses filled with an unknown concoction. The bright pink liquid glitters in the light as he hands it to me.

'Thank you, but um . . . what is it?'

'It's the guardsman's punch. Cantforth makes it. I'm not sure even he knows what's in it – it's a different colour every time he makes it.' I cautiously bring the glass up to my nose to give it a quick sniff test; it is pungent enough that I am sure it has just singed off all of my nose hair. Smelling somewhat like a berry-scented nail polish remover, it reminds me of Bran's university flat parties where I'd create my very own cocktail from all of the almost-empty bottles of spirits that had been left over at the last party. I take a cautious sip and am instantly sent into a fit of coughs.

'Jesus Christ. Is this the stuff you clean your weapons with or what?' I laugh in between my minor choking fit and my eyes water.

'It'll put hairs on your chest that will,' Davidson pipes up, chuckling at my disgusted expression. 'Hurry up and down it and find a partner. We're about to start,' he adds, strumming a warm-up chord on his guitar.

'Wait . . . a partner?' They don't reply so I quickly throw the acidic mixture down my throat and cringe at the taste. I wouldn't be surprised if I could now breathe fire. The small group of guardsmen cheer and Mo gives me a rough slap on the back. Secret initiation complete. I'm grateful for the shot of liquid courage as Tiny plays the intro to a rather up-beat folky tune and I am tugged by Mo towards the cleared space in the centre of the room. Just as Chaplin and Davidson fill out the melody, Mo grabs one of my hands, placing his other respectfully on my waist.

Dancing. We are bloody dancing!

For someone who can barely walk in a straight line, dancing can only really end in one thing: an injury. I try to protest, the nuclear bomb of a cocktail not quite enough to strip me of all of my self-doubt. Mo releases my hand, but as quickly as it is free, it is claimed again by another. Freddie.

'I believe that the first dance should be reserved for the host should it not?' He gives Mo a playful nudge as he pulls me from his hold, replacing Mo's heavy palm with his long fingers. As he rests his other hand against my hip bone, my body betrays me, and I draw an audibly sharp intake of breath. I try to repress the feeling of warmth as it pulses across the whole left side of my body. My cheeks throb with redness, and Freddie softly chuckles.

'Is that right? Does that still count if the original host

leaves his guest to fend for herself as soon as they step through the door?' I quip, the strain to my voice doing little to hide how his hands have affected me.

'Mo seemed to have it all covered. Who knows, maybe you can find a new boyfriend that doesn't have "arsehole" scribbled across his forehead.' The tingling up my body subsides at this, and my mood sags again.

'A soldier?'

He nods.

'My mum made that mistake years ago . . . I'm not sure I want to follow in her footsteps.' The light on his face also neutralises and he is back to his true Freddie self. My right hand that rests in his grows increasingly damp and I quickly pull it free to rub it against my jeans.

'Sweaty hands, I'm all slippery and gross.' He shakes his head with a small upward turn of his lips, and quickly grasps my hand again, holding it even tighter than before.

'I once had to sleep in a tent with Mo on exercise. I never knew sweat like it. I thought it had been raining and the tent was leaking but turns out that he had just taken a fancy to me in the night and given me a rather tight hug. We were both soaking wet through with his sweat. A damp palm is nothing, I assure you.' He shakes his head, amused with the memory and no doubt noticing my nauseated glance over at Mo, who is dancing with a group of soldiers that I have yet to be introduced to. They take it in turns to swing each other around to the folk tune and freestyle in the middle of their small circle.

Without warning, Freddie skips me into the middle of the room, spinning me around to the increasing tempo as though I am weightless. Laughing hysterically, every other step I take ends up on top of Freddie's shoe. Luckily for me, he isn't still wearing his beautifully polished boots – a quick look down, which results in me swiftly headbutting Freddie's extremely solid chest confirms that he's swapped them for a pair of soft white trainers.

'I had an inkling that you may be a toe-stomper, so I changed them whilst you were with Mo.' He speaks directly against my ear so I can hear him above the music. All of my senses are filled with him. He is pressed so close that I notice how his musky aftershave is laced with bursts of citrus, the perfect combination of sweetness that wraps me up into the cloud of him. I can't tell if it's the lethal alcoholic potion or the thrill of his proximity – his hands on my waist, the smell of his cologne rubbing against my blouse, the way we skip together across the room at breakneck speed – but I am intoxicated.

Freddie dances us into the group. We weave between them as they clap and stomp to the beat. Not a single face is stoic and still now. They are animated, electrified, and I feel alive in a blur of Freddie.

The music reaches its climax and our feet finally come to a halt. I breathe heavily through my smile, each expansion of my chest pushing me further into him, and I feel his racing heartbeat against me. As Freddie looks down at me, I don't even care that my hair sticks to my cheeks and tickles at my lip; I don't care that a sprinkling of sweat dapples my forehead. He runs his rough thumb across my face, swiping away the hair and catching at my bottom lip in the process, as he tucks the stray behind my ear. The last little bit of tension leaves my body, and, for the first time all night, I truly feel like myself.

Then, he blinks twice and drops his hands from me abruptly. Before I can even say anything, he strides away wordlessly and disappears behind the curtain.

Chapter 9

Even as the band begin their second song, I can't drag my eyes away from the direction that Freddie made his quick getaway. Have I done something wrong? I discreetly sniff to see if my deodorant has let me down with all of the unexpected exercise. Nope, all clear. It was going so well, and for once I didn't even say anything embarrassing. I sigh and look to the ceiling in frustration, and when I refocus on the present another glass of pink punch is being wafted under my nose. Cringing at the smell, I accept the drink from a smiling Mo and swallow the whole thing down in one go.

'Come on, we're wasting a good song!' Mo's accent is stronger as he shouts over the strings. He pulls me beside him in the circle. In the middle, an older-looking man with a bushy moustache attempts to dance. He kicks his legs erratically and swings his head from side to side so hard that it looks as though it's about to fly clean off and smash through the window. Each of the guards give their own two-step dance around the circle and I instinctively join them. The blond and brunette from earlier slide in together and launch into a choreographed routine so well polished that you can see the hours they have put into rehearsing it. It reminds me of the dances you'd make up on the primary school playground at break time. The lighter haired of the two jumps down into a squat position and bounces around to the beat as the darker-haired man kicks his legs over him in a well-practised move, and I dread to think how many times he got an accidental boot to the head in rehearsals.

'Riley and Walker – the platoon entertainment. Every time we get deployed, they give us a little performance to keep up morale. They even showcased their own version of *Cats* the musical in the middle of the Belizean jungle.' Mo leans over again to fill me in. I make a mental note to ask if there would be any chance of getting a repeat performance.

Riley's attempt to do the robot to the folky tune is interrupted by Walker, who gives a slapstick show of pretending to slap him in the face. Riley plays along, giving an exaggerated flick of his head with every false slap, a hyperbolic expression of wide-eyed innocence on his face. He's really giving this act his all. My stomach cramps from laughing too hard.

The song comes to an end and the comedy duo take their bows to a rapturous applause. With no room for a break, another folk tune commences. This time, all of the stragglers still milling around in the wings come together and line up with a partner. Mo stands opposite me, mouthing: *Follow my lead.'*

The partners beside us begin to dance their own version of a Scottish ceilidh. After bumping into the back of the moustachioed man who almost danced his head off, I learn his name is Dick. I'm not sure if it's derived from Richard or the more common insult, but he seemed proud to introduce himself nonetheless. And, despite falling over my own feet *and* everyone else's, I manage to survive the song without any injuries.

'Okay, I'm done! I need a drink.' I laugh as I fall back onto the leather sofa. Mo and Riley plop down either side of me as Walker brings up the rear carrying a half-empty bottle of whisky. He pretends to sit down on my lap and cleverly manoeuvres his way beside me, pushing Riley further down the couch. Stealing the bottle in retaliation, Riley swigs it straight. The bottle gets passed down the sofa and we each take a mouthful. I hardly flinch; even tasting how I imagine petrol to taste, it has nothing on the pink cocktail I had been gifted previously, so it goes down relatively easy.

'So, everyone just calls everyone by their surnames?' I turn to Walker and Riley, interrupting their bickering over who got the larger shot and who is to blame for the fast-depleting alcohol.

'Pretty much. You can call me Jamie if you want, but I probably won't answer to it. Even my mam just calls me Riley now. Wait . . . what's your first name again?' Riley turns to the other half of his duo who dramatically clutches at his heart.

'Nope, not telling you now.' Walker crosses his arms over his chest, his childish streak unveiling itself in full force.

'Hold on a second! You two are the best of friends, you work together every day, but you don't even know his first name?' I slur my words slightly, utterly baffled.

'Aye, I'd take a bullet for him, but it's just never come up. I've probably seen it on Facebook or something, but I don't remember.' Riley shrugs. The more I learn about men the more I believe that we are not even the same species.

'So then, Walker, what is it?' He looks at me sheepishly and mumbles something incoherently. 'Huh? What was that?'

'Courtney.' He almost coughs it out. Both Riley and Mo choke on their respective drinks, clamouring over the bombshell.

'Okay . . . okay . . .' I struggle to respond. The whole sofa is in hysterics, even Courtney Walker, although his blush would give mine a run for its money. 'Walker it is then.'

The next hour is a blur of dancing and drinks swigged between breaths. Swinging each other around to the music, I feel like I've actually made a few friends. Mo practically lifts me off the ground in a rather surprising twirl and I don't even stop to panic at him feeling how heavy I am.

The room hasn't quite stopped spinning since then. My feet don't even feel as if they are touching the floor as I stand against the fireplace, using the mantel as a crutch, impatiently waiting for Freddie to return.

In my drunken stupor, I decide he has had enough time avoiding me; I am not letting him get away with ditching me on the dance floor like Daniel Harris did to me at my year six school disco. Stumbling across the dance floor, I sweep aside the curtain with a theatrical swoosh.

Behind it, bookcases scale the walls with dusty cloth-bound and leather-bound books. The dark wood shelves soften the harsh artificial lamplight, and a soft glow falls across the room. This must be the library. I had almost forgotten the real reason for my being here. My bubbling frustration subsides as I breathe in the view. It is *sublime*. A rickety ladder is fastened to wheels and I picture myself clambering up it, and sliding across shelves of ancient books, living out all of my *Beauty and the Beast* fantasies of hiding away in a castle library, using only pens to hold my messy bun in place.

A soldier I have yet to meet suddenly appears and, in my drunkenness and my intoxication with the sight before me, I don't notice him until we have fully collided. He is only an inch or so taller than me, so we are face to face as he steadies me. Like most of them, he is clean-shaven, and his light hair is neatly clipped, but there's something about him that makes him less intimidating than the rest; his jawline is soft and rounded and his brown eyes are so large that I can see each splatter of hazel across his irises.

'Ah, you must be Maggie,' he says as he releases me, though his hands hover either side of my shoulders, as if he's making sure I am going to stay upright. 'I'm Cantforth . . . Cai. And I have a feeling that . . . *this* may have a little something to do with me.' He points his finger up and down my body as I sway, having to clutch either him or the curtain to steady myself every now and again. 'Ever so sorry!'

'Hi! You must be pink cocktail man.'

'I am indeed. Although I can fetch you a glass of water if you'd like?' He goes to leave but I quickly catch his arm.

'I'm actually looking for Freddie. Have you seen him?'

'Freddie? Who's . . . oh, you mean Guildford? Yeah, he's over there, at the bar.' I follow his outstretched arm around the bookcase. Sure enough, a small bar – lined with various bottles and glasses – is tucked into the corner. Freddie leans on it, one hand nestled into his curls and the other rolling the liquid around in his glass, just like he did with his hot chocolate.

As I wobble my way over to him, it isn't long before he is snapped out of his reverie by the sound of me stumbling over my own feet. I wave, and he lets out a slow breathy chuckle and flicks his hand in a lazy salute. Finally reaching the bar, I try to casually slide onto the stool beside him, but the seat spins and I slip, banging my elbow against the bar. Freddie's reflexes manage to catch me before I fully flop at his feet. Guiding me to the stool this time, he holds the seat still so I can hop onto it properly. Once I'm safely on top, he pushes the entire stool forward so my legs meet the bar, and I can lean against it like him.

'Are you okay?' he asks quietly, not taking his eyes from my elbow. I rub it, the pain dull thanks to the alcohol.

'Yes, yes. All good. It wouldn't be me if I didn't go somewhere new and leave with a few more bruises.' He just nods his head in acknowledgement and stares again into his whisky. 'You keep disappearing. Just ditched me like you needed to get home before midnight, or your trousers would turn into cabbage leaves or something.'

'I think you must have been watching the pirated version

of *Cinderella* as a child.' He swigs from his glass with an amused twitch of his lip.

'That is more than a possibility actually. There was always that one guy down the pub handing them out for a quid. I once saw a version of *The Lord of the Rings* where it was just four men, high in a forest walking around with one pretending to be a wizard. Pretty confusing for a ten-year-old. Still haven't seen the proper version.'

'You are joking? You have never seen *The Lord of the Rings*? Not even *The Hobbit*?' His quiet and subdued demeanour has been replaced with a childish expression of curiosity.

'Nope. Not a single one. From what I gather from the one I did see though, it's just about men with hairy feet going on a walk, right?'

He expels an exaggerated gasp. 'Blasphemy!' He points his finger towards me, and I half expect a medieval priest or some hairy man with a patchy neck beard who works in HMV to come around the corner and drag me away to punish me. 'Although . . . actually that pretty much is what happens when I think about it.'

'Ha!' It's my turn to point at him this time.

'You do realise I'm going to have to make you watch it – the extended editions, no less – even if I have to strap you to a chair in front of the television in the guardroom for eleven hours.'

'Eleven hours? Bloody hell. You're lucky if you can hold my attention for more than ten minutes these days.' Although the thought of being with him for that length of time is fairly appealing – hairy wizards or otherwise.

'If I watch the *Lord of the Rings* then you have to watch a documentary with me. Or *Pride and Prejudice*! Has to be the 2005 version though, with Matthew Macfadyen as Mr Darcy. The *better* Mr Darcy. And I will die on that hill.' Getting a little too passionate about my Jane Austen adaptations, I blush, averting my eyes from Freddie.

'You're not wrong.' When I look back to him, he is smiling. 'Macfadyen was a far more true likeness to the book than Colin Firth being all sexy clambering out of a pond in only his shirt.' And just like that, Freddie is, to me, sexier than any man in period costume, dripping wet and head over heels in love. He watches – and *reads* – Jane Austen? This man really is a mystery, but more than ever he's an enigma that I must solve.

I must have been staring at him a little too long because he speaks again, snapping me out of my look of hypnotised awe. 'But a documentary?' he asks, with intrigue. 'What kind of documentary we talking?'

'Any historical period of your choice, except the Tudors. They can get a little boring after a while.' I point to the window behind us. The White Tower is lit up and framed in the panes.

Freddie extends his hand to shake. 'Fine, deal.'

I go to wipe my hand on my jeans again, but he grabs it anyway and shrugs. I smile, and we shake on it. It's a date! Well, it's probably not, just two friends hanging out watching a few films, but . . . it's definitely more exciting to say it's a date.

'So, you're a bit of a history geek?'

'And you are a fantasy nerd.'

'Touché.' He raises his glass to me slightly, before taking another sip.

'It's pretty hard not to be a little bit of a history fangirl in this place. Wellington has probably walked through this very room, and some of these books even look old enough to have been his.' I feel myself getting animated again, and swing around on the stool to look at the shelves that line the walls. A little flutter goes through my stomach at the thought of how many fingers have touched their pages.

'I've never thought about it like that.' Freddie turns to look too, and we both stare at the colourful spines for a while.

'Doesn't it make you feel so . . . full! We are living *inside* history. Each step we take in this place has already been trodden by kings and queens, and the people who have quite literally created the life we live in.'

'Imagine what they would think if they could see what it's become! Mo's horrendous dancing could bring anyone back from the grave.' We chuckle together. 'Has he exposed you to his famous sprinkler move yet?'

'No! I feel like I'm missing out now.'

'I'm surprised! He's normally more than happy . . . Remind me later and I'll ask him. If you're really lucky, he might even throw in the lawnmower one too.'

I tear my gaze from the books and nod. Freddie doesn't look at me when he speaks next: 'You know, they might be talking about you in the same way in a couple of centuries.' I grin self-consciously. 'Who knows . . . ?' he adds, taking yet another swig from his drink, actively avoiding my gaze.

'Ha! The only thing I'll go down in history for is perhaps burning the place down while trying to make a cheese toastie.' He finally meets my eye, and his teeth make an appearance in his smile. 'Fancy another dance? I absolutely *have* to see this "lawnmower" move now.' He nods wordlessly and gets to his feet, offering a hand to help me down from my own stool. I accept gladly, still wobbly on my legs.

This time, we dance like we're at an under eighteens disco rather than a village ball. Mo shows me both the sprinkler *and* the lawnmower, which involves him dramatically miming the pulling of the choke and mowing some wonky lines across the dance floor. I even learn the 'chainsaw' move from Walker, which involves quite a lot more hip thrusting than I think is generally considered safe when using dangerous machinery. By the time the music stops, the whole room is at it.

Once the band retire their instruments, Freddie, Walker, Riley, Mo, Chaplin and I all collapse onto one of the larger sofas. Despite its size, we're all bunched together, and Walker ends up pretty much sat on Riley's knee. I am pressed so tightly into Freddie's side that he moves his arm from between us and throws it across the back of the sofa behind me.

'So, you and Stiff, huh?' Riley nudges me suggestively and Freddie retracts his arm.

'Oh, no, no . . .' I laugh, trying to mask my discomfort and the disappointment I feel at the loss of Freddie's closeness. 'He owed me, so he brought me up here with the promise of seeing the library. I have to admit, I was intrigued at what you guys get up to in this place when you're not standing still outside. To be honest, I was secretly hoping there would be some handsome men behind those bearskins, but I am still waiting on that one.' I wink at Riley as he pretends to be shot through the heart.

'Come on, I've never had a girl resist these.' Mo stands up, flexing his biceps under his shirt. When I only raise a playful eyebrow to his biceps, he begins to bounce his pecks, adding: 'Okay, okay, how about this?'

'Sit down, Corporal,' Freddie grumbles.

'No taste!' Mo huffs and sits back down – but despite his best efforts to look offended at the whole group's rejection of his 'talents', the dimple in his left cheek tells me that he too is only teasing.

Dick comes around the corner, then. His moustache is slightly damp with drink and he sucks at it drunkenly. 'Sorry, I was earwigging,' he says, although it's a little muffled by the thick dark hair in his mouth. 'I would give my life for any of these blokes, I really would.' He claps Chaplin on the shoulder with a fatherly smile. 'But I would not let them lay one finger on my little girl. I've seen far too much of them and what they get up to in the Irish bars in Soho to let them get anywhere near my daughter.' All of the lads nod in agreement.

'He's not wrong. Riley tried to have a dance-off with a girl last week. She thought he was having a seizure and got the manager over,' Walker teases, still sat on his friend's lap. Riley stands up abruptly, sending him flying to the floor and Walker lands with a thump on his arse. He stands up quickly, rubbing his tailbone, but seems to feel his jest was worth it.

Freddie has gone quiet again, hands folded neatly in his lap. He simply observes what's happening in front of him and makes no attempt to involve himself or acknowledge me. Thankfully, Cantforth makes his way over with a tray of shots. This time, they are luminous green, but despite the fact they look exactly like a vial of poison from the movies, I swig two down unflinchingly. The others do the same and Cantforth plops himself down on the floor with the tray of empty glasses.

'You're probably better off on the dating apps – Tinder, and that.' Cantforth adds his two pennies' worth into the conversation. I redden in the knowledge that I have the whole royal guard giving me dating advice. 'Girls never have a problem on those kinds of things, and you're far prettier than most others so you'd probably be fighting them off on there.' That's it – I feel myself flush full tomato. Compliments always send my mind into overdrive. What do I do now? Just thank him? Is that vain? Agree with him? Even more vain. Compliment him back? Something about the drinks maybe? Or his hair? But that's just awkward.

Honesty is the best policy, I suppose. 'You'd hope that would be true, but I downloaded Tinder a few days ago, and not so much as a nibble.' I embarrass myself even more admitting my failure and I'm grateful when none of them laugh at me.

'Right then, you'd better show us this horrendous profile . . .' Walker extends his hand, gesturing for my phone.

'Wh-what? Horrendous?' I stammer, self-conscious.

'Men would swipe right for Kermit the Frog on these

apps – they really aren't picky. You probably just need some help with your profile because in all honesty I'd pick you over a Muppet any day of the week,' Mo clarifies.

As I reluctantly slide my phone out of the pocket of my jeans, Freddie leans over to me and speaks in a low voice. 'Are you sure? You don't have to, you know – they're all drunk.'

'It's fine. And so am I,' I reply, a little disgruntled that he would choose now to involve himself. He only shrugs in response and I hand my phone over to Mo, offering him the password openly. The worst thing they'll find on there is probably a picture of a rash that I had on my back a few weeks ago and wanted to compare to all of the Google Images results that suggested I had a medieval skin disease.

'Oh, Maggie.' Mo sighs, looking at me in despair. The others are crowded around him, scanning over my profile. They all give me the same pitiful look.

'What? Is it the picture? The bio?'

'Maggie, you may as well have written "I'm not interested" or "I have zero personality". To be honest, some people might even swipe right for that, but then they can barely even see your face in this picture.' He angles the screen towards me. He has a point; the photo is taken from quite a distance and all your eye is really drawn to is my dad and the White Tower. I'm essentially just a blurred ginger blob in the corner.

'You're right. I know you are. I just don't . . . really do this stuff.' I look to Freddie, but he is staring straight ahead, sipping his drink mechanically, and back to being a robot it seems. Perhaps it's crowds he struggles with.

133

'We will fix it. Tonight! Right now, in fact.' Riley pops out from behind the wide expanse of Mo's back, with a giddy expression.

'Oh, no, no . . . you don't have to do that.' I protest, making a weak grab for my phone. It is in vain, however, as they're already swiping through my photos on my phone. My embarrassment – initially held at bay by the alcohol – is beginning to creep back onto my cheeks. Cantforth tiptoes over quietly and places another drink in my hand, and I am grateful for the Dutch courage it affords me.

Between sips, I nervously chew on my lip, hands folded in my lap as if I'm waiting outside the headmaster's office, ready to be scolded. Quiet muttering and muted whispers pass between the group until Walker finally pipes up: 'Well, if we wanted to make a profile for your cat, we have hit the mother lode.'

At that, Freddie stands suddenly and snatches the phone out of Riley's hand. I'm confused as to what could possibly have annoyed him, but he turns to me and points it at my face. He's taking photos of me, lots of them, moving side to side to capture each angle of my stupefied expression.

'She looks nice enough now, why not just take some new ones?' Freddie says bluntly, still snapping photos.

'Well, they're not going to be any good now, are they, Mr Paparazzi? Unless you're going to use them for a ransom letter!' Mo grips his shoulder, taking account of my look of surprise and slight fear. He pries the phone gently from Freddie's grip and sits down with a bounce on the cushion at the other end of the sofa. I have to swallow the sudden bad taste in my mouth. That was . . . odd. Sobriety hits me hard, and I wish Cantforth would wander past like the mind-reading barman he apparently is and top me back up. The reality of the situation dawns on me and if Mo weren't an exceptionally muscular Fijian man who is built like some sort of demigod, I'd have taken my chances to wrestle my phone back off him.

Chaplin stands up this time and gently picks up my phone, before walking towards me and offering a kind hand for me to take. The sympathy in his face is instantly calming and I accept his offer without another thought. No one else follows as he leads me back through the curtain and over to the bar. He grabs a large bottle of spirit off of the shelf and pours it into a glass, topped off with a squirt of lime juice. I accept it and drink it down; it's surprisingly pleasant and I'm grateful for his tenderness. He makes one for himself and sits quietly beside me. Taking my phone from his pocket, he opens it up and places it on the bar in front of me, opened onto one of the many photos taken by Freddie.

I can't tell if it's the blurriness of my eyes as they swim behind the alcohol, but the one he has chosen isn't actually atrocious. In fact, I can honestly say that I look almost pretty. My eyes are open wide, and the soft lights of the Mess illuminate all of the different shades of green in my irises. My mouth is parted in surprise, pushing out my lips; they're a soft hue of pink, which matches the booze-induced flush across my cheeks. Freddie captured me so off guard that I didn't have chance to screw myself up into my awkward hunched state. Chaplin beams his silent smile beside me, nodding his head. I return it, a soft warmth growing in me. The feeling is foreign . . . but I *think* I feel genuinely beautiful.

He picks up the phone again and mimes taking a photo. Understanding that he means to take more, I nod my head, a smile still tugging at my cheeks. He demonstrates a pose whilst sat on the stool, leaning on the bar with his head lolling into one of his hands and gestures for me to do the same. I follow his direction as he snaps a few quick photos. He gives examples of a few more angles that I try my best to replicate, and, when I giggle at his attempt at a pout, he clicks another candid photo of my genuine laughter.

After just a few minutes of modelling, two sets of strong arms are wrapped around my shoulders as Mo, Riley, Walker and Freddie appear and hop in for a group photo. Mo rubs his teasing hand through my hair, sending it into every wild direction. Returning the favour, I reach up to place him into a headlock, rubbing my knuckles across his hair. There is absolutely nothing stopping him from releasing himself from my playful grip, but he accepts it like a good sport. After Walker and Riley steal away all of the attention again to wrestle one another in the middle of the floor, Freddie retrieves my phone from Chaplin. Before returning it to me, he takes his own sleek phone out of his pocket and types what I can only assume to be my phone number into it. Averting my gaze as he finishes up his covert task, he crosses back to me and discreetly slides my phone into my back pocket and settles his eyes onto his colleagues as they roll around on the floor at our feet.

'Now I'll be able to call you,' Freddie says into my ear in a low voice, neither of us taking our gaze from the other. With great difficulty I maintain my poker face, concealing the fact that my heart is beating so hard against my chest that it would be a high scorer on the Richter scale.

The alcohol may be to blame, but something about this moment feels natural. Pulling up the photo taken only seconds ago, I realise I slot into this scene so effortlessly. For once in my life, I don't stick out like a huge ginger thumb. To be laughing like a maniac with guys I have only met a few hours before already seems like the norm, almost homely. Each one of them is entirely different from the other, all of them with different stories, and yet not a single one of them is judged. Nor do they judge me. Teasing me like one of their own, they've accepted me as I am and, for once, I am entirely at ease.

I send the photo to Mum. It would make her smile.

Chapter 10

I t was a mistake. A huge mistake.
    I groan as I roll over in bed. My brain throbs against my skull so hard that I am sure it is about to explode and throw its contents across the room. Ugh, why did I even imagine that? Retching at the mental image, I realise that the prospect of the contents of my stomach being projectile-vomited across the room is a lot more likely in this very moment.

I jump up, but the sudden motion makes me gag again and I have to steady myself on my headboard. Trying to navigate my room to get to the bathroom feels like trying to find my way through the Matrix. The carpet looks extremely appealing; the grey fluff with two half-eaten packets of cheese and onion crisps, an empty packet of microwave rice, and my underwear strewn across it could well be a memory foam mattress in a fancy hotel at this stage. Falling to my knees with as much elegance as a spider wearing roller skates, the urge to vomit rolls over my whole body and I shake, trying to hold it in. I'm sure I have seen Cromwell in this very same position before, making all kinds of noises to relieve himself of a large hair ball.

With little time to spare, I crawl on my hands and knees to the toilet – just making it in time. When the worst is over, I lie my cheek on the seat and close my eyes, unable to lift my head. The toilet seat is surprisingly comfy; in fact, I think I'm just going to stay here for the rest of the day.

The loud ringing of my phone wakes me up from my power nap, with my face still smushed against the hard plastic. Crawling back through to my room, I feel another wave of nausea overtake me as I see Kevin's name lighting up the screen. I don't answer it. I already know he is calling because I'm late. Reluctantly, I shuffle around my bedroom with as much elegance as a slug who had just snorted a line of salt and is burning from the inside out. After brushing my teeth, I take one last regrettable look in the mirror and notice I have a rather sexy outline of the rim of the toilet seat engraved into my cheek. Too hungover, and still slightly too drunk to care, I salute Mum on the way out and trundle off to work.

On the way, I can barely bring myself to say 'good morning' to Holly and Duke, the inseparable pair of ravens. Duke is the biggest and oldest of the conspiracy; he is easily the size of a small child and has been known to fight a few over a packet of crisps. But it is Holly that is the most terrifying. The two are mated, and wherever she goes, he follows, hopping along behind her like her biggest fan. And it's easy to see why: a stunning creature, her feathers are always perfectly sleek; she is the undoubted queen of the ravens – and she knows it. Even I feel judged by her as her black eyes track me across the courtyard. I imagine her tutting and muttering about my slouch or my creased shirt. Often, I see her smoothing down Duke's feathers, like a wife adjusting her husband's tie for work as he squirms at her fussing.

Under her watchful gaze, I haul myself away from the fence post that I had propped myself against and drag myself onward. Already well over twenty minutes late, I am feeling so fragile that I can't even muster up enough energy to be annoyed at the prospect of having to be on White Tower safe duty tonight.

Kevin only receives a grunt from me as I pass through the office; he shouts something in response, but I cover my ears. My body reacts to his voice in the same way it does to my iPhone alarm; I feel it in every one of my synapses and each one sends a pulse that spurs on the urge to throw up again. I flop down at my desk and lay my head on the cool veneer. The closed blinds of the ticket booth cast out most of the light, but everything still seems just that little bit brighter and more invasive today. Groaning, I shrink further into my cardigan and 'rest my eyes' for a moment.

'Margaret, what on earth are you doing? It won't be long 'til that queue reaches Buckingham Palace.' The sound of Kevin's voice and the obnoxious clicking of his heels stirs me from my nap. Groggily, I nudge the mouse of my computer and the locked screen flashes up brightly in my dark booth: 14.35 p.m. I have managed to nap for almost four hours undetected! Why haven't I done this before? Rubbing the sleep out of my eyes, I quickly snap up the blinds and log on before he can reach me. He rounds the corner and I swing back on my chair to meet him.

'Huh, did you want something?' He surveys my booth and looks me up and down. I quickly wipe away the dried-up drool from the corner of my mouth as he narrows his eyes. Not finding whatever he desired, he waltzes away with a huff.

By the time five rolls around, I have managed to find three spots to successfully skive off and nap in. One: of course, just at my usual desk, not taking any extra precautions to hide – there are certainly perks of being the least liked in the office as no one bothers to take any notice. Two: under the shelves in the store cupboard that Kevin will only go into every now and again to let out an offensively squeaky fart, and that's a small price I am willing to pay to sleep off this hangover. And three: I got a full ten minutes of kip sat upright on the toilet, face nicely wedged against the toilet roll holder, with my knickers still around my ankles. Not at all my finest hour but when it feels like someone is playing a game of pinball inside my brain, I'd sell a kidney for a ten-minute nap.

It's still abusively bright when I finally step outside at the end of the day, lumbered once again with the bag of change. Flipping the fiery ball in the sky the bird, it takes a few moments before I can fully open my eyes. Not to be dramatic but the world feels like it is closing in on me: the crushing pain of my persistent headache, the heavy bag dragging down on my shoulder, my hair flicking into my face and having the audacity to tickle my neck. I am one annoying itch away from throwing a full temper tantrum and just lying down on the cold concrete.

Almost as if the wind heard me, it blusters, and I get a mouthful of my red strands. Groaning loudly, I throw the bag on the ground, plonk myself down on the kerb and rub my eyes so hard I am sure I can see my headache in motion, flashing painful lights across my eyelids.

'Bloody hell, and I thought Riley was the human embodiment of a hangover this morning . . .' I stand up quickly at the voice. Too quickly as it happens; the floaty spots in my vision return, and Freddie has to catch my arm as I stumble.

'I have no idea what was in that pink stuff, but it was sent by the devil.'

His hand still holds on to my forearm as I clutch my head in pain. One of his long fingers rubs back and forth slowly. Pain melting away, all I can focus on is the warm friction of his fingertips, the instinctive comforting motion that instantly sends my skin into a burst of pleasurable warmth.

'That's my fault. I should have told you the first and only rule of the Mess—'

'Don't talk about the Mess Club?' I interject. The joke is terrible and the shot of burning pain that follows my laugh at said terrible joke is even worse. Freddie rolls his eyes with another of his outward-breath laughs. His fingers still press softly against me, absentmindedly caressing my skin. I don't think he even realises that he's doing it.

'No, you can talk about it all you like, I'm pretty sure no one would believe you. The one and only rule is: never accept a drink from Cantforth. He fancies himself as some sort of nutty professor, concocting all of these potions that I'm pretty sure could be used as explosives.'

'Come on, man, you had one job.' He chuckles, sweeping a hair from where it had been trapped at the corner of my mouth and tucking it behind my ear – making it the neatest strand currently on my head.

Coldness hits my arm as Freddie releases it, and the sudden absence of his touch is so noticeable that I have to actively stop myself from reaching for him. At last, I manage to open my eyes fully without feeling like I have a Viking axe wedged into my skull, realising as I do so that he isn't tightly bound into the red tunic and buff belt of his uniform. Although he does still look startlingly formal, buttoned into a perfectly ironed white shirt and a pair of tight grey dress trousers. I wonder if he owns a pair of jeans, or even a T-shirt. Does this man ever just lounge around on the sofa in his pyjamas eating leftover pizza? Umber curls are tousled on top of his head, still slightly damp from a shower, the only part of him that doesn't look like it has been plucked straight out of a catalogue. The sleeves of his shirt are rolled past his forearms, and I notice how his strong veins poke through his milky skin as he balls his fists by his sides.

'Are you going somewhere?' I ask, since he does look ready to conduct a business meeting or go on a date with some fancy socialite who does her weekly food shop in Harrods.

By way of response, Freddie bends down to pick up the sports bag filled with money and tosses it over his shoulder with such ease you'd think it was empty. 'I was on guard at half past eight this morning and usually seeing you rushing to work is my sign that it's around nine. I could tell you were late as my back was aching by the time you emerged. And I remembered what you said about your boss punishing you and thought you could use some backup . . . with the ghosts . . .' He gestures to the bag as he trails off awkwardly.

I don't even know which part of that to process first. The fact he looks out for me each morning he's here? The fact he remembered our discussion about the cellar? Or the fact he has come to help me in case I am afraid? In the distance, I spot Bob closing the main gate, herding out the last few stragglers and chasing down a few who were attempting to leave with the fluffy headphones of their audio guides fastened to their ears.

'I'm not sure you know what you've got yourself into. You may be a big strong soldier, but I won't be holding your hand when the ghosts try to hold the other one. They say it's a little girl down there. Someone from the press office once heard her singing apparently,' I quip with a laugh. His eyes widen just enough for me to notice. Truthfully, I want to be serious with him. I want to ask him about last night, about why he invited me there only to disappear as soon as I allowed myself to get comfortable with him.

Except . . . I think I already know the answer. For goodness' sake, he took a picture for my Tinder! Those aren't the actions of a man who wants me for himself. Freddie is just a friend. Barely that, come to think of it, since I *still* hardly know anything about him. The sooner I accept that he's not interested in me, the better. How could a man who looks like he has just walked off of the set of a Hollywood film ever take notice of someone like me romantically? I'm just one of the lads. I've always been one of the lads.

'How exciting. I hope she knows a bit of Metallica or maybe some Iron Maiden. I could show her my air guitar.' It's my turn to roll my eyes then. Evidently pleased with his joke, he walks off with the bag of money still slung over his shoulder. When I don't follow, he shouts across the crowd: 'Are you coming? Or do I have to hold my own hand?'

'Not holding your hand!' I holler back as I jog to catch up with him, trying my hardest to ignore the hangover that hasn't quite dissipated.

When I finally catch up with his long efficient strides, he doesn't look at me but instead pulls a small box out of his pocket and hands it over. It's a box of painkillers. 'I thought you might need some of these.' Thanking him, I dry-swallow two, too impatient to shift the pain to wait for a glass of water.

There is no worse time to be walking through the Tower than now. Streams of staff rush to leave over the drawbridge that Freddie and I are entering across, and curious eyes scan over Freddie. His lean figure and Disney prince mannerisms make him a magnet for longing glances or jealous stares. Their eyes are then, by default, drawn to me, and with every glance I become more aware of the fact that I pale in comparison; my face is no doubt crawling with evidence of my heavy night, my hair resembles a stray cat plopped on my head, and my body is, as always, awkwardly large. Not fat, not thin, just a mass of gangly limbs and wobbly bits. To save face, I wave each of them goodnight and smile politely, but with each group we pass, I instinctively inch further and further back from Freddie until there is a comfortable distance between us.

It's the thought of the cameras that really make me itch. The beefeaters, my dad included, like to joke in their tours that they never have to worry about their children sneaking around and getting up to no good in the Tower.

'*Not only do they each have ex-sergeant majors for parents,*' my dad always tags onto the end of his tour with a cheeky grin, '*but they also have thirty-two ex-sergeant-major godparents for neighbours, and nothing gets past them. Even if they did miss anything, the cameras that cover every inch from the White Tower to Tower Hill station will catch them. So, when we're not here you can guarantee someone will report where they are, what they're wearing, who they're with, what time they come home, and what they have for breakfast.*'

To my dad, who has seen me more in the last year than he did for the first twenty years of my life, I am and always will be eight years old. I suppose it doesn't help that I have never been one to party or sneak around with boys, so now anytime anyone sees me do something not entirely kosher, it is a marvel, one that invites people to talk. Every step I make is documented and fed back to my dad – and the other beefeaters who are equally protective – to the extent that I had at least five of them ask me when I split with Bran if I would like him to be 'taught a lesson'. It really is no wonder that I am twenty-six with only one notch on my bedpost; in fact, the closest I've come to romance in the last year is accidentally skimming hands with the good-looking checkout boy in the supermarket when he handed me my bag for life.

Every now and again Freddie turns his head to search for me, and each time he finds me even farther away than the last. He says nothing, nor does he wait for me to catch up to him, he just nods his head quietly in acknowledgement of the passers-by and beelines for the White Tower.

Once we reach the wooden steps up into the Tower, I remember that I'm the one with the key and rush to overtake him. By the time I reach the door at the top, my breathing is laboured. Though I try my best to hide the fact that I am verging on an asthma attack from just climbing a few steps, I'm forced to take a big wheezing breath. Gently, Freddie takes the key from me with his free hand, unlocks and pushes open the door, allowing me to pass through into the armoury first.

Suits of armour propped up on display clink as we walk together across the floorboards. 'How long have you worked here?' He breaks the silence of the dark room, where the soft reflection on the rack of helmets from a faraway window illuminates part of his face. He looks like he did in my dream.

'Too long. It was just meant to be a temporary thing after uni. Dad was here, and I've always wanted to be one of the wardens. They are walking history books, know everything about every detail of these walls and get to immerse themselves in it every day. But I got stuck in the ticket booth, just looking at it from the outside.'

'Can you not transfer?'

'I tried. I got the degree, spent months studying. Dad would even bring me up here and test me on it. I think it was his way of trying to bond with me, you know, after Mum, but they wouldn't even give me an interview. So, I've just kept it locked up . . .' I say knocking on my temple. 'Dad still talks about it, tries to get us to come up here to practise just in case, but the moment's gone.'

'Why would they not? Give you the interview, I mean.' He's stopped walking now and looks at me with great intrigue.

'There's some talk that the beefeaters, and their kids by extension, are not well liked by the new management. Dad said it's because we know too much, so we tend to stray from the pre-approved stories that they want the public to know. I had the audacity to care about the history in a *historical* attraction. I even spent a traumatic few months trying to really kiss Kevin's arse and be a half-decent ticket office employee, so they had nothing to hold against me and might think about promoting me but here we are. None of it worked, so I gave up trying and there's no chance now. Their "official" excuse is that "the top hat probably wouldn't fit" over my hair. Very strict uniform policy apparently.'

'Go on then . . . regale me! What's this one?' Freddie points to a monumental suit of armour lit up in a glass case. The codpiece immediately draws one's eye. The long metallic shaft is erect and, no word of a lie, the width of a fist. It screams 'overcompensating for something'. It would be around Freddie's height stood on the ground but elevated on display, it dominates both of us. Almost as wide as it is tall, the breastplate is slightly curved to account for a more rotund figure and metallic gauntlets the size of small planets are fastened to the arms. All I can think is I am glad Freddie is with me or my imagination would run away with me, picturing the beastly suit springing to life like a juggernaut and chasing me across the room.

'That there is the armour of a man who liked to make up for his underperforming cock by making a codpiece so large it could take your eye out.'

'Is this the kind of story you learnt for your interview? If so, I can maybe see why they wouldn't want you teaching history to kids . . .' he teases, the ghost of a smile visible in the reflection of the glass.

'Okay, okay, that is Henry the VIII's armour from 1540. It was incredibly expensive to make at the time, because he was such a tank of a man.' I point to the cabinet beside it with spare gauntlets and various metal pieces suspended on display. 'There's actually little bits and pieces called garnitures to fasten to it that give it different functions. It means that this one piece of armour has the function of four. Brilliant engineering. The codpiece is obviously more about showing off though, of course. I'm not sure why he'd want to make . . . *that*—' I gesture to the baked-potato-sized piece '—a bigger target for the enemy. You can't help but stare at it can you?'

Freddie chuckles and nods his head in agreement. 'It is rather magnificent.'

149

'Apparently when the Victorians first displayed it, they'd let women come in and rub it to help with fertility. Although I don't think I'd fancy it. His syphilis was probably so rampant, I'd be worried that I'd catch it just from touching that thing.'

He pulls a face that implies both disgust and amusement. 'He's hardly the poster boy for fertility either, is he? What about this?' He is smiling down at a tiny suit of armour. It's barely three feet tall and luxuriously embossed across the helmet with scales that lead into the peak of the helmet, moulded to look like the top of a dragon's head, which matches its pauldrons on each shoulder. Welded to the crown of the helmet is a metal dragon, posed in a terrifying scream – although from a distance, it looks like a pointy mohawk.

'They are not one hundred per cent sure on the story behind that one. Some say it's the armour of various princes but there's one story that suggests it was designed for an entertainer with dwarfism, Jeffrey Hudson, who belonged to the Queen Henrietta Maria of France in the seventeenth century. He ended up fighting in the English civil war triumphantly and was promoted to become a captain.'

Freddie seems fully engrossed and listens attentively, scanning the artefact in awe.

'I think I would be more terrified at a suit of armour that small charging towards me out of nowhere on the battlefield than I would be of that great thing. Henry would have been horribly slow in that, I'm sure.' He looks back to the looming iron cast of the infamous king, and then places the bag of money, our forgotten task, on the floor to bend down to the height of the miniature armour. He surveys it with great interest for a few moments, every now and again looking back to me with a boyish smile. I feel like any moment now he's going to press his face to the glass like a child in an ice cream shop that has too many flavours to choose from.

'Incredible, simply incredible. Imagine how much this suit has seen.' Freddie shakes his head in disbelief. A little glow of pride spreads through me, thrilled that someone is listening to me, to the stories I tell. And enjoying them!

'I could show you the shields too if you like? Ooh and there's a breastplate with a cannon ball shot right through it over there! Or I could show you the cannons themselves?' I'm in my element now, and I can't hide my excitement.

Freddie doesn't laugh or mock my fervour, only smiles and nods his head. A flash of white teeth teases from behind his lips, so close to cracking a blinding grin. 'All of the above.'

In my head I throw my arms around him and thank him over and over, but I repress the giddy impulses and stretch my arm towards the next exhibit. 'This way for the beginning of your tour, if you please, sir.' He obliges with a very slight spring in his step.

We leave the duffel bag of money at the base of the armour, to be guarded by King Henry himself, and lose track of time passing through each section of the armoury. I don't even stop talking when the last of the sunlight sets, and we are left in almost complete darkness with only the dim lighting of odd display cases to guide us.

I am halfway through explaining the way the windows

151

were designed for the cannons to be winched in through them when Freddie's phone vibrates loudly in his pocket. He slides it out, takes a single glance at the caller and puts it back into his pocket, his face as indecipherable as it is when he is donning his bearskin. 'It's almost seven!' he announces abruptly, ridding himself of the boyish excitement in an instant. I deflate, losing my animated warmth. It's as though a spirit has sucked all of the excited confidence out of my body, leaving me as lifeless as itself. My facts forgotten, all I can think is that Freddie is about to do another of his disappearing acts.

'Oh, yes, of course, the safe. You can go if you need to.' We wander back where we started, and I pick up the bag, nodding to Henry in gratitude for watching over it. 'I can do this. You probably need to get back to work, never off duty and all of that . . .'

'No, no, no. You promised me ghosts and I haven't seen any yet, so I can't leave now.' He plucks the bag from my hands again and steps aside for me to lead the way. Warmth flushes back through me in a wave so overwhelming I actually do a little skip past him.

I don't make eye contact, but I hear his low chuckle, and add: 'Please ignore whatever that was – I don't know either.' For once, though, the embarrassment doesn't overtake me. The sound of Freddie's laugh and the thought that I could make it happen again gives me more of a rush of pleasure than anything Bran ever did in bed. Although, that's not too hard; he spent most of the seven years rubbing the bone of my pelvis and never getting any closer to hitting the target.

He follows me down the stairs, and the deeper we go, the more the fear creeps in. I stop halfway to ask if he wants to go in front of me – I making up a half-hearted excuse about 'guests first' – but he gives a smug smirk and ushers me to go on. When we reach the crooked door, we both stop to stare at it for a while. His smirk disappears swiftly once he feels the draught that tickles at his ankles.

'Are you ready?' I ask him with a sideways glance. He twitches nervously and chews at his lip – though when he realises that I have caught him in a moment of weakness, he stops, coughs, and straightens his posture.

'Yes, yes, indeed.' His hands grasp at the handles of the bag, and he twists them uncomfortably as I start for the door. 'Wait, you were only joking about the ghosts, right?' He looks adorable; brows furrowed and his lips drawn the whole way into his mouth.

'You'll see.' As I push open the door, a gust of cold air greets us from the other side. Freddie takes a step back instinctively, as if readying himself for an imminent attack. I stifle a laugh but before I can tease him, he steps into the hazily lit corridor, the bag raised above his head, and charges down the stairs into battle. I watch him from the top, blinded by laughter as he lets out a shrill battle cry. By the time he reaches the bottom, he has completely disappeared into the void, like a penny dropped into a well.

'Erm, I don't actually know how to get into this thing.' He shouts up through the darkness. Shoulders still shaking with hysterics, I don't even think twice in joining him. I take the stairs quickly, no hesitation.

'Come on, Maggie, where's your battle cry!' There's a hint of laughter in his voice, the soothing bass of it all the encouragement I need to let out an animalistic cry, taking the last few at great speed. Just as I reach the second to last step, I overestimate the curved edge of it and fly forward, hurtling straight towards the safe. That same sodding one that tries to kill me every time. You really would have thought I'd have learnt my lesson by now – it must be all of the concussions. Falling almost in slow motion, I brace myself and cover my face, not wanting to have to explain yet another black eye. But the impact never comes.

When I emerge from behind my hands, I find myself firmly wedged into Freddie's chest. I feel the curve of his pecs against my cheek and the ripple in his bicep wrapped around my waist. Despite not being the most petite of women, I am completely enclosed in his body. I couldn't be closer to him if I tried. In this intimate proximity, the soft scent of peppermint cuts through his woody cologne and I immediately come to the conclusion this is how I want to go: smothered to death against the soft linen of Freddie's shirt, under the pressure of his perfectly sculpted muscles and drowned in whatever his aftershave is called.

'How you have survived this long is humankind's greatest mystery. Can you not go a single day without almost smashing your face into something?' His chest vibrates with his words and bounces faintly with a chuckle.

I reluctantly withdraw from his embrace and awkwardly swipe my hands down my trousers. 'Would you believe me if I told you that I have never broken a bone?'

Before I can even finish my sentence, he has his answer. 'Absolutely not.'

'Okay, yeah. I think I broke my nose at one point.' I point to the crooked mess on my face. 'But nothing major.' I can hardly make out his features in the low light, and he must be having the same issue as he takes one of his long fingers and runs it softly down my nose, tracing its higgledy-piggledy path down my face.

He mutters something inaudibly to himself and turns back to the safe. 'Do you have the code?' he says through an awkward cough.

'Yes, sorry, I'll do it,' I mumble as I shuffle past him to get to the safe and turn the dial. It clicks and grinds into the silence that has settled over us, before popping open with a light ping. Freddie stuffs the bag inside. He has to hold it there as I creak the metal door closed, and I slam it quickly when he whips his arms out.

Once the door is fully bolted, I turn back to him. Our closeness is made even clearer as my boobs skim across his chest with the movement. But he inches ever closer to me. Chest to chest, the worry that he may be able to feel how hard my heart is pounding against my ribcage only makes it beat faster. I have to tilt my face up to his to avoid smashing it straight into his neck – as tempting as it is to see if his aftershave tastes as amazing as it smells. Okay, that was weird.

I distract myself from my stalkerish thoughts by skimming my eyes across his face. His expression is soft, relaxed, and I envy his composure. I am absolutely sure that if the weight of his body wasn't pinning me to the safe, my knees would have given way and I would be in a puddle on the floor. One of his hands touches my cheek in a hesitant embrace, his thumb swiping the escapee hairs from my eyes. My body responds by pressing back into him.

Freddie's hand grips my face with a tender firmness, his face lowering to mine. We're so close that his breath ghosts across my lips, and every inch of my skin begs for him to close the gap.

Suddenly, the light that cascades down the corridor shuts off with a pop, plunging us both into total darkness. The spell between us broken, I leap away from Freddie both in terror and in realisation of what was about to happen. He springs from me in the same motion.

'What the bloody hell . . . ?' Freddie half whispers, half growls into my ear and I can't deny the rush that it sends through me almost makes me push myself against him again.

Another gust of cold wind rushes past us down the stairs, slamming the door at the top with an echoed crash that reminds me of the present situation, and the supernatural experience that we may or may not be having. 'Okey-dokey, time to go.' We both bolt up the stairs, Freddie steadying me from behind as my erratic sprint sends my clumsy tendencies into overdrive. When we reach the door, I try the lock, but it doesn't shift. Giving it a rather unceremonious kick from the bottom does nothing either, not so much as a creak under the pressure.

Freddie places his hands on both of my shoulders, and I jump at the contact, but he shuffles me to the side with a polite, 'Excuse me.'

He slams into the four-inch-thick wood with his shoulder. The sound of the impact reverberates around the dark stairwell, and I wince at the thought of his bones ricocheting around in his body. No luck: the door remains stuck fast. This time, he places both hands either side of the doorway and takes one of his booted feet to it, and the lock clatters to the floor as the latch snaps clean off. And with that, he grabs my hand and pulls me out of the door, up the stairs, back through the armoury, and out of the Tower.

Chapter 11

Once our – well, mostly my – panting subsides and my heart rate returns to a healthy equilibrium, a chilly silence settles over us. Freddie looks past me, his shoulders angled towards the steps. I see in his face, as it pulls tighter, his eyes growing blank and dull, that he is distancing himself again. Raising a finger to my lips, I trace my Cupid's bow lightly. It tickles the same way it did under his breath. From the force of the memory, I shudder, both longing for his touch to return, and cringing at the awkwardness of his clear regret.

A strange animalistic cry diverts our attention and no doubt interrupts Freddie in the middle of mapping out his escape. Stood on the White Tower south lawn, in front of a small collection of ravens, are Tiny, Mo, Chaplin, Riley, and Walker. Tiny stands a little in front of the troupe and wears his forage cap with the peak facing backwards.

Freddie notices and groans beside me. 'I thought he may have a little more sense than that.' He descends the steps.

Unsure whether I will be invited to follow, I remain fixed in place. When he reaches the ground, he pauses to summon me with a sharp flick of his head. Hesitating for a moment, I think again about the cameras. What will Dad think if he sees me here, out in the open, with not one, but a handful of guardsmen?

'Maggie?' Freddie hasn't moved from the bottom of the stairs; his face is now creased with confusion. Taking a slightly shaking breath, I join him.

The group spot us as we pass over the green, and Riley waves, with such fervour his whole body sways from side to side. I return his wave with a chuckle, and the others nod their heads in recognition too. Mo even offers a mock salute. Freddie shakes his head, the stony expression still not thawing from his face. Once we reach them, I quietly ask Mo what on earth Tiny is doing to the poor ravens. When he squawks, I wonder if he has completely lost it.

'It's the ravens' roll call. Tiny's a new recruit, so it's his turn to check all of the ravens are in and show them the proper respect.' He finishes his explanation with a wink. Everything makes sense now. There is no 'ravens' roll call', and the ravenmaster and her team are the ones that put each bird to bed. This is a good old-fashioned initiation prank.

Tiny ceases his shrill cawing and stands to attention with a sharp click of his heels. He unravels a worn piece of paper and calls the first name: 'Duke.' He raises his hand up to his backwards cap and salutes Regina, definitely not Duke. Chaplin beside me gives one of his silent laughs.

'Holly,' Tiny continues in the same manner, sharp proper

159

salute following his 'call'. He dutifully runs through each of the ravens: Merlin, Rex, Regina, Edward, and finally Lucie. By the time he reaches the youngest, all of us are shaking with silent laughter, struggling not to give the game away. He goes to bow – to the conspiracy, I think, who have paid him zero attention thus far. As he steps forward and leans down, Holly lets out a threatening call and hops towards him with her wings outstretched at her sides. She has over doubled her size and Tiny all of a sudden looks . . . well, tiny. Duke follows his mate with equal ferocity. Tiny lets out a yelp as the two peck fiercely at the polished toecaps of his boots, and he flees across the grass, but the mating couple aren't so easy to shake off.

Walker lets out a 'PAH!' unable to keep in his silenced laugh any longer. We all follow suit as Tiny turns around. He throws his head back and groans.

'Oh, for God's sake. Really?' the bony boy asks his colleagues in a mix of annoyance and embarrassment, still side-stepping Holly and Duke's attack. When his eyes fall on me, he flushes a shade of red and purple that I never thought possible. I pull a couple of Cromwell's cat treats from out of my pocket and throw them towards the greedy birds. All of the ravens, including the two bullies, immediately forget their previous engagements and chase over to gobble them up. Tiny mutters a humiliated 'thank you' as he returns to his fellow guards.

'That was great, Tiny. Really professional!' I say, but, though I genuinely mean it, it comes out sarcastically and his face goes darker still. At this rate, I am worried he will pass out from all of the blood rushing to his head.

Freddie doesn't say anything throughout, and as the humour of the last few minutes dissipates, he feels like a stranger again.

Mo distracts me from my thoughts of Freddie as he addresses me from across the group. 'How's the Tinder been going today? Pinging away with matches?' I look at him, momentarily confused. In my periphery, I notice Freddie roughly shove his hands into his pockets. 'You know, after we improved your account . . .' he clarifies.

'Oh! You know, I haven't even checked it. I forgot all about that.' I'm pretty sure that my cheeks are now giving Tiny's a run for their money.

'Come on, Mags, let us have a look.' Walker and Riley both flank me from either side, pushing Freddie further away. I am actually intrigued to see if their overhaul of my account worked in any way, so I dig my phone out of my pocket and open up the app. The explosion of red notification dots that emerge from behind the loading screen has me genuinely thinking that my phone has a virus for a second. I don't even remember swiping on so many people, but I supposedly have twenty different matches, six of whom have already messaged.

Mo lets out a 'whoop' and claps me on the shoulder and Chaplin wiggles his eyebrows suggestively. Tiny and Freddie stand away from the huddle that has formed around my phone, the former keeping his gaze nervously fixed on the ravens as they play with each other like feathery puppies.

The latest message is from someone called Aaron. He's twenty-nine and opens with: *So what are you on here for?*

161

Not so much as a 'hello'! I may be a complete dating novice, but I even I know that that actually means: *I'm here for a quick and easy shag. Are you going to be difficult about that?* I pull a face at the lads, and they nod their heads in agreement, clearly coming to the same consensus. I unmatch him without replying; that's the best thing about these apps, I don't even have to bother being polite.

The second is from Stephen, 32. He goes for a chat-up line: *'R u a parking ticket? Because uve got fine written all over u ☺.'* I click back onto his profile; it says he's a 'consultant'. To be honest, I have no idea what that means but his pictures show him in acid-wash trousers that end three inches too high up his ankles and a shirt that shows a hell of a lot of chest hair. The photos combined with the irritating text speak and emojis firmly establish him as a prime fuckboy candidate.

Okay, maybe I am being a bit too judgemental. The whole process feels like a game, deciding who you're too good for, and who is out of your league just from some crappy photos. I decide to give him a chance, and reply: *'Does that mean you have to pay me now?'* That's flirty and funny, right?

'Bloody hell, Mags. When did you become a flirty minx, eh?' Walker nudges my shoulder playfully.

I open the third message, fully engrossed now in the game of online dating apps. Henry, 28, is next in line. He sticks with the boring, but classic: *'Hi, how are you? x'* I pretty much return his message word for word and my group of wingmen all groan at the mundaneness of it. I move quickly on to the last one.

Angus, 30, sends me a funny gif of a man lifting up his sunglasses in pleasant surprise at whatever is happening in front of him. The silly moving image gives me a little confidence boost, making me feel desirable. The bar really is on the floor at this point. I search for a while for a gif to reply with and settle on one of Audrey Hepburn in *Breakfast at Tiffany's* pulling down her own shades to get a better look at the scene before her. I giggle as I press send, realising that the two gifs look as if they're competing.

Taking a break from my phone, I look up at the guardsmen. They're uniformly dressed in their camouflaged combats except for . . . Freddie has disappeared. Again. I look around to see if I can see him walking away but he's long gone.

Suddenly, I'm no longer in the mood for Tinder.

'I'm not sure any of these are screaming marriage material . . .' I sigh. 'Sorry, lads, I'd better head off or my tea's gonna be cold.' Classic excuse, and realistic if I was in year five and playing out in the street on my bike with my classmates, but I'm a grown woman who is terrible at lying. They don't believe me, but they go to say their goodbyes anyway.

'Wait one sec,' Walker interjects. 'Five dates,' he declares, as the rest of the party look at him confused.

'What you on about now?' Riley voices what we are all thinking.

'I challenge you to go on five dates, five different blokes, and I guarantee that you'll be coming out with a husband.' Walker looks pleased with himself as he finishes his explanation.

'Why five?' I chuckle, both embarrassed and intrigued by his gusto.

The fresh-faced soldier shrugs. 'Sounded like a decent number. And I might have only known you for five minutes, but it doesn't take a genius to work out that one bad date would have you giving up on love for good.' Am I that easy to read?

'Fine. Five dates.' I shake his hand, tying myself into our unwritten contract, not quite knowing what I'm letting myself in for.

'You'd better keep us updated,' Mo says, with Chaplin nodding his head enthusiastically over his shoulder.

'Of course. I can't do this crap without the help of my platoon of wingmen. See you later, guys.' All of them see me off and I walk quickly around the casemates and back home.

Dad does actually have my tea on the table by the time I get there. It isn't any definable meal; the plate is arranged with sausages, chicken tikka kebab skewers, a slice of bread, a sprig of broccoli, and all tied together with thick gravy. I'm pretty sure that Dad has raided the 'whoopsie' section at the supermarket, and whatever had yellow reduced stickers on it has ended up on that plate and is now being doused in ketchup. My mum was the chef in our house. Dad was constantly at work, and she had little better to do in our garrison town than work her way through her dozen Gordon Ramsay cookbooks each month. Her lasagne was famous wherever we moved to. All of the other military wives begged her for the recipe, but she'd just give a coy smile and swear it was a family secret. She never did tell anyone that she just made it up as she went along.

'You didn't have to do all of this,' I tell him as he gestures for me to sit down on the sofa opposite his armchair. 'Looks great!' I add with a smile. It's a white lie but he's trying – and the beam he gives me makes it worth it.

We eat in relative silence. The splutter of the near-empty sauce bottle and the scraping of knives and forks the only noise that raises over the *Carry On* film playing lowly on the TV in the corner. Dad chuckles to himself at a few of Kenneth Williams's slapstick blunders and I am pretty sure I hear him giggle – yes, giggle – at the array of innuendos.

'Foxes have been about again.' He speaks up through a mouthful of sausage. 'They've been doing their filthy business in Richie's rose bushes.'

'It's supposed to be good fertiliser, isn't it?' I say, wondering why he has plumped for this topic.

'Aye, it is. But he keeps standing in it when he's pruning. Traipsed it all through the house yesterday. Trixie went mental.' The village gossip is thrilling, as always. 'Little buggers have been going for the ravens too. Ravenmaster had to beat one of them off with her walking stick when it went for little Lucie the other day.' Okay, I take it back: I'd pay to have seen that.

'That's terrible. Are they all right?' I ask, and he nods.

'You see any of 'em, Richie says you're welcome to use his hose by the shed to scare 'em off.'

'Cheers, will do.' Let's be honest, I probably won't.

'Erm, Simon, you know Simon, in the control room . . .' Oh God, here it comes. This is how Dad always starts off his awkward lectures, the ones where he isn't angry per se but feels he has to say something to fulfil his role as father, when someone has whispered in his ear.

'He said he saw you on the cameras at close on five this morning.' Trusty Simon never misses a trick does he. 'It's not that I mind you always coming home late at the minute, God no, you're an adult – I know that. I was doing much worse at your age. Just where had you been? Bob wouldn't tell me.' Bless Bob and his mantra of 'I didn't see anything'. He is perhaps the only loyal man left on this earth.

'I went out to the library and then met some friends for a drink on the way back, which turned into a few too many drinks. The hangover made me late again this morning, so I was on safe duty.' Well, it's not really a lie. He nods his head, not completely convinced, and takes a swig from his cup of tea. We both feel awkward now, and I can tell that he's trying not to pry but his protective dad side is hard to suppress, even when his child is now the age he was when he was married.

'They all talk – you know that. Just be careful. You don't want to be getting a reputation, like that Lizzy Mackintosh.'

Lizzy Mackintosh was the sergeant's daughter where we lived on base in Germany for a while when I was only about eleven. She was *beautiful*, the envy of the whole garrison. The wives would watch her front door whilst her dad was away, and when soldiers started coming and going all day, always looking very grateful as they left, the rumours began that she was the woman they would go to, to cheat on their wives. They made her life hell, and we weren't allowed near her after that. It wasn't until a few years later, when her whole family had been posted else-where, that we all found out that she was doing a sport physiotherapy course at college and had been helping all of the troops who were injured from training and their military exercises.

Dad always uses Lizzy as an example. She was doing a good thing, but in army communities gossip spreads like wildfire. They could transform a kitten into a lion if they were bored enough. He knows that I'd never be up to no good, but this place runs on reputation, and my reputation is a direct reflection of his. I assure him that I'll be careful, that I'll give them nothing to talk about and quietly he goes back to his *Carry On*.

By the time I get up to my room and out on the balcony, both Cromwell and Lucie are waiting. I hold Cromwell on my lap, keeping him apart from his feathery rival and for once he doesn't resist. He enjoys the comfort of a cuddle as much as I do. I take half of a sausage out of a square of kitchen roll and toss it to Lucie. She catches it mid-air and chomps it with her beak before swallowing. Cromwell mews in jealousy and I dig the few remaining cat treats out of my pocket.

Once they're happily fed, I address the both of them. 'I thought this place had stopped being a prison?' My audi-ence is silent. 'My own thoughts are enough to deal with, analysing every bloody move I make, reminding me of all the stupid things I've done and said at inopportune moments. But no, I can't function without the whole world having something to say. Dad's pulling this protective father act now, but did he ever care what Mum and I were up to the other half of the year that he wasn't around? No, he didn't. And what is so bloody wrong with me being happy, eh? Does everyone just want me to sit around like some matron, sewing by the fire and smiling nicely?'

I push my face into Cromwell's fluffy shoulder. I wish I could scream. It feels almost foreign to be angry. I know who I am, I know where I live, I know that on paper my life is perfect. But I feel caged. 'And why does that man disappear like Harry frigging Houdini every time things start to get good? Just as I think I've found someone who lets me be me, lets me cry, lets me speak more than a sentence, he vanishes in a puff of smoke. The one man who makes my mind feel like it's been galvanised, who makes it feel like every cell of my body has all of a sudden been awoken and every tiny fibre gained its own impetus, can leave me, just like that. No apology, no goodbye, no damn explanation.'

I am in full rant mode. Neither Lucie nor Cromwell dare to make a noise. I think even a human would be lost for words at this spectacle. 'Is the real me that insufferable? Why would he make all the effort to see me if he's just going to piss off at the drop of a hat?'

Lucie crows softly. I notice my arms are prickled with goose bumps. The quiet interruption snaps me out of my frustrated trance, and I realise why I'm so upset. I like him. I like Freddie.

'No! I don't *like* him,' I say to the bird, but of course it's more to myself. 'I hardly know him. I've met him what . . . like four, five times? You can't *like* someone who's practically a stranger!' The night is mild, the wind non-existent, but

168

a coldness spreads through me. 'And besides, he's in the army. I always told myself that I would never end up like Mum. I can't live a life of not knowing where my husband might be one week to the next. Doing countless Christmases and birthdays alone. Every week after Dad called from whichever secret location he was in, I would hear her cry herself to sleep. Imagine only speaking to the love of your life for ten minutes each fortnight and knowing that it could be the last time you ever hear from them. Half the time she cancelled plans for a phone call that never came. She was always waiting. Waiting for a call, waiting for him. She never got to live.' This is where the tears fall, big fat ones that roll down my cheeks. 'Even if by some miracle, he likes me in his own messed-up way, I just can't.'

Cromwell shifts out of my hold and leans against my chest. He drags his rough tongue against my cheeks, collecting the salty beads before they can splash onto my blouse or his fur. Freddie gave me hope these past few weeks, something to wake up for each day. Every day I took a new risk to see him – and be seen seeing him. The guardsman and his stiff posture and strict manners were a surprising breath of fresh air, a distraction from the monotony of the same walk to work, the same conversations with the same people. And who wouldn't end up liking him when he stood up to Bran like he did? He's the one person who has really, truly *seen* me . . . since Mum.

'Eurghhhh.' I vocalise my frustration, but it's half-drowned out by a convoy of sirens that pass over Tower Bridge. 'Mum would have understood. She would have known what to do.'

Lucie hops closer and pecks me softly. I stroke her down her beak and she lets out a contented squeak. From the corner of my eye, I spy Cromwell, battling with himself over whether to seize his opportunity and pounce. Clearly deciding better of it, he relaxes from his readied stance and lies back into my lap, pawing at my leg. With each loving knead, he shoves my phone against my leg, and I dig it out of my pocket. Maybe I should text Mum; maybe sending my worries into the void might help me find some answers, even if she can't give me any directly.

The list of notifications on the lock screen distracts me from my plan. All of them are accompanied with the little flame icon of Tinder, some messages, some new matches. I swipe it open, a little excited for the attention.

Angus has replied to my gif, which was replying to his gif, with another gif. The new one is Jim Carrey waving manically, and I send back one of Forrest Gump. I wonder who will break and actually send words first.

Henry has also replied, continuing our boring small-talk conversation with: *'I'm good. Have you had a nice day?'* It's nice enough, polite even. But has anyone ever actually said anything other than 'yes, thanks' or 'my day was nice'? I can hardly reply telling him I had the hangover from hell, which left me expelling hot lava from both ends of my body at six this morning, can I? I give him the socially acceptable and very British: *'Yes thanks, you?'* and move on.

The rest of the messages are almost all the same story – either very blunt *'You wanna meet?'* texts or the dreadfully dull *'Hi, how are you?'*

Just as I am about to give up, a new message pops up at the top of my screen from someone called Caleb. I open it straight away, silently hoping that it is more entertaining than the rest. Thankfully, he skips the introduction altogether.

> Caleb: *Maggie, you look like the kind of person that people write songs about.*

I read it again. And again. Six times over in fact. Is it weird that my first reaction is a little tear? He probably says that to everyone on here. We're all in the same place for one thing: to pull. If this is what he says to every girl, he mustn't have a shortage of interest.

I slide open his profile before I decide on a reply. His first photo is a black and white professional photo of him playing the guitar rather wildly on stage. His hair is down to his shoulders – or it would be if it weren't defying gravity as the photo catches him mid head-bang. The next one is more relaxed: he's sat at the wooden bench of a beer garden, clutching a pint. He is smiling at the camera. His teeth are slightly crooked, but they suit his alternative look. The imperfection of them makes them almost as good an accessory as his silver nose ring and black leather jacket. His other photos are a variation of the two: gig shots and chilled-out social settings. Even if I am just one of a hundred, I can't ignore the irregular beat of my heart as I imagine him saying those words to me, and meaning it. I am hopeful about this one.

I decide to play it safe with my reply, not act too keen.

Maggie: *Oh yes, and what genre would I be then?*

Caleb: *Hmmm . . . well, you're too interesting to be a ballad. You'd be a folk song. One of those folk songs that tell stories of faeries, that are passed down through generations as your beauty becomes myth.*

Caleb: *Not just your beauty of course, but there's a depth to you. You aren't just melody, or lyrics, each part of you is an art in itself but all together . . . wow.*

My breath catches in my throat. He's good at this . . . My mind goes completely blank when I come to reply. What are you meant to say to the man who just gave you the nicest compliment you've ever received? At least with him safely behind the screen, I have time to compose myself and think of a collected response.

Maggie: *You seem to know an awful lot about your music. What is your go-to?*

Caleb: *Would it be too cliché to say my favourite is folk?*

Maggie: *Just a little . . .*

Caleb: *Okay, okay, I am more of a rock and metal kind of guy. Bit of Judas Priest, Misfits, Megadeth – all that. My band is a bit more chilled than that tho.*

Maggie: *That certainly explains the leather jackets!*
Do you gig much?

I try to slowly drip-feed his own interests to him. He can't not like me that way, and I went through far too many various emo and punk phases as a teenager not to use the knowledge to my advantage.

We go back and forth for a while, asking each other silly questions and he scatters in various other compliments. When I check the clock again it's past midnight. The events of the evening were a good enough distraction from the pounding in my head, but my body begins to catch up with me again. My eyes are heavy with sleep and the bright glow of my phone is making them sting, so I stow away my phone and head to bed – already excited to read his reply in the morning.

Chapter 12

I am going on a date. The first proper date I think I have
ever been on. Bran doesn't count – he invited himself
over to my house in my second year of uni and pretty
much just never left again. Caleb and I have been chatting
non-stop for the past week – even in the shower I find
myself mentally replying to his array of compliments and
exciting anecdotes about his life in a band. After seven
consecutive days of him asking to meet me for a drink,
and me responding with a range of excuses about how I
am too busy on that day, when really I am just festering
with anxiety, I have finally plucked up the courage to meet
him tonight.

Don't get me wrong, I want to get out there! And I'm
well aware that the only way to do that is to go for drinks
with a man I've never met. I might not have ventured out
further than the bounds of Tower Hill in I don't even know
how long, but other people do this kind of stuff all of the
time . . . I mean, *everyone* is on all of these dating apps,

right? Loads of people my age have met their partner online – a girl I went to school with is even married to someone she met on Tinder, with a baby on the way. How bad can it be?

'Plenty of women have also become victims to their Tinder dates,' the little voice in my head reminds me. In fear of ending up like one of the poor women you read about all too often in the newspapers, I have been repressing the urge to ask Caleb for a DBS check and two forms of photo ID. But deep down, I know I can't keep living my life hidden away in a tower because I'm too afraid of the 'what ifs'. Plus, the heavy knot that is permanently sat in my stomach is surely enough to keep me on my toes and on the look-out for a threat.

So here I am, at the bus stop, waiting for the number fifteen bus and trying almost painfully hard not to be sick all over my shoes. I check the time on my phone and check it again against the LED sign under the bus shelter. One says six minutes, the other says four. They both end up being wrong. It takes a full ten minutes for the first bus to come, and it almost drives away as I stand on the pavement fumbling for my Oyster card. It's a very London thing to be irrationally irate at the thought of having to wait more than five minutes for public transport. Back home in Yorkshire, it would be a miracle if the hourly bus ever made it at all. Whenever we ended up living there for a decent amount of time, I'd always end up stuck in town, waiting for Dad to fetch me because my return bus never arrived. And we had no fancy bus shelters with electronic timetables – you were lucky if you got a bench, and even luckier if it wasn't smeared with a strange-looking substance.

After clambering up the stairs, and almost falling back down them in the process as the bus jerks away from the kerb, I get a seat upstairs, but it's so jampacked with people leaving work that I have to awkwardly ask an older lady to move her handbag. She huffs as she slides it onto her knee, and the cross-stitched dogs that decorate it seem to give me an equally dirty look as I sit down next to her. My legs are too long to fit comfortably behind the seat, so I have to shuffle to the side and sit with my knees in the aisle, which in turn means that every time someone else gets on, I have to shift gauchely.

The pure discomfort of the situation makes me so anxious, I no longer feel the initial nerves I had about my date. I can't figure out if double anxiety just cancels each other out, or I am one bump in the road away from having a panic attack and getting my hysterical snot all over the old lady's disapproving pooches.

Checking off each stop on my phone, I try and distract myself by taking in the view. We pass St Paul's Cathedral just as the evening sky casts an orange glow across its ivory dome, as though the sun itself is caught in its marble pillars. Pink blossom on the courtyard trees flurry against the bus as the top windows clip the overhanging branches. If the overwhelming smell of weed and urine didn't linger in the air, it would be quite the angelic scene. We pass down Fleet Street and the Strand. Old pubs line the streets, their time-worn wooden signs juxtaposed against the bustling pavement of walking iPhone carriers who wander these streets each morning and evening but have probably never even noticed them there. All down the Strand, various churches are nestled in between office buildings. As my phone ticks over to 6 p.m., I hear the Church of St Clement Danes, which sits on an island in the middle of the road, toll its bells to the melody of the old nursery rhyme 'Oranges and Lemons'. Despite the cacophony of exhausts and telephone chatter, the chiming bells ring out clearly across the street, and it is strangely calming, a little tiny pocket of tradition to break up the erratic monotony of city life.

As we approach Trafalgar Square, I fidget in my seat again and glance at the time; I am half an hour early – just in case I get lost or sweaty and need to cool down before he arrives. I hop off at the very last stop and am pushed out into the tidal wave of commuters. Involuntarily, I am swept past the lions that lie proud, surrounding Admiral Nelson atop his column, and almost take out an unsuspecting tourist who had stopped in the dead centre of the pavement to take a photo. Rushing a string of apologies for pinballing off her shoulder, I am once again carried away by the crowd.

Caleb arranged for us to meet at some pub just outside of Leicester Square and, as much as I want to scream every time a group walks four abreast towards me, thus forcing me to take my chances against the mopeds in the road, I am quite grateful that our date is happening somewhere so public.

The pub is called Richard's Tavern and is tucked away down one of the side streets next to Chinatown. I barely even notice it as I almost walk past; the sign is faded and rusted at the edges. Pushing open the two sets of doors, the smell of tobacco is sticky in the air. Instantly, every eye in the room is on me, all five of them – one of the patrons at the bar has a pirate's eye-patch covering over one of his – and I avert my gaze hurriedly. The décor looks as though someone has picked up one of the Kray twins' old East End pubs and dropped it slap bang in the middle of central London. The red carpet is a patchwork of dark stains, the slot machine in the corner is switched off but buzzes obnoxiously at irregular intervals, and the barman – a tall ugly man – polishes a glass with a rag that I'm sure was once white, but is now more the colour of the dirty water in a mop bucket.

Captain Eye-patch leans over a packet of pork scratch-ings that he has opened out onto the bar. He wears a suit that looks so old and full of dust, I wouldn't be surprised if he had stolen it from the coffin of someone dead for half a century. He sits across from a third man, who looks like he could be the grave-robbed owner of said suit. His blondish stubble stops just below his watery blue eyes; the tips of his fingers are blackened and grip a pint glass of a liquid almost as dark.

I give them all a smile. Actually, I'm sure it looks more like a grimace but being stared down by three men who look like they haven't seen a woman in a scarily long time is not something I like to be doing with my Friday evening.

'Good evening.' I shakily address the barman with a nod. He grunts in response. 'Do you have any Diet Coke?' He lifts up a can of full-fat Coke and slams it onto the bar, and I jump at the noise.

'Two fifty,' he grunts. I drop the money onto the sticky bar quickly and take the can to the furthest-away seat possible.

Perching myself on a stool at a table by a window, I notice it opens out into an alleyway with a prime view of the opposite building's wall and a split bin bag. Two mice scurry away from the contents as a rat almost the size of Cromwell comes stalking from the other side, taking the goods for himself.

Reminding myself what I'm actually here for, I stare into my can of Coke, trying to remember all of the conversation starters that I found on some random article about perfecting first dates. The only one that comes to mind now is: 'What is your biggest regret in life?' But I'm not sure how well that would go down. 'Hi, good to meet you for the first time ever. What is the thing you hate most about your life that you probably can't even talk about with your closest friend, but might want to share with a stranger you met on the internet?'

Nervously, I scratch at the back of my hand; the skin turns blotchy and red in the pattern my fingernails draw. This is definitely somewhere Jack the Ripper would have hung out, hunting for his next victim.

The doors squeak open again. Sneaking a glance at the entrant, I try not to seem too keen. A tall dark-haired man strides across to the bar. He's wearing skinny jeans and a denim jacket with various pin badges lining the lapels. Even from this distance, I can tell that his hair must pass his shoulders, as it's swept back in a messy bun at the back of his head. Surely that's Caleb. He really does look like a rock star. Excited nerves flutter in my stomach as I watch his impressive frame lean over the bar and order a drink from the barman, who seems considerably happier to serve him.

With his rum and Coke in hand, he finally turns around. The butterflies in my stomach stop dead and fall with a thud in my gut. It's not Caleb. He flashes me a smile but they're not the same crooked teeth from the photos, nor the same angular face. I'm almost disappointed that I'm not on a date with him.

As he walks away to the other side of the bar, I go back to staring into my can. I have a little more faith in the pub now that the clientele consists of more than a pair of staring old men and a gravedigging pirate. Perhaps it takes a while to get going, or alternative types like Caleb like the 'rustic' appeal of it – hipsters love stuff that to anyone else looks like a heap of crap.

Twenty more minutes go by. He's officially late. In the time I've been waiting, I've finished off my Coke and am now desperately trying to ignore the screaming in my bladder, not really wanting to find out the state of the toilets – if they even have one for women that is. Only one other person has passed over the threshold since the entrance of the attractive Caleb-hopeful, and it was a rather beautiful woman that I can only assume is his girlfriend.

Feeling like a fool, I am just gathering my denim jacket ready to leave when the door creaks once again. An older gentleman – around my dad's age – strolls in and, noticing me stood in the corner, heads straight towards me. Worried about getting caught into a conversation with an old man who most likely uses his age as an excuse to get handsy with young women in public, I shake my head at him.

'Er, I'm sorry, I was just leaving. I have to, er, meet someone,' I stutter, feeling a little rude but really not in the mood for a conversation just after being stood up.

'Maggie?' he asks, a little spit clinging to the corners of his mouth. 'Sorry I'm late.'

I can't bring myself to even move. I stand, jacket still clutched in my hand, staring at him open-mouthed. A leather jacket, like the one on his profile, hangs on his shoulders, but the rest of him is completely unrecognisable. His hair has receded all of the way back to the top of his head and the dark strands are sparse in comparison to the grey ones. Scanning down, I notice his jeans are covered in holes – and not the hipster sort that come ready ripped into the fabric despite costing half of your month's wages. Paint is splattered across them and across his hands too. It looks like Caleb is less rock star and more painter-decorator, which wouldn't be a problem if he didn't look as though he's on the waiting list for a hip replacement. His nose is bulbous and red, his cheeks a similar shade; he's either already been drinking or has drunk so much in his incredibly long life that he is permanently stained the colour of red wine. I have never been averse to an older man, but this is just taking the piss.

On my first ever date, I have been catfished.

'Can I get you a drink, love?' He has a thick cockney accent, and he fits into the scene around us like a piece in a puzzle.

'I'm w-waiting for Caleb?' I finally splutter out, hoping

to God that this man is simply passing on a message from his attractive grandson.

'He's right here, darlin',' the old man replies, gesturing up and down his body. I shudder. 'My photos are a bit old, I know.' I'm pretty sure they didn't even have colour cameras when 'Caleb' was the age he appeared to be in the photos on his profile. They certainly didn't have the iPhones that lit up the foreground of the gig pictures.

'I don't mean to be rude, but your profile . . . it said you're twenty-nine?' I press, though I tread carefully, afraid of offending him, since some men get volatile if they think they're being rejected. The time a man spat on me after I ignored his catcalled advances springs to mind.

'Bloody thing, I've no idea how to change it. It was automatic. It doesn't bother you I'm a bit older, does it?' His brown eyes scan down my body as he replies, making my skin crawl. Earlier, I decided to wear a short summer dress, to push myself out there, to be a new, more adventurous me. Now I regret having so much cleavage on display.

My mind is working overtime. No one knows I'm even here. I couldn't tell Dad – it felt too awkward – and now I recognise I have made a horrible, *horrible* mistake.

'Oh, well, no . . . it's okay,' I lie, trying not to insult him. Avoiding his gaze, I look past him and see the whole bar staring at us. My cheeks flush and a wave of heat washes over me, burning at the bottom of my throat. I have no idea what I am supposed to do now. Do I make an excuse and leave? Would he get angry if I did? Do I stay for one drink, to appease him? But then what if he gets the wrong idea?

'Sit yourself down, I'll get you a drink.' He makes the decision for me. I plop back down into the chair, and a cloud of dust disperses out of the cushion and makes me cough. Caleb walks over to the bar and chats to the barman like they're old friends. They both turn to look at me and I give them another grimace in place of a smile. The man with the eye-patch chuckles to himself.

Think, Maggie. Bloody think. Maybe he's a nice man. I suppose I'm used to chatting to the beefeaters and they're better company than anyone I've met my own age. But they don't pretend to be a twenty-nine-year-old guitarist to lure you to a pub that looks like a murderer's den, I remind myself.

The only logical thing that my panicked mind can decide on is going to the toilet. I'm not sure if it is my bladder speaking for the rest of me, but Catfish Caleb is on his way back with two dirty glasses of tar-like lager and I have to leave now or I never will.

I excuse myself when he arrives back at the table. I briefly wonder if it looks strange to be taking my jacket along with me, but I'm sure all men are taught not to question what a woman takes into a bathroom. It takes me a little while, but I finally find the door, tucked away in a dark corridor of the pub. As it swings closed behind me, the repulsion hits instantly. The scent of urine is inescapable, and despite the fact I have seen no person venture this far into the pub in the hour I've been here, the floor is damp with puddles and there's enough rubbish strewn across it to support both the fat rat and the family of mice in the alleyway. I can't decipher what colour the paint should actually be, but there's a multitude of colours, all equally chipped away and all four walls are scrawled in thick marker pen.

Now I'm away from the curious eyes of my 'date' and his peculiar pals, I can finally throw together a plan. A small window peeks over the top of the end cubicle, but I am five foot nine and twelve stone, and the chances of me being able to parkour myself up high enough to reach it are slim . . . but not impossible, and I am rapidly running out of options.

The cubicle that houses it has a little handwritten sign on it that reads 'OUT OFF ORDER'. I try to force it open, but it's locked from the inside.

'Fuck.' I breathe to myself. My plan crumbling around me. So, I can't go over it, and I can't go through it . . . I look down at the floor, with suspicion. My Dr Martens are swimming in a damp pool. Various hairs and a stick-on nail float on the surface. Sighing, I get to my knees, the beautiful pale hem of my dress absorbing some of the liquid. Gripping the bottom of the door with one hand, I use the other to reach under it and grasp for the lock. The bottom of the door digs uncomfortably into my shoulder and an unfortunate section of my hair ends up in the puddle, but I finally grasp the bolt on the other side. The metal is stiff but after a lot of wiggling, I manage to slide it across with a jolt. I breathe a sigh of relief, until the wet strands of my hair wipe themselves against my back. Gagging, I clamber to my feet, trying to shake some of the wetness from my hands.

What's behind the door isn't much of a relieving sight

either. A dead mouse is curled up next to the sanitary bin, and the toilet itself is blocked to the rim with a stew of tissue and vomit. I gag again, almost adding to the pile.

Trying not to inhale too much of the biohazard of the bathroom, I kick closed the toilet seat and mount the lid. As my escape route comes into view, I'm grateful to find the window already slightly ajar. I give it a small shove and it opens all of the way out into the neighbouring alley. With the upper-body strength of a wet lettuce, I have to put one of my legs onto the cistern to lever myself onto the window ledge. My foot catches the flush on the toilet and a wave of dirty water overflows from under the closed seat lid, showering the floor. So that's where all of the liquid has come from. I suppress another gag and thrust my head out of the window in the hopes of locating some fresh-ish air.

After throwing my jacket out first in hopes it may break my predictable crashlanding, I swing my leg onto the ledge, which is long enough for me to shuffle down it and manoeuvre myself so I'm able to slide backwards out of the window. First one leg. Then the other. Just as I'm thinking that I should have had more faith in my parkour skills after all, I discover that getting both my arse and my belly out at the same time is a near impossible task, as the extra pounds I carry on both sides wedge me into the window frame. An auntie of mine once said I was 'blessed with a childbearing figure', but I sure as hell don't feel blessed hanging bum first out of a dirty window with the skirt of my dress still on the inside with the rest of me.

After some very inelegant worm-like wriggling, I

manoeuvre more of my torso downwards, and my belly is freed – though unfortunately my dress is not. I pause to consider my next move.

The last obstacle is my boobs. I was quite proud of the way they sat lovely and high on my chest in this dress when I left after work, but now they're yet another thing in the way of me escaping. And, much as I am desperate to flee the premises, I really would like to do so fully clothed.

If the universe hears me, it gives me the middle finger: I manage to wiggle myself free, spurred on by the sound of footsteps approaching, but my dress doesn't cross the finish line with me. Feet firmly planted in the alleyway outside, tits to the wind, my dress hangs limply from the upturned latch. Tugging it free only rewards me with a loud rip as the window refuses to release it, but, since there is no way I am standing in central London wearing little more than my knickers and a pair of boots for any longer than I have to, I persevere with increasing levels of desperation.

When the damp fabric is finally back in my grasp, I throw what's left of it over my head. Quickly realising that it barely retains the function of covering my nipples, I replace it with my jacket and wrap the shredded material around my waist, thanking God that I decided to save the thong for the second date. Successfully looking, and smelling, as if I have walked off of the set of a horror film, I start my walk of shame home.

Luckily for me, the District Line has seen far worse than a twenty-something mostly naked and reeking of an old man's catheter bag, so no one bats an eyelid as I rest my head against the dusty window, desperately trying not to cry, the whole way back to Tower Hill.

The ravenmaster is on watch when I get home. Once a month, each beefeater has to take a turn on the night shift. Although I'm not sure shift is the right word – they mostly just sit all night in the Byward Tower, either snoozing in an armchair or watching the array of DVDs that they have collected over the decades, pausing occasionally to shepherd out the drunken guests from the bar and shepherd in the drunken residents who are coming home. In my experience, it can take a good few rings of the bell to stir them from their power naps.

The ravenmaster, however, opens the door to me before I can reach it. Merlin is perched on one of her shoulders, his talons curled into her knitted cardigan. When I'm standing up straight, the ravenmaster barely reaches my chest, losing most of her height to the worsening curve of her back, so Merlin and I are almost face to face and I'm sure he gives me a sly wink.

As I go to thank her and begin the tedious walk along the cobbles to bed, the ravenmaster silently waves me in to follow her into the Byward. The tears that have been threatening the whole way home sting at my eyes, holding on for dear life, but I trail after her obligingly – and completely, utterly mortified.

Behind the heavy door is an octagon-shaped room of stone. Various engravings of beefeaters gone by line the walls, all of the way up to the high ceilings, and I feel their eyes on me immediately. I attempt to cover myself as much as possible, but it's little use. Aside from the portrait of the Duke of Wellington, similar to the one in the guards' Mess, the décor is painfully stuck in the 1960s. The desks and cupboards are all a strange orange shade of veneer wood and a boot polisher the size of a fridge stands barely used in the corner. The only things from this side of the millennium are the plush armchairs. Their chunky leather jars strangely with the rest of the room, as if they've been cut out of a magazine and stuck onto an antique photograph.

The ravenmaster hands me her watchman's coat and I slide it on over the top of my makeshift outfit. The coat is a bright scarlet wool that on the ravenmaster reaches her shins, but on me it sits tightly against my mid-thigh. I thank her quietly as a sweat breaks across my face. An open fireplace roars on the other side of the room, and the heat has turned the stone room into a sauna, despite the fact that the ravenmaster is wearing enough layers to rival a French pastry. She has four of the ravens joining her tonight: Rex, Regina, Edward, and of course Merlin. The other three sit on the backs of the chairs dotted at the desks around the room. During the day, those seats are occupied by beefeaters as they share old military stories for the hundredth time. It's quite funny to see them replaced by the sleek birds – I imagine them gossiping to the ravenmaster through the night, divulging their own secrets. Strangely the sight soothes me, and the tears lodged in my throat dissipate a little. Who could feel sorry for themselves coming home to this?

I go over and stroke Edward's feathers. The ones on his head stick up at all sorts of angles, earning him the nickname 'Slash'. He nips my fingers playfully when I stop, so I continue to smooth them down, only for them to spring straight back up again once I lift my finger.

Usually, the table in the centre of the room is strewn with papers and forms, but today it is covered in various plates of bird seed and indistinguishable red balls of food. The ravenmaster sits behind the desk in an office chair that swivels, her petite hunched frame looking bizarre in something so modern. Her shoeless feet hang as awkwardly as they would if she were suspended from a great oak, and I can't help but think she'd be more comfortable sat up in a tree.

'Mercurial men are often hiding secrets.' She doesn't look up when she delivers another of her prophecies. Again, it seems as if her advice is coming too late. Caleb, the lovely and witty man over text, turned out to be double my age and a catfish to conquer all catfishes. Perhaps her divinations are a little delayed in her old age.

I nod in thanks for her wisdom, not wishing to diminish the few times she actually manages to speak. 'I am yet to find a man who isn't hiding a secret, to be honest.' I half-laugh, but my joke pangs a painful jolt through my chest. My intention was the same as always – to make a joke out of the thing that makes me uncomfortable – but suddenly the room swims before me. Perched together, Rex and Regina are submerged as I try hard to swallow my tears back down. I refuse to let myself cry; I have been crying far too much for someone who lives rent-free inside a castle.

189

'Not all secrets are what they first seem,' she continues. Again, pretty sure that Caleb – if that is even his real name – is just an old man trying to get into the pants of someone thirty years younger. 'Except anything that ex-boyfriend of yours ever spouted – he's just a massive cockwomble.'

My tears are forgotten as my face creases in uncontrollable laughter. I have never heard her speak so directly, and I certainly haven't heard her swear – albeit in her own quaint little way. She even gives a chuckle. Her head shrinks further into her shoulders as they shake with her timid laughter, looking pleased with herself and her insult. How she even knows about Bran, I have no idea. The ravenmaster is the last person to listen to the whisperings of the staff, but somehow, she always finds a way to know exactly what is going on, all whilst being a recluse.

'Thank you,' I say through fresh tears – this time of laughter.

'Get to bed, child. Oh, and Maggie, the all-seeing eyes shall be no problem for you tonight,' she adds as she slowly shifts to sit before the computer that whirs in the corner.

'Goodnight.' As I head back to the door, she's already back to separating the sunflower seeds out of her bird food so waves me off without looking up. With one last wave to the birds, I close the door behind me and continue my walk home, no longer ruminating over the failures of my date and instead simply giggling like a child at the word 'cockwomble'.

Chapter 13

It takes me another few days before I can face Tinder again. The Grenadier Guards still haven't been back to the Tower since I last saw them at the ravens' roll call. Each morning on the way to work, I take the same route through the courtyard, looking out for the bright white plumes stuck into their bearskins. And every morning I am disappointed. I tell myself it's because I could really use Riley and Walker's cheery double act, and Mo's advice on how not to get catfished by old men on the internet right about now. But Freddie still lingers on my mind.

Despite the fact I caught him making a note of my phone number after the party in the Mess and despite the fact that he said that he'd call, I haven't heard from him once. I suppose I should be grateful. He has made the whole 'learning from my mother's mistakes' thing much, much easier.

I have decided that since I have told no one about the incident with Catfish Caleb, and the only people who know are the patrons of a pub that I will never again visit in my life, I have no reason to be embarrassed. So, I'm going to try again, learning from my mistakes. Plus, Samantha and Andy have spent all morning talking about the many men and women they have falling at their feet. Andy goes to the extra effort to speak *fortissimo* when telling our colleagues that none other than my ex-boyfriend has been in and out of her inbox whilst he thankfully avoids mine. Frankly, if two people who share the personality of a toothbrush with an attitude problem can find someone to love them, then there's surely some hope for me still.

Clicking open the app, I take a moment to block and report Caleb, and, pushing down the lingering feelings of shame that seeing his photos reignites, begin swiping. When a tourist looks on course for the window of my booth, I duck down behind my desk and they luckily divert to Andy, who I hear audibly groan.

Quickly it becomes apparent that the profiles are just a cycle of the same few distinct characters on a loop. First up, the 'fuckboy': usually vaping or flashing off his clenched jawline, in jeans so tight that they should belong to his little sister, and a bio along the lines of 'here for a good time, not a long time' with a variation of the creepy sideways-glance emoji. Then there's the 'car guy': always stood beside a car that clearly isn't his, followed by more photos of exhaust pipes than his own face, and a bio that is full of jargon I can't understand – about cars, obviously. The 'peaked in uni guy' comes up a lot too; his photos are almost all taken in some strange fancy dress or in a club, clutching vibrantly coloured alcopops, and they include the name of the university in their bios too, just so you don't forget that they have some degree you didn't even know existed.

Of course, being me, there's always the 'military guy' too; for some reason I come across a lot of American troops. In their photos they're normally lying in their combat uniform and boots on a skinny bed, and their distance is often a good few thousand miles away, clearly deployed and looking for an English rose to send them a few pictures of their boobs to, you know, 'boost morale'. There's also the 'Dad guy'; he doesn't have his own children, but all of his photos are of him either holding a cute baby, or a dog. Always paired with the bio, 'not my baby', just to make sure you know he's a caring bloke but not tied down with a sprog of his own. I can almost guarantee that the loving uncle look is just for show and the only part about a baby they actually care about is the process of making it. Being London, every now and again there's someone travelling and 'only in the city for three days, looking for someone to show me around whilst I'm here', which is just code for 'I'm trying to sleep with someone in every different country I travel to'.

It would be an understatement to say that none of them could be considered husband material, but I carry on swiping in spite of the disappointing clientele. It's quite entertaining flicking through them all and assigning them a category; any that are even slightly unique get a rare right swipe, and so far there have been a whole three of them. And, of course, I match with none.

Over the course of the next week, I gain a grand total of four new matches, three of which must have changed their minds because only one has actually decided to start a conversation. Jake, 28, wastes no time in trying to learn everything about me, and I have to remind myself that if he asks for the name of my first ever pet or my mother's maiden name then it's probably a scam. But he sticks to the safe stuff, like *'how are you?'*, *'where are you from?'*, *'what's your favourite colour?'*, and *'what's your choice of weapon in the zombie apocalypse?'*

We spend a long while discussing the latter, as I have spent many a lonely night watching zombie movies wondering why everyone is so desperate to actually survive. I mean, why bother blowing out the brains of the undead only to live in a world that's considerably worse than the one you started in? Plus, I just don't think I'd have the energy to rebuild civilisation. But when I share these ruminations, I think Jake is a little taken aback and simply replies: *'I think mine would be a chainsaw.'*

After that, I decide it's probably best to not be so honest. Changing tack, I let him take the lead and the next hour is filled with me responding a little overzealously to him recounting his '1RM' for each and every lift and arguing over whether he would be able to 'bench' me, which tires me out just thinking about. Being a little less myself seems to work; once he has exhausted gym chat, Jake asks me out on a date, and before I can chicken out, I agree.

We arrange to meet at a restaurant in Shoreditch. It's within walking distance of home, and I plan every tiny detail of my route to settle my nerves. Shoreditch is a place full of far cooler people than me. I could have come out here dressed only in the netting of satsuma packets and I'm sure no one would look twice, especially if I am taking photos against any of the graffiti-covered walls. Even the vandalism is fashionable.

The restaurant is one that Jake suggested, called 'The Medicine Ball' and I wait around the corner, not wanting to be too early and get caught out again. I give it five minutes after our scheduled meeting time before I head in, but it was all a waste of time – I still arrive before him.

Not wanting to make things even more awkward by walking straight back out again, I take a seat and look around. It is for the first time that I realise I greatly misjudged the name. When Jake suggested 'Medicine Ball', I was thinking apothecary-styled bar, you know, dark academia vibes, the kind of place where women wear dresses like Keira Knightley's iconic green *Atonement* dress and smoke cigarettes in long pipes. Unluckily for my presumed dress code and my imagination, the name is far more literal. It is one of those themed restaurants, the kind that you see all of the time on Instagram, where they make it look amazing, but they spend more time on making it picture-perfect than actually functioning as a restaurant. It is decorated to look like an old school gymnasium, with basketball hoops fastened to each end of the room, and markings on the floor to depict the crisscrossing lines of a court. I don't have too many fond memories of these rooms; I spent most of my PE lessons sat at the side, permanently, to the knowledge of my PE teacher, on my period.

I have never quite understood these places going for the 'someone forgot to pay the electricity meter' aesthetic, but the lights barely illuminate the table in front of me as a waiter, dressed in a tracksuit with a whistle hanging around his neck, delivers me a jug of water. After pouring myself a glass almost blindly, I sip it slowly and deliberately. The waiting is making me itch.

Five more minutes pass before the door opens again. A tall blond I recognise as Jake from his profile photos swans in, a slight swagger in his walk. Rugby player muscles stack his shoulders high and wide; he looks like he could tackle a bear, and no one could have any doubts about who would win. His bloated biceps – along with half of his left nipple – are exposed in a tank top, and he almost puts me to shame in my cleavage-framing dress, with his chest puffed out like a pigeon. On paper he really shouldn't be attractive – the whole of his face looks as if it has moved just a jot to the left, his nose is slightly askew, and his ears stick out noticeably – but there's actually a sexiness in his ruggedness, the imperfection making him more alluring if anything.

Everything about him seems almost opposite to Bran, and thankfully he is the antithesis to Caleb. The heavy nerves that have settled on my chest lift ever so slightly at the knowledge that I have not been catfished for a second time. The restaurant is mostly empty, so it doesn't take him long to spot me and a smile spreads across his face, revealing a pair of deep-set dimples that soften his slightly imposing first impression. He waves enthusiastically as he crosses the room, growing taller and taller as he nears. When I stand up to greet him, he towers over me, and a little flutter runs through my stomach.

'Maggie, you look . . . lovely,' he says. I am painfully aware that I'm overdressed for this place. Jake looks as if he has come straight from the gym, protein shaker and all, but I chose to come in a baby-blue dress that clings to the top half of my body and fans out in a flowing skirt down to my knees. I decided against heels, and I am grateful for that now, but that doesn't negate the embarrassment of turning up to a glorified leisure centre café dressed as if we are off somewhere remotely nice.

'Thank you. It's great to meet you,' I say as we both take our seats again. 'Been to the gym?' I motion to the bottle that he sets on the table.

'Nope.' I wait for him to elaborate and, when it becomes clear he isn't going to, laugh uncomfortably, a little taken aback by his blunt response. He continues to smile, not visibly as uninterested as his answer suggests.

'So, what do you do?' I enquire, realising I never actually asked about his occupation in the initial Tinder grilling.

'The gym, mostly.'

'Oh . . . I meant your job.' I laugh again.

Jake lifts a glass of water to his lips and attempts to reply with his mouth full of water. A little spurt rolls down his chin and he chuckles, still with his mouth full, as he wipes it away with the rag of a strap on his shirt. 'Yeah! The gym, training and that, a bit of bodybuilding,' he adds after he finally swallows.

'So . . . you do bodybuilding shows and things like that? That must be so hard on you . . . mentally as well as physically.' I try my best to act interested. Bodybuilding is hardly my *Mastermind* specialist subject but anything that jumpstarts the conversation is A-okay with me.

'Yeah, it's a bit hard.' Thankfully, the waiter saves me from having to try to muster a response to that riveting contribution.

'What can I get you both to eat?' he says, leaning over my shoulder to look at the menu in my hands. His prop whistle swings back and forth, intermittently hitting me in the cheek.

The menu is sparse, to the extent that it almost feels post-apocalyptic. There is a section for choosing from a selection of rice – by which, I mean you can plump for white or brown. The rest of the menu is mostly dedicated to different ways you can have your chicken breast cooked, or if you really want to be fancy, there's a salmon option too.

'Chargrilled chicken and brown rice please, Reece,' Jake recites without even looking.

'All right, Jake,' the waiter replies, evidently recognising my date. 'How are the lads? I saw you hit the two-eighty dead.' They shake hands, though it's really more of a clap.

'Man, it was mental. Pushing the two-ninety this time. Got to up the macros for a little bit. I feel like a tank.'

The conversation continues in similar fashion, and I look between them, smiling and nodding, as though I'm part of it. Even if they did include me, I wouldn't have much to add. They may as well be speaking a foreign language, and I give up listening after they start talking about supplements and the like, perusing the menu again instead as I wait for them to finish their little catch-up. The fact that I barely got five words out of Jake, yet he's having a full mothers' meeting with the waiter, makes me think that he would probably prefer to be on a date with him.

Reece finally takes my order after I've read the whole thing twelve times. I spoil myself with the lemon salmon, white rice, and even go crazy in adding some tender stem broccoli. I tell myself that I'll just go to McDonald's afterwards, to get some proper food.

'So . . . where would you go in the zombie apocalypse?' Jake asks after a brief silence. I am beginning to worry that he may know something I don't about the undead getting ready to stage their attack on the world. Either that, or he really has no other conversation starter . . .

'Erm, probably just stay at home,' I say, a little uninterested, reminding myself not to go on yet another rant about the pointlessness of my survival.

Not satisfied with my answer, Jake spends the next forty-five minutes describing in great detail what one should do when faced with the army of the undead. He pretty much just plagiarises the plot of *Shaun of the Dead* but continues with great seriousness, talking more than both of us in the entirety of the evening.

'So essentially, you'd go to the pub and wait for it all to blow over?' I laugh after listening to his meticulous plan.

'Pretty much, yeah.' He's completely straight-faced, the joke going straight over his head, and I realise he isn't even aware that he has stolen his entire plan from an Edgar Wright film.

I clear my throat and attempt to steer the conversation away from zombies before he tries to describe the plot of *Train to Busan*. 'Have you always lived in London?'

'Yeah.' I sigh. Clearly, this is going to be a long night . . .

We eat in relative silence, and Jake keeps his eyes trained on his plate, as if taking his eyes off it would make it grow legs and run away. Mine tastes about as good as expected, and I spend most of the meal trying to decide what's drier: Jake's conversation or the salmon. By the time we finish, I am itching to leave. This was absolutely not worth getting out of my pyjamas for.

Like any good feminist, I offer to pay half, but Jake insists on paying and leaving a hefty tip for his friend. As we exit the dimly lit restaurant, I am hit with the same feeling as leaving the cinema in the middle of the day; it is 7.30 p.m. but the summer sunlight is blinding, and I have to squint up at Jake as he follows me out. We stop to have an awkward parting.

'I've had a great night tonight . . .' he says.

'Really?' I interject, unable to hide my surprise. He's smiling, has barely stopped in fact, but I had assumed from his lack of any kind of communication that he wanted to escape as much as I did.

'Yeah, you're all right,' he says in what appears to be a compliment.

'Thank you,' I reply, a little awkwardly. I falter then, thrown by the validation. Am I being too quick to judge? Tonight hasn't been a *total* car crash, and it has certainly been a step up from Catfish Caleb. He is a half-decent human being, just not a great conversationalist. *And just not a Freddie*, a little voice in my head adds. I shake that thought out of my head and turn my attention back to my actual date.

Most unexpectedly, Jake begins to lean in, doing that awkward face that men pull when they're about to kiss you: eyes closed, head tilted, lips slightly parted. *Fuck it*, why not? Freddie may not want to kiss me, but this man does. I lean in too. I need to be more adventurous, more spontaneous, and what is more out there than kissing someone who an hour ago was a stranger?

Our lips almost meet when I feel his hot breath on mine. I snap open my eyes, and shut my mouth closed as if it had been forcibly stapled shut. Fish. It was me who ate the salmon, but the odour is so pungent on his breath that it smells as if he has eaten the entire cast of the *Little Mermaid*. I quickly divert the kiss into a hug and use the moment that he can't see my face to gag over his wide shoulder. Hugging Jake is almost identical to hugging a tree. His body is rock solid from all of his training and not a single part of him moves under my embrace.

When I pull away, he's blushing. I feel awful for embarrassing him, for rejecting him, but I think he would be more grateful for that than the alternative, which is me throwing up a little into his mouth.

'Thank you for tea, Jake. It was so nice to meet you,' I say, trying my best at a warm smile, which he returns. 'I'd better be heading home . . . I'll, uh, text you.' He waves me off and when I have walked a comfortable distance away from him, I look back to see him heading into a gym that I now realise is positioned directly over the road. Rolling my eyes, I turn back and walk my mapped-out route home, thoughts of getting into bed and snuggling with Cromwell occupying my mind.

Chapter 14

With the evening ending far earlier than expected, I arrive back at the Tower just as the light begins to retreat behind the casemates. My path along the drawbridge is illuminated by the evening's blushing haze, and each individual cobblestone glows as the night draws in. Deep into the moat I see Charlie and Timmy both stretching their legs – though it looks more like the fluffy dog is walking his beefeater owner. Charlie waves once he finally notices me and, pointing at his empty-headed companion as he barks into the breeze, shakes his head with a grin.

Back in the haven of my home, the emptiness of my unfulfilling date subsides. Samuel Johnson once said: 'When a man is tired of London, he is tired of life.' Except I do get tired. Tired of the rush-hour Central Line Tube when I have four sweaty armpits in my face, tired of the sound of sirens all hours of the day – I even get tired of weirdly themed and absurdly overpriced bars and restaurants. But I could never tire of the Tower, of this welcome.

When a woman is tired of the Tower, she must have lost her head. The annoyances of the cameras, the rules, the gossip . . . they're nothing compared to the feeling of seeing the stone walls on the horizon, being absorbed into its story as you cross the threshold. That same feeling reignites each and every time I return.

Holding on to the rich pleasure that the Tower affords, I take the long way home, to see her in all her glory. Down Water Lane, the Bell Tower greets me first; its smooth thirteenth-century stone stacked high, and my eyes follow it up to the tiny white shed that houses its eponymous bell at the summit. The wall that stretches out from behind it is scarred from the shrapnel off of a bomb dropped nearby only decades before, the collateral damage leaving both its mark and its tale; and beyond that, Traitors' Gate swims in the tide of the Thames that infiltrates the outer wall. The black panels are reflected in the murky water, redundant from their duties; the only prisoners now are the spirits that were never emancipated.

As I turn left under the Bloody Tower archway, the weather- and time-beaten faces of lions carved into the curved stone watch me as I proceed up the cobbled path. Edward and Merlin stand on the ruined wall beneath the White Tower, and they both hop over towards me. Edward's dishevelled feathers fluff out all the more as he greets me with a shake, and Merlin cocks his head, waiting patiently for me to fetch him something edible from my handbag. I dig out a couple of cat treats from the bottom and they each catch one in turn before getting back to the mischief they were no doubt creating before I arrived.

As I round the White Tower, a voice calls my attention before I can get back to my marvelling.

'Maggie!'

'Ayy! There she is! Mags!' another voice calls out. I follow the source as my name echoes around the courtyard.

'Maggie! Over here!' My eyes snap to the far corner of the Waterloo Block. Riley and Walker hang precariously out of one of the tiny windows. Walker is crushed under his blond companion as they wave like children in my direction.

I wave back, trying to mask my thrill at knowing they have returned and who else may be lurking behind them. As if by magic, the window to the room just over from the pair swings open, and my heart catches in my throat as I anticipate the face that will emerge from behind it. A face I have been aching to see.

'Here she is, everyone. Our plain old Maggie!' Mo gives me a wink as his curly dark hair leads him out of the frame. Freddie is probably just busy, I tell myself, trying my hardest not to look disappointed.

Riley wolf-whistles as I get a little closer. 'Someone is looking FIT. *Please* tell me my dating app expertise has—'

Before he can finish, I run over to beneath the window, shushing him erratically, attempting to draw their attention towards the ravenmaster as she passes the Old Hospital Block, heading straight towards us. She is definitely not the sort to gossip, but my reaction is instinctive. The three guardsmen, with their well-trained reflexes, duck down and out of view.

From the void, I hear a faint groan along with Walker's

slightly strangled voice: 'You really need to stop eating so many pork pies.'

Suppressing a giggle, I offer the ravenmaster a wide, sheepish smile instead. Only when she nods in reply do I see the little conga of ravens hopping along the ground behind her. In single file, Rex, Regina, and Holly all follow her like she's a mother duck.

'Our parents tread the frozen river first. They crack the ice, their feet get wet, sometimes they even sink. They take the risks, so your feet stay dry. But not following their path doesn't always mean going in an opposite direction. You just have to avoid the cracks.'

Her words of wisdom feel more on the nose than ever before. I can't hide the bewilderment on my face, and I make a mental note to check my bedroom for listening devices.

'Sometimes you just need to dip your toes in. No harm comes from wet socks.' This is where she loses me; in my book, walking through a damp spot on the kitchen floor in your socks is up there with a paper cut and a watery eye as one of the most soul-destroying minor grievances. Sometimes, I think I would rather take a punch to the boob.

I voice this thought, but she simply shakes her head and waddles off, the Pied Piper of ravens followed out by her murder.

'And it'll give you athlete's foot too!' I shout after her. She doesn't turn around, only raises a hand to dismiss me and I laugh.

'Psst.' Turning back to the windows I see Riley's face

peeking out from under the windowsill. 'Is the coast clear?'

I nod my head, still smiling from the ravenmaster's didactic conversation.

'Well?' Walker emerges once again. 'Tinder? Fellas? Success?'

'*Sex?*' Riley excitedly interjects and is greeted with a slap on the back of the head from Chaplin, who pokes his head up behind Tweedledum and Tweedledee to give me a smile.

'Absolutely not. And I am certainly not going to shout about any of that out here.' As usual, I am burning red.

'Well, come on up then!' Mo says declaratively as if it is the most normal thing in the world to just pop up to the royal guards' guardroom to tell them all about your failed dates.

Before I can make an excuse or protest, the door that Freddie led me through to the Mess pops open and Chaplin's cheery face pokes out. His cheeks are as red as mine, but presumably from the fact that he has managed to run all the way down from the second floor in thirty seconds rather than from embarrassment. Before I can overthink, I throw a furtive glance over my shoulder, and I follow him.

This time, instead of going all of the way to the end of the corridor, Chaplin opens up one of the doors and leads me up an old staircase. All of my new friends are waiting for me with eager eyes when I reach the top. Bar one, that is.

'So . . .'

'I blame all of you,' I declare with an accusatory point at them, though I'm smiling.

'Oh, God . . .' Walker mutters.

'Maybe we should ask Cantforth to make us a few drinks before you tell us?' Mo adds.

'Absolutely not – never again.' They laugh. 'But a cup of tea would do nicely.' Tiny is elected, as the youngest, to go and make us all a pot of tea and the other lads lead me out of the stairwell and into their guardroom.

It smells about as nice as you'd expect a room housing fourteen men to smell. Riley must have noticed me turning my nose up because he quickly dives across one of the single beds and gasses the place with at least half a bottle of Lynx Africa. I give him a grimaced smile as the assault on my senses makes my eyes water.

Trying my hardest to look casual, I scan the room for any sign of him, but I am ultimately disappointed: other than the four who carted me up here, there's only Davidson, half-hanging off one of the beds, fiddling with the frame as he talks on the phone.

'He's not here,' Mo leans down and says in a low voice, clearly having noticed my analysis of the place.

'Who isn't?' I feign cluelessness, but he sees through me, throwing back a glance that says 'you know exactly who I'm talking about'. 'Is he okay?' I add then.

'Family duties call.'

Family duties? What does that even mean? I think back to the jewellery box and the phone call from the night we met. 'An order . . . errand for my father,' he had said. At the time, I had assumed it to be a slip of the tongue, a military man so used to orders that the word has become part of his daily vernacular. But now 'duties'? I remind myself that

208

Mo, too, is a man of the military. I am more than likely just overthinking. Perhaps he simply means a funeral or wedding.

'I hope it isn't anything too serious.'

Tiny comes back then with a pot of tea and as many mugs as he can hang on to his long, skinny fingers. I thank him as I slide one of them off and fill it.

'Come on then, Mags. The suspense is killing me,' Riley pipes up just as I drop the teaspoon of sugar in.

'Are we all sitting comfortably?' I tease as Mo, Chaplin, and I sit on one bed, and Tiny, Walker, and Riley cram onto the one parallel. The three opposite lean forward, their faces propped up in their hands like children waiting for a bedtime story.

'*Well*, spoiler alert, but the first date ended up with me covered in someone else's piss, making a quick exit out of a very small bathroom window . . . naked.'

It takes about an hour for me to fully recount the story of my traumatising first date with Catfish Caleb and my terribly boring date with Gym-Bro Jake. Of course, they all find my humiliation hilarious and, actually, talking about it out loud, I can almost see the funny side too.

'Well, you sure know how to pick 'em, Mags.' Riley exhales after I finish my story.

'I blame the profile you made me. It attracts all of the weirdos.'

'You'll be thanking us when you find the love of your life.' Walker winks.

'I'm not sure if I can ever face that app again.'

'You can't give up now!' Riley protests as if it is him that I'm finding a boyfriend for.

'Protein shaker was at least an improvement on the old man, so by that logic, every date you go on will get slightly better. Maybe give it a couple more and who knows you might end up on a date with someone as sexy and charming as me,' Mo chimes in and I roll my eyes.

Chaplin taps me on the knee and holds up three fingers and shrugs. 'Three more?' I ask and he nods. I deliberate over it for a moment. What do I have to lose? I did hit rock bottom on my very first try, so it surely must be up from there, like Mo says. And I did shake on it with Walker.

'Fine, I will go on three more dates. If I don't find the man of my dreams, then I am deleting Tinder from my phone, and we will never speak of this again.' Chaplin smiles, and the others follow suit.

Maybe if Freddie had been here, if we had another evening like we did in the White Tower, if he had at least called, I wouldn't have been so easily convinced . . . But he hasn't, I remind myself. And with that, we pull up the app on my phone and start swiping again.

'How about this one?' I present my phone around the room with what I thought was a half-decent profile. An instant chorus of grumbles offers a resounding 'no' and I take their advice as gospel for the rest of the evening.

Chapter 15

Jake sends me a few texts intermittently, but as soon as they get past the *'What you up to?'* texts that always end up with him telling me he's in the gym, we have little else to talk about and, much like on our actual date, the conversation quickly fizzles out.

I'm grateful when I finally get another match a few days later, with one of the guardsman-advised right swipes coming good. As soon as I see his profile, I remember that Toby earned his 'like' mostly for the picture of his cat wearing a little cowboy hat. He's in his mid-thirties and most of his pictures are high-angle selfies, but they're not horrendous. They show off his dark stubble nicely, and the one shirtless mirror selfie he kindly includes displays a lean figure; it's toned, but not to the extent of Jake, who apparently even does bicep curls in his sleep.

Toby: *Hey Gorgeous. Xxxx*

Maggie: *Hi! X*

Toby: *You're so hot for a redhead. Aha xxx*

Ah yes, the classic backhanded compliment that every ginger is so familiar with. When I don't reply he messages again.

Toby: *Always wanted to get with a ginger. Does the carpet match the drapes? Aha xxx*

Okay, so Toby certainly isn't going to be one of the lucky five that I take on a date. So, I resolve to fire back:

Maggie: *If you're meaning long enough to braid, then yes, I've got a French plait in both right now.*

Maggie: *Aha xxx*

Just as I am about to close down the app, I get a new message. Felix, a rather dashing blond that I matched with weeks ago, must have run out of other people to talk to. He is the Australian surfer dude type. His dark blond shaggy hair is tousled in long waves around his tanned face – every teenage girl's wet dream. I can't deny, I did do a little excited squeak when he matched with me for the first time.

Felix: *Do you have Snapchat? I'm not on here much. X*

Okay, maybe I was so focused on the sea-salt-tousled hair that I may have overlooked a few minor red flags . . . no self-respecting man in their twenties still uses Snapchat. That app is only used for two things: teenagers making mistakes, mostly in the sending nudes department, and married men cheating in a way that can't be traced. I think about ignoring him, but the picture of him in his crazy-coloured swimming trunks flashing a tattoo that wraps around his thigh encourages me to give him a chance.

Maggie: *I'm afraid not. You can text me? X*

I know you shouldn't really give your phone number out to strangers on the internet, but I am a fool for floppy hair.

Felix: *How about we just go on a date? Skip the small talk . . . x*

A second red flag . . . it would be pretty reckless to meet a total stranger without enough of a conversation to establish that he isn't a serial killer. But, *again*, he looks a bit like the grown-up version of Jeremy Sumpter's Peter Pan, and six-year-old Maggie would kick me if she knew I'd turned down a date with the first love of her life . . .

Maggie: *How does dinner at Ricci's in St Paul's sound? X*

I have no idea who the woman in those little red bubbles with all the confidence is, but she certainly doesn't sound like the same woman sat in her pyjamas trembling whilst she presses the send button.

Felix: *Great! I'll book it for 7 p.m. tomorrow? X*

Maggie: *Perfect, see you then x*

I have to take a few deep breaths after hitting send on the final message and it takes me exactly half a second to regret the entire exchange.

'Bloody corgis,' Riley mutters to himself for the sixth time in the half hour since I snuck up into the guardroom to tell the lads about my impending and spontaneous date with Felix. Riley sits hunched over at the end of his bed, furiously polishing his boots. The lads had returned again to the Tower after a short guard at Windsor Castle where one of the royal corgis, who had popped in for a cheeky visit, took quite a shine to Riley's perfectly bulled boots, making them his bed for the rest of the sentry duty.

'Here, Tiny,' he shouts to the youngest member of the platoon. 'How would you like to earn fifty quid? Buy your mum something nice?'

'No way! I'm not doing your dirty work,' he replies, and Riley moves on to his next victim.

'My dearest friend Courtn—'

Walker cuts him off before he can finish: 'Not a chance.'

Riley makes his way around the room, asking every one of his colleagues, before his gaze finally settles on me. Clearly deciding I would probably just make the boots worse, he ceases his moaning and gets back to work with the brush.

'Is the bearskin heavy?' I ask. My hair hangs down the ladder of the spare bunk bed as I press my feet against the ceiling, blood rushing to my head.

Mo tosses his bearskin at me, and it lands softly on my stomach. 'Fur stretched over wicker. It's more of a pain trying to keep them on when it's windy than having to worry about it giving you neck ache.'

Stroking the soft fur, I realise the only weighty part is the metal curb chain at the base. With a struggle akin to a seal attempting to climb a tree, I pull myself up, not forgetting to whack my head on the ceiling as I do so. Hopping down from the bed I stick the bearskin on my own head.

'This is poorly designed, no?' I point to the curb chain as it rests on my chin. 'Surely it should be around your neck, to fix it in place.'

'It's not meant to. We're infantry foot soldiers – it's there to stop you getting a sabre in the face from the posh gits on horseback,' Riley answers and Chaplin leans over the side of his top bunk and pretends to strike down with a sword.

'Now it functions as the most irritating bit of kit to have to polish. Speaking of which . . . Anyone fancy doing mine for me?' The sound of fourteen clear nos from the entire platoon prompts Riley to give a loud groan.

Lifting the bearskin off of my head, I place it back at the end of Mo's bed.

'Maggie, can I ask you a question?' Walker, who has barely spoken since I arrived, pipes up.

'Of course you can,' I reply, slightly alarmed about where this is going but trying to keep my concern out of my voice.

'Your parents, they managed, didn't they? Doing the distance thing?' His youth is made even clearer as his brow slopes and his dark eyes shine with a childlike worry. My heart sinks at his question.

'Is everything okay?'

Gesturing to his phone with a sad smile, he nods. 'Just the missus. Struggling.'

I have never told the lads about Mum; I haven't had the right opportunity. How can I tell him that my parents' marriage only lasted because my mum gave up every part of herself to wait around for my dad? How do I tell him that the army made my dad miss almost every important event in both mine and Mum's life? How do I tell these lads, who moved away from home as teenagers to devote their lives to a job, that it will always come before anything else that they want, especially love? Most of all, how do I tell them that I blame my father for Mum never living her life?

I don't.

'They were married for twenty-five years. It was tough, but they managed. It's not just you strapping lads who have to be strong once you've signed up, you know. Your partners are essentially in the army too, in their own way. Except they don't get paid for it.' I sit down beside him on his bunk.

'Mum struggled a lot . . . it's lonely. Lonely for all of you too, I imagine, in foreign countries, or even just being

216

here, but you have each other. Mum only had me for company.'

'I'd rather have you than listen to his moaning all the time.' Mo points to Riley who throws his polishing brush at him. Walker looks pensive, a rawer version of his usually chipper self.

'Honestly, Walker, I'm not sure you ever get used to it – you just find ways to deal with it.' It's not a lie, but it's the sugar-coated version. 'Get her tickets to Trooping the Colour and it will remind her what you work so hard for and make her even prouder of you. And who doesn't find a well-disciplined man in a red tunic sexy, eh?' Walker offers a soft smile but it's clear his mind is ticking distractedly behind his eyes.

'You think so?' Mo jumps up and throws his tunic over the top of his vest and stands proud with his hands on his hips.

'Hmm, on second thoughts . . .' I tease and he sits down with a chuckle.

'You've only got eyes for Stiff, haven't you, Maggie.' Riley wiggles his eyebrows as the redness burns on my face.

'Absolutely not,' I fib. 'I'm going on a date with *Felix*, remember?'

'Yeah, yeah, yeah,'

'Anyways, I haven't seen him in an age. I can hardly remember what he looks like!' I quip, in an attempt to use the mention of the one missing guardsman as an opportunity to gain some of the information I am desperate to hear.

'He's been lording it up in Scotland last I heard.' Riley

gets up to retrieve his brush, before resuming the scrubbing motion. 'I bet he doesn't have to polish his own bloody boots.' Before I have a chance to ask what he means, Mo stands up and nudges him, causing the wooden handle of the brush to mark the finally clean shoes. The ensuing scuffle distracts both of them from giving any more information. 'Now does anyone feel like polishing a buff belt? Twenty quid?'

By the time my date with Felix rolls around, I've had to stop myself from texting him to cancel upwards of six times, changed my mind about my outfit twelve times, and vowed never to date again about eighteen million times.

Ricci's is a small Italian restaurant sitting under the imposing gaze of St Paul's Cathedral. Small bistro tables line a veranda with climbing vines framing the whole scene, and, from your seat, you can see right up to the vast dome of the white marble monument.

For the first time, my date has beaten me here. Felix sits in the corner, leaning back against his chair with one of his legs propped up on the opposite knee. He wears an open-collared white cotton shirt, shorts and a pair of navy boat shoes, and his deep tan ties the look together, giving him the air of someone who has just stepped off a plane from a beautiful exotic island. Felix seems to be the epitome of the laid-back surfer type I had hoped he would be, and I get a little giddy realising that he wanted to go on a date with me.

'Hi . . . Felix, right?' I say, fidgeting a little in front of his table.

He barely moves a muscle, only gestures towards the parallel seat and I sit. I clutch my handbag on my lap and sit up pin-straight on the very edge of my seat. It feels like I have just been invited into a meeting with my boss, who lounges across his desk casually, but is preparing to fire me without an ounce of remorse.

'It's so nice to meet you!' I chatter through my nerves. He looks at me through thick eyelashes, like he's studying me, moving a pondering hand to his chin as his eyes flicker up the full length of my torso. My body instinctively squirms under the intensity. 'I really love it in this place, I mean, look at that view.' I point to the glowing structure beside us, but Felix doesn't move his gaze.

He smoothly manoeuvres his body so that he is leaning towards me on the table and runs a hand through his hair in a practised motion before he speaks. 'Maggie,' he says, his voice deep and smooth. 'How would you feel about heading somewhere a little more . . . private?'

I blink blankly at him, confused. Only the front-of-house stands at a plinth at the furthest corner from us, the other tables void of any other patrons. 'I think we've struck lucky,' I reply. 'It looks like this place *is* pretty private tonight. It's like it's been hired out just for us.'

I give him a smile and he shifts forward even further. 'I mean go back to mine . . . The view isn't so bad there either.' His voice is a little gruffer this time.

I try to brush past it: 'Better than St Paul's? I doubt it! What are you going to have? I think I'll go for the carbonara. Have you ever tasted it here? It's heavenly – very befitting of the location.'

'Look, we both know the reason we're here.' He reaches under the table and gives my thigh a stroke. 'So, let's just skip the food and go straight to dessert . . . if you know what I mean?'

I choke on my own saliva. 'Oh, I, well, I'm not . . . I . . . I don't normally do any of *that*—' I gesture wildly with my hands, not really sure what I am trying to mime '—on a first date.'

My face burns hot, and I find myself wishing the idle waiter would bring me a glass of water to busy myself with. 'It would be nice to have dinner though, and we can see where things go in the future.'

Felix stares at me, face twisted in disgust, as if I have just told him that I eat babies for breakfast or something. 'Sorry . . .' I blurt, worried that I have offended him. 'It's not that . . . not anything to do with how attractive you are . . . you're very attractive. I'm sure it would be . . . nice. But I just, well, these things, I . . . sorry.'

He gets to his feet, and he's a little shorter than I was expecting. 'I suppose I had better get us some drinks then,' he says, and I relax, giving him a warm smile.

'That would be lovely, thank you. I'll just have a lime and soda please.' He disappears inside and I lean back against the chair, letting out a sigh.

Part of me – a rather large part – is a little doubtful of this date now. I almost don't want to take it any further, knowing the endgame is only to get into my pants. Perhaps I gave him mixed signals agreeing to meet him without even a conversation – or maybe I'm naïve to believe that anyone on these dating apps wants anything more than whatever is in between my legs. But I *did* promise the guys three more dates, and I'm here now so if nothing else, this is an easy tick.

Feeling awkward sat alone, I peer over to the restaurant doors, to see if I can see Felix at the bar. He must have nipped to the toilet, I think, and I pull out my phone to pass the time. No messages. Still nothing from Freddie, and thankfully nothing from Bran either – it turns out that whatever Freddie said to him has been more effective at scaring him off than anything I have ever managed and for that I'm grateful. The only notification I have is from the app that tracks my period, which kindly tells me that I should expect her arrival within the next twenty-four hours. Brilliant.

Ten minutes go by and there is still no sign of Felix or my drink. I keep looking around hopefully, but the scene never changes. After a little while longer, the waiter comes over to my table with a deadpan expression, one of those people who look both twelve and forty-five all at once. He doesn't greet me, nor smile, only mumbles: 'You know he's gone, right?'

I swallow down the bile that has risen in my throat and take a couple of deep breaths through the threat of tears. I can't cry in front of this guy – he probably barely makes enough an hour to justify being on his feet all day, never mind expecting him to mop up my waterworks too. With a pang, I remember I did the exact same thing to Caleb not too long ago. Catfish or not, knowing I made someone feel as worthless and rejected as I feel right now adds a hefty dose of guilt into the mix of uncomfortable emotions.

'Yes.' I smile, trying my best not to show him that I am hurt by the rejection. 'Thank you.'

'Do you wanna order anything?'

'I'll have the carbonara, and a large glass of rosé, please?' He scribbles my request down on his notepad.

No failed date is going to stop me from getting that damned carbonara. As he walks away, I call to him across the tables. 'Actually, can you make that a bottle, please?'

Once I have a wine glass filled to the brim, I take the opportunity to get back on my fruitless search for a half-decent human to date. This time, I abandon my judgemental system; it clearly isn't working and perhaps I need to be more open-minded.

I continue to slide through countless profiles with my free hand as I eat, and long after my plates are cleared. When a barmaid from the inside brings me my second bottle of wine, she sits down beside me to aid me in my search. Her hair is dyed half black, half electric blue, and shaved all up the back, revealing a stunning mandala design, and every inch of her skin seems to be adorned with some kind of piercing: her dimples are accentuated with two silver-balled studs and she has managed to fit three piercings into her tiny nose. Thick eyeliner frames a delicate set of green eyes. After half an hour of her lurking over my shoulder telling me which way to swipe, I learn that her name is Jenny.

'He looks like he'd definitely have the clap,' she offers in her deep voice, a West Country twang softening her appearance. I follow her advice, and swipe left on Liam, 25. I'm not quite sure what about a photo of him on a hotel balcony screams 'I have an STD!', but I trust her judgement.

We carry on like this for a while and I end up matching with another handful of Jenny-approved men. A bottle deep in cheap wine gives me the confidence boost I need to move past this minor setback with Felix and get straight into messaging one of them.

Oliver, 30, intrigues me most. Most of his pictures are of him smiling, beautifully thick dark hair bouncing around his kind face, and a clay-coloured birthmark maps onto his cheekbone and forms an island around his eye. There's a benevolence in the way he looks. He seems like the kind of guy to do that thumb-rubbing thing when he holds your hand.

'You need to message first, show him you're confident and you know what you want.' Jenny gives me a little pep talk as we decide what to send. 'He looks like a soft boy, you know, all the jumpers. Maybe something sweet, but sexy.' I think it would be easier for me to sprout wings and fly across to Cambodia than to be sweet or sexy.

'Can you do it for me? I'm not great at this.' I slur, passing her my phone.

'I'm sure you are!' she rebuffs, kindly.

'Hmmm . . .' I lay my head on her shoulder and type:

Maggie: *Hey, you look nice*

Jenny snatches the phone out of my hand with a half laugh, half sigh. She taps out a message, her long nails clacking fiercely across the screen, and hands it back to me with the message already sent. 'Here.'

Maggie: *Sooooo, when are you going to be taking me on a date then? X*

'Right, I need to get back to work. Good luck!' she says as she gets to her feet.

'Thank you,' I reply. 'I should probably be getting off now too. Shall I come inside to pay the bill?' I reach for my bag with a wobble, almost tumbling from my seat.

Jenny waves me away and simply says, 'Already done. You needed it.' Her kindness sends a fresh wave of emotion through me, and I have to work hard to stop myself from crying.

'You're the best,' I say a little too ardently and it makes her chuckle.

'Go on, get home safe.' And with that, she disappears inside, and I stumble away into the night.

Chapter 16

A few days since my third date, which very much continued my string of bad dates, and I'm still feeling dejected as I walk to work. Cromwell has decided to join me this morning. Snaking in and out of my legs as I stride, he wraps his long tail around my ankles.

'You better not be trying to trip me up, young man,' I say to the fluffy creature at my feet as I have to do a little hop over him to avoid us colliding.

He answers by doing the same again and I narrow my eyes at him, but before I can berate my fluffy companion properly, the soft buzz from my phone in my pocket steals my attention. Without so much as a beat, it is in my hand and I am scanning the name on the screen, my heart leaping at the prospect of it being his. With all of my attention focused on the phone in front of me, I completely forget about my mischievous cat and stumble over him. To add insult to injury, the text is sorely disappointing, with no AWOL guardsman in sight; instead, it is Bran's words that I read.

Bran: *Come with me to the British Museum. I miss you.*

I stop dead in my tracks. That used to be a weekly occurrence for us before he found corporate parties. We'd have a date every Sunday and we'd either wander around the museum or sit quietly together in the British Library archives, looking at anything we were allowed to get our hands on.

Those are fond memories, tinged with sadness now. That was the point in our relationship where I thought I would spend my life with him. I picture the last three dates: Caleb, Jake, and Felix. Maybe Bran isn't as bad as I thought? Maybe I will never do any better than him? Are all men just awful? Thinking about it, most of the great romance writers were spinsters . . . Have I been hoodwinked into believing that men will love you unconditionally?

Maybe my standards are too high, maybe someone who looks like me should settle for what they can get. I can't claim to be beautiful; I hardly have people falling over me to tell me that I am. Well, aside from creepy old men who tell me their wives had hair like mine thirty years ago. I have nothing to give to guys. No money, no amazing career, no supermodel figure.

Cromwell headbutting my calf stirs me from my cogitation.

'No, you're right,' I say to him as if he has offered some sort of voice of reason. 'I have a date later, and I at least need to finish this stupid challenge of Walker's, so we're going to pretend that I'm not some sort of anxiety-ridden

226

freak who can't stand the sight of her belly in or out of clothes, and I am going to whack on that really uncomfortable push-up bra from Ann Summers and with my tits at my chin I'm going to make him believe that I'm sexy and confident . . . and then show him that I have an equally sexy brain, of course.'

As I finish my own pep talk, a knight strides past me, a broad smile breaking through his dark stubble. One of the actors who performs for all of the kids in the Tower, and one of the most beautiful men I have ever seen in my life, has clearly just overheard me talking to a bloody cat about my boobs at half eight in the morning.

'Morning,' he says with a smirk, flicking his long dark hair back, and sending my cheeks rosy.

'M-morning,' I stammer in reply.

Oliver is leaning against the side of London Bridge Tube station when I reach him. Despite my usual struggle to match profile photos with the actual face, I spot him straight away. He's built like an athlete, wide and strong, but dressed in a soft woollen jumper and brown corduroy trousers. He reminds me of one of those giant teddy bears that obnoxiously fill half a room, and which, no matter what your age, make you immediately want to curl up in the stuffing and go to sleep.

Hair the colour of black obsidian puffs out from under a camel-coloured beanie hat. It's pushed back on his head so none of his face is obscured, and I notice that his nose slopes dramatically and his jawline casts a shadow on his neck, drawing attention to the sharpness of it. The powerful features are softened by his plump lips, which settle naturally into a soft smile. Everything about his look is a perfect mixture of authority and tenderness.

Hiding just out of his eyeline behind a conveniently parked-up bus, I decide that I'm going to take a new approach, a confident one. I throw back my shoulders, so I stand at my full height, flick the stray curls out of my eyes and, for the first time ever in my life, I strut. To the casual London bystander, I more than likely look absolutely insane, but in my head, I am putting Tyra Banks to shame and am half expecting to be talent-scouted straight into London Fashion Week. The spell is very quickly broken, however, when my ankle rolls over an uneven paving slab, and I accidentally find myself clinging on to a passing stranger for stability. Shooting me a dirty look, the passer-by shakes me off, and I fight the urge to shrivel up in embarrassment. Luckily, though, Oliver still faces away from me, so I resume my long-legged strides, ignoring the hot blush of embarrassment as it spreads across my face.

When I reach him, I place a flirty hand on his shoulder.

'Oliver?' I say, my voice low in timbre. 'It is so good to finally meet you.'

My accent is so posh and proper that I actually question whether the words came out of my own mouth. When he turns to me, I notice his birthmark isn't there framing his eye, and I falter. That's a bit of a strange thing to photoshop in – usually people filter their photos so hard that you can barely see so much as a freckle.

Too focused on the birthmark, or lack thereof, it takes

me a while to realise he hasn't greeted me back. In fact, he's just staring at me, eyebrows furrowed.

'Erm . . . I think you have the wrong person,' he says eventually, with a confused look still etched into his face. My mouth drops open; I can hear the blood thumping in my head, and I have a sudden urge to cry uncontrollably from the mortification of it all.

'Ah, oh, yes, I . . .' Before I can form an actually coherent sentence, a hand grabs mine and another figure swoops in beside me. A swift kiss is planted onto my cheek.

'Maggie! Hi, I was waiting inside the station, but spotted your crazy hair from across the crowd.' The real Oliver is the one clutching my sweaty palm. His birthmark softly stains around his eye and down the cheek closest to me – impossible to miss. When I turn back to apologise to the stranger that I had weirdly attempted to seduce in the street, he is already gone.

I face Oliver, mouth still agape. 'Are you all right?' he asks, and I shake out of my humiliation and offer him a false smile. That is the last time in my life that I pretend to be confident. Everything about me has shrunk, and I feel as though I might simply disintegrate. If I tried to get onto one of the Tube trains now, I'd drop through the gap between the train and the platform and join the mice in gutters.

'Yes, sorry about that. Hi. It's nice to finally meet you.' I'd usually go in for a hug, or at least a wave, at this stage but he's skipped all of that and has already locked his fingers around mine. There are too many thoughts, mostly my own internal monologue continuously heckling me, to process that fact right now. And he's doing the thumb-rubbing thing!

Looking up at him, I realise he is really nothing like the poor stranger. His skin is much darker, a milky brown like treacle fudge and a constellation of freckles cluster down both his cheeks. He isn't quite as tall as I imagined either – whilst just tall enough that I have to look up at him, in a decent pair of heels I'd most definitely take the higher ground. As he beams at me, I notice two deep dimples kissing at both of his cheeks. His teeth are so perfect and white I self-consciously close my mouth so as not to disappoint him with my own considerably less perfect set.

Shifting his hand from mine, he wraps an arm around my shoulder, and I wryly note that I have had more physical contact with this man, three minutes into meeting him, than I have in total in the past couple of months.

My mind betrays me and flicks back to Freddie in the basement. The way he caught me as I fell, the sensation of my soft body pushed against his hard chest, how safe I felt wrapped in his strong arms. A familiar tingle climbs up my legs and spreads through me as I remember the way I felt each ripple of movement under his shirt.

Where is he now though? I remind myself firmly. *He hasn't attempted to contact you for almost a month. He isn't thinking about you; he doesn't care about you.*

The tingling ceases and I look back to my actual date who I realise has been talking all this time, and I have not taken in a single word of it. Oliver doesn't seem to notice. '. . . so my sister said that I had to get on some dates. She hated my last girlfriend, but I think she'd like you. You don't seem too bothered about makeup and all that stuff. Lily doesn't like people who care too much about the way they look.'

I fake a laugh. 'That's nice.' Little does he know it took me almost two hours to get ready and I *am* actually wearing quite a lot of makeup. I question whether he thinks I was born with the thick black line that flicks out across my eyelid. At least he was attempting a compliment.

Oliver takes my wide smile as an invitation to carry on. 'I've got something planned for later, but I thought I'd keep it as a surprise. You'll never guess what it is!' He looks pleased with himself and his chest puffs out. 'It isn't until half nine-ish but it's a twenty-minute walk away so I thought we could stop for some dinner first?'

Backhanded compliments from before are all forgotten – he has well and truly captured my attention.

'Sounds good to me. Do lead the way,' I say, genuine excitement unconcealable on my face.

We walk hand in hand across London Bridge and Oliver talks the entire way. I learn that he's doing a PhD in Philosophy and spends most of his days in the University College London library immersed in the work of the greatest thinkers in history. Half a mile of the journey consists mostly of him fanboying over Rousseau. Most of what he says is too complex for me to follow along with whilst we walk in the midst of the bustling city, but he talks with such fervour I am transfixed. The hand that isn't clasping mine gestures wildly, and he occasionally has to apologise to a commuter who gets caught up in the passion and receives a whack across the shoulder.

231

'He was such a pioneer. I would give anything to spend just five minutes in his company.' He turns to me, eyes blazing in zeal. It really is *hot* to see someone so passionate about something they love. I make a mental note to research everything I can about Jean-Jacques Rousseau when I get home.

'Anyway, sorry, you have let me run away with myself.' A light blush settles over the smooth skin of his face. 'I get a little too excited – I apologise. Let's talk about you for a bit!'

'Don't apologise!' I say a little too quickly. 'It's cool to find someone so dedicated to their work. It all sounds fascinating! Anything I have to say would be far less interesting.'

'No, no, give yourself more credit than that! What area of history do you specialise in?' My cheeks ache from the constant strain of such a wide grin.

'Well, I have a few really . . . I love military history – it's quite important to me because of my family. Oh, and I also really enjoy medieval literature. In fact, you must know *The Letter of Alexander the Great to Aristotle* – being into philosophy? I did a university module on Medieval Science Fiction, a real paradox I know, but it was so fascinating . . .' I am bubbling with enthusiasm at getting the opportunity to talk with someone who gets as excited about a subject as I do.

'But that's fiction, not fact. You know that, right?' he interrupts, taking me by surprise.

'Yes, of course. I just think fiction from any point in history can tell us so much about the world at that time.

Particularly medieval fiction . . . getting a window into the imaginations of people a thousand years ago is captivating. I guess my main interest in history lies within people, what the lives of those like you and me would have been a century or a millennium back.'

'But Aristotle has far better works to stretch your mind. You should read some of his actual work,' he retorts, but I tune out, my excitement fizzling, and I keep my mouth closed for the rest of the journey.

I'm a little perplexed when we reach Tower Hill Tube station, although I suppose I've never told Oliver where I live so he wasn't to know he's just led me back the very way I came. My guard is instinctively raised, my eyes scanning in all directions for familiar faces.

'So, this is us.' He gestures to a restaurant when we reach the riverside. The whole outside is crowded with a jungle of perfectly pruned flowers and ivy climbs its walls. Aside from the constant hum of the city, it's easy to imagine this place in the heart of a tiny English village. The summer evening is warm enough to take a seat at one of the little tables on the bank. Oliver, proving himself to be a gentleman, pulls out my chair for me and, after I plop myself down, we awkwardly fumble as he tries to push me under, only succeeding when I half-stand up and shuffle forwards.

Tower Bridge is lit up in the setting sun and its light shimmers on the surface of the Thames. Thankfully there is another building separating us from the Tower and its watchful gaze, and I relax into the evening.

We spend much of the meal talking about books as our

food goes cold in front of us. I learn that Oliver has quite the soft spot for romance books, and I can tell by the way he holds my hand across the table and compliments me that he has learnt much of his dating skills from them as well.

'Oh gosh.' He stands up with a start, looking at his watch. 'It's almost time to go.' We have been so engrossed in learning about one another that two hours has slipped by without either one of us noticing.

Oliver rushes to pay the bill, despite my protests, and takes my hand and leads me to our next destination. We don't walk far. Ten metres in fact, around the other side of the building that has concealed me from my home all evening.

'Every night for hundreds of years the Tower of London has been locked up in a special ceremony called the Ceremony of the Keys,' Oliver announces with a sparkle in his eye. I haven't the heart to tell him how well acquainted I am with this ceremony. One of the few things I haven't told him tonight is where I live, and I was hoping to keep it that way. But the only alternative is going on a first date in my house surrounded by members of my extended family . . . that's like taking your one-night stand to your grandmother's funeral.

The warm blanket of comfort that had settled over us after such a perfect date is ripped away and I tremble without it. Not looking at Oliver as he continues his lesson, I desperately search for a way to avoid having to go inside, to be seen on a date *inside* the Tower.

'Maggie?' Oliver says, noticing my distracted features.

Snapping my attention back to him, I smile as best I can and give his hand a squeeze. The usual expression of soft happiness returns to his face, and he resumes.

Bob, with his military precision, opens the gate exactly on time – and with it my last hopes of escape slip away. Managing to wriggle my hand free from Oliver's kind grasp, I tuck my hair down the back of my dress, hoping to at least dim my most recognisable feature. There's no getting past Bob, though; he recognises me almost instantly as he takes the tickets from Oliver.

'Ooh hello there, M—' I quickly put a finger to my lips and gesture to Oliver who is distracted in looking about the Tower in awe. Bob's eyes widen in understanding and he nods. With softened eyes, I thank him silently and, grasping my date's hand once more, I manoeuvre us both into the middle of the crowd, desperately praying that the other excited guests will provide cover from any other Beefeater.

'Isn't it amazing,' Oliver remarks, pointing at the Middle Tower. I nod in agreement, trying to shield my face with the hair that is left poking out of my clothes.

'So much history,' I add quietly, keen to hide my discomfort.

Tonight's watchman is Richie, and he commences the small pre-tour that prefaces the ceremony, standing up on a block to project his voice over us as he makes a few jokes, that I too can recite by heart. Despite his bird's eye view, I remain undetected by my next-door neighbour, and I breathe a sigh of relief as we are led down to Traitors' Gate to prepare for the main event. Still keeping prisoner of my hand, Oliver smiles warmly at me and I forget where I am for a moment and relax into his touch.

Walking the familiar road down Water Lane, a guardsman in his red tunic and bearskin is visible at the sentry box in the distance. It's not until we reach our end point at Traitors' Gate that I notice the white plume that juts out of the side, and I try to suppress a gasp. In my efforts, I end up holding my breath, my body drawn so tight with anxiety that I am sure I might snap.

The synchronised click of hobnails echoes around the walls as the escort of four more identical guardsmen descend the hill, pairing and forming up in twos under the archway of the Bloody Tower. It's only when I dare to raise my eyes from inspecting the cobbles beneath my feet that I see them: Riley first, then Tiny towering behind him, then Walker. And, at the very back, shrouded in shadow, for the first time in weeks: Freddie.

Instinctively, I tear my hand out of Oliver's. If he looks at me, I wouldn't know. Freddie and I lock eyes in a stalemate, neither of us caving and breaking our gaze. My heart hammers in my chest, and when I manage to draw a breath, it barely fills my lungs. Emotion overwhelms me – mortification, anger, sadness, all wrapped up in a pang of longing – but, much as I'd like to run, I am stranded, as the Chief Yeoman Warder, the boss, approaches the ceremony, bearing both the keys and a lantern.

Freddie is the only one without his rifle, meaning he must be tasked with carrying the lantern tonight, but, with his eyes still fixed on me and mine on him, he fails to notice as the brass handle is placed into his outstretched hand. The centuries-old light clatters to the ground, one of its glass windows shattering across his boots. Balking at the smash and following gasp from the crowd, Freddie finally breaks the trance between us and scrambles to the ground to collect the damaged lantern.

'Now that is definitely not part of the ceremony,' Oliver whispers to me. 'Must be an amateur, not what you'd expect from a trained guard . . . what a klutz.'

My heart aches. I want to run up to Freddie, take him by the hand and drag him away into the White Tower again, but the chief barks his orders and he is once again stood to attention, this time gripping the dented lantern tightly in his fist. The glass crunches under their heavy boots as Richie joins them and all six men set off on their march off to the gates.

My breathing is ragged as I watch them walk away. Why of all people is Freddie the one in today's ceremony? I've been so desperate to see him for a whole month and then he finally pops up when one of these stupid dates is finally going well. I have missed him far more than I ever thought I could. Just seeing him – remembering the way his warm breath felt against my lips, how his body felt pressed against mine in that fleeting moment in the White Tower – makes Oliver pale in comparison. Suddenly, I don't want to be here; I know now that these 'dates' have been nothing but a futile distraction. And they haven't even worked.

Interrupting my thoughts, the escort party returns, the gates behind them locked fast. It's Cantforth's voice that calls the challenge: 'Halt! Who comes there?' His rifle is pointed at his colleagues and the two Yeomen in the middle.

'The keys,' the chief replies.

'Whose keys?'

'King Charles's keys.'

'Pass King Charles's keys – all's well.'

All of the guardsmen, aside from Cantforth who returns to his position guarding the Middle Drawbridge sentry box, continue their march back through the archway and join the rest of the platoon who are positioned across the Broadwalk Steps. The group of spectators are invited to follow, and we watch as the officer in the middle with his tall bearskin draws his sword. I hide away at the back, and I hardly hear as Chaplin plays the 'Last Post'. All I can think about is getting Oliver out of here.

As soon as that final note dies on the cool breeze, I drag him by the hand, back down the cobbles towards the exit.

'Maggie, where are we going? I wanted to ask the beefeater a question,' Oliver complains. Turning back to him, I am bordering on hysterical: eyes widened and a sweat hanging on my brow. My chest heaves as I look at him.

'I want to go home!' I snap, as Bob comes out of his security box to meet us, offering to unlock the gates.

A wounded expression crosses Oliver's face and my stomach drops at the sight. 'I'm sorry,' I say, trying to relax my breath. 'I . . . erm, I just need to get back. I've had a lovely evening – wonderful, even.' His expression still sticks as I squeeze his hand. 'Easily the best date I've ever been on.'

'You mean that?' he asks, his eyes holding a little hope.

My last evening with Freddie comes to mind – the White Tower safe, the tour of the armoury, the almost kiss – and my hands shake. *Not a date*, I remind myself.

'Definitely.'

'I can walk you home if you'd like?' Oh, bloody hell. Why does this have to be so difficult? I have mere minutes until everyone else catches up with us.

'Don't be daft,' I try to laugh, but it comes out like a strangled bird call. 'I wouldn't ever ask that of you. It's no trouble at all – you get on home.'

'Really, I insist.' The sound of chattering approaches. They're coming.

'Look, Oliver . . . I live *very* close by so there really is no need.'

'It doesn't matter if you're five minutes or five miles away! You never know who's lurking about these streets. I'd quite like to go on a second date with you so can't have anything happen to you before then.'

That makes me falter. For the first time ever, someone wants a second date . . . with me! A real-life, good-looking man *actually* wants to see me again, and I haven't scared him off either! Why, whenever anything goes right, is timing always against me? Quickly I drag my thoughts back to the pressing matter at hand: 'No, no! I . . . well, I . . . erm . . . live *here*.' I gesture behind me, the Middle Tower shadowy and imposing in the moonlight.

'Very funny.' He laughs, a little too hard. 'This is the Tower of London. No one lives here.'

If I had a pound for every time someone told me that – mainly Deliveroo drivers who take three hours to find the place and give up before I get my takeaway – I could probably buy the White Tower for myself.

'Nope, not a joke, I'm afraid. It's a long story, but my dad works here, so I live with him.' He furrows his eyebrows in an expression that I can't decipher; it's either surprise or still confusion. Most likely both.

'You're actually not kidding?'

'Not kidding. Sorry, I don't really have time to explain it all now, I *really* need to go.' I throw a furtive glance at the crowd making their way towards us.

'So, this whole date has been . . . where you live? Why didn't you tell me?' He frowns.

'I didn't want to hurt your feelings, and by the time I had the guts, it was too late. I'm sorry.' He stares at me a little wide-eyed, flicking his gaze from my face to the stone towers.

'Bloody hell.' He snorts, clearly exasperated, and rubs his palm up and down his face.

'But I really did have a great time tonight! I mean that. And, if you still want to, I'd love to see you again, maybe just a bit further away from home . . .'

'Yeah, I'd like that.' He smiles. Satisfied that I've managed to save the first good date I've had, I go to walk away, still desperate to wrap things up, but he grabs my hand and pulls me back to him, pressing his lips to mine before I have time to acknowledge what's going on. When my brain finally catches up, I push him off, only to be met with his rejected expression once again. Out of the corner of my eye, I can see the red flashing bulb of one of the Tower cameras. In any other place, any other moment, I would be floating; this would be perfect. But with Richie, and Dad, and Freddie – God, *Freddie* – and goodness knows who else mere metres away, watching my every move, my mind is reeling and his kiss only sends me into fight or flight. My whole body vibrates with tension, and I feel a few short breaths away from a panic attack.

'I'm not . . . I just . . . It's just that there's a lot of cameras,' I gabble nervously. 'And a watchman. And I know *everyone*, and . . .'

Before I can finish, he is bending his face down to mine, eyes closed, whispering: 'Forget about them. It's just me and you that matters . . .' He moves in for a second kiss, lips puckered, but before I can shake him off the sharp bang of a door slamming against the wall echoes around Tower Hill.

He whips his outstretched arms away from me in alarm, and our attention is drawn to the Middle Tower. A chorus of boots slap against the cobbles, rhythmically marching towards us.

'Step back!' barks the deep, familiar voice of Freddie. Still in his tunic and bearskin but having swapped the lantern back for his rifle, he is flanked by the lads, their cheery expressions nowhere to be seen. My heart is on the floor, as is my pride.

'Fredd—' I start, looking between him and my date frantically.

I am interrupted. 'What the fuck!' Oliver exclaims shakily. All of the air is sucked out of me, and my chest burns.

'Step back from the lady!' Richie barks from behind the

241

guardsmen, the quiet old man that I see tenderly watering his roses each morning replaced with a terrifying tank of a person. 'Be on your way.' His face is growing redder by the second. Oliver jumps back obediently. 'You have precisely five seconds to scarper before I set these lot on you like dogs,' Richie continues in the same clipped tone, gesturing to the armed guards.

My date doesn't need telling twice. He quite literally runs from me, not looking back. I haven't moved; I can't move. I want the Thames to overflow, swallow me up and carry me away.

Richie moves forward. 'You all right, Maggie love?' He is back to the tender neighbour, his voice soft and kind again.

Walking past him I head straight for Freddie, over-flowing with emotion that I can no longer keep a lid on; all of the anxiety, tension, longing, joy, and sadness of the evening culminating in . . . anger. I'm angry with Freddie, and I can't stop myself. I'm fuming at him, for disappearing, for coming back at the worst possible moment, for inter-rupting, for his whole bloody confusing existence in my life.

'You had no right,' I say through gritted teeth, poking him in the chest with a weak finger. Freddie's face is blank, expressionless, as I see it up close for the first time in weeks. There is a darkness in his aimless stare. His features are taut and tense, and I notice that his knuckles are white as he grips his rifle so tightly, he cuts off his own blood circulation.

'Take it that was another flop, eh Mags?' Riley's upbeat voice emerges from his grinning face.

'It wasn't until *he* bloody ruined it.' The other guardsmen hold their tongues as I continue my fierce stare at Freddie.

'Go home, Margaret,' he says coldly. The ice of his tone summons a single tear that rolls down my cheek.

Head down, I take off, and I don't stop running until I get home.

Dad never bothers to lock the front door, not having to worry about burglars inside one of the most protected fortresses in the world, so I swing it open, and it slams against the inside of the wall.

'Mags! Is that you?' Dad calls groggily from his bedroom in the basement.

I try and keep my voice calm, level, despite the way my hands tremble and emotion claws at my throat: 'Yes, Dad, only me. S-sorry, I think I've had a bit too much to drink.'

'All right, darlin', get yourself off to bed.'

I creep up the stairs and when I finally reach my room, my legs almost give out from under me. Everything in me feels strangled. I'm moving but each pang of muscle is constrained, like a thousand hands are grabbing me all at once and I'm too tired to fight them off. Overwhelmed, my mind can only settle on my insecurities, I need to be angry, and the only thing I have to direct my hatred towards is myself.

Tearing off my clothes, I stand naked in front of the mirror. I don't want to be me; I don't want this mind, this stupid body that holds me back. Maybe if I were beautiful, none of this would matter. My dates would all go well. People wouldn't mock me for the mere thought that a man could want me. I wouldn't have to rake through the chaff of men to find anyone to love me. Then going on a date with a beautiful, intelligent man wouldn't be such a novelty. I wouldn't be single at twenty-six and feel like I'm running out of time.

If I were beautiful, Freddie might feel about me the way I feel for him.

My body doesn't feel like my own. I'm pale, sallow, aside from the purple stretch marks that are sewn across my thighs and stomach like scarred scratches from a lion's claws. Dragging my hands across my body, I pinch at the folds of my figure until it hurts.

I should stand on my balcony like this, let them see me, all of me. Sometimes it feels like my body is the only thing I have control of, the only thing that is still mine, but even then, I don't want it. I'm bawling now. Full heaving sobs that shake me from head to toe. I shrink to the floor and press my hands into the carpet.

Without a doubt, I am never going to hear from Oliver again. Sure, it was only one date, but he was the one person who enjoyed my company enough to want to see me again. Apparently, it was too good to be true.

And Freddie! He yo-yos into my life at all of the wrong moments and then bounces straight back out again without warning, dangling his friendship before me like a carrot to a donkey. And as soon as it is almost in my reach, he snatches it back and just about snaps the thing in two in front of me. You only have to look at the way he greeted me tonight, after I have spent every waking moment thinking of him, to realise that he could never feel the same about me.

Remembering the way that he looked tonight, the emptiness of him, the coldness, sends another sob rattling
through me. Worst of all, I don't blame him. Why on earth
would he ever want to look at me? Everything with Bran,
and now this! I am tragic. Each night somehow ends in
tears, in embarrassment, in shame. Tonight probably made
him realise why I have no one in the first place, why Bran
messed around with other people, why Andy and Samantha
can't stand the sight of me.

Looking in the mirror at myself, hunched over and
blotchy from crying, I look pathetic. Exhaustion takes over
and, laying my head on the floor, and clutching my knees
to my chest, I let sleep overcome me.

Chapter 17

Cromwell's rough tongue raking across my eyebrow stirs me as the sunlight streams through my balcony door. As I lift my head, he nestles himself across my neck, his fluffy ears tickling at my own. My whole body is either numb or throbbing with my strained night's sleep on the floor. Clutching the small cat against my chest, I clamber to my feet and plop us both down onto my bed, wrapping us in my duvet. Cromwell purrs happily in my ear and it momentarily softens the heaviness on my chest.

The humiliation of last night has dissipated over the course of the night, replaced with a feeling of numbness, where even emotion seems too overwhelming, and all my brain can coherently think about is the fact that I cannot exist for today. I used to have these turns as a teenager, when the stress of moving to a new school every six months caught up with me and I would retreat into myself. Hide for a day or two. Even Mum couldn't coax me out.

Normal people have a bad date and move on. If it's

really bad, they might get a bit of second-hand embarrassment when they're daydreaming at work, and sometimes
even have to do a retrospective facepalm. Then they can
just carry on with their day, pretending like it never
happened. But in the Tower, tales spread like wildfire and
it's impossible to not have gossip thrust upon you. It's no
wonder people were once killed in these very walls because
of rumours. Even less than twelve hours on, I'm sure there
won't be anyone left who hasn't cringed at my failure.

I know only one thing for certain: I won't be going on
that fifth and final date that I promised the lads – or any
date ever again for that matter.

Rolling over, I go back to sleep with Cromwell's soft
purrs in my ears for another four hours. Freddie's face
haunts my dreams, stalking like a phantom. His disappointment, the coldness of the look he gave me, is tattooed
on my eyelids, inescapable as soon as I close them.

When I wake again, a hollowness has spread through
me, and I have long missed work. My phone buzzes on
my desk intermittently, and someone even rang the door-
bell half an hour ago but left again when they realised
that I wasn't coming.

I can't face it. The Guard rarely get called out for
anything short of bomb threats, so for them to be wheeled
out to scare off a date of mine will be the talk of the place.
I'm sure all of them in the ticket office will be beside
themselves laughing at the idea that I had even found a
date to begin with. They can live without me for today.

When Dad comes home for his lunch at midday, he
finds me still in bed. To my gratitude, he doesn't say

anything, only leaves and returns with a cup of tea, that now sits stone cold on my bedside table. There's no way that he hasn't heard. Richie will have told him on his way home from his post this morning, and if he didn't, someone else will have.

It's only when the sun has long set close to midnight that I finally decide to get up – though I don't stray too far, wrapping my dressing gown around myself and heading out onto the balcony. Lucie, having once again avoided being put to bed, is sat waiting in her usual spot and does a little hop on the wall when she sees me emerge. Settling myself down in one of the patio chairs, I gently stroke her beak in silence. I have little to say to her today – or, actually, I have too much to put into words and, despite spending the entire day swaddled in my duvet, I'm exhausted.

We sit like this for a while, listening to the sirens and shouting over on Tower Bridge, and I watch the planes as they cross the starless sky and imagine the people on them, who they are, where they're going. I wonder what the Tower looks like from where they're sitting.

I can see the houses of the Old Hospital Block from my balcony, the dark brick contrasting with the white stone of the Constable Tower. The flashing lights of a TV fill the arched windows; a thirteenth-century structure but still as much alive as when it was filled with log fireplaces and medieval weaponry. It's a collage of time, a palimpsest of history. Tower Bridge is lit up just off to the side, over-looking its elderly neighbour with its bright blue accented configuration.

In the midst of all of this, I am tiny. Not only in size, but significance. I almost feel like an imposter. A working-class Yorkshire lass whose clothes are all bought in cheap high-street shops and whose idea of a nice meal is a Toby Carvery should not live in a place lived in by royalty. What have I achieved in comparison to them?

Although, I *can* confidently say I've never killed anyone, so perhaps I am in a position to take the moral high ground.

Accepting my insignificance, weirdly, makes me feel slightly better. Who will care in ten years if I went on a few shitty dates? Who will remember the girl who looks a little bit rough around the edges when she gets to work? None of this really matters.

And I do know that it could always be worse. Some if not most people would look on me with envy, tell me I'm the luckiest girl in the world. And maybe I am. I live rent-free in a palace. But loneliness can't be filled by an interesting postcode. Whether I live in a palace or not, my problems still hurt; the way my chest feels as if it's been crushed by a steel-toecapped boot is still real, still valid.

Just as I am about to say goodnight to Lucie for the evening, I hear my name being hissed. I look around hesitantly, hoping it isn't a wise old spirit intending to offer me some advice.

'Maggie! Over here,' the whisperer calls again. I turn back to look at the east wall opposite and nearly keel off the balcony in shock when I notice a figure leaning over the battlements.

'What the . . .' I suck in a sharp breath.

'Shhh, Maggie! It's me.' Freddie's curly hair flops across his face as places a finger to his lips to quiet me.

My heart leaps in my chest at the sight of him. The thrill of seeing him again, his anger defrosted, buries my own anger. I rake a hand through my wild hair, suddenly painfully aware that I am only dressed in my dressing gown. What was I saying about him always catching me at a bad time?

Freddie waves his hand, beckoning me to come to him.

'If you hadn't noticed, there's a thirty-foot drop preventing that . . .' I point out, in my own hushed tone.

He shakes his head, a slight smile just visible in the distance. 'Beauchamp Tower, ten minutes.'

Without another word, he disappears back along the wall and out of sight. I stand gaping after him, rooted in my spot. Only when Lucie hops down off the wall and pecks me sharply on the toe do I finally come back to reality with a yelp.

'You didn't have to do it so bloody hard,' I say, hopping on one leg and rubbing the targeted toe with my hand. She moves forward to get my other foot and I leap out of the way. 'Okay, okay! I'm going, you sadist.'

Lucie flies back over the inner wall and disappears into the black night as I make my way back into my room. As always, my entire wardrobe is piled high on the floor. Attempting to find a half-decent outfit, which will hopefully make Freddie forget that he's ever seen me in my worn-out dressing gown, I dig through the heap. About halfway down, I find Cromwell nestled into the cup of one of my bras, buried under various odd socks and a T-shirt.

When I unveil his hiding place, he mews loudly in protest, and I cover him back up again hurriedly.

It takes me a long while to decide what to wear, although part of me recognises that I'm stalling. After last night, I'm afraid to face him, not sure what's left for him to say. He ruined everything for me with Oliver, yet not one part of him looked as if he did it out of affection of any kind. I know now, once and for all, that he means a heck of a lot more to me than I do to him. Why else would he drop me so easily? Even a friend doesn't leave without saying goodbye. But he disappears without a trace and only reappears at exactly the moment when he is the last person I'd wish to see.

In the end, I decide on a T-shirt and jeans, and leave the house. The Beauchamp Tower is across the other side of the site from my house, nestled between the doctor's tall house, and the edge of the King's House. Freddie is stood exactly where I saw him in my dream those few long weeks ago, beneath the flickering lamp, leant against the cold blue metal of the post. If I weren't looking for him, a little too desperately for my own liking, then I probably would have missed him completely. Only his curls are illuminated. The rest of his body is shadowed by the towering buildings surrounding him and the trees in the courtyard, which are full and thick with leaves.

I try to follow the most shaded route possible, hiding my face from the cameras dotted along the Jewel House until I am stood before him. I take a breath ready to speak, but before I can he slips his hand into mine and drags me through the door into the relative privacy of the

251

Beauchamp Tower. Only when we are immersed in total darkness in the cold stone room, where I can barely make out the outline of his tall figure silhouetted in front of me, does he slide one of his wide palms into my hair, the other snaking along the top of my back and pressing me into his chest. I can't tell if it's his heartbeat I hear, thumping against my cheek, or my own racing in my ears, but his breastbone rises and falls in a series of deep breaths. His thumb strokes back and forth across my scalp and the hand on my back squeezes me closer and closer, as if he's afraid of someone coming along and tearing me away.

When Oliver touched me like this, when his hands clutched at my cheeks, all I wanted to do was run, get as far away from him as possible. But this, this is otherworldly. Freddie's body is firm under his clothes but there is a softness in the way he holds me. He makes me feel fragile, but not helpless or vulnerable, not weak.

'Are you okay?' he breathes, his mouth so close to my ear I feel his lips dancing across my lobe. Pleasure rattles through me and holds all of my words and thoughts hostage, and all I can do is nod against his shoulder.

Time passes as if the world just stopped counting and we're frozen together, like the bodies of Pompeii, forever preserved in ash, spending eternity still clutched to one another in a beautiful embrace. So, when he finally moves away, reality hits like a ton of bricks. For the first time, I'm aware of the cold draught of the old stone room, the emptiness of it mirroring the way I feel now I am released.

Neither of us say a word, but he pulls out the lantern

that I watched him smash only the night before and strikes a match to light it. The momentary spark teases the clearest picture I've seen of him all night and, as he lights the candle inside, he's cloaked in a soft glow that fills his eyes with tiny fires.

'I hope they don't mind me borrowing this.' He gestures to the lantern. The glass windows are decorated with golden twists of metal and engraved with a likeness of the Tower. Only now one of its windows is missing and a small part of the heavy base has caved in on itself, consuming the soft pictures on the brass. I eye it nervously, worrying about how much trouble Freddie must be in and imagining tonight's watchman noticing it missing and closing down the Tower to look for it.

'Don't worry, I told them I was taking it to try and, erm, fix it up a bit. I didn't fancy using the main lights in here. That would be practically asking for them to find us,' Freddie says, as if reading my mind.

I haven't said a word to him yet. My body is still quivering from his touch. As he closes its tiny door, it emits a lambent light that softens his blunt features in shadow. He is ethereal, a muse for the pre-Raphaelites, wild hair and a perfectly sculpted profile. With the Tower's stone framing the image, I could almost wonder if I've fallen through a painting and met with one of Leighton's knights.

'I want to show you something I found the other day,' he continues, carrying the lamp over to the door. 'Would you like to see?'

I don't move and he pauses in the doorway.

'I was handling it,' I say with a shaking breath, unable

253

to suppress my feelings any longer. 'Last night. Why? Why did you have to . . . do *that*?'

'I heard you shout, Maggie.' He crosses back to stand before me, his glassy eyes filled with the flame of the lantern. 'I was worried about you.'

'*Worried*? Don't say that like it's obvious!' I can't help but grow passionate, his words only drawing my anger back to the surface. 'Your face! That wasn't worried. You told me to go home, like I was a child. You made me feel like everyone else does; like a problem that you wanted to go away. I really thought you were different.'

'I never . . . that wasn't . . . I didn't mean that – not at all.' He reaches for my face, but I don't let him touch me.

'You ruined the one good thing to happen to me in weeks. He's the first guy who's been kind to me, who actually wanted me! And for what? Just to remind me that I seem to have no control over my own life!'

'I swear to you, Maggie, that it was never, *never*, my intention. I acted on impulse. I thought you were in danger; I thought I was doing the right thing. Clearly I was wrong. I've made a horrible mistake and I'm sorry.'

Sinking to the floor I sit with my knees tucked up to my chin, looking at the wooden boards under his feet, which creak as he shifts his weight back and forth.

'You never called,' I whisper, the real root of my anger finally finding its voice, though it sounds as though it came from someone else's mouth.

'I know. I'm sorry,' he breathes, lowering himself down to sit beside me. 'I wanted to.'

'But you didn't.'

'No,' he says with a sigh. 'Things in my family are . . . complicated. I'm not good at getting close. You mean a lot to me, Maggie. You're a good friend.'

Friend. My back instinctively straightens and, though I stay firmly rooted, I feel as if an invisible force has dragged me far across to the other side of the room, into the darkness. That hug . . . I'd thought the way Freddie brushed his fingers across my body, and pulled me to him, had meant more than it did. Again.

'Maggie, I could spend hours in your company. In fact, I want nothing more than to spend every moment I can with you, and it hurts me to know I made you feel any less than the fascinating and remarkable woman that you are. I've never met anyone like you. You are so unlike everything I've ever known . . . but maybe that's the problem.' He doesn't make eye contact, seeming far away inside his own mind, fighting with himself.

I swallow down his words with great difficulty. Why is it that everything with Freddie has to confuse me so much? Anyone could listen to the first two thirds of that speech and assume that this is some tender declaration of love, yet he always makes sure to finish each of his monologues with something to make me doubt whether he likes me at all. What bloody 'problem'? Why is there *always* a problem? Perhaps I shouldn't have listened to the raven-master; perhaps I was right to doubt him, to push him away. But I didn't just dip a toe into my mother's mistake . . . I plunged straight in and now I am gasping for breath. I am drowning in my affection for him.

'God, I've missed you, Maggie Moore. Seeing you last

255

night . . .' he continues, and I flinch as he finally looks up at me. 'I told myself, as soon as you caught my eye framed in the arch of Traitors' Gate, that I am going to be here for you. I want to be here for you. I think I got a little too carried away with that vow last night and only made things worse. But from now on, this friendship is no longer part-time. I promise you I'll be doing no more running away.'

I don't trust myself to speak and only nod my head in reply. He has finally confessed his feelings for me, his feelings of *friendship*. I am embarrassed. I am embarrassed by how I've got this so wrong, of my yearning for his affection, at the way my body now trembles before him.

Frantically, I try to pull myself together – Freddie can't see my disappointment. It isn't his fault that I fell for him so blindly, my heart free falling from the moment he held me again tonight. I can't expect him to catch me – that would be like expecting a cobweb to ensnare a bowling ball as it hurtles towards a black hole. Unrequited love is bad enough, but I know from romcoms that it is always considerably worse when the object of your affections realises you are accidentally hopelessly in love with them.

'What was it that you wanted to show me?' I push through the heaviness of my body that readies me to sink through the floorboards and disappear, and instead clamber to my feet, offering Freddie a hand to join me. He stands using his own strength but still takes my offered hand in his. After a soft squeeze, he swaps out my palm for the lantern and leads me up the round staircase.

Freddie leads me up to the first floor and across the

room. It is chilling to only see it lit up in parts, the dim lamplight flashing across the marred brickwork.

The Beauchamp Tower is famed for its carvings on the walls. A great many prisoners have been held here throughout history, some for years on end, and, for as long as the Tower stands, the etchings they made will keep their memories alive. It's not just names, detailed illustrations of family crests and religious symbols also adorn the stone, so beautifully placed and so intricately carved that it almost feels as if this is the way it was intended to be decorated.

Some of it feels more timeless, as though it could appear on a modern-day school desk or in the pages of a teenage girl's diary. A small heart with an 'E' scratched into the middle of it, for example. Granted, the 'E' stands for Queen Elizabeth, carved by her Italian tutor after her older sister tortured the poor old chap, but it's interesting to see how the human desire to mark their love, whether romantic or patriotic, has been carried down through millennia. The Victorians valued these raw slices of humanity so much that, as they dismantled a few of the Towers, they saved the bricks that had been inscribed and placed them all together in here. I find it hauntingly beautiful to think that such stories live on in these walls – even if I do worry that one of the many Johns, Williams, or Edwards might still lurk beyond the veil, ready to seek their revenge on whoever lives within these walls again.

Freddie comes to a stop in front of one of the names. My own – 'Margaret' – is scrawled in shaking letters diagonally across the wall. He turns back to me with a pleased smile, still lifting the heavy lamp to keep it illuminated.

Beaming back at him, I trace the letters with my fingertips, the cold stone a shock against my skin.

'Margaret Pole,' I murmur, without lifting my hand from the wall.

'Yes, I saw it and had to bring you here. You share a name with quite a remarkable woman it would seem.' My heart leaps in the knowledge that he has spent time alone in here, reminded of me by the scratchings of the stone.

'She's fascinating, isn't she? I wonder if more people would remember her if she had been some beautiful, young queen. She is always forgotten when people talk about Henry VIII's tyranny,' I lament.

Like many women in history, Margaret was brought to the Tower for her son's sins, rather than her own. Because she was a little too outspoken for the king's liking, Henry imprisoned the elderly countess when his actual quarry fled to exile in Italy. When her arrest did nothing to have her coward of a son return and face up to his treason, her execution was ordered.

But she was a mother. She had pushed that monstrous chicken out centuries before anything like an epidural existed to help, so she wasn't going to go down without a fight. She had more bravery in her left toe than all of her yellow-bellied sons put together. Rather than submitting to her fate, she refused to lay her head on the chopping block. Instead, she remained steadfast, proclaiming that the block was for traitors, and that she was not one.

The executioner had to hack her to death where she stood.

'She was such a powerhouse. Imagine the strength it

took to stand there, looking your executioner in the eye, seeing yourself reflected in the axe and still not giving in.' I shake my head, in awe of the physical reminder of her, still standing half a millennium later. 'Some say they hear her ghost, screaming across Tower Green. I'd love to just sit and talk to her. Everyone remembers Anne Boleyn's story, but she isn't the only strong woman to be condemned here.'

I am getting animated again. Freddie shifts the lamp slightly, so it's my face that is illuminated by the light as opposed to the brickwork. His eyes are fixed on me the whole time. As our eyes lock, I am overcome with the urge to kiss him, and I have to remind myself that kissing a man when you get excited about the story of a woman's execution is a little bit insensitive. Not to mention the fact that I know for certain that it would mean a one-way ticket to rejection town now he has made our friendship abundantly clear.

'Do you think this place is haunted too?' Freddie says, looking around into the empty void in the room and I am grateful for the distraction.

'Have you never heard about the Beauchamp Tower exorcism?' I reply, giving him my most sinister smile.

'E-exorcism?' he stammers, his Adam's apple bobbing as he swallows nervously.

'Yup. For years they had visitors complaining of the feeling of a hand pushing them down those very stairs.' His gaze follows the direction of my hand as I point towards the staircase that we clambered up only moments ago.

'It got so bad that they called in a medium to see if she

could talk to the disturbed spirit. When she asked the empty room for a name, she was overcome by the urge to move into this corridor.' I lead him behind a rope that closes a section off to the public and scour the wall for the right name. Settling on the carving 'Thomas', I place my hand against it.

'They managed to find out that Thomas had been a prisoner here, alongside his friends. He'd watched each day from that window as his fellow captives were marched down to Tower Hill for execution, but he died before he could meet his end in the hangman's noose. His spirit was trapped here, in Beauchamp, never being emancipated because he never served his full sentence.' Freddie raises an eyebrow, pity etched into his features. He steps forward and caresses the name as I did. He visibly shivers with the contact.

'The medium suggested an exorcism. Not the Catholic priests splashing holy water and head-spinning demon kind, but they got one of the officers of the Tower, someone with power, to formally dismiss him. He'd been waiting centuries in purgatory just to be discharged, to be told that he had served his time and was free to go. Supposedly a gust of wind swept through the whole of the Beauchamp Tower, and no one was ever pushed down those stairs again.'

'Rather sad really,' Freddie notes, his hand still against the carving.

'Yeah.' I breathe, with a frown. 'I hope he's at peace now.'

Freddie drags his fingertips across the rest of the wall, and they dip in and out of the crevices.

'Hang on a minute,' I say, after a brief epiphany. 'Your surname ... it's Guildford, isn't it?' He looks at me confused for a moment and nods. I walk down right to the end of the dark corridor, and he tails after me timidly.

'Lord Guildford Dudley,' I declare. Freddie moves the lamp closer to better see the carving. The Dudley family crest sits alongside his name, immortalised in the stone. 'Both our names are in here.'

'Fascinating,' he murmurs. It is hardly audible, and I could almost believe he's actually talking to the wall.

'Poor Lady Jane Grey's husband. The Nine-Day Queen. She was barely sixteen when Bloody Mary sentenced them both to death. And she had to watch from a cell next door, as he was dragged out of here and executed, all whilst witnessing her own scaffold getting built. He carved her name in here too, such a bittersweet memento of their short love.'

He looks genuinely affected by this, his face so soft and full of a deep appreciation for what lies before him. I am quite envious that I am not the object of such a gaze.

'A few great loves have been seen in this place, most of them resulting in a far from happy ending . . . except one, my all-time favourite. Have you ever heard of Lord Nithsdale?'

Freddie shakes his head, listening intently.

'He was arrested and brought here after the failure of the first Jacobite rebellion; he was an important figure amongst the Scots, so the king sentenced him to death on the charge of treason. He had only been married to his wife, Lady Winifred, for mere days before his capture but she travelled with only her handmaids from Scotland to

London to beg the king's forgiveness. If that wasn't badass enough, when the king refused, she visited her husband in the Tower on the day before his execution. She and her maids snuck in another set of clothes under their skirts and kept passing in and out of the cell to confuse the beefeater guarding him.'

'I can see where this is going, and I can see why it is your favourite story,' Freddie interjects with a broad grin gracing his face.

'They dressed this huge, hulking great Scottish bloke, beard, and all, in a maid's clothes, and just walked straight out past the beefeater, who didn't bat an eyelid, and out of the Tower. And the two of them lived a long and happy life together in exile.'

'Ha, I wouldn't fancy having to explain that one to the Chief Yeoman, that's for sure.' Freddie laughs in the light of the flame. 'How did he explain the beard?!'

'Perhaps he hadn't met many Scottish women before!' After a brief spell of echoing laughter, we settle into a comfortable silence.

'Anyway, *Lord* Guildford,' I break the stillness of the room, before my racing thoughts can start up again. 'Are you sure that you're not too proper to have plebeian friends like me?'

Freddie does a double take, his face contorted in alarm. 'No, no, not at all. Who told you that?' he rushes.

I point again to his surname sketched on the wall. 'Your name is popular amongst lords.'

He visibly relaxes and nods his head a little too hastily muttering: 'Ah, yes, yes, indeed, of course.'

Seeing him so unsettled intrigues me, distracts me from the throbbing in my chest. I can't help but press further: 'Why? What did you think I meant?'

He opens his mouth to speak but closes it again. A brief moment passes before he says anything. 'I owe you honesty, but I don't want this to change how you think of me. I should have told you sooner.'

It is my turn to look confused, a lump of anxiety forming in my throat. My mind rushes with all of the possibilities of what could possibly be coming next.

Noticing my discomfort, he grasps my hand in his. 'Promise me?' His eyes are beseeching, brows sloped, with anxious lines creasing his face. I nod nervously – although if I'm honest I'm unsure if I can keep it.

'I wasn't meant to be just a guardsman. My father . . . Well, my father is the colonel of the Grenadier Guards. As was his father before him and his father's father, and so on. The post has been passed down through the family, and as the eldest son waits, they become officers of the guard.' He looks at me cautiously, as if he's afraid that I'm going to run away. The gravity of what he's saying dawns on me: in aristocratic terms, his family is second only to the king. So, that's what 'family duties' meant . . . I subconsciously fiddle with the cheap nylon hem of my T-shirt.

'That was supposed to be my fate. I am the eldest, but I always saw the job as my . . . duty. It was never something I looked forward to. My father raised me to be a soldier, not his son. He has all of these expectations of me, but that's not . . . what I want for myself.'

I am still reeling from the blow of rejection, but I can't

help but be warmed by being invited into his confidence. Despite everything, I feel closer to him than ever.

'Anyway, my younger brother, Albert – Bertie – adored all things military from the moment he picked up one of the toy swords my father bought me for my tenth birthday. So, when he began to envy me for my inherited fate two months into my training, I went straight to my father and relinquished my post. Father had little choice but to offer it to Bertie. He was hideously disappointed and forced me to join as the lowest rank whilst he made other arrangements.' Freddie coughs into the last part and looks back at the scarred wall for a moment. 'I didn't mind that so much. It was never the army that scared me, just the expectation, the responsibility, I suppose.'

'Why would he be disappointed? At least one of his sons still fills the position,' I ask, the politics of nepotism not exactly my specialist subject.

'When my father passes, I will inherit his title. He was almost sick knowing that his title will be passed to a son who is no more than a number or statistic in the infantry. I think his exact words were . . .' I didn't think it possible, but Freddie puts on an accent even more cut-glass than his own and launches into an impression of his dad: '"Our family are leaders, have been for centuries, and shall be for centuries to come. You shall not prevent that with your cowardice. Think of your family."'

There's a familiarity in the way he jokes, the way his eyes flicker with a sadness that can't quite be covered up.

'Hold on . . . *title*?' The words almost don't make it out before I choke on them. All this time I have been embarrassing myself in front of someone so important his family are practically royals.

Freddie looks embarrassed, his eyes averted and shuffling back and forth on his shoes. 'The future Earl of Oxford at your service,' he mutters with a mock bow.

'You're having me on!' I splutter, but I already know he's telling the truth. It would all make sense: the boarding-school accent, the uptightness, the way the others treat him with an air of superiority despite officially outranking him.

'I'm afraid not.'

I don't know why it's this last admission that floors me. Even without his father's title, he's a viscount in his own right. 'My lord' is the way I should have been addressing him this whole time, as if I am some debutante crooning for an advantageous match at an Austenian ball. Except I wouldn't be at the ball. I would be his maid, his servant, washing his dishes and making his bed.

We don't only exist in different tax brackets, we live in entirely different worlds, and I vastly underestimated how different we are. It's no wonder he doesn't think of me like that; I really did never have a chance. Not that I ever really believed that the man who looks as though he was sculpted by gods would fancy the girl who is more akin to the artist's off cuts all melted together. He really did mean it when he said the 'problem' is that I am nothing like him. An earl can hardly be caught dead dating a commoner now, can he? Friends it is, then . . .

'Wow . . . so did you ever get a chance to meet the queen?' I joke, knowing that, whatever American tourists might think, it's rare even when you *do* have connections.

'A great many times. She was my godmother,' he replies with a soft smile, no hint of irony. My face drops at this unexpected curveball. When my gawping continues and I am unable to form any actual words, he chuckles and says: 'Some of my favourite times as a child were spent in her gardens. I always felt lucky to know her. I think perhaps she's the reason that I enjoy being in the guards so much – she always talked of them so fondly. My father is an old friend of the king, so we still go back to at least one of those beautiful gardens every year.'

'You know . . . you might be the only British person who can actually answer in the affirmative when an American asks them if they had tea with the queen,' I blurt in my astonishment.

Freddie laughs. 'She always had the best biscuits too.' He talks as if he's just continuing my joke, but I know he's deadly serious.

'Wait . . . Does this mean that I am supposed to curtsey to you?'

'Please don't. I felt so bad when my father made the lads at work salute me that I begged them not to.'

'Good, because I have the elegance of a chicken having an asthma attack so I'm sure I'd manage to headbutt you or something if I had to do that.'

'Ha! Well *that* I would like to see.'

'Hmm . . .' I squint my eyes at him in a playful glare.

'So, you don't think any different of me?' Freddie asks, suddenly reverting back to seriousness.

'Well . . . I think that your family have a title that I thought only existed in Jane Austen novels. And I am also

266

now *very* conscious of the fact that pretty much all of my clothes are from the charity shop. But other than that, I am very flattered that someone so important would like to be my friend.'

Before I can see the response on his face, he has me pulled back into his arms in another crushing hug. Caught by surprise, my eyes are wide, arms stuck at my sides – I have no say in how long this hug may last. And I don't know how long I can make this 'friends' thing last either.

Chapter 18

It's almost light before we leave the Beauchamp Tower. I go first, leaving him and the redundant lamp lurking behind the door, awaiting the perfect time to sneak away. My mind swims and if I try and think about any one part of the evening too much, I just might cry. Focusing instead on getting home with enough time for a brief nap before work, I practically run through the courtyard. In lieu of the crowing of a cockerel, I hear Duke and the deep timbre of his caw serving as an alarm clock for the rest of the Tower.

Each step I take up to my bedroom creaks obnoxiously, practically screaming 'she's been up to something' to my dad downstairs. Being quiet probably won't make much difference anyway; I'm sure it won't be long before someone in the control room calls to snitch on me for coming back at half past three in the morning.

With a nap as fast as a wink, although still dream-infested, I am back out in the courtyard once again. My work uniform is creased in places I didn't even know could get creased and each pace I take feels sluggish and slow. My eyelids are so heavy that opening them feels like a chore and I walk most of the way under the White Tower with them closed. I'm sure it's the physical manifestation of the weight of Freddie's honesty last night, and I make a mental note to vent to Lucie and the others later.

The smacking of boots against the floor startles my eyes open wide and I look over to the guard's post accusingly. They have a habit of doing that, standing to attention when you least expect it, emitting an echoing boom, which is amplified by the architecture and sure to disconcert everyone within a hundred-metre radius. You can quite often see the glimmer of a smirk on their faces after an unsuspecting tourist lets out a little yelp. Standing still for so long, they look for any kind of entertainment and getting the opportunity to shout at or scare a naïve audience comes in at the top of that list.

Of course, when my gaze lands on today's guard, it is Freddie who is in possession of that oh so familiar smirk. I can't help but go over to him, and throw him my own wry smile, bending down into a wobbly curtsey before him, and pretending to hold up my many skirts. From the side of my mouth, I mutter: 'Bastard.'

He can't contain the little puff of air that slips between his lips in a muted laugh. Trying to reclaim the discipline of his face, Freddie twitches under the fur of his bearskin and gives me a curt nod that I return, before turning on my heel and continuing on my commute.

*

'We thought *you'd* died,' Kevin sneers as I walk through the door.

'Thought or hoped?' I say under my breath.

'I would have wanted to die after your little date,' Samantha jeers from behind the boss. She doesn't look at me, but over to Andy who covers her mouth to let out a giggle.

'Me too! Imagine getting caught by all of those guards! I'd have dropped down dead on the spot,' Andy pitches in, covering up her poisonous words with another innocent laugh.

'Come on, girls . . .' Kevin says, and for a second I wonder if he's actually going to behave like a manager for once. 'We should all be more shocked that Princess Maggie is actually going on dates. *How* did you manage that one?' he finishes, seemingly less worried about trying to disguise his insults.

'The cheek to have done it right on your own doorstep. What's the phrase? Oh . . . don't shit where you eat.' Andy puts a finger into her open mouth and pretends to gag.

'Next time do it in the bushes and actually come in to work. I am never covering for you again.' Samantha's bemused expression shifts into one that finally reflects the rotten core she carries around with her. All I think when I notice it, is how well she'd play a demon in a horror film.

By now, I've heard enough. Well, I'd heard enough before any of them actually started talking, but now is when I finally decide to uproot myself and flee to my desk.

'Oh, and Margaret, you're on safe duty for a week,' Kevin

shouts after me – Andy and Samantha still screeching beside him.

I roll my eyes with my back to them all. It hurts, but the only way I can stand up to them is to not cry. Their hatefulness isn't worth my tears, and I shouldn't give them that satisfaction.

Freddie is waiting for me when I can finally leave the stifling office, and I'm pleased that he's keeping true to his word – no disappearing, no awkwardness, no part-time Freddie. I give him the first smile I have been able to muster since I saw him this morning.

'You, sir, are going to be the death of me. You could have given me a heart attack!' I joke as I shove the bag of money into his chest playfully. He accepts it with a laugh. 'Anyway, how did you know I'd be on safe duty again?'

'That "curtsey" of yours . . .' He mimes the inverted commas with one hand, clinging to the heavy bag with the other. 'It took you at least twenty minutes to get back up again. There's no way you were on time after that performance.' He lets out a hearty laugh that vibrates all the way down my spine. 'I'm pretty sure my grandmother manages it better, and she has two metal hips.'

'Well, that is the first and last curtsey you'll ever get from me.' I poke him in the ribs as we walk, and he cringes, turning his smiling face towards me.

'Good riddance.' He returns my contact by tapping his elbow against mine.

'I didn't think you'd be able to handle seeing the ghosts again. You aren't going to get all scared, are you?'

'I have no idea what you are talking about.' He smirks. '*I* am part of His Majesty's Armed Forces . . . I cannot feel fear.'

'Pah!' I exclaim. 'This time I'm going to record you and you can show His Majesty the video over your Christmas dinner if you like?'

We reach the White Tower before I can even clock where I am. We've walked the entire way, practically leaning into each other, in a world of our own. A nervous pang makes me hesitate for a moment, but Freddie opens the door and places his hand lightly on my back to guide me in. His fingertips tap a slow, playful rhythm just above my bum and any thoughts of anyone or anything else dissolve.

'Tell me about *your* family,' he says, as we enter into the dark exhibition.

'What would you like to know? My story certainly isn't as exciting as yours.'

'Everything! Parents, grandparents, siblings.'

'Well, it's just me and Dad at home now. My mum . . . she passed away a couple of years ago – just after I graduated. My parents were divorcing but she got sick right after she left. It didn't take long for us to lose her.'

'I'm sorry to hear that . . .' he says quietly, his eyes expressive in the dim light. 'Were you close?'

'I grew up a pad brat, so we lived on military bases across Europe, moving every six months or so. You couldn't be closer than us two to be honest. She was the only person that I didn't have to say goodbye to every couple of months.' I notice my accent growing even stronger as I reminisce about my childhood. 'Once I moved to uni, she . . . couldn't

272

handle it. Her life was so isolated, spending most of her years as a single mum, hardly making friends before she would have to leave them again. I think her body just gave up, followed her mind, and we lost her not long after that . . .'

Freddie places a hand on my shoulder and gives it a supportive squeeze. 'Sorry. You don't have to say anything else. I didn't mean to upset you.' It's not until he says this that I realise I'm crying. A salty droplet drips onto my lip, and I hurry to wipe them away.

'It's okay. It's nice to talk about her. I think you'd have liked her. She used to make the best roast dinners you've ever tasted. Her lamb . . . ugh, I'd do anything to have one of her lamb dinners again. She'd bake her roasties in duck fat until you could audibly hear them crunch when you bit into them. And, oh . . . her gravy! It was none of that watery crap that ends up just drowning your vegetables. It was thick, heavenly stuff with little bits of meat in it. I could drink it!'

'Please tell me she gave you her recipe? It's been a good few years since I had a proper roast dinner.'

'I think I'd end up killing you off if I tried cooking. The best meal Dad and I can conjure up between us is pie and chips. All frozen, of course.'

He shakes his head, teasing disappointment.

'Don't you have a chef who could deliver one to you on a silver platter if you click your fingers?' I add, smiling.

'I wish. The closest I come to that is the chef at Buckingham Palace when we go on guard there. He is an *extremely* friendly Italian chap called Christian whose

273

dinners always come with a side order of a slap on the arse and a questionable wink. The food isn't even worth it, to be honest. The number of times I have had to order pizzas to the palace is dire.'

'The guardsmen can order pizza to Buckingham Palace?' I ask, my eyebrows raised.

'Maggie, *you* order pizza to the Tower of London. Why is that a surprise?'

'Oh yeah.' Both of us laugh now. 'Should we?' I ask.

'What . . . Order a pizza? Right now?'

'Yeah, why not?'

'Why not?' Freddie agrees. 'I'll even pay, *if* I don't have to go all of the way into the cellar.'

'I'll take a pepperoni.' I outstretch my hand for him to shake and he squeezes it tenderly.

He follows me to the cellar door, Deliveroo already open on his phone. I take the stairs alone with trepidation. 'Hi. Hello. Good evening . . .' I say to the walls with each step.

'Maggie!' Freddie calls from the door, which is propped open with one of his shoulders as he leans against it.

Keeping my focus on the task ahead, I reply with only a 'Hmm?'

'Which address do I send it to? Is it literally just the Tower of London?'

'If only it was that easy.' I turn around on the stairs and peer up at him, almost submerged in the darkness at the bottom. 'You're better off just putting the Tower Hill Starbucks in and I'll just have to walk out and get it.'

'Starbucks? How is it easier to find a Starbucks than a medieval castle?'

'You tell me! I once had a driver call me up *ten minutes* after his arrival asking: "Which building is the Tower of London?" I genuinely thought that a big old fortress in the middle of London would be hard to miss but obviously not.' He lets out a little snort that echoes in the doorframe.

Turning back around, I resume the task at hand. Fearful of another accident, I tread carefully down the last few steps and make it onto the floor before the safe without any semblance of a fall. Going through all of the regular motions, I safely stow the money away, before beginning my ascent. A breeze catches in my hair and spreads goose bumps up and down my arms. Only pausing to shiver, I make it all of the way up the stairs without having to flee in terror.

'See! I don't know what you're such a wimp about.' I poke Freddie in the chest as I reach him. 'Thank you, guys, have a lovely evening,' I shout into the cellar before slamming the door shut.

A pair of hands grab at me suddenly. Instinctively, I let out a scream, but it more closely resembles the sound of a stuck pig. My whole insides feel as if they have lurched either up or downwards and my heart is pumping so hard it feels as if it could cause a tsunami in my bloodstream.

'Boo!' Freddie's deep voice resounds in my ear.

'You little . . .' I swing round with such force I'm sure I could have knocked him clean over if his quick reflexes hadn't dodged my clumsy limbs first. He doubles over in laughter, his hands spread across his knees, as he pulls his

275

eyes tightly closed, wrinkles fanning across his face. The pitch of his laugh only heightens with each wheezing breath, and I can't help but join him in his euphoria. Each movement of his body is poetic. The shaking of his shoulders, the way he flings his head back, spilling his curls back from his forehead, and they burst from him like the crown of a Roman god. His laughter finally breaks with a few deep breaths and his cheeks glow red with a youthful blush.

Unable to take my eyes off of him, I simply stare, my cheeks aching from my smile as his chest heaves up and down with the exertion of his little prank. Breathless, he sweeps forward and grips my shoulders.

'Who's the wimp now, hmm?' A little laugh still clings to his words.

I push out my bottom lip in a childish pout and grumble: 'Arsehole.'

He's closer to me than I first thought, and I can feel his hot breath against my mouth. I'm sure he is normally much taller than this, but somehow we are face to face. Irises the colour of Neptune skim across my face with such intense interest it's as though he is counting each of my freckles individually. The seconds tick painfully slowly as each peach fuzz hair on my face is subject to his gaze. In turn, I track the six o'clock shadow down his jawline, repressing the urge to kiss the line on his neck where it ends.

His gentle fingertips push my cascading curtain of hair back away from my face, as his other hand cups my chin and cheek. Instinctively, I push myself further into him, his hand hiding the blush that spreads across my face as my breasts skim against his chest.

He's going to kiss me. I'm sure he is. He's leaning in . . . I am wrapped up in everything Freddie. I can't control myself as my eyes flutter closed and I wait for the contact my body is longing for.

It never comes. The abusively loud ring tone of Freddie's phone results in us both jumping backwards as if we are teenagers caught kissing behind the bike sheds at school. He clears his throat before answering, actively avoiding looking at me.

'Yes. Yes. You're here? Okay. Right. We'll be right there.' His voice, sharp and staccato, echoes around the room. It suddenly feels as if the temperature has dropped, and I draw my arms across my chest.

'Pizza,' Freddie says to me as he shoves his phone back into his pocket. He turns to leave but I catch his shoulder lightly. Turning back to face me, he still refuses to meet my gaze, instead distracting himself with a cobweb or two in the corner.

'I'll have to go. You wouldn't be able to get back in. You put the Starbucks, right?' My voice sounds a little hoarse. Freddie nods.

I have to brush past him to leave. My body rubs against his, causing him to visibly flinch away from me. Fighting the urge to look back at him, I rush out of the Tower and back down Water Lane. My shoes thunder against the cobbles, and my chest heaves with heavy breaths.

What the hell is going on? What *was* that? The almost kiss. The way he pressed against me. Then how he shunned

277

me, closed off. None of it makes sense. How can he explicitly tell me just last night that we are nothing more than friends and then try to kiss me not even twelve hours later? Perhaps he was possessed.

Bob smiles at me from his little hut at the main gate. I prop my cheery façade back on.

'All right, Maggie. Off out, are ya?' he says, jangling his ring of keys over the half door.

'Just a takeaway tonight sadly. In theory I should be straight back in, but you know what it's like.'

'Bloody useless is what it is. I was stood 'ere waiting three-quarters of an hour for Lunchbox to come back in after chasing his Chinese all over the city earlier.'

'Lunchbox? Chasing? Bloody hell, he must have been hungry.'

Bob chuckles. 'I'm pretty sure I saw him cracking open a tub of chow mein going down Mint Street. Poor Sandra probably only saw a couple of prawn crackers by the time he got home.'

'Brilliant.' I giggle. 'On that note . . . I'd better hunt down my pizza.'

Bob limps to the gate and unlocks it for me. He too is a veteran, although didn't quite qualify to be a Yeoman himself. He was a paratrooper, shot in the leg in Afghanistan and had to be discharged before he did enough years. They all see him as one of them though; from the banter to the housing, this place is essentially a retirement home for soldiers, sailors and airmen who aren't quite ready to hang up their uniforms.

When I reach Starbucks, it's no real surprise that the

delivery driver is nowhere to be seen. I also realise that I have zero way of contacting the driver, having left in such a flustered rush that I failed to think about the fact that it is all on Freddie's phone.

After a few minutes I decide to walk up Tower Hill to scout the main road for any delivery drivers who look a little perplexed. I shoot Bob an exaggerated eye roll as he watches me pass the gate again.

'That'll teach you for being lazy!' he shouts after me, and, throwing the middle finger over my shoulder, I hear him chuckle.

It takes me twenty minutes of marching back and forth around the bounds of the Tower to find the delivery driver, who is sat on a slab of concrete beside All Hallows by the Tower – the little church whose bells toll three minutes earlier than all of the other bells across the city. He's smoking a cigarette, his bicycle propped up against the wall of a restaurant.

'Hi! Is that for Freddie?'

'Huh?' he says. His face is gaunt, and he is almost as thin as his bike. A prickly shaving rash covers most of his cheeks and he rubs it absentmindedly.

'The pizza?'

'Some kid thought it was funny to order to Starbucks and put a note wanting me to take it into that place.' He points to the Tower behind me.

'That was me. I live there,' I say sheepishly.

He scoffs, 'Yeah, right. No one lives in there.'

'Er . . . but I do. Quite a few people do actually.'

He laughs a little too loudly and, when he notices that

I am not joking, switches to grumbling incoherently. The scrawny man stubs his cigarette out on the concrete and walks over to his bike.

'There you go.' He shoves the pizza box towards me. I take it quickly, reluctantly thanking him.

Bob does a sarcastic cheer when I finally ask him to let me back in. He looks at his watch. 'Twenty minutes . . . a new record that. It might actually still be lukewarm.'

I slap my hand against the bottom of the box, the grease transferring onto my skin instantly. 'Nope, stone cold. They probably didn't even bother cooking it.'

We both laugh as I wave goodbye.

Freddie comes pacing down Water Lane just as I pass the Bell Tower. His heavy boots strike the cobbles with such force that I question whether he could crack them, and as I get closer, I notice that his face is lined in a deep frown. He only notices me once he reaches Traitors' Gate, and he stops dead in his tracks. His shoulders loosen, and he visibly releases a breath, although his regimented posture remains.

I give him an awkward wave, raising the pizza above my head triumphantly. He jogs the rest of the distance between us, his boots now silent and he reaches me in no time.

Taking the pizza from me, he straightens again. 'Are you okay?'

'Worried I'd run off with your pizza, eh?'

'Something like that,' he says quietly.

'Well . . . Luckily for you, it is clap cold, so I wasn't as tempted.'

We make our way back up into the White Tower and sit down on parallel cannons. The box of pizza lies open in between us both, with Freddie encouraging me to take the first slice. Ripping the cheese away from the rest of the slices, I try to drop the end into my mouth, but the grease has dampened the bread and it flops around awkwardly until I can finally catch it in my teeth. Freddie smiles and shakes his head in the way I am becoming so familiar with and takes a slice for himself.

He shifts his fingers uncomfortably down the crust, a slight grimace hijacking his smile. He looks at his own hands and then rubs them against his trousers, as if to rid them of invisible dirt.

'Don't tell me you usually eat pizza with a knife and fork?'

A guilty look flashes in his eyes. 'There are some habits from my childhood that I haven't quite managed to shake.'

'Wait there . . .' I say, deciding against mocking him this time.

I scuttle down a few of the gloomy corridors until I reach one of the staff break rooms. Grabbing a pair of plates and one set of cutlery – in my mind it is still blasphemy to eat pizza with a knife and fork – I hurry back to the cannon exhibit. Breathing a little too heavily from my little jog, I hand them to Freddie, whose face colours lightly.

He gives a nervous laugh. 'You didn't have to do that! I would have gotten over myself. I can eat just fine out in the field on exercise when I have been crawling around in dirt and without access to running water for a week. But my head just gets the better of me when I'm back in the real world. Thank you, though.'

'That's okay. It's just something else that makes you interesting, even if this is quite possibly the oddest thing I have ever witnessed.' He's sat on the barrel of the cannon, his back hunched over a tiny plate of pizza. The knife and fork are dwarfed in his hands as his arms bend awkwardly upwards. Both of us take note of the peculiar scene and laugh at ourselves. I'm sure I look just as strange. The grease of the pizza does me no favours, having coated my hands, as I keep having to stop myself from slipping down from my own cannon. Everything feels just right, yet I can't quite shake the desire to grab him by the collar and finally close the gap that neither of us can seem to cross.

'Tell me more about her,' Freddie says after a comfortable silence. 'Your mother, I mean. If you'd like to.'

I swallow the last mouthful of pizza and smile. 'Hmmm, where to begin? Okay so she almost exclusively made us listen to old Nineties house music in the car. You know, the sort of music that you would only hear in clubs in Ibiza. Every car ride became a rave; she even had glow sticks in the glove compartment. I still have no idea why she loved it so much – she never went to the clubs, or even partied that much. She would just say that music made her happy. She was so disappointed when I grew up loving melancholy ballads, and even more so when I turned my attentions to angry rock songs . . . Somehow, she'd always manage to drown my music out with her own CDs, and we'd end up dancing together in the kitchen.'

I can see her now, twirling on the tiles as she sang the

wrong lyrics to a song that she had played a thousand times. Her hair would swirl with her, the soft curls that she spent her life trying to tame were set free and stuck up in every feral direction. Small hands would clasp mine as she'd pull me into her whirlwind, drawing out my teenage angst, my self-consciousness until I too was as carefree as a bird.

Almost forgetting I had company, Freddie reminds me of his presence as he leans forward and swipes his thumb gently across the corner of my mouth. I blush as he licks it clean.

'Sorry, tomato sauce. It kept distracting me,' he mumbles awkwardly, blushing too, as if he hadn't realised what he was doing until he did it. 'I wish I could have met her.'

'I wish you had too.' And I do. I wish she had known him instead of Bran, that she could see how I light up when I'm close to him, how just catching a glimpse of him in the corner of my eye makes my body come alive, like a flurry of blossom caught in a whirlwind in my stomach.

'My mother once taught Bertie and I how to ballroom dance. Together of course, so she made us take it in turns as to who would play the role of the woman. She could be very severe, but she loved to dance too, like your mother. Sometimes I'd catch her, alone, dancing as quietly as she could in the sitting room. I am sure she was training us up so she could dance with us when we grew tall enough.'

'And do you?'

'Bertie was far better than I ever was . . . Father put a stop to me dancing eventually. He would take me on long hikes and runs to prepare me for the army instead. I danced with her once, when he was away, but my brother is her favourite ballroom partner. Albert has always been much closer with our parents than I am.'

'Can you teach me?' I ask in a moment of impulse. Just the way he talks longingly about dancing makes it clear that he misses it. With a glimmer in his eye, he accepts and stands up to offer me his hand. Leading me into the open space in the centre of the exhibits, we have an audience of ancient weapons, bodiless armour, and wooden horses.

'Wait, can we even do it without music?' I falter, nervous at being so close to him again.

He simply nods as he draws my body towards his. A practised hand snakes around my waist, the other chassés up my arm until it settles in mine. Despite all his previous reassurances, I can't help but think about my sweaty palms. He catches my eye and, seeming to read my mind, his grip tightens. Gently, his hand around my waist guides me forward until my figure rests against his.

Friends. *Friends, Maggie*, I have to remind myself as my heart donkey kicks in my chest.

Freddie hums as he sways us to his own improvised tune. His face is close to mine and the vibration of his humming travels through me like an electric shock. I submit myself to him as he moves us both together fluidly as if we are one being. We don't take a single step, only lean into each other. I sigh into his hold.

We stay like that for a while, until his song diminuendos to an end. Without wasting any time, his slow dance tune transforms into a more upbeat jig. With a wide smile, he pulls away from me, only taking one of my hands with him as he too transitions into a more lackadaisical dancing style.

'I can't admit to knowing any house music, I'm afraid,' he says interrupting his sporadic beat, as he spins me, deftly catching my arm as I stumble against him.

His laughter becomes our music as we dance like a drunken aunt and uncle at the end of a wedding.

Mid way through our air guitar-off the creaking of the White Tower door startles us into silence. We stop dead. Freddie looks to me as I look to him, his expression now absent of humour. I feel the colour drain from my face as the familiar churning settles back into my stomach.

I mouth the word 'Ghost?' half hoping that it actually is a member of the disturbed dead, rather than a real-life human.

He shakes his head slowly and places a finger to his lips to encourage my silence. My chest heaves from our exercise and I try to control my breathing before it runs away from me. Freddie, of course, shows not even a hint of exertion; he is calm, controlled.

Taking me again by the hand, he crouches as he leads me across the room. The old wooden floors groan from both ends of the room as my heavy feet and those of our intruder inelegantly creep around. Freddie and I duck behind the horses and watch from under its wooden belly the boots of a beefeater, who scours the room with the light from his torch licking up and down the armoury. You can practically see the cogs turning in Freddie's head as he scans the area, planning our escape.

My heart is well and truly lodged in my throat as our little pizza night has quickly turned into some military operation. I can't help but think of the Prince Griffin of Wales, who once tried to escape the White Tower in the thirteenth century. He tied his bedsheets together out of the window, but it didn't quite go as well for him as it does in the movies. The sheets snapped and because he had dressed in his armour, he landed straight on his head and snapped his neck.

'We're not going out of the window, right?' I whisper as Freddie leads me forwards again, countering the movements of the beefeater.

He looks back at me, perplexed.

'No, right, yes, of course we wouldn't. Stupid thought.'

He silently laughs, shaking his head.

My knees are crippled from the amount of crouched walking we have done – about five yards to be exact – and the sight of the door is even more of a relief when we near it.

'Follow me,' he mouths before counting to three on his fingers. Distracted by the latest addition of a signet ring on his little finger, I miss the cue and he practically yanks my arm out of the socket as he makes a dash for the door. Letting out an involuntary squeal, I accidentally alert our pursuer to our position.

'Oi! You! Stop right there!' It's almost a relief when I hear Lunchbox's voice call out. There are few people in this world that I can outrun, but luckily Lunchbox is one of them. Plus, with the help of Freddie whipping me out of the door and down the stairs, I travel at a pace that is giving me motion sickness, so the old beefeater really does stand no chance. When we reach the bottom, Freddie pulls me under the staircase, placing his hand softly over my mouth as Lunchbox pounds down the stairs and off in the opposite direction. Only when he is out of sight does Freddie let go and we both laugh in unison.

'Are you okay?' Freddie asks between laughs.

'Yep! That was definitely a better plan than falling head-first out of the window.' His confused look returns. 'Prince Griffin? No? Never mind, I'll tell you another time.'

The golden clock chimes nine o'clock and Freddie excuses himself to prepare for the Ceremony of the Keys, leaving me to walk home. And though I'm alone, I feel less lonely than I have in years.

Chapter 19

For the next two weeks, I wake up every day to a text on my phone from Freddie. They range from a simple 'good morning' to photos of Riley asleep in precarious positions. Since the day we almost got caught by Lunchbox, Freddie and the rest of the Grenadiers have been in Wales for a training exercise. It started off as an exciting trip out of London into the countryside to actually do the jobs they had signed up for – or as close as you can come to warfare when you're firing a few guns and climbing up a hill in Brecon anyway. But after twenty-four hours Freddie sent me a rather un-Freddie text saying: *'We have done nothing but sit in the pissing rain and I am in clip.'*

Which is army speak for no longer functioning as a human and hurting even in parts of the body that no one knew existed.

I did almost stop to ask if Walker had stolen his phone until he sent me a drowned-rat-looking selfie, his face smeared in a mixture of cam cream and dirt, as though he had just climbed Everest. Yet, somehow, he still looked like he could be on the cover of *Vogue*. It really isn't fair.

I am almost certain that he has texted me at the same time each morning just to get me up for work. And his plan has succeeded. My body clock now wakes me up at 8.45 a.m. and instead of cursing at the world, the first thing I do is smile.

Even the ticket booth doesn't seem such torture when I know that by dinnertime, I will have heard from him again, even if I would prefer it if he was waiting for me outside.

Today, however, my phone has remained silent all day. It's not like he owes me communication, so I can't be annoyed, but it's amazing how a few words from the right person can make the days just a little easier. Instead of inevitably waiting by the phone, I take another wander down the steps into the pet cemetery when five rolls around.

The ravenmaster is in her usual spot, as though she hasn't left. Regina and Rex accompany her this time, with Edward keeping watch from the battlements.

'Evening.' I smile at each of them, and oddly enough they all give me a similar bob of the head in return, ravenmaster included.

We assume our usual positions side by side and settle into our silence. After a few moments, I slide my phone out of my pocket and sigh when it's only Cromwell's face that stares back at me, clear of any messages from any guardsmen.

'Patience, child,' the ravenmaster mutters. 'Your mind

runs at a thousand miles an hour. By the time you decide you're happy, you convince yourself to be miserable again.' Ouch. It seems the ravenmaster has forgotten to be ambiguous and cryptic and gone straight for the jugular. She isn't wrong, though. I put my phone away, sheepishly.

She pulls her normal trick and places a pile of seeds on each of my legs, binding me to the bench and encouraging my stillness. With only my breathing to focus on, I work hard to clear my mind of thoughts, which is far more difficult than it seems, and spend the next immeasurable bout of time filling my lungs and expelling my tense breath. Only after a robin and a pair of starlings clear my trousers am I permitted to move again, and I have to hand it to the ravenmaster, I *do* feel considerably more at ease. Clearly, she's more in tune with my emotions than I am.

After giving Rex, the neediest of the trio, a stroke of his beak, I excuse myself with a thank you to the ravenmaster and head back up the stairs. At the top, I come face to face with the heavy black doors of the Byward Postern. They are a daunting pair that have stood there since the thirteenth century, and it always fascinates me to think how many hands have pushed them open in that time. Once the royal entrance to the Tower, it was also the sally port, meaning that beyond those doors lies a dark passageway that soldiers would have used to sneak out of the Tower during a siege to ambush the enemy in the night. You'd think that with doors the size of two men it wouldn't be so effective, but it's so tucked away that most people forget it exists – and it still works as a hidden exit.

As I turn to leave, back over the tiny bridge that stretches across the moat and towards home, the doors swing open, and I am pulled in before I can even register what the hell is happening.

The sheltered passage is dark and damp, and it takes a short moment of erratic blinking for my eyes to adjust before I realise that the arms that ensnare my waist and the hand that covers my mouth belong to a certain curly-haired guardsman. Knowing that I am not being kidnapped or ambushed should have made my heart rate settle, but seeing his face again only makes it pound harder.

Freddie releases me and I immediately wrap my hands around his neck in an excited hug. I can't help but do a little jump against him as he returns his arms to my waist and buries his head in the hair against my neck.

'When did you get back?!' I excitedly whisper, grateful that, in this dark corner of the Tower, the need to be secretive and put on a modest show for the cameras isn't necessary. I wonder how many forbidden lovers have hidden away in here to steal a kiss or spend a precious moment alone. Not that Freddie and I are lovers, of course. Just two friends reuniting away from the scrutinising gaze of CCTV cameras.

'This afternoon,' he replies with a smile. 'I thought I'd surprise you.'

I practically throw myself at him again and hold him close. I am half expecting him to shake me off, to move away, but he doesn't. Instead, he relaxes into my touch.

'Do you realise how difficult it is to get signal to text you from the arse end of nowhere every day?' He laughs.

'Yesterday I had to get on Mo's shoulders just to be able to send you a message.'

'Well, I very much appreciated it. I haven't had to go down in that cellar for two whole weeks now because your texts have been my alarm clock. I'm almost missing little Barbara.'

'Barbara?'

'The ghost. I named her just after you left so she wouldn't scare me so much.'

Freddie shakes his head with a smile and pushes my hair back from my face in a motion that feels so natural we barely take notice of him doing it.

'You know you could have texted me to meet you! You didn't have to kidnap me.'

'It keeps you on your toes. And like I said, I wanted to surprise you. But I definitely need to give you some self-defence lessons – you're far too easy to kidnap. I was expecting you to put up a bit of a fight at least.'

'Well, we *are* in the Tower of London. Who knew what I was up against? It would be futile to try and punch a ghost. If you wanted me to beat you up, you should have just asked.' I finish my point by giving him a playful punch on the shoulder. Acting as if I have just shot him, Freddie jolts backwards, his face contorting in faux pain.

'I've missed you.' His face suddenly is serious as he makes his confession.

I mask the bolt of electricity that shoots through my body, leaving a tingling path in its wake. 'After only two weeks! I must be great company.'

'Or Riley, Walker and Mo's company is *so* bad that yours

becomes better by default?' Freddie's light-heartedness returns, although he avoids my eyes. 'I, er, actually had something to ask you.'

My breath catches in my throat. What if he's changed his mind? What if he doesn't just want to be my friend anymore? Is he going to ask me on a date? My cheeks grow hot.

'Walker would not shut up all the time on exercise about this little challenge thing he set you and I remember you told me that after I ruined the last one you were throwing in the towel.'

I dare not breathe in case one tiny interruption from me would sway him from his path.

'Well, there's this thing, this gala, that I have to go to next week, and I wondered if you'd like to come? You could tell Walker that it's your fifth and final date. You know, to shut him up. Don't feel like you have to or anything. It's raising funds for the restoration of the castles across Scotland. I thought that maybe . . . perhaps it might be something you're interested in anyway? I don't know very much about it myself, but there are a few people going that I am being . . . encouraged to network with, for work, and . . . I wanted to make it up to you. I truly am sorry, Maggie. Plus, I thought it would make the socialising a little easier if I went with a friend.' He chokes out the last few words, and they're rushed, as if they've taken all of his effort to say.

'I . . .' I start uneasily. A fake date. I try to hide my disappointment, but I know my face swims with it. Of course, he would never date me seriously – the guy seems to drop the F-word into every conversation we have. Friends, friends, friends. As soon as I accept that the easier this will be.

The thought of castles, though, Scottish ones at that, makes me want to take his hand and march him there right now. But there's a huge difference between living in the Tower of London, and everyone believing you're a class above everyone else, and actually meeting those people who belong in a royal palace. Yes, we have celebrities and people with fancy titles in and out of this place all of the time. But it is run by the working classes, by veterans who spent years working their way through their respective branches of the military, gaining each promotion because of what they do, rather than who they are. We all live in a castle, but it is just another posting. The Yeomen haven't changed; they don't think they're better than anyone else, and they certainly don't get any more money. No one has been to private school, and most still work paycheque to paycheque.

Freddie's world is entirely different. Someone like me, with a northern accent, a wardrobe full of charity shop dresses and absolutely no idea about table manners just doesn't slot in easily.

'It's just, well, are you sure you want to bring someone like me?' It comes out before I can stop it, and his face pangs with a look of confusion.

'What do you mean someone like you?' he interrogates defensively.

'I *mean*, I know I live in a fancy place like this, but there's more class and wealth in your pinkie finger than there is in me.' I grow hot and itch at the collar of my blouse.

'Oh, Maggie . . .' he says with a sigh. 'First of all, I know plenty of people with more money than sense who are very far from classy. Just because you're not a millionaire doesn't mean that you don't belong. I think that you are *brilliant*. I would be honoured to bring "someone like you".' He exaggerates, miming the inverted commas that punctuate the sarcasm of his tone.

A smile stretches onto my face cautiously. As long as I am with Freddie, I know it will all be okay – after all, he offered to defend me against the paranormal, how much worse can a few rich people be?

'Okay!' I agree. 'What's the dress code?'

Chapter 20

I should not have worn a thong. I stand at Monument, shuffling side to side in an attempt to move the string somewhere that doesn't feel like I should be able to taste it. Freddie promised to pick me up just out of the eyeline of the Tower at the two-hundred-foot column that memorialises the Great Fire of London. As I wait, I hum 'London's Burning' under my breath, just like Mum used to when I was a child.

The dress that I hurriedly bought yesterday, and which almost gave me a heart attack when the cashier told me the price, clings to my hips and legs. I keep having to remind myself that a little rope burn in my arse crack is better than everyone seeing every seam of my granny pants. The fabric is the silky kind where everyone would be able to see if you've gone to the bathroom and dried your hands on the skirt. Emerald in colour, I like to think it draws out the green of my eyes.

Usually punctual, to a degree where I am sure he has

the ability to appear out of thin air, Freddie is surprisingly late. Everyone who walks past is either a tourist or a white-collar worker headed to the train station for their stupidly long commute home, or to the pub to brag to their colleagues. Stood by myself and dressed in a way that is far outside of my comfort zone, I fumble with the clutch bag I managed to borrow from Richie's wife, Trixie, next door. My hair is thick with product, and each time I nervously fiddle with the ends, or run my hands through it, I find myself having to unstick a patch that has gone rather crispy.

'Come on, Freddie,' I say under my breath, rocking on the heels that have made me so tall I am starting to think I may suffer with vertigo. They're already cutting into my toes and the arches of my feet are getting dangerously close to cramping. Just as I begin toying with the idea of sitting on the pavement, the discomfort of my shoes a higher priority than getting London muck all over my expensive dress, a car finally pulls up on the road in front of me. It is a sleek stallion of a car with a glossy paint job and blacked-out windows. It can only either be Freddie, the rich heir, or some high-class London drug dealer, and I am very relieved when it's the guardsman who slips out. Although today's uniform is a black dinner suit that looks classy, it also does a lot to show off the contours of his arse.

Freddie is smiling already, matching his perfectly white teeth to his perfectly white shirt, which I'm surprised to see he has left unbuttoned at the top, no tie in sight.

'I am so, so terribly sorry that I'm late,' he says when

he reaches me, pressing his hands to my bare arms instinctively and giving them a little squeeze.

'It's okay.' I smile.

'If I am being totally honest, I know your track record of being punctual is a little patchy, so I thought it best to tell you to be here a little earlier.' He winks, and I shove him as best I can when I am still in his tender embrace.

'I'll have you know I am very punctual when it comes to doing the things that I actually want to do,' I say with a faux huff, making him laugh. Freddie holds me at arm's length then and stares at me for a little while; though he initially focuses on my face, his instinct betrays him, and he does a quick scan down my body, making the both of us blush.

'You, erm . . .' He coughs. 'You look . . . very pretty.' And with that, he releases my arms and opens the door to the car for me to climb in. I bump my head on the top as I bend down in my heels, but the blow is surprisingly soft. Only when I'm sat comfortably in my seat do I notice Freddie pull his hand away and close the door; he had pre-empted my clumsiness and was there yet again to stop me getting hurt. I'm grateful for the heavily tinted windows that mean Freddie can't see me as he shuffles around the other side of the wide car. He slides in far more elegantly than I did but I put that down to practice.

'Thank you, Carol, we're ready to go now.'

'No problem, sir, madam.' The chauffeur looks to both of us through the rear-view mirror and then pulls away smoothly.

We get a little way down the road before Freddie takes out a little wooden box. Popping the little hook out, he lifts up the lid to reveal a selection of silk handkerchiefs and ties in every colour imaginable. He selects two different colours of green and lifts them up towards me. Squinting, he moves each fabric closer to my dress before settling on one that is almost identical in colour. He folds it with brilliant dexterity and slides the handkerchief into his top pocket after he has tied the tie neatly. We sit in silence, me blushing, him perfectly composed, both matching in dress. He is taking his role as my fake date far more seriously than I ever thought he would. I shimmy down into my heated seat and try to hide my smile.

We aren't travelling for long before we pull up outside of a rather fancy hotel. The concierge greets us as he opens the car door before Carol has come to a complete stop.

'Good evening, madam,' says the man, who looks not unlike the penguin waiters in *Mary Poppins*, with his neat bow tie and the same face that seems to be worn by all of the others in the same uniform.

He offers me his hand and I am whisked out of the car and up the carpeted marble stairs before I can check if Freddie is following behind. I can barely acknowledge the beauty of the hotel as the overly attentive staff encourage me down what feels like a conveyor belt of services. Someone takes my denim jacket from over my arm, and someone else hands me a programme of sorts, whilst another fills my other hand with a flute of sparkling wine. They each accompany their gestures with words, but the overstimulation of it all means I can only think for long enough to give them each a swift nod.

My chest grows tighter and tighter as bodies swirl

around me in the lobby. Soft piano music plays in the background, but it's almost drowned out by chatter and false laughter, and it tips me over the edge. Noticing a bathroom, tucked away from the smooth perfection of the room, I slip into it before another suited employee can corner me.

To my dismay, the bathroom is equally overwhelming. If I were staying at this hotel and they offered me this as my room, I would be more than pleased. The ceiling is draped in a thick creamy material, and each alcove is embellished by golden carvings of vines and flowers. The mirrors are enclosed in gold frames like the ones you'd find in the national gallery, so when you look into it, you see yourself as a portrait. Mine is a portrait of a woman out of place. My hair is already askew, the top sprouting tiny frizzy curls, and the rest sticks to the sprinkling of sweat on my face and along my back. Red cheeks, red lips, red chest; I am flushed from head to toe, and I visibly breathe as if it is laborious to do so. A patch of sweat leaks onto the fabric of my dress and I sigh into my hands. I shouldn't have come. I haven't even made it into the damned party yet – I've been defeated by a foyer.

I dampen a towel and swipe it across my face and chest. Not one of those scratchy paper towels that disintegrate as soon as you rub it on yourself – but a literal towel. I am far too easily impressed. There's not much I can do for my hair at this point except drag my damp hands down it and hope the new curl pattern is better-looking than this one.

Taking a few deep breaths, I step back out into the lobby and immediately feel like I've just stepped out onto a busy road. Bodies fly past me, and I close my eyes for a moment. If ever I was anxious, Mum used to make me play these silly distraction games.

'Your mind can only focus fully on one thing at a time,' she would say. 'Go on, A to Z of boys' names.'

A . . . Angus. B . . . Billy. C . . . Callum. D . . . David. E . . . Elliot. F . . .

'Maggie, there you are! I've been looking everywhere for you.'

Freddie.

He doesn't go to touch me like normal, but instead stands at a distance, far enough away that I wouldn't be able to reach him if I tried. But he still scrunches up his eyebrows, terrible at hiding his concern.

'Sorry, had to stop off for a nervous wee.' I laugh. He gives a quick smile, clearly fake and gone almost as quickly as it came.

'Come on, I want to introduce you to a few people.' He strides off ahead of me, and I have to duck and dive through the busy hotel to keep up with his long legs, all whilst trying my hardest not to sweat even more obviously than I already have.

Freddie turns to give me one final smile before he pushes open two quilted doors, plunging me headfirst into a tsunami of grandeur. Women are dotted around the room wearing no less than actual tiaras and long gowns of silk. The men who funnel around these regal beings are in suits much like Freddie's, thick rich fabrics perfectly tailored to their wearer. I feel cheap wearing the dress that I purged my bank account for.

Leading me through bodies, dodging around waiters and their flutes of never-ending drinks, Freddie doesn't stop to notice all of the eyes that follow us. I feel like a debutante stepping out into the ton, except they and I both know that I would be better suited to serving them canapés. Whether their eyes are actually watching me I don't know for certain, but the itch that climbs up my chest and claws at my neck tells me they are. Covering my face with my hair, I scratch that itch, imagining what they are thinking: how ugly I am; how I have to walk with my legs slightly apart, so my thighs don't chafe; how my sweat seeps through my dress; how I am an embarrassment to an accomplished and beautiful man such as Freddie. I allow my nails to rake across my chest, and they leave behind dark lines like the Red Arrows across a clear sky.

My date only stops when we reach a small group of couples. Each one is tall and skinny, like an artist's mannequin, and draped in the finest of clothes.

'Everyone, this is my . . . friend, Margaret.' That confirms it: the whole date thing is just for Walker's benefit. It's another punch to the gut, but I can't lose face in front of all of these beautiful people. I stop scratching and straighten my back, forcing a smile onto my lips. They each nod, not a single word uttered to me. One particularly angular young woman steps forward, and I realise I can see each of her bones as if she were a skeleton wrapped up tightly in a sheet. She outstretches an arm that is so thin it looks as if holding up the weight of her hand for too long would make it snap in two. Foolishly, I think she's offering to shake my hand, but as I go to take it, she snatches it away, moving it more firmly into Freddie's eyeline. He lifts her hand to his mouth to kiss it and, no doubt unconvincingly, I try to make it look as though I was simply moving to scratch my shoulder awkwardly.

'My lord,' she says, her voice like honey, dripping with a warmth that sends a shiver up my spine. She is both terrifying and strangely comforting.

'Drop the formalities, Verity. You and I have known each other far too long for such customs.'

She puts a bony hand to her mouth and giggles softly. 'You are looking *very* well.'

'And you are stunning as ever.'

I smile uneasily at the others, feeling as if I'm intruding on a private moment. None of them return it.

One of the men eyes me suspiciously. 'What do you do, Mabel?' he says, clearly making no effort at all to remember my name.

'I, erm . . . well, I work in tourism,' I say, attempting to make my minimum-wage job sound slightly fancier.

'Oh, my friend did that on her gap year,' his partner says, pronouncing 'year' more like 'yah'. 'Where are you based? Asia? Greece? She took Singapore. Would you believe she was once tipped a Bentley by one of her clients? Terribly rich you see.'

'Just London at the moment.' She gives a small 'humph' and returns to sipping her drink.

'What an interesting hairstyle!' another of them adds. This one is blonde, naturally. Her hair is slicked back into a tight ponytail, and I am almost certain that she cannot move her face because of it. 'Reminds me of . . . Oh Pandora, what is that dog of your grandfather's, with the hair?'

'A golden doodle. Great huge stupid thing. Yah.' She giggles.

'Yes! That is exactly it! Very Eighties.'

I instinctively fiddle with the ends. 'I've realised after many years that it's probably best to just let it do what it wants. It has a mind of its own really.' I try not to show them any weakness – they're like wolves, always aiming for the fleshy parts.

'Hmm, I can tell,' the blonde muses.

'Do you ever straighten it? You know there is a way to do it semi-permanently now with chemicals? Far neater!' Verity has moved on from her intimate conversation with Freddie and now twirls a lock of my hair around her nail. She drops it and wiggles her fingers in disgust. 'Works best on very coarse strands apparently, so I'm sure it would take well.'

'I like *Maggie's* curls,' Freddie interjects, taking us all by surprise. The Botoxed faces around us barely conceal their shock. 'Haven't you noticed how each strand of her hair is a different colour to the one beside it? She's hiding some sort of magic in there, I'm sure. And I'll have you know, only the sexiest of people can pull off a curl.' He points to his own mop of ringlets, which look as if they have been perfectly placed one by one. All of the women look to each other, stunned into silence, their eyes the only part of them communicating.

Pressing my hands to my cheeks to attempt to cool them, Freddie turns to me and mutters: 'You okay?' I only nod in reply and, satisfied with my answer, he resumes an earlier conversation with the partner of the blonde woman, who is also blond and, quite frankly, could almost pass for her brother. His hair is a little darker but has the same thin and fine texture. Their noses both turn up slightly on the ends and their teeth, although perfectly uniform, flash a large amount of gum each time they give a false smile. I would have assumed them siblings had his hand ever moved from the curve of her bum at all throughout the conversation. From silently listening to Freddie's conversation, I learn that his name is Alexander, although Freddie refers to him affectionately as Al, and that the blonde girl's name is Xanthe.

The other couple is formed by Pandora, who adds a little 'yah' suffix to the end of each of her sentences, and her boyfriend Hugo, who laughs a little too loudly at whatever anyone, and mainly himself, says. Verity is the only one without a partner, and she clutches to Freddie's arm. I find myself tucked behind her, forced out of the circle of laughter, although I am not too fazed; my mind is still busy replaying Freddie's words over and over until I am smiling to myself like a weirdo.

I cast around the room. White tablecloths shroud round tables, and gypsophila and white roses surround each extravagant centrepiece – a little stone statue of a floating cherub. Each one has their own guardsman too: a cleanly dressed waiter stands beside every single one of the tables, armed with a bottle of champagne, ready to refill each sip taken by the guests. It all seems a little excessive to me. I haven't been to many posh dos, but I know that I'd much rather have a pub lunch and a pint over this any day. I bet the food they offer here won't come close to a steak and kidney pie, and the sparrow-like portion sizes will be no match for the mountains of food the pubs back home provide.

People cluster in exclusive groups to 'network'. In the centre of the room, a few men congregate around a gentleman whose medals are so heavy, they hang at a slant across his chest. Clean-shaven, tall, lean, and exceptionally handsome, it's difficult to work out how old he is. Going off the medals alone, I'd say he's probably in his sixties, but the years have certainly been kind to him. The gaggle of peacocking men all laugh obnoxiously loudly at intermittent intervals, causing a few disturbed heads to look in their direction. Mr Medals is clearly the one to impress.

Once I finally stop people-watching and trying to pair older gents with their wives, I turn back to the group I was meant to be with. The circle is completely shut off to me now, Xanthe's beautifully slim and toned back is forming a brick wall that I really can't be bothered to skirt around.

A new face sidles up to them, a rather short and round man who strains to reach up to Freddie to whisper into his ear. Whatever he says, Freddie doesn't look at him. His attention has finally returned to me, and he holds my gaze. Brows furrowed, a darkness settles over his countenance, and he nods stiffly, eyes still locked with mine.

'Freddie dear, is everything okay?' Verity enquires in her sotto voce, not forgetting to lay her palm on his arm. I get a little twang of pleasure when he shakes her off.

He moves with purpose away from the group, pausing as he reaches me long enough to slide the fabric of my dress between his fingers and offer a short apology. By the time I register what is happening, Freddie, in the way he promised never to do again, has disappeared without me.

Without him, the idea of standing around with Verity and her flock of swans becomes increasingly repulsive, and I make the executive decision to track down someone with a tray of the slightly too sharp prosecco – which I am now realising might be actual champagne – to see how many free drinks I can cop before someone notices.

Making my way to the edge of the room, my target is in my sights. A very young waitress stands away from the crowd, taking discreet sips of the drinks on her tray when she thinks no one is looking. Jumping when she notices me beside her, she instinctively straightens her back and avoids my eyes.

'It's actually pretty gross, considering how expensive it is, isn't it?' I say, and the waitress releases a breath to let out a nervous chuckle.

'Just a bit.'

I take one of her glasses – one of the ones she hadn't been lapping like a dog on a hot day – and return it empty seconds later. 'Do you mind?' I ask as I go to reach for another. The young girl shrugs and I take a flute and leave her to it.

Even if I had wanted to mingle with another of the guests, who could pay off my student loan with just their cufflinks or handbag, I couldn't, because they each avoid my eyes as I wander past and they instinctively close the gaps in their circles. My fingers tap an irregular beat against my palm as I glide through the gala and my chest grows more and more itchy until I cave and scratch it, once again summoning a deep redness.

Out of the main hall, I desperately search for a quiet room or, even better, Freddie. It surprisingly isn't hard to find him as he stands in a quiet corner of the lobby. I am just about to call out to him when I notice that he's stood in front of the man with the medals from earlier. His back is to me, and they are too far away to hear any of their conversation, but if Freddie's expression is anything to go by, it isn't just a simple friendly chat they're having. He looks as he does when he is on sentry duty: hard, unwavering, intimidating.

He hasn't seen me, so I sneak along the edge of the lobby, camouflaged between the hordes of staff and actual living trees. Finding a seat in a little waiting area just metres away I can finally hear them. I tremble with a mixture of guilt and the fear of being caught, but I can't stop myself.

'You have a duty to your family, Frederick. Mhairi is that duty.'

'I know, sir,' Freddie responds. He is stood to attention, more tense than I have ever seen him before.

'Who is she?' the decorated man demands.

'No one, sir.'

'No one, yet you bring her here. Bring her here to make a mockery of us all.'

'That was never my intention, sir.'

'You have always wished to rebel, Frederick. You have always been ungrateful for the opportunity this family

308

afforded you. I have organised this evening for you, to get Argyll on side, and you have purposely sabotaged it.'

'I am sorry, Father.'

Eavesdropping only ever gets you hurt. That was a lesson I was taught as a child, which clearly I didn't take in. Even if I didn't have a bad habit of immediately overthinking and assuming anything bad is always about me, it's hard to believe that this isn't. The Earl of Oxford and his son are embarrassed at my being here. It's one thing feeling unwelcome, but to hear the two people you want to impress the most discussing how unwanted your presence is . . . well, it turns the feeling from a tough punch in the gut to a bulldozer.

Had Freddie even told me that his father would be here, I would have been far more reluctant to accept his invitation. I suppress the tears, not wanting to embarrass myself so publicly or embarrass Freddie even more. Leaving my heart and my pride on the sofa, I stumble back across the lobby until I find myself trying to clamber up onto a bar stool. In my heels, it takes four solid attempts to successfully park myself onto the spinning seat.

'Can I have a vodka and lemonade please,' I say to the barmaid, as she stands to attention, waiting for me to finally make my order

'A single or double, madam?' she says, almost robotically.

'I don't suppose you can do a triple can you?' She doesn't laugh. 'Double please,' I clarify after an awkward pause.

'That bad already huh?' a voice says beside me. I look a few seats over to a woman, petite and pretty, swigging back a glass of red wine.

'Mmhmm,' I murmur taking a long draught of my drink. 'I came here with the promise of castles and, so far, have heard not one word about them.'

The stranger laughs. She's a redhead too, but her hair is perfectly smooth and bounces around her face. Despite being sat on the rather uncomfortable stool, her posture is perfectly straight, and her sleek black dress holds not a single wrinkle. I'd say we're probably around the same age, but she holds herself with an air of maturity that I haven't quite mastered yet.

'I'm Katie,' she offers, a hint of an accent on her words.

'Maggie.'

'You've found the best seat in the house here, Maggie. It only gets worse when they start throwing their money around. I just came for the free bar.'

'Australian, right? The accent?' I enquire, and she smiles again.

'I'm three glasses deep and that's when it usually shows.'

'That I can understand. I'm a Yorkshire lass, and one sip of alcohol has me sounding like Sean Bean. I'm sure you get sick of people mentioning it?'

'Not really – only when they ask me to say something. You know, all of the stereotypes.' Katie rolls her eyes dramatically.

'How come you've wound up here?' I ask.

'Moved over here for uni and just never left. This climate is more my natural habitat, I think,' she says, gesturing to her hair. We talk for a while, but she doesn't mention her job, or much about her life, only asks about me. I can tell there's a story in her somewhere, but she's being coy about it.

She does, however, give me a run-down of who's who. It turns out there are a range of lords on parade: Lord Austen of Bath, Lord Choudhry of Fulham, Lord Featherstone, Viscount Wise, and the Earl of Cornwall. All older gentlemen with rounded bellies and a wife much, much younger and much, much better-looking. There's the odd baroness too – including Baroness Asquith-Beatty and Baroness Norton, two absolutely terrifying older women who wear neutral pantsuits like they're wearing armour.

'But the main attraction tonight . . .' she continues, 'is the Duke of Argyll and the Earl of Oxford. The duke leads the Scots Guards, the earl the Grenadiers, so they're both old friends and old rivals.' The mention of Freddie's father, of his power, reminds me of their conversation and my stomach churns again. I swig down one of the sambuca shots that Katie has ordered for us to disguise the stray tear as an eye-watering reaction and continue listening to her talk.

'They've been chums for decades. Well . . . no one here is really friends, more they are good for each other's image, so they stay at one another's estates annually. The duke is hosting tonight, and no doubt the saving the castles thing is all bullshit to raise a bit more cash for his estate and whatever other business is on his mind. The earl is difficult to catch in public, so this is all a performance for them, to show the closeness of their families. How come you're here, anyways? No offence, but you don't seem like one of these toffs.'

'None taken,' I say. 'I was invited by a friend, but I've been ditched. I'm not too sure why he invited me, to be honest. It's definitely tarnishing his image to be seen with

311

me.' Katie pushes another shot towards me, and we clink the tiny glasses together before both throwing them down with a little cringe. 'Are you here alone?' I say, still reeling from the bitter shot.

'I . . . erm, came with a friend too. Looks like we both got ditched.' She looks around, eyeing the other guests with a drunken vigour and raises her glass to me sarcastically.

'Is this seat taken?' a man rasps, interrupting our conversation as he looks down at the stool beside me. His hair is the same colour as the ravens, and even shines blue under the light, in the same way that Lucie's feathers do. It's long, but not untidy, slicked back at the top and then curling around his ears, not a single strand out of place. His white teeth glow against his complexion; skin the colour of a warm mug of coffee, and his eyes the colour of the beans. There is the look of a movie star about him, so, of course, I gesture for him to go ahead.

'You came with Guildford, right?'

'I did . . .' I say cautiously, unsure whether I should admit to it now that he so clearly regrets bringing me.

'Hang on . . .' Katie pipes up from across the bar. 'Your "friend" is Freddie Guildford? The Earl of Oxford's son?' She looks flushed as I nod.

'Oh, bollocks. I didn't . . . I mean, you could have told me!' she exclaims, clearly unnerved at the knowledge that she was gossiping about my friend and his family.

I laugh. 'It's okay, really,' I reassure her, and she asks the barmaid for another glass of wine, her lips becoming the same shade as her dress.

'How do you know him?' the man enquires. He has the same impression of authority as a police officer, and I feel obliged to respond.

'He works at my home,' I say, only realising from his taken-aback expression how odd that must sound. 'I live at the Tower . . . of London. I met him on guard there.'

'The *Tower* of London,' Katie interrupts again, eyes wide, and I can see just from her expression how her mind is racing with thoughts.

'It's not what you think, really.'

'So, you've met the family then, and Mhairi?' the raven-haired interrogator continues.

'Erm . . .' I start. 'We haven't been friends for too long really. He only invited me because I'm into history.' I can't help but feel as if I have done something wrong.

'Who are you again?' I ask, my voice a little shaky.

'Excuse my rudeness. I'm Theodore. You met my sister, Verity, earlier. I went to school with Freddie – we boarded together.'

'Ah.' I nod my head, hoping that the less I say, the sooner he leaves.

'Lovely news about his engagement to Lady Campbell, isn't it?'

Engagement? I choke on my drink; the vodka burns a little more than it did before. I feel it run down my chest and set fire to the rest of my insides. The fire steals all of my oxygen and I struggle for breath. I grip the side of the bar, but it doesn't seem to steady me. A thousand thoughts rush through my head, yet I can think of nothing at all.

'Oh speak of the devil, here they come now,' Theodore

313

says, excessively cheerily. 'Countess Guildford, Lady Campbell, may I introduce you to the viscount's guest, Maggie.'

Two ladies float towards me. Both equal in beauty, together arm in arm, they steal the show. Freddie's mother wears full-length lace opera gloves and a fur shawl that covers the shoulders of her caramel-coloured dress. Her hair is a dusty blonde, tied up in the style of a monarch, a few pearls laced between the strands. There is no doubt that Freddie is her son; they share the same explosive eyes, a colour I can't quite define between blue and green, impossible to look away from. She is regal in every definition of the word, and I am scared that if I let go of the bar I will pass out at her feet.

Lady Campbell, his fiancée, is frustratingly beautiful. If Freddie is modelled from the same stuff as Michelangelo's *David*, she is painted by the brush of da Vinci. She's radiant. Her hair is pin-straight, smooth, and falls in a waterfall of a thousand different tones of mahogany. I question whether she is wearing makeup at all. Her cheeks are dusted with light freckles and a natural rose kisses at her round cheeks and plump lips. She wears a floor-length satin gown, the colour of a twilight sky, and she towers over almost all of the guests in modest heels that show off her natural height. She should be on the cover of magazines. Hell, I'm sure she *has* graced a few.

What delivers the final, fatal blow is the necklace that clings to her dainty neck. Fat sapphires are fastened onto a delicate silver chain, matching both her teardrop earrings and her ocean eyes. It's the same sapphire necklace that came in a glossy wooden box, the corner chipped, the wood splintered, as it crashed to the floor on the day Freddie and I collided. This beautifully ornate cathedral of a woman is his and has been since the moment I met him.

Katie deftly turns her stool away from us as a group forms. She shields her face from the new guests with her thick hair and I have to stop myself from turning her seat back around, so I have some sort of backup, even if it is from a tipsy Australian I only met an hour ago.

'A friend of my son you say?' the countess says to Theodore. 'I've never heard him mention a . . . Maggie?' She hasn't looked at me, only addressing the instigator of this ambush.

Lady Campbell ignores them and comes straight for me. I want to run, but I'm trapped against the bar.

'Hi, I'm Mhairi. It's lovely to meet you,' she says, her voice as smooth as her hair, a subtle Scottish burr only adding to the comforting tone. She grasps my hand to shake.

'Ah, uh . . . sweaty,' is all I can splutter out. She laughs softly. Even her laugh is perfect. I look down at her hand, which still clutches mine tenderly. A diamond the size of an acorn sits on her ring finger, framed by an elegant gold band. The fire in my chest makes its way up to my eyes and stings at the corners.

'Are you okay?' she asks, bending down to get a better look at my face, concern knitted into her brows. *Come on, Maggie, pull yourself together. The quicker this is over the quicker you can leave.*

'Sorry, yes . . . it's great to finally meet you.' I try to blink away the tears, but they blur my vision for a moment.

'Freddie has told me so much about you.'

'He . . . has?' I say, perplexed.

'Yes, of course! I'd love to visit the Tower. I haven't had an opportunity to come down yet, with me being up in Scotland most of the time.'

'You'd be welcome any time. I can give you a tour,' I say with a smile, but with each kind word she offers me, I feel my heart chip away a little more.

He told his fiancée about me. I know he said we're just friends, but, over these past few weeks, I really thought, by the way he touches me, the way he almost kissed me, that there was something more. I am here as his date, for goodness' sake! If he wanted me, if he felt anything for me at all, why would he tell her? Because he feels nothing, I tell myself.

'Oh, that would be lovely!' She claps her hands together and her eyes disappear with her smile. 'You'll have to come and stay at our house in Scotland too! Mi castle es su castle, if you will.' She laughs again.

How can one woman be everything I have ever wanted to be? Be everything that I am not? I feel ridiculous for ever having thought, hoped, that Freddie could have feelings for someone like me when he's actually in love with my complete antithesis.

Freddie's mother finally shifts her attention towards me. She reminds me of a headmistress, and I cower into myself just from her gaze.

'How is it that you know my son, young lady?' Her voice

is soft, calculated. Every intonation is carefully planned, I'm sure, to terrify me.

'I, well . . . I, erm . . . it's . . .'

'Come on, dear, we haven't got all day.' Now I am sure it is universally known that, like telling someone to 'relax' when they are hysterical, telling someone to hurry up whilst they are clearly struggling with that task only makes the problem worse.

'Maggie lives in the Tower of London, Countess.' Flawless Mhairi comes to my rescue. Of course she does. She probably rescues stray puppies in her spare time.

'I see,' Countess Guildford replies. 'Is Lord Bridgeman still taking up his residency there as constable? He hosted a rather lovely dinner for us in the Queen's House a few years back.' She directs the latter part towards Mhairi.

'Sadly not, ma'am. Lord Herbert was recently instated,' I squeak out by way of reply.

'Oh, Herbert! Brilliant chap. I must call him.' Of course, she knows everyone with a fancy title. 'Your father must be ex-military, yes?'

'Yes, ma'am. Engineers.'

'Not commissioned though?'

'No, ma'am.'

'What school did you attend whilst your father was away then?'

'Actually, I moved with them. Although, it's funny; people say I have finishing-school posture because my mum told me off so much for slouching that I can still hear her voice saying "stand up straight!" each time I relax my shoulders.'

317

I laugh to myself. Mhairi does too, more out of politeness; the countess is unamused.

'But you didn't actually go to finishing school?' she says, sharply.

'No . . .' I lower my head, the heat rising again to my face. 'How long is it until the wedding?' I turn to Mhairi, changing the subject. The words have to squeeze past the cork in my throat that bottle-stops my tears. I know that learning the details of Freddie's relationship will be torture, that I am only upsetting myself, but I can't help myself. The more I hurt, the more I will want to forget him. The more I don't want to be with him, the less I'll care about how these people look down on me.

'We're hoping to have a winter wedding in Balmoral. Perhaps December! Scotland is so magical in the snow.' She smiles, her mind visibly wandering. This year. He is to be married this year.

'That's lovely, so . . . lovely,' I breathe, clambering to my feet and adding, with false gaiety: 'I must nip to the loo.' I am desperate to excuse myself before my shortness of breath turns into a full-scale panic attack. 'It was so nice to meet you. Maybe we will again . . . Mi castle es, er, your castle et cetera.'

Mhairi gives me a smile farewell.

'It was so great to meet you too, Mrs . . . Countess Guildford.'

She rolls her eyes, but I'm already rushing away. As I push my way through the lobby, it swims before me. Everyone in my path moves out of the way, whipping past me like blurred comets. Blood pounds so loudly in my ears that it blocks out any whispered commentary from onlookers.

Flying through the ornate doors, I discover it's raining. Fat droplets smack me in the face, stealing my breath for a moment. But I don't stop, I can't stop, until I am far away from this place. The unfamiliar streets are empty, aside from the odd car crashing through puddles by the side of the road. The darkness and the rain have driven everyone else away, and I don't pass another living soul. Eventually, I come to a stop, realising I am completely lost.

Clinging to a railing, I cry, sobbing against the wind. I slump down against the cold metal, and my mascara leaks into my eyes but I hardly notice them burn. As I raise my face to the sky, the water splashes against me in an onslaught of damp bullets. I stay this way for a while.

How could I allow myself to fall for someone like Freddie? How could he not once tell me that he is getting fucking married? My skin feels itchy at the thought of what I have done to Mhairi. She has no idea how many times we've almost kissed. How many times he has touched me so tenderly, been so intimate, that there is no way that we are only friends. I am officially the other woman.

My head in my hands, I let out an animalistic noise, somewhere between a grunt and a scream. The slamming of a car door interrupts my meltdown. Shuddering, I whip around to assess the danger, just about making out through the downpour a Rolls-Royce pulling in sharply a little way down the road. A black and white blur rushes towards me. Freddie, in his pristine suit, is quickly in front of me, placing his jacket over my shoulders. It isn't long before the rain is dripping from the ends of his curls. He holds me by the arms in a familiar embrace, keeping me at a little distance to get a good look at me, those beautiful eyes tracking across my face, checking for any injury.

'Are you okay?'

'I'm fine,' I say, brushing him off. The driver of the Rolls is parked at the side of the road, the door still open.

'Maggie? What's going on? Why did you leave? You should have come and found me.'

'I have to get back, before the Keys.'

'Maggie, I *organise* the Ceremony of the Keys. Don't lie to me!'

He reaches for me again, and I erupt: 'Don't fucking touch me.'

He jumps back. 'Wha . . .'

'I met your fiancée, Freddie.'

His face drops and he turns away, a hand shooting up to push his hair back from his face.

'I knew that falling for someone like you was always going to hurt. I knew that I would always have to live with the fact that I am just not good enough. But I thought, for just one foolish moment, that we had something special. That maybe you were the first person to see me for what I actually am. I wanted that so desperately. I live my life like a ghost, so when you came to me, and you kept coming back, I thought . . . I just . . .' Crying takes over. I bury my face in my hands and it physically overcomes me. 'But like you said to your dad, I'm no one.'

'To my . . . ? Oh.' I see the realisation dawn on Freddie

in real time. 'You weren't meant to hear any of that, Maggie. I'm sorry.'

'Well, I did,' I say through broken sobs.

'My father . . . it's complicated.'

'Why did you even invite me here? You must have known your family would hate me, and that your friends would look down on me. Did you do this to mock me? The stupid girl who fell in love with you and thought for one second she might have a chance with the high and mighty Guildfords. How hilarious – what a spectacle. I'm not a *freak show*, Freddie.'

Cold fingers grasp my cheeks, and Freddie looks at me as if a star has just fallen from the smog-filled sky and landed right in his hands. His thumb swipes gently under my eyes, in an attempt to wipe the makeup that tries to escape with the rain.

'Don't you dare look at me like that. You have no right to look at me like that. You have a wife . . .' I break for a sob '. . . you have a fucking wife.'

'She's not my wife, Maggie,' he says, his voice quiet, soft.

'Oh, I'm so sorry that I am six months premature. The woman you are going to marry, then. That beautiful, classy, educated woman who was at the same party you invited me to!'

'It's not like that!' he rushes. 'I didn't know she was going to be there; she was never meant to be. Please . . . You don't understand.'

'Pah! And that makes it so much better, does it? What is there to not understand about that massive rock on her finger! You're engaged to her, yes?'

He nods.

'And you're getting married this year, yes?'

He nods again, shame enveloping him.

'Then I want no part of you. I'm not going to chase a taken man. And I certainly won't sit around to be his mistress, his dirty little secret. I can't watch you be with another woman. I can't . . .'

'It wasn't meant to be like this. Please, believe me. I wanted . . . I *needed* you here.' My heart finally cracks, an earth-shattering wave that flows through me and puts the thunder to shame.

'It's my fault. I got the wrong idea, somewhere in this stupid head of mine, I thought we were something more. I am so, so sorry for falling for you, Freddie Guildford. I really am.'

'Maggie, don't say that. Please. Please . . .' He reaches for my hand but decides against it. I shiver, the coldness of the night finally settling on my bones.

'I need to go home,' I whisper, wiping the rain from my face as it drips from the tip of my nose.

'Take the car.'

I want to be stubborn. I want to tell him to take himself and his stupid car with its stupid heated seats far away from me. But I know that would be cutting off my nose to spite my face – I left without my jacket.

Crossing my arms over my chest, I turn back towards Freddie. He's in pain – I can see it in his face. He rubs his face roughly, and I feel sorry for his sopping curls, which are absorbing most of his frustration as he rakes a hand through them.

Once he's certain that I'm not just going to run off into the night, Freddie walks over to the passenger-seat window. Carol, the chauffeur, rolls down the window and he leans through it to give her instructions. The back door is still open; the leather seat has a puddle forming in the middle of it. Freddie beckons me over as he moves around the car to open the door on the other side. I do as he says. We're both silent. I can tell he is aching to touch me, to hold my hand to help me into the car. But instead, his fingers just twitch, itching to be placed on my skin. But he only shields my head from the roof again and slams the door.

'Carol, please make sure she gets home safe, and don't leave until she's inside the gates,' Freddie says.

'Yes, sir,' she replies with a swift nod.

He goes to close the still-open car door on the other side, by the puddle, and pauses to look at me, the rain bouncing off the back of his soaked suit jacket. 'Goodnight, Margaret.'

His cold tone cuts through me. Not a single emotion balances on his words, and he closes the door with a thud. The locks audibly slot into place and Carol speeds off down the streets of London.

As we pull away, I notice that the rear window is dappled with raindrops. The world and its lights are smudged in each tiny bead. Each one transforms into a jeweller's loupe, magnifying brake lights, shop lights, streetlights, like a melancholy Christmas tree. Freddie gets smaller and smaller, until he fits inside one of the droplets. He hasn't moved an inch but watches the car as we drive away. The distance between us is immeasurable now.

Chapter 21

As I leave for work, I notice that Richie is harvesting his roses this morning, scratching his head, and muttering about how the leaves at the bottom of them are always turning brown. Joe, one of the younger beefeaters, who's partly dressed in his T-shirt and braces, laughs hysterically as he releases his two spaniels to cock their legs and piss against the bushes. Richie swears loudly, in between his own laughter and I shake my head affectionately at the scene.

'Morning,' Joe hollers over to me when he spots me. Richie follows suit with his Cornish grumble, stopping his spaniel-swatting briefly to give me a wave.

'Oh, you little bastard!' he shouts as one of them uses the momentary break to recommence squatting in the soil. Joe's laughter roars between the walls, and I have a little chuckle to myself as I continue on my way.

'Morning, Linda,' I say to the beefeater on the corner as I pass her. She sits outside of her house in a little deckchair, picking tiny strawberries off of her plant and popping them into her mouth.

'Good morning, Maggie dear.' She smiles and chucks me a strawberry, which I, surprisingly, manage to catch.

The casemates are bustling by the time I reach the North Bastion. Beefeater Jolly walks towards me in full uniform.

'Morning, Ginge,' he calls with a cheeky smile, tipping his hat as he passes. His beard is predominantly dark, as opposed to the grey of most of the others, and he is one of the few who can still see his toes for his belly. Jolly always stops for a quick chat or at least a smile – hence his name. As an ex-marine, on paper he should be absolutely terrifying, but Jolly will always make an effort to give you a laugh. He hasn't quite left the navy behind and spends his spare time speeding up and down the Thames in the lifeboats, so you can always rely on him to share a story or two – albeit most of them relaying the discovery of something ridiculous, disgusting, or both bobbing down the great London river.

I don't even reach the end of the cobbles before Timmy the Newfoundland is bounding towards me, released from his lead by Charlie. He charges at me, his jowls swinging from side to side, flinging slobber against the stone fronts of the casemates. The size of a baby polar bear, his fluffy fur bounces with every step and he looks utterly adorable. If this is the way I die, crushed under this lovable beast, then so be it.

Just before he reaches me, Timmy flops down on his back, flashing his grey fleshy stomach. He wriggles against the ground impatiently, imploring me to rub his belly, and

325

I bend down and do his bidding. Charlie catches up after a few moments and I give him another familiar salute. As always, he chuckles and says: 'Mornin', hen.' Then adds, to his dog, who still lies spread-eagled on the ground, tongue lolloping: 'Come on, you big lump, let Maggie get to work.' Timmy gets up, much to his dissatisfaction, and trundles off with his owner again.

The ravenmaster is stood just outside on the wharf peering down into the moat. She notices me too and nods her head in acknowledgement, a little leaf falling down across her face from the motion. Smiling back at her, I complete the last stretch over the drawbridge and out to the ticket office.

It's been two weeks since the gala, and two weeks since I last saw Freddie. After Carol dropped me off, it took me three days before I could face anyone. I'm not sure if it was the rain or the emotional exhaustion but I didn't have to lie to work about being ill. My body felt, and still does feel, like it's made out of lead. My head is cloudy, as though filled with cotton wool, and thinking about any of it is painful. There's an emptiness in my chest, a coldness, where the wind has blown its chilly breath through the void where my heart used to be.

But now I am back to my usual mundane routine, and I'm first in this morning. In fact, I'm so early that even the rats haven't had chance to go back to their hiding places. They scurry across the floors and I retch at the thought of where else they've been all night. The pleasures of working (and living!) on top of centuries-old underground networks . . .

'Right, you manky scamps, that's it,' I shout towards the greasy balls of fur, who have spent so much of their lives in London that they have forgotten they're meant to be afraid of humans and just sit staring at me from across the room. I grab a broom out of the storage cupboard and chase them. Though I start off by using it as a jousting pole, attempting to herd them towards the door, I quickly have to change tack after five minutes and barely a flinch from the rodents, so I slap the bristles against the floor, which soon gets them shifted. After twenty minutes and all of the energy I had saved up for the entire day, they are out of my eyeline and now someone else's problem. Before I sit down, I grab two rolls of cling film from the staff kitchen and suffocate my chair in the stretchy plastic. Sticking some on my desk for good measure, I finally plop myself down with a squeak.

Charlie's Arseholes walk in after a few precious moments of silence, already giggling. They don't see me.

'Have you heard? *Apparently* there've been guardsmen all over looking for Maggie. Rachel in accounts reckons she's been up in that guardroom "entertaining", if you get what I mean,' Samantha speaks loudly, her vocal fry so prominent I am sure it must hurt her throat.

I lean back on my chair, the cling film creaking loud enough to make them aware of my presence. 'Samantha, did you brush your teeth this morning?'

She's taken aback. Blushing, from both being caught and my peculiar question. 'What? Why?' she says sharply.

'Well, it's just when you shovel so much shit out of your mouth every single day, your breath really stinks.' I waft

327

my hand over my nose and sit back up in my chair, leaving them all speechless.

Freddie hasn't attempted to speak to me; the guardsmen Samantha is referring to are Riley and Walker. I don't think any of them really know what's happened and they both keep trying to get me to come over for another party. The mere sight of a bearskin has me hiding behind anything and anyone I can possibly find. I have withdrawn back into my normal life, just existing, without any interruption from tall and handsome soldiers.

Each new day is exactly the same as the one before. The day drags on and before I know it, I am walking along the cobbles of Water Lane back home again. Months could pass by, and I'd have no idea – bar the ground beneath my feet changing from green grass to crunchy leaves to slick ice and back again. I am so zoned out, from myself, from the rest of the world, that I am numb to all of it. I spend most of my walk in my own head, reminiscing, walking past spots that are now inextricably linked with him in my mind.

Today is the same. Retracing the steps that I take every morning and evening, I realise I have already forgotten the last eight hours and all I have to look forward to is doing it over again tomorrow. Handing out the same smiles to the same people on their way home, I keep my head down, avoiding spotting another landmark that might make me dwell.

The clinking of hobnails against the cobblestones snaps me out of my wandering thoughts. Only a select few people sound as if they are wearing tap shoes when they are marching around this place and all of them are members of the one group I wish to avoid at all costs: guardsmen.

I look around for somewhere to hide. For one mad moment, I toy with the idea of jumping into the river that flows through Traitors' Gate, but quickly come to my senses after realising the water is almost black. I hotfoot it past the Bloody Tower, towards the Middle Drawbridge. After hopping over one of the short railings I don't quite land on my feet so crawl on my hands and knees around the back of the sculpted polar bear. The marching continues, and I look up; I'm sure my arctic friend is judging me. I shush him with a finger to my lips like the heroes in those action films do when a child has uncovered their hiding position.

The guardsmen finally pass, and I emerge from my hidey-hole. When I manage to get one leg back over the railing, the ravenmaster appears out of nowhere, as though she was waiting to ambush me. She thrusts a pair of plastic gloves into my hands and walks off into her little room of supplies.

The chilling sound of the slamming of a butcher's knife against a wooden board reverberates around me as I pull on the gloves, and she soon re-materialises with a bloodied bucket of offal and makes off with it. I can only assume she wants me to follow and so I awkwardly traipse after her. From this position, I can see right over the top of her head, and I am almost sure I see a little bird's egg nestled into the matted patches of her hair.

When we reach the south lawn, the ravens flock from every corner of the Tower, summoned both by the promise of food and their master. They bundle together in their conspiracy at our feet and wait patiently for the ravenmaster to throw the first mouse. Merlin hops over to me and pecks at my shoe impatiently, and I take that as my cue to thrust my hand into the slimy bucket and toss him his dinner.

As we watch the ravens tearing into their dinner, the ravenmaster's timid voice says: 'Stories only make sense when you stick around for the ending.'

'Easy for you to say. What's yours?' I retort, surprising the both of us. She looks at me for a moment, her face unreadable, then turns back to her birds and dumps the entire bucket out in front of us.

'I'm sorry. I didn't mean to . . .' She cuts me off by spinning on her heel and shuffling away. The familiar sick feeling grows in me, knowing I have upset her. The bucket clatters as she tosses it into the store cupboard.

'Are you coming?' she calls back, using her wrinkled hand to beckon me forward. Still feeling guilty, I oblige obediently and jog to her side. Edward also takes the invite and flutters over to be carried to our destination on her shoulder. She leads me across the courtyard, around the back of the chapel, behind the safety rope, and into the Devereux Tower. The ravenmaster's house is secluded from the others, hidden in a corner of the inner wall. It is one of the houses that no one ever wants to go in, which probably suits her quite well now that I think about it. The courtyard in front of the door is built over the crypt of the chapel, which is filled with the miscellaneous bones discovered across the Tower that couldn't be identified. If legend is to be believed, the Devereux Tower is haunted by a nursing mother, who breastfeeds her baby in the window, and I am almost certain it isn't just her who wanders here. The basement must back onto the crypt, and I've heard stories of there being a spooky well down there and wet footprints being found outside of the door.

I can't deny that my body is betraying me; on one hand I am so terribly intrigued and flattered to get to see the inside of the ravenmaster's house, but on the other my fear of the place means I have to fight the impulse to flee.

The diminutive woman swings open the door and waddles in, not waiting to see if I am behind her. I catch the door before it closes and follow her in. The hallway is cramped and dark, the walls on each side crammed with bric-a-brac, which all looks as if it was plucked straight out of the bedroom of a witch. Edward flutters off of the ravenmaster's shoulder as she makes her way towards a door. He lands at the very end of the hallway and perches himself in a line of taxidermy birds and a few other avian skeletons, which gives him the look of a Madame Tussaud's wax figure coming alive. Walking slowly down the hall, I eye jars of all kinds on the shelves, stacked high up to the ceiling. I notice one labelled 'crushed bone' and I decide to not let myself speculate what species said bones came from.

I tail my host into another room, the arched windows allowing for a little more light to creep into the house. The room is bare, aside from a large leather armchair in one corner and hundreds of photos wallpapering the walls. Each one cages the miniature face of a soldier, men and women alike. I walk towards one in which a young man is crouched down on a sandy surface, his dark hair cropped and a moustache ornamenting his beaming smile. Scanning across the photos surrounding it, I notice that of the hundreds of photos, there are around thirty different faces, just repeated in various new poses – each six-by-four contains wide smiles, all worn by people dressed in their military uniform.

The ravenmaster takes her seat slowly, as if it pains her, and looks up at the walls.

'I was an army medic for just over twenty years.' She stops to clear her gravelly throat and then continues. 'I was in the Falklands when I was younger than you are now. I should have got out after that, some of the things I saw. But I didn't, I stayed and, I saw what happened in Ireland, and still went and did several tours of Iraq and Afghanistan, each one worse than the last.' She coughs again, unused to the strain of speaking for so long. 'By the time it got to my very last tour, I didn't think I could handle it anymore. I had seen too much, lost so many people. So, to stop me from leaving, the army put me on admin in an Afghan field hospital. I thought it would be just paperwork, you know, noting down what had happened, prescribing medication. But . . . they just kept dying.'

My heart sinks. I don't need her to tell me who all of these people are. I think I already know.

'So many bodies came through those doors, and I was tasked with organising their return. I had to box them up like toy soldiers and ship them home.' She gets up now and stands beside me, my eyes still fixed on the photographs. 'These are all of the men and women that I had to send home in body bags.'

'I'm sorry,' I breathe. She doesn't look at me.

'I got out after that. Came here, and my birds looked after me. I couldn't face people anymore, so it was nice to have them.'

She sits back down in her chair. It makes so much sense; she keeps her distance from everyone because she's too scared to lose anyone again. My heart breaks for her as I scan over the sea of faces before me.

'Can I get you something to drink?' I say after a short while of silence. I can tell that sharing her greatest traumas has taken it out of her, and she looks frail and weary in the corner. She nods gently and I do what us Brits do best: brew a pot of tea to make everything feel just that little bit better.

Once the sun sets and the room grows shadowy, I leave the Devereux Tower with the promise of visiting again for another cuppa soon. We've spent the last two hours going through each of the photographs in turn, with the raven-master telling me each person's name and a short anecdote about them. Despite the pain it must cause her, she smiles through it in a way I don't think anyone in the Tower has ever seen before. It's as though she's finally finding her peace, sharing the lives of those who have been locked away in the darkness of this room, and her mind, for so long.

I only leave her once she begins to doze in the armchair. She pauses whilst telling me a story about Lance Corporal

Scott, a young dog handler whose dog refused to leave his side long after he'd passed, and resumes her soft snoring. On my way out, I have to compose myself in the dusty mirror in the hallway. I couldn't help but weep in hearing her story, and the grief I feel for her, and the people she spoke of, is written all over my face.

When I get home, Dad is sat in his usual seat in the corner. His belly peeks out from between his trousers and his T-shirt, and he sits running his hand through his beard.

'Hullo, Mags. Do you want me to get you something for your tea, love?' He stands up out of his chair, ready to wait on me with a smile. I say nothing, only move forward to pull him into a tight hug. He wastes not a single moment in hugging me back, his hands tapping across my shoulders playfully.

'You all right, kid?'

I nod against his shoulder. 'I just wanted to tell you that I am so proud of you.' I squeeze him tighter.

'Proud of me? What for, eh? All I've done is polish off that entire packet of custard creams, and you know that's nothing special for me.' He chuckles, his broad chest vibrating with the motion.

My dad has always taken everything in his stride; though hard as nails, he's still a soft soul and one that would never burden you with his troubles. I feel guilty that I am only now realising what a strain he must have been under, to have left his family, to have seen the things that the raven-master saw, and yet always come home with a smile on his face, ready to do anything he could for me and Mum.

'I love you, Dad.' He knows my meaning in all of

this – I'm sure he does. He taps me on the head with an affectionate palm.

'Love you too, you soppy git,' he answers, and, after giving me another pat, moves away. 'Now let me make you some beans on toast.'

I accept with a smile. He toddles off into the kitchen, coming out not too long later with two plates. One is buried under a blanket of cheese, and he takes that one for himself. I notice he's made sure to pile my beans in the middle of the plate, so that the toast, cut into triangles, is not quite touching the tomato sauce. As a child, I'd always moaned if the bread became too soggy; he'd remembered.

Taking our plates down to Mum's room, we eat in a comfortable silence until he eventually kisses me on the forehead, kisses Mum, and descends to the basement for bed. The emptiness of losing Freddie is pushed to the back of my mind for one single evening.

I'm early to work again the next day. Bran leans against the side of the office, smoking a cigarette. I observe him for a moment, so far undetected. Every woman who walks past becomes subject to his wandering eyes, scanning them from head to toe. Seeing him stirs little more emotion than repulsion for me now; I can't even find it within myself to be anxious about having to confront him.

Moments later I'm spotted. He drops his cigarette in a panic, stamps on it with his heavy boots and then walks quickly over to me.

'Marg—'

'Can't you just piss off?' Rolling my eyes, I cut him off

335

and dodge under the arm he has outstretched with the intent of hugging me. I walk straight past him, and he jogs up behind me like a little lost puppy.

'Margo, wait up! I just want to talk to you, come on. You owe me that much.' *That* gets my attention. I swivel around with such force, he flinches as though I'm about to hit him, and I know my face looks thunderous.

'Owe you? Fucking owe you?' I spit out, punctuating my phrase with a cold laugh. 'You really are more deluded than I thought. The only thing I owe you is an invoice, billing you so I can afford to go to therapy to undo all of the emotional trauma you put me through.'

He is stunned, only stares at me like a deer in the headlights, as I put my face so close to his, I'm sure he can smell that I am not wearing his god-awful perfume.

'I was so blinded by everything with Mum, I stayed with you because I thought no one else would ever understand. I thought that after all you did for me that maybe I did owe you something. But you just took advantage of me, of my grief, of my dependence on you, which you had assured by isolating me from anyone else. You made me feel worthless. I lived every day wondering why I wasn't enough. I gave you everything, yet you still slipped and fell in between another woman's legs. *Three times!*' I'm on a roll now, boiling over with hatred for him. If I get much more passionate, I think I will end up frothing at the mouth.

'Mar—'

'Shut up and let me speak.' People are watching now. 'You are the most self-centred, arrogant pig I have ever met. Every time I think about you, I don't hate you, I hate myself. I hate myself for not being strong enough to leave you the first time. I hate myself for allowing you to steal so many years of happiness from me. I hate myself for feeling like I deserved it, like I deserved to never be told that I'm beautiful, or smart, or funny – or just worth something. You made me believe it was my fault that *I* was being cheated on because I couldn't satisfy you. But I realise now that people like you are never satisfied. And it's you who didn't deserve me.'

He scoffs, turning his lost-puppy innocence into the classic defensive conceit.

'Andy told me you got dumped by your little toy soldier. Did he have to have another bit on the side too? At least it took him a bit less time than me to realise you're the most uninteresting, useless woman anyone could possibly find.'

I want to slap the smug smile off of his face. Or even better, tear his head clean off his body and use the dense skull as a bowling ball to take out Andy as well.

'You know, Bran, we could sit down on that bench over there and I could insult you all day without stopping for breath. But I wasted seven years on you already, and I don't have a single piece of energy left to throw away on a man who didn't make me come once in all of that time. Don't come here again. Don't contact me. If I never think about you again, it'll be too soon.'

I stride into work without looking back. Once I am inside and have shut the door, I catch my breath for a moment before giving myself a high five, which instantly

337

makes this whole situation a lot less cool. Relief washes over me. I hadn't even realised that he was weighing so heavily on me until now. Everything is all of a sudden fresher, lighter. And for the first time in over two weeks, I properly and wholeheartedly laugh.

Chapter 22

A quiet knock at my front door sends Cromwell flying down the stairs like a guard dog, giving me little choice but to answer it. Dad is spending the evening in the Keys, and I will no doubt find him asleep outside, slung over a cannon, on my way to work in the morning. I wander slowly down the three flights of stairs, wondering who it could be. With this postcode, I am immune to any cold callers, and chatting on the doorstep with one of my neighbours in my dressing gown is certainly not what I'm in the mood for right now.

When I get to the ground floor, there's another soft knock. I sigh before opening it, but it quickly turns into a choke when I see the face on the other side. Freddie stands before me wearing his combats and beret, another identical uniform folded neatly over one of his arms. His posture is rigid, but his face is soft, his eyes a little glassy, his brows sloped. I panic and drag him inside the house by his arm. Behind the wide expanse of his shoulders, I notice his rifle, propped up against the umbrella stand. I slam the door shut behind me and it rattles the picture frames on the walls in the hallway.

The problem with living inside a thirty-foot wall is that there is plenty of height, but very little width, meaning my hallways are incredibly cramped. We are chest to chest and both breathing heavily.

'You can't be here,' I say, bluntly.

'I saw your father in the bar. Well . . . outside of it, having a nap.' He isn't trying to be funny; his face is firm, unmoving from its serious mask.

'I don't want to see you, Freddie. Please just go.'

'Maggie . . .' His façade falters. He lifts his hand to grasp mine, but once his fingers skim my knuckles, he decides against it and takes off his beret and twists it in his free fist instead. 'Please, just let me explain myself. If you don't want to see me again after that, then fine . . . I won't bother you again. But at least give me a chance to tell you the full story?'

'What else is there to say? And even if I wanted to, I can't. There's nowhere truly private in the Tower of London – I know that better than anyone. Just go back to your fiancée.'

'Lord Nithsdale,' he blurts out, lifting up the spare uniform. 'You told me that your favourite story from the Tower was the Scottish lord whose wife travelled all of the way from the Highlands to break him out. And she did so by dressing him, the six-foot-something, bearded Scotsman in her maid's clothes and he walked right out past the Yeoman Warder, and they lived happily ever after.'

'Yes . . .' I say suspiciously.

'Well, I . . . well, I wasn't sure that you walking around this place with a six-foot-three maiden in a granny's dress would be all that subtle. So, I thought it might be more inconspicuous to dress you up like me instead. I have a patrol to do, and no one really looks past the uniform. If it worked once it could work again, right?' he offers, a tentative smile on his lips.

The cold void in my chest warms. He wants to see me, and he has a plan to make it happen. He's thought of the risks, he's remembered the stories I told him, he's gone to all of this effort . . . I hesitate. I've always been a soft touch when it comes to Freddie, but I can't just forget all of my doubts. The lies, the hurt, the *fiancée* . . .

But, amongst my indecision, the ravenmaster's words echo: 'Stories only make sense when you stick around for the ending.' Maybe if I give Freddie the opportunity to finish his story, I'll be able to make more sense of it. If nothing else, it would be quite nice to have some closure. After my run-in with Bran, I'm no longer afraid, and, if I'm being honest, more than ready to tell another man where to shove his lies.

'Half an hour,' I concede, grabbing the uniform out of his hands and slipping into the bathroom. It almost fits, and I am momentarily embarrassed that I'm the same size as a soldier but remind myself that I possess something that they do not – a pair of tits – and that makes me feel a little less self-conscious.

'Perfect,' Freddie says when I finally emerge. 'Except . . .' He reaches up to the beret and adjusts it slightly. 'There we go.' He smiles.

He opens the door and collects his rifle, and I follow him nervously. My hair is tucked down the back of the shirt and it scratches at my back, making me shuffle uncomfortably as we walk along, scouting the premises for anything untoward.

Freddie clears his throat. 'So, you know that I told you about my family, and how I gave up my commission in the Grenadiers . . .' he starts, keeping his eyes on his patrol. I hum a yes in reply and he continues: 'Well, my father still wanted me to take up a commission in the Household Division, in the guards. Each of the regiments works in the same way – eldest sons of the colonels are commissioned in as officers, until they can take over from their fathers.' Freddie pauses to steal a little glance at me, but I don't make eye contact. 'The Duke of Argyll, Mhairi's father, is the colonel of the Scots Guards, and Mhairi is his only child. As a woman, she can't join the guards, unless she's in the band, and she has about as much rhythm as a donkey having a seizure.'

So, there *is* something she isn't perfect at – noted.

'The duke needed to find someone to fill the empty officer's position and one day take over his colonelcy to keep it in his family. Our parents have been friends for my whole life so, naturally, my father and Mhairi's father arranged for us to marry. That way, the duke can fulfil his role of providing the Scots Guards with a son to succeed him, Bertie gets to become the Grenadiers' colonel, just as he has always wanted, and my father no longer has the shame of his heir being *just* a guardsman. The only time I have ever seen my father look proud of me was the day I told him I'd marry her.'

342

'An *arranged* marriage?' I splutter. He looks at me with a pained expression. 'Sorry! I, just . . . how am I meant to respond to that?' I mumble guiltily.

'I *am* almost thirty.' He shrugs. 'I never really had anyone. Mhairi is a good friend. If I couldn't marry someone I loved, then at least I knew I wouldn't be lonely. And she's beautiful, smart, funny . . .' He twists the knife in my gut, and it feels more like a claymore, disembowelling me in one swipe. 'And most of all, she understood.' I barely notice how far we've travelled until he opens the gate of the moat for me to pass through; it's inky black, lit only by Freddie's torch and I am glad that he can't see as a small tear drops from my lashes and onto the uniform.

'And I mean this in the best way possible, Maggie, but when you came along you messed everything up. I have always hidden, behind my father, and then behind my uniform, but when you crashed into my life . . .' He pauses for a moment to take a deep breath. 'You were right in front of me, staring me down. I couldn't reach out and grab you, but you were the first person who didn't feel a million miles away. I found myself thinking about you, looking for you, seeking you out . . . and it terrified me. No matter how hard I tried to shake myself out of it and remind myself of my father, Mhairi, my duties . . . I didn't want any of those things as much as I wanted you. I couldn't stay away from you, so I didn't. And I fell in love with you.'

He scratches his forehead with the top of his torch, and I welcome the silence for a moment. Catching my breath, I absorb the last ten minutes. Freddie fell in love . . . with me? He doesn't love Mhairi, but he *has* to marry her. Something about this feels far worse than him just being a cheating arse. So, my love isn't unrequited . . . it's just forbidden. If Freddie chose to be with me, it would ruin his whole life: his family, his job, his reputation.

We're still moving through the Tower, and he speaks again when I don't say anything. 'The only time I've ever pulled out my title at work was to organise the guards so that my platoon was always the next to come to the Tower. I begged my little brother not to let any other Grenadier platoon take our place as they do normally. I volunteered us for every single guard, skipping our leave dates, just to be here. The lads hated me for ages, until I explained myself. And it *may* have helped that I took on as many patrols as I could to placate them. I just had to be near you. I stood myself at that same sentry box every morning at the exact same time with the hope of seeing you again – even if it was just a brief glimpse as you flew across the courtyard. And then you welcomed me into your orbit, and everything changed. With you, I finally feel like myself.'

'Hang on just a second, you rearranged the schedules of the entire King's Guards . . . to see me?' I turn to face him, stopping us in our tracks, and he scratches the back of his neck.

'Of all of the things I've told you tonight . . . *that* is what you are most surprised about?' Nervousness melts away from his face, replaced by a broad smile. He shakes his head and a curl escapes from the side of his beret. 'Yes, I did. His Majesty's Guards were disrupted and reorganised just so you could petrify me in that god-awful cellar!' He laughs, and it fills me with a feeling of the sublime, like the moment I first stood on the south lawn and looked up at the White Tower in her moonlit glory. That crisp coolness that bubbles down your body like the fizzing of pop.

'See! I knew you were scared!' I point a teasing, accusatory finger at him with a smile. But even as I say it something in my chest cracks, and I drop my arm to my side again. None of this changes the fact that he's going to be married. Platonic or not, he's a taken man, and if the wedding doesn't go ahead, it will tear his family apart. I think of myself in his shoes. If I had to choose between the love of someone I have only known for a handful of months or my parents, I would choose them any day. I would sacrifice any ounce of happiness to see my mum again. To see the way her face would light up when my fifteen-year-old self would rap to some horrendous pop song I'd learnt all of the words to, to dance maniacally with her in our kitchen again, or even to hear her moan at me to tidy my room. I could never ask Freddie to give up the one thing I long for.

'Freddie . . .' My tone is serious, and his eyes flash with concern. 'We can't be together. I could never live with myself if you gave up everything you knew for me.'

He hardens, almost as though drawing a shield. 'My whole life is dictated to me, Maggie.' He turns around sharply, and I practically butt heads with the barrel of his rifle. 'Every single day, someone tells me when to sleep, when to wake up, what to eat, what to wear, who to fucking marry.' His voice is raised, but it trembles, as if he's holding on to his tears so tightly that it shudders with the effort. 'The *one* thing that I chose for myself was you.' His tone softens, and he places his torch into his pocket, plunging us into darkness. With his free hand, he puts his palm to my cheek, and I wrap my own fingers around his, swiping my thumb over his knuckles.

'Freddie, I love you, but I heard your father at the gala. Choosing me would be losing everything you have. I can't let you do that – you'd only grow to resent me. My mum gave up her life to travel the world with my dad, to raise me, and I watched her retreat so far into herself that we lost her a long time before she passed.' He swipes a tear from my cheek, the moonlight reflecting off his own glassy eyes. 'I'm sorry, but we can't see each other again.'

'Maggie . . .'

'Please don't make this harder than it already is. This is the only way both of us will be able to go back to some sort of normality.' I lift his hand from my face, plant a soft kiss on his knuckles, and lower it back down to his side. 'Goodbye, Freddie.'

It's my turn to disappear. So, I walk away. Retracing the dark path that we came down, tears stream their hot trail down my face and hit the soft earth of the moat at a rate fast enough to refill it. The Middle Tower and the Byward Tower are lit up by the busy lights of South Bank, and the tip of the Shard glitters to replace the stars tucked away behind clouds of smog.

My breathing becomes laboured. I am excruciatingly aware of every single fibre of my being: the way the label of the combat trousers scratches at the bottom of my back, the throb of a fresh blister in my boots, the puffiness of too many tears already setting in around my eyes. I want to unzip my body and toss it aside.

I feel like an addict. The withdrawal from Freddie is instantaneous and all I want to do is run back to him. One taste and I am hooked again.

Not letting myself look back, I clamber out of the moat and stumble home over the cobbles.

When I reach the casemates, both Richie and my dad have only managed to make it halfway through their respective doors before collapsing in their hallways. Richie lies flat on his front, his legs sticking over the threshold; Dad, on the other hand, has managed to end up backwards, his head snoring on the doormat. I grab a few coats from our shared cloakroom and drape them over the two beefeaters as makeshift blankets, before stepping over Dad and heading straight for bed.

Cromwell is curled up in the middle of my duvet, but springs up as soon as I enter the room. Slowly, I peel off the borrowed uniform. My hands tremble as I fold it neatly and shut it up in a drawer out of sight. As I go through the motions of my night-time routine, washing my face, brushing my teeth, and climbing naked into bed, my tears finally dry up.

Chapter 23

One month later . . .

A loud knock wakes me. I am sprawled on top of my covers, dressed in the same clothes I wore to help Richie in his flower bed after work yesterday.

'Maggie?' My dad's voice follows his knock. 'Maggie love, are you awake?'

I grunt in the affirmative and he opens the door.

'Bloody hell,' he says when he notices the spectacle before him. 'You'd better get yourself washed, kid. Bob has just radioed from the main gate saying someone is out there asking for you. Didn't give a name but it's some woman. Bob made sure to tell me that she's very pretty.' I raise an eyebrow sleepily.

I run a hand over my face and it's grainy with dried dirt. Groaning again, I heave myself out of bed and give my hands and face a proper scrub over the sink until both are red raw.

'I can come out with you, if you'd like? In case it's someone you don't want to talk to,' Dad says from the other side of the bathroom door. I toy with the idea for a moment. If you don't know how much of a literal teddy bear my dad actually is, he looks pretty intimidating at first glance. He would make a very good security guard, but then again, if someone did want to cause trouble, I'm not sure they'd choose to do it outside of a place famed for its security.

'Thank you, but I think I'll be okay. You should head into work.' I place my hand on his shoulder and kiss him on the cheek. I notice one of the buttons of his tunic is undone, and quickly slide it in for him.

'That one is a real bugger,' he says with a laugh. 'Thanks, love.'

Once I look a little more presentable, we walk out of the house together, but he leaves me at the Salt Tower to begin his day. The Tower is busy, and I have to weave between groups and wait patiently for endless streams of tiny schoolchildren in hi-vis jackets, carrying backpacks bigger than they are.

I have no idea who will be waiting for me at the gate, but for once I don't feel anxious. Well, maybe a little, but I choose fight over flight today. Bob gives me a wave when I cross between the Byward and Middle Towers.

'Never seen her before in my life. Lovely lass, bit proper and the like. Thought we were having a visit from that Kate Middleton for a moment.' He gestures to a willowy, mahogany-haired goddess, who stands up straight beside the security cabin. Mhairi. As Bob alluded to, she's perfectly dressed in a long tight skirt and a flowy pink blouse. Her hair is a little untamed compared to when I saw her last, unrestrained by any pins or a sleek up do, and instead it flows around her oval face in a shroud of whisky-coloured strands.

My stomach drops at the sight of her. The last month has passed by without so much of a whisper from Freddie. He's clearly also stopped pulling strings in the chain of command because the Grenadiers haven't returned to the Tower once. Each day on the way to work I slip into the Byward Tower and check the rota before the watchman on guard wakes up from their nap. But each day I am disappointed. Day and night, I sit on the bench under the White Tower, as still as the guardsmen I watch, until they retire for the evening, and I am left staring into the empty sentry boxes as the night fills them with shadow. I gave up checking last week. I thought it might help.

I turn to leave before she spots me, but I'm unsuccessful.

'Maggie!' she exclaims, her eyes widening merrily at the sight of me. Rushing forward, she embraces me like an old friend, planting a kiss on my cheek. I tense up under her hold, taken aback by her strange familiarity. 'Oh, sorry, do excuse me,' she says, noticing my discomfort. 'I've been meaning to visit you for such a long time just to do that.'

My mind whirs, as I try to work out her meaning. Surely she should want to harpoon me, not hug me. Maybe she still doesn't know. Laughing awkwardly, I reply: 'Well, I'm honoured. Would you like to come in? I can show you around.' Of course, I don't really mean it; even as I offer, I'm secretly hoping that she will leave again, and I can go back to lamenting her fiancé in peace.

'Oh, that would be *wonderful*! Thank you.' She places her bag over her shoulder, and we fall in step alongside one another. 'How have you been? I didn't manage to catch you before you left the gala.'

'Ah, yes, sorry . . . I meant to say goodbye, but I had to leave early because of the curfew of this lovely place. How are you?' I return her question without really answering.

'Oh, Maggie, I can't tell you how happy I am. I have been so unbelievably happy.' I wish it didn't but hearing her say this feels like watching her gorge on a rich banquet whilst I'm starving.

'I actually had something else I wanted to talk to you about . . .'

Oh shit, here it is. The hug was just to lure me in, let my guard down. She is an orchid mantis, enticing in her prey with the promise of a beautiful flower, before she pounces, striking me down like an unsuspecting butterfly. I swallow hard when I realise that she has come to a stop outside of Traitors' Gate. Catherine Howard had a similar experience. Called here to answer to her crimes of adultery, she faced the ultimate punishment and gave her life for her betrayals of the heart. Only she was executed by the king, her husband, whereas my execution will be one of embarrassment, ripped apart by the sweet woman I have hurt without ever getting as close as I desired to the man I love.

I stay silent, a lump wedging itself in my throat. Mhairi seems to struggle with herself for a moment, her mouth opening and closing until it spreads into a . . . smile? Before I can decide if it is the grin of a deranged villain, I am dragged into yet another embrace, her grip is so tight I couldn't escape even if I tried.

'I can't thank you enough, Maggie, I really can't. Thank you, thank you, *thank you*.' Her voice trembles close to my ear. Knitting my brows together in confusion, I pull away. Tears stream down Mhairi's face but it still hasn't lost its cheer.

'Thank me for what?' I question.

'Hasn't Freddie told you?' The sound of his name is like a punch to the gut, and I have to keep swallowing past the growing lump and the salty tears that pool in my eyes. 'He's here, so I thought . . .'

'No. I haven't heard from him.' I have to clear my throat to be able to speak, and Mhairi grasps my hands in hers, tears still flowing down her own face, not making her a drip less perfect.

'Oh, what a stubborn little creature!' she exclaims shaking her head. 'Maggie, look,' she says flipping our still-clasped hands, so I see her fingers plainly. The diamond that weighed down her ring finger has gone.

'Y-you're not . . . you're no longer engaged?' I splutter and she nods her head, beaming. 'But . . . how? What . . . ?' I can't hide my perplexity.

'Freddie,' she sighs lovingly, taking a little handkerchief out of her handbag to dab at her eyes, and instantly restoring her composure. Seriously, not a blotch in sight. 'Because of you – or more *for* you,' she corrects herself, 'he called off our engagement.' I have to grip on to the fence of Traitors' Gate, or I think I may just end up in the sluice. 'He came to me in Scotland and told me everything.

That he couldn't go on living this lie anymore, knowing that he'd have to give up so much for something that neither of us really wanted. Maggie, I agreed straight away to end our engagement. I couldn't let him lose you for some marriage that would only make our archaic parents happy.'

'So that very same day, we both went to his father and told him the wedding was off. Freddie really stood up to him! He said he would rather relinquish his title and resign himself to a life as a guardsman, working his way up like everyone else, if it meant he could be with the person who makes him happiest.' I can't look at her as she speaks; my brain has gone into overdrive and her words swirl around in my mind, knocking their hefty weight into my skull as I try to make sense of them. 'He meant *you*, Maggie. You made him realise who he wanted to be, made him feel like he was actually worth something, outside of his family name.' She shakes my hands to punctuate her words, as my mind wanders adrift

'He shouldn't have . . . His family. I told him not to.' I'm not making sense.

'I know. Which is why he did it without telling you, I suppose. To show he wanted this whether it won you over or not. Maggie, I've never seen him stand up to his father like that. You should have seen it! The old man had no idea what to do. I think he knew he had no choice but to just let us both walk away. For the first time, Freddie chose his own fate, and he is far better for it. Please don't think you have forced him into a life of alienation, because living the life he had before you, he was alien even to himself. When you came along, everything changed.'

'But I don't understand. Why are you so happy? I've ruined your life . . .' She only laughs at my response.

'You've saved us *both* from a life of hiding, from living for everyone except ourselves. When I saw that look of relief on his face, when I heard how he fought for you, how he defended his love for you without a single care if anyone approved or not, it gave me the courage I needed. I . . .' She trails off, blushing through her freckles. 'I have been in love with someone else since the first day I set foot in my university.' Her expression takes on a dreamy gaze, and I can tell she's thinking of her lover. 'We've dated in secret for almost ten years, stealing moments when no one else is watching, savouring each second because we don't know when we will be alone again. She was – she *is* – the one thing I live each day for. I tried so hard to bring her into my life, she came everywhere with me, but being so close yet not being able to touch one another was torture.'

Her face clouds over at this. 'Up until a few weeks ago, Freddie was the only one who knew. He agreed to the marriage in the knowledge that it would shield me and her from my family. But seeing him fight for you, refusing to let you be some dirty little secret, I realised that Katie deserved to have a partner who isn't ashamed of her too.'

Katie. The beautiful Australian, ditched by her friend and finding comfort at the bar. I knew we had something more in common than just the colour of our hair.

'So . . . I finally proposed to her. She waited for me through everything, knowing that I would one day be married to a man, and yet she stayed. I knew the love that Freddie felt for you, because I had been hiding mine for a decade.' A dusting of pink brushes across her cheeks; it's clear that talking about her emotions isn't something she's used to. 'I wasn't afraid anymore, about whether or not I would be accepted, so Katie and I tackled my parents head on. We went hand in hand to their sitting room, told them we were getting married, and I didn't even wait to see if they approved or not. We walked straight back out and here I am now. We're living together in Brixton!' She claps her hands together. 'Oh, and you absolutely have to come to the wedding. It'll only be small, but I'd love for you to be there.'

She is glowing. If she was pretty before, she is ethereal now. Every inch of her is animated, there is life in her every pore, and she radiates a genuine happiness. No one could look at her and not be warmed through with contentment themselves.

'I'll be there.' I smile, and she embraces me again.

'And you must bring Freddie Guildford as your date! It's a bride's orders.'

Freddie! I have been so carried away in Mhairi's happy ending that I haven't had time to think about my own. He defied everyone, everything . . . for me. But why hasn't he told me any of this himself?

'He knew you'd blame yourself, Maggie,' Mhairi says as if reading my mind. Her face is softened, and she raises her eyebrows encouragingly.

'Can you excuse me for a second?' I rush, the epiphany finally clicking into place. She nods her head energetically and I run, practically floating along the cobbles as I barge my way through the crowds.

'Excuse me. Sorry. Sorry! Coming through!' I hurtle past the Bloody Tower and up the steps until two bearskin hats, white plumes and blood-red tunics fill my vision. They are the only objects in focus as my vision tunnels around them. My heart throbs and I feel it in every corner of my body. I sprint up to him, vault over the miniature fence and . . .

'Tiny?' I say to the wide-eyed teenager in front of me. He is the one with the gun in his hand, yet he looks terrified at my proximity to him. 'Shit!' I mutter and step back over the gate. 'Sorry, Tiny.'

My face prickles with heat and I audibly groan. 'I don't suppose you have any idea where Freddie is, do you?' I add in a murmur.

'King's House,' he squeaks from out the corner of his mouth, his face the colour of his tunic. I look to the King's House. A lone guardsman stands at his post, shoulders wide, posture strong, his bearskin tilted ever so slightly in my direction. And that's when I see him. His eyes are covered by the fur of his uniform, but his pointed lips and chiselled chin are enough for me to be sure this time.

'Thanks, Tiny,' I throw over my shoulder, already retreating. I cut across Tower Green, much to the chagrin of the nearest beefeater, who booms: 'Keep off the king's grass!' But I don't stop; there is no diverting my course now. Rex and Regina scarper out of my way as I fly between them. And out of the corner of my eye, I notice my dad, silently smiling at his Bloody Tower post.

Freddie drops his rifle to the ground to catch my hurtling body. Within seconds, I slam into him, and he wraps his arms around me firmly. My breathing is heavy; my body pulses against him. I push the fur away from his eyes to make sure it really is him, and teary irises return my gaze, those tiny fireworks of cyan and sage. Without wasting another second, I kiss him. Under the thousands of eyes and cameras, I kiss him, and he kisses me back.

Epilogue

Two months later . . .

'So, Andy walks in with this smug look on her face, way too pleased with herself. She swans over to show me her lock screen, and what do I see? None other than my ex's naked torso, balancing the time and date across his nipples.' Katie's eyes widen as she struggles to swallow down the mouthful of IPA without doing a dramatic spit-take. 'When I tell you I laughed! Jesus, I *howled*. I don't know what she expected from me, but it definitely wasn't that. She just spouted all of this crap about how I had been so awful to him and it's no wonder he cheated on me, et cetera, et cetera. So, I got up—'

'And punched her in the face?' Katie interrupts, deadpan, and I can't help but laugh at the image. We sit together at the bar in the Keys, and she slots into the scene perfectly in her crisp red suit.

'I wish! I just walked away. She'll get her karma when

Bran gets up to his old tricks again. I did try to warn her, but she wasn't having any of it.'

My new friend rolls her eyes and takes another swig of her pint.

'But it gets even better. That's when Kevin arrives. He tells me that they're going to have to discuss the whole "leaping over fences to snog King's Guards" thing with HR. And I don't know what came over me, but I turned around and told him to stick his job up his arse. If he wasn't already made entirely out of nicotine and Red Bull, I think his heart might have stopped.'

Katie whoops triumphantly and bumps our glasses together to cheers the discovery of my backbone.

'And since I had nothing left to lose, I told him that it was actually his dear little Samantha who blabbed about his affair all those months ago, and I walked out. Haven't been back since.'

'Ha! I'd pay good money to see the CCTV from that room. What are you going to do now?'

'I have a couple of interviews, museums and the like, but in the meantime, Trixie next door has got me some temp work with this veterans charity. So, I've been doing a bit of work helping ex-forces get back on their feet and stuff. Everything about it just feels . . . right.' I think back to the ravenmaster and how a cup of tea in her living room has become a permanent fixture to my Wednesday evenings. With every week, she seems to say more, relax more, and I smile into my drink at the image. 'Anyway, enough about me. I want to hear all about the honeymoon!'

Mhairi and Katie didn't waste any time getting married. Just a month after Mhairi came to tell me the news, me, Freddie, and Katie's parents all got on the bus up to Gretna Green to watch them finally get their happily ever after.

Katie is more than happy to tell me all about their Parisian artists' retreat, scrolling through at least a thousand photos. She has to quickly skip over the life drawing of her new wife and asks Baz for another drink to hide her blush.

The ringing of my phone saves her from any embarrassment. Freddie's name lights up the screen, and despite it now being a very familiar sight, I still get a little giddy seeing it.

'Hello! I, er, need your help,' his voice sheepishly says through the speaker.

'On my way,' I say before hanging up. I turn back to my drinking partner, who is fully engaged in a conversation about Australian politics with Baz. As Godders joins in with the impromptu seminar, I excuse myself to go to my boyfriend's rescue.

Catching sight of him makes my heart swell. Freddie and Mo stand in the window of the guardroom both fumbling around with a bow tie that the former has slung around his neck. I have only planned to give him a little tour of my house and meet my dad for a drink or two in the Keys, but it's clear just from the worry etched across his face that it means so much to him to get it right. I pause for a moment to watch him from a distance, my body warmed by the sight. When they finally notice me, Freddie slaps away his corporal's hands and straightens out his suit with a grimace.

'A bow tie?' I laugh as he almost offers me a pout in his frustration.

'Can you help?' He rakes a shaking hand through his hair, pawing at the bow tie defeatedly with the other.

'Maybe you're meant to twist it this way, and then loop it over like that?' I stand in front of him, making my own clumsy attempt to tie it. He gives an exasperated sigh, his brow furrowed so low that the lines fork across his face like lightning.

'Hey! Look at me.' I cup his cheeks in my hands, swiping a thumb over the cusp of his strong jaw until he relaxes. 'It's okay, I promise.'

He exhales, more calmly now, tilting his head against my left hand. 'I just really can't mess this up.'

'And you won't. My mum really wouldn't have ever cared about a stupid bow tie. She'd probably have laughed and said you look like a magician. Dad too for that matter.' I stand up on the tips of my toes to kiss between his eyebrows softly and let go of his freshly shaven face. Turning back towards his bag, the contents of which has been strewn across his single bed, I pick up his 'blue, red, blue' Household Division tie.

'How about this one instead?' I say, holding it up.

'Perfect.'

There's no way that he doesn't know how to tie a tie, but I move back over to him to do it myself anyway. His tense frame, clad in a sleek suit, his regimental pin badge wedged into the lapel, eases under my hands. I muddle up the knot and have to take a moment to lean back and picture my dad teaching me when I was a kid. Freddie takes my pause as an invitation to steal a soft kiss. His lips feather across mine and I instinctively push myself further into him. Smiling as he pulls away, I drop the tie and shove him lightly on the shoulder.

'I need to concentrate, you arse.' He laughs as I tug the red and blue striped material and attempt it again, successfully this time. When I'm finished, he presses his lips to mine once more. It's tender and intimate; there's no distinction between us when he kisses me like this; I become him, and he becomes me.

'Unless Maggie is going to kiss me like that after she's done with you, then will you both please get a room!' a voice shouts across the shared bedroom, and Freddie stops just long enough to throw a balled-up pair of socks at Walker, who is making gagging noises from his bed a few metres away. I don't have enough time to get embarrassed before Freddie kisses me again.

'We should get going,' he murmurs. My face clearly betrays my feelings of disappointment because he offers me one last peck before dragging me gently by the hips towards the door.

'Have fun! Do try to come back with your head still attached to your body!' Riley shouts.

'I reckon it's his dick he'll have to watch out for.' Mo laughs heartily from his bed space beside the door – just close enough for Freddie to reach out and slap him across the back of his head.

'*Guys*, it'll be fine.' I chuckle as they all raise their eyebrows.

'Good luck,' Walker mouths as Chaplin claps him over the shoulder with a smile.

At Freddie's request, we're both dressed as if we're about to attend the Oscars, not just meet my parents. He even went as far as to buy me a brand-new red dress.

'I want to do this properly,' he said to me a month ago, as I lounged across his lap in St James's Park. 'It needs to be perfect.' I resisted the urge to remind him that my dad, along with hundreds of others, watched as I leapt into his arms and shoved my tongue down his throat. But it's sweet that he wants to make a good impression. We walk hand in hand from the Waterloo Block, down the secret passage and the casemates to my home. Lucie, Merlin, and Edward fly over just before we reach the front door, and Freddie takes a packet of biscuits from a canvas bag that he had picked up on the way out and releases my hand to bend down and feed the greedy birds. I join him, squatting next to them as Lucie hops towards me and nestles her beak into the folds of my dress.

'You brought those especially?' I ask Freddie once their little bellies have been satisfied and they skip away merrily.

'I pinched them from the guardroom. I thought that I had better get on the good side of your friends, so they don't go telling any tales about me.' He winks and I bring him in closer.

When we finally reach my front door, Freddie hesitates, another trembling hand raking through his curls. I reach for it, give him a little squeeze, and push open the door. It is silent when we walk in, with Dad no doubt already in the bar and preparing for his own meeting. Freddie doesn't let go of me as I walk over to the closed door to Mum's room and push it open.

There's a note in the middle of the table, propped up by a little box of lemon cakes and a packet of custard cream biscuits. In loose handwriting the note spells:

'I thought I'd give you some alone time with Mum. I bought you her favourite and my favourite for pudding. See you soon. Love, Dad. P.S. Save me a biscuit!'

Looking at the pile of sugary treats, my heart swells, and not only because of my sweet tooth. I simply couldn't have planned it more perfectly. Freddie has his arms wrapped around my waist as he reads the note from over my shoulder, and I feel his cheeks press against my neck as he smiles.

'Good afternoon, ma'am. I'm Freddie. It is an honour to be here.' He lets go of me to introduce himself to my mother, addressing the wall of photographs. Placing his bag on the table, he pulls out four different Tupperware boxes. When he opens them, the contents are still steaming.

'You cooked?' Suddenly, I am overcome with the urge to cry but I hold it together . . . just.

'Of course. I thought we could have dinner with your mum. I, erm, spoke to your dad the other day on the phone, to ask his permission, hence the . . .' He gestures to my dad's gift of a dessert, looking to me with a sheepish glance. 'I asked him to join, but his words were: "I'm sure we will have many dinners in that room together, lad. You just go and meet my Hilary first." I hope that's okay?' The tears that had threatened to fall just moments ago roll down my face and I sweep them away with a grin and a nod.

'The kitchens aren't that great in the guardroom, so it's as much of a roast lamb dinner as I could manage.' He lines potatoes, vegetables, and meat along the table before pulling out a pot of gravy.

'Thank you.' That's all I can say as I reach up to kiss him on the cheek. I barely say a word as we eat, whilst Freddie, dressed to the nines, tells the walls all about himself, all about us, and all about everything I have ever told him about Mum. My silent tears slide onto my empty plate.

When we are finished, I take the plates up to the kitchen to give them a quick rinse. On my way back down, I hear him still chattering away, more softly now but still just loud enough for me to hear him.

'If you're wondering what my intentions with your daughter are . . . I just want her to be happy. If she is happy, I am happy. I don't believe that I'd ever experienced happiness in its true form until I met Maggie. She made me realise things about myself, about who I was and wanted to be . . . She saved my life. I couldn't say that I would give up the world for her, because she *is* the world. And I'll be her moon, always within her orbit. Any time there's darkness, I'll be there, casting as much light as I can muster so she doesn't have to wander blindly through the nights. My intentions are to be everything for her that she is for me.'

You know that feeling when you go outside and breathe in for the first time on a winter's morning? And the fresh air's icy touch spreads the whole way through your body with every inhalation, as it wakes up each and every one of your cells. That's what Freddie is; he makes me feel anew with each breath. He is the wind at the top of a Scottish mountain, which I get lost in as he envelops me and leaves my cheeks pink.

I lean against the doorframe with a smile. He is stood to attention, gazing at a photo of Mum on the day I was born. Somewhere in the bundle of blankets is me, with my fresh bones slightly squashed from birth. Mum looks radiant, her crazy curls even wilder than usual as they caress her cheeks, and her skin glows into the flash of the camera.

'You have the same smile,' Freddie says, sensing my presence.

'You think so?'

'Definitely.'

'You would have made her cry with that speech.'

'Good cry?'

I nod. 'We'd better go, before Dad gets jealous that Mum has spent more time with you than he has.' With one last salute to Mum, he grabs his jacket, and we make the short journey over to the Keys.

Mhairi has joined Katie by the time we get there – and so have all thirty members of the Yeoman body, including the ravenmaster in one of her very rare public appearances. My dad is perched on a stool at the very back of the room, sat up so straight I am almost certain he is going to pull a muscle in his neck. Resting his hands against his knees, he too is dressed like he has a meeting with the king, accessorising his blazer with his long row of medals.

He briefly turns around to fumble with the light switch for the cabinet behind him and the glass case illuminates to reveal a huge axe crossed with a beefeater's partisan. He looks happy with himself, probably thinking he looks like some tyrant king from *Game of Thrones* or something.

'What's going on here then?' I roll my eyes with a laugh.

Freddie swallows, visibly intimidated by the court of beefeaters who have turned out to greet him.

'We've come to welcome your new fella to the Keys,' Richie pipes up and I eye him suspiciously.

'And show him how many people will be after him if he breaks your heart,' Charlie adds.

'I give you my full consent to bury me in the moat if I ever did because that would mean that I have lost my mind,' Freddie announces to the room, catching my eye with a smile.

My dad rises from his chair and walks slowly over to Freddie, who keeps his posture rigid, showing off his discipline. When he reaches him, Dad places a hand to his shoulder. I think if I tried, I could probably hear Freddie's heartbeat from a mile away.

'Good lad. Now, son, are you going to get this old man a pint?' Dad chuckles, pulling my boyfriend into a rough one-armed hug. Freddie noticeably relaxes as the both of us exhale in unison.

'Of course, of course.' My boyfriend quickly swipes a sheen of sweat from his brow. 'Pints all round?' he declares to the room, and I have never seen them all move so fast. Baz practically leaps over the bar to begin pouring as Freddie slides his wallet out of his pocket. He gets rather a lot of pats on the back, and I practically have to fight Godders and Lunchbox off just to get to him.

As I take my place at his side, Freddie hands a few notes over to the bar.

'Well, I don't think that could have gone much better,' Mhairi observes. Her hand rests proudly on Katie's thigh, and they share a doting look. Freddie wraps his arm around my shoulders and squeezes me to him.

'I think, in this place, any result where you get to keep your head is a good one,' Katie adds, making us all chuckle. She and Riley would get on like a house on fire.

From his arms, I watch the beefeaters bustle around the bar. Freddie's pulse has finally calmed and thumps softly against me. My dad catches my eye from his regular spot nestled between Godders and Charlie and he raises his glass to the both of us.

I always thought happiness came perfectly packaged. A skinny body, a nuclear family, blonde hair, a six-figure salary, all tied up in a pretty bow in the fairy-tale happy ending. But it turns out that true happiness is just a bar full of beefeaters and the knowledge that someone loves me just as I am.

Acknowledgements

This novel would never have existed without Molly Walker-Sharp. You took a chance on me and believed in me when I scarcely believed in myself. You have given me an opportunity that most people have to spend their lives in search of, and I can never put into words my gratitude (if I could, I'm sure that I'd need your expertise to edit them for me anyway!). Every single step of the way you have guided me and encouraged me each time that I couldn't 'see the wood for the trees'. Not only have you helped me achieve my dream of being an author at least forty years before I thought it would be possible, but you have given me the confidence that I have been searching for my whole life. Thank you really isn't enough.

There is so much more that goes into publishing a book than I could ever imagine. Thank you to the entire team at Avon and HarperCollins and the freelancers that work alongside them. Maddie Dunne-Kirby, Gaby Drinkald, Ella Young, Emily Chan, Raphaella Demetris, Sammy Luton,

Georgina Ugen, Hannah Avery, Emily Gerbner, Jean Marie Kelly, Sophia Wilhelm, Peter Borcsok, Caroline Young, Claire Ward, Dean Russell, and Anne Rieley; this whole process would fall apart without the tireless work that goes on behind the scenes and I wish I could share all of your names on the cover alongside my own. A massive thank you to Helena Newton for your incredible talent at not letting even a single rogue comma slip through your net – and for spending so much of your time having to delete the overwhelming number of times that I had written that Maggie 'blushes'.

Without stating the obvious, I wouldn't be here without Mum and Dad. As I get older, I see more and more how you made so many sacrifices to provide me with a life in which I wouldn't be held back by anything. You held my hands on paths you've never walked yourselves, wiped away my tears when it didn't work out (and even when it did), and you have always believed in me. Thank you, Dad, for getting the coolest job on the planet and putting up with me for a lodger, even when you've had to spend the last year bringing me cups of tea whilst I'm sat in my pyjamas swearing at my laptop. Most people are unaware of the sacrifices you have had to make throughout your life to now be able to reside in a palace, but there is not a day that goes by where I am not proud of you. And Mum, thank you for getting me through every single day, you are my best friend. From proofreading my Harry Styles fanfic when I was thirteen years old to proofreading my university dissertation, your unwavering support is the reason why I am here right now writing this.

I know I would be in trouble if I didn't mention my family, but I would never dream of leaving you out – Nanny, Grandad, the Browns, the Nortons, the Keys, and Ben. If I have nothing else in the world aside from all of you, I would still be the luckiest woman alive. Thank you for teaching me how to love and how to be loved, unconditionally. And everyone's favourite family member: my little dog Ethel, thank you for saving my life.

The beefeaters of the Tower of London deserve infinite thanks, from more than just me. I could write books about every single one of you as individuals and yet I would never do justice on just how interesting and wonderful you all are as people. I have gained a family and I cannot tell you how proud I am to say that. Special thanks to Gary and Tamika, the best neighbours and friends this old soul could ask for.

To the Scots Guards, thank you for being my introduction into the Guards and giving me such a privileged view into your lives – somehow you even managed to get me to enjoy the sound of bagpipes!

Cameron Wilson, thank you for being my very own Guardsman Google and answering my never-ending questions about all things royal guard no matter the time of day. Katie McCann, you saw the very first chapter I wrote for this novel and have encouraged me constantly ever since – there is no one I would rather be mistaken for my sister. Cai Cherry, thank you for always being my biggest fan. No matter what you go through yourself, you never forget me, and I'll never forget that.

George, you will always be my first love, thank you for inspiring this story.

Most of all, thank *you*, reader. I am grateful each and every day for how many people have engaged in my story, both of my own life on social media and this fictionalised version. Social media can be both a blessing and a curse and I am thankful that I have been shown such compassion and love from the people that interact with the content I create. Every moment of the last couple of years has been an almighty privilege and it is the kindness of strangers that reminds me why I do this and that keeps me going.